One
Enchanted
Evening

C
___
CENTURY

1 3 5 7 9 10 8 6 4 2

Century
20 Vauxhall Bridge Road
London SW1V 2SA

Century is part of the Penguin Random House group of companies
whose addresses can be found at global.penguinrandomhouse.com

Penguin
Random House
UK

First published by Century in 2023

www.penguin.co.uk

A CIP catalogue record for this book is available
from the British Library.

ISBN 9781529136159 (Hardback)
ISBN 9781529136166 (Trade paperback)

Typeset in 12/16.5 pt Palatino LT Std
by Integra Software Services Pvt. Ltd, Pondicherry

Printed and bound in Great Britain by Clays Ltd, Elcograf S.p.A.

The authorised representative in the EEA is Penguin Random House
Ireland, Morrison Chambers, 32 Nassau Street, Dublin D02 YH68

Penguin Random House is committed to a
sustainable future for our business, our readers
and our planet. This book is made from Forest
Stewardship Council® certified paper.

One Enchanted Evening

To Desmond, who, after 50 years
is still at my side

Acknowledgements

My books are never created from only my imagination. I think of a book as an arch. The author may well be the keystone, but they wouldn't stay in place without all the other people keeping them there. There will always be people I forget to thank but I'm going to do my best!

Thank you to my particularly supportive and meticulous editor, Selina Walker, and her enormously helpful assistant Charlotte Osment.

Thank you to my managing editor Laurie Ip Fung Chun and to my eagle-eyed and wonderfully helpful copy editor, Richenda Todd, without whom I would look exactly as stupid as I am. I couldn't manage without her saving me from huge mistakes.

Thank you, writing buddies Jo Thomas, AJ Pearce, Judy Astley, Milly Johnson, Bernardine Kennedy, Catherine Jones, Janie Millman, Sarah Steele, Kate Riordan, Mandy Robotham, to name a few.

Thank you, Bill Hamilton, and the entire team at A. M. Heath for being the best agent and the best agency.

Thank you to the geniuses in Sales and Marketing. Sarah Ridley, Hope Butler, Claire Simmonds, Evie Kettlewell, Mat Watterson and Lindsey Tan – you're all brilliant!

Thank you to all the PR team. Charlotte Bush, Klara Zak, everyone at EdPR.

Thank you to Meredith Benson and the rest of the audio team.

Thank you to the creative people who give me such lovely covers, especially Ceara Elliot who does an incredible job.

Thank you to Helen Wynn-Smith and Annie Peacock from the production team, who make sure everything is running smoothly.

Thank you to Burleigh Court hotel for telling me about country house hotels.

Chapter One

❦

Dorset, Spring, 1966

Just for a moment, Meg was on her own on the station platform. She had travelled into deepest Dorset and it felt like another world. It was just after two o'clock in the afternoon and everything was very still. She had time to take in the hanging baskets, the tubs of scarlet tulips, narcissi and blue grape hyacinths, the sense of peace. It was an unseasonably hot day for April and waves of heat shimmered above the platform.

Then her mother, Louise, hurried into view. 'I'm so sorry I'm late, darling! And thank you so much for coming at such short notice. It was such a relief when you said yes!' She took Meg into her arms and they hugged each other hard.

'It's OK,' said Meg. 'The moment I said, "My mother needs me," the manager accepted my notice without question and allowed me to leave straight away.'

'Let me look at you! It's been far too long since we've seen each other. I love your hair like that.'

Meg ruffled her dark brown locks disparagingly. 'It needs cutting again really, but keeping it stylish was

1

so time-consuming! Apart from having to keep going to get it trimmed, I was supposed to stick down my fringe and the bits at the side with Sellotape when it was wet and I couldn't be bothered. Now it's just curly and does what it likes.'

'It's very attractive and I like your dress too. The colour brings out the green of your eyes. Though it is quite short.'

'Too short? It's only just above my knee, not halfway up my thigh.'

In fact, Meg didn't have many dresses: she spent most of her time in kitchens wearing chef's whites and checked trousers or in black dresses with aprons for when she was working as a waitress. When she wasn't working, she mostly wore slacks, but it was so hot she had felt a dress would be more comfortable to travel in.

'It's lovely,' Louise said, not sounding quite convinced. 'But we're a bit behind the times in Dorset. Swinging London is a long way away. The only thing that swings here are the church bells.'

Meg laughed, glad to see her mother hadn't lost her sense of humour in spite of her worrying new job. 'I've brought my working gear. I don't want to frighten the horses with my modern ways.'

'Cows mostly.' Louise took hold of Meg's case. 'Good journey? The last bit is so pretty, isn't it? Are you hungry? I can make you something when we get back, but we should hurry.'

'It's OK. I ate on the train – sandwiches and leftovers from an event last night.'

Meg followed her mother, who had set off at quite a lick into the car park which only had two cars in it. Louise stopped by a pale blue Mini Traveller. 'This is us.'

'Oh, Mum! A Mini,' said Meg. 'How dashing. This would be perfectly at home on the King's Road.'

'I know! Andrew – he owns the hotel – bought it for my use. Purely for practical reasons, of course.' Louise laughed. 'I can't tell you how relieved I am to see you. I couldn't decide if I was going to murder the chef or he was going to murder me. But whatever, it's all going to hell in a handcart!'

'I was delighted to have an excuse to leave my job,' said Meg. 'I'd got awfully bored with cooking nursery food for rich bankers. This will be the perfect job before I go and work with my French chef.'

'It's so exciting that you've managed to arrange that. In Provence? So you'll be near Alexandra?'

'That's right. Antoine, her husband, who's a count—'

'I hadn't forgotten!'

'—helped me arrange it after their wedding. It's going to be terribly hard work and I don't think the restaurant will pay me, but I'll learn such a lot it'll be worth it.'

'They won't pay you?' Louise was outraged.

'No. I'll be learning so that's my payment. In the old days young chefs had to pay old chefs for the privilege, so things are a bit better now.'

Louise pursed her lips in disapproval. 'Well, I do hope you won't find working down here as boring as what you were doing in London. They're not rich bankers, but most of our clientele like what they call "simple food". In fact, everyone gets what the chef decides to give them.'

'Please don't worry, Mum. I'll do anything you need me to do. My French slave driver doesn't want me for a while, anyway. You can have me all summer, or however long you need me.'

Louise put Meg's case in the back of the car and walked round to the front. 'Get in, darling. It's not locked.'

As the car pulled away, Meg said, 'Now tell me everything! I've been dying of curiosity ever since you rang. I know it's been awful for you, but I feel quite excited about it. You know I love a challenge.'

Louise swallowed. 'We have a big function coming up, a lunch. The hotel does it every year and it's quite a moneymaker for us. It's been going on for years. It used to be for the birthday of the squire and all the tenants came and celebrated. There aren't many tenants left now, so other people are invited too. Since the war, people have had to pay for the lunch themselves, but they still love to come. Some of them travel from quite long distances. Andrew made sure I knew all about it before he went away.'

'Where has Andrew gone? It seems a strange thing to do just before this big event.'

'Well, his father moved to France some time ago and he has just died. Andrew has had to go and sort out the estate. He rang me last night to say it's all in a frightful muddle. We're just hoping that as Andrew's been running the hotel for a couple of years and really

4

loves it, he'll inherit it, but we don't know.' Louise paused. 'He's left me in charge, although I was only taken on as a receptionist and office manager.'

'And it's not easy?'

Louise shook her head. 'I'm still new to the job and the moment Andrew was out of the way, the chef, Geoff, who I'd never liked but didn't have much to do with, turned into a tyrant.'

'Well, I'm here now, so you can sack him.'

'If only I could! But I have to run major decisions past Andrew's son, who I've never met and has shown absolutely no interest in the hotel since I've been here.'

Meg laughed. 'Don't worry, Mum. Foul-mouthed, bullying chefs are the norm. I've worked with dozens of them. It'll be fine. Now tell me about the hotel.'

'Oh! Nightingale Woods is the most gorgeous old Georgian house with perfect architecture,' said Louise, obviously glad to move on from the chef. 'When I read the advert in *The Lady*, I looked it up in an old AA Guide that was in the staff room at school and fell in love!'

'In love?' Meg was startled. She'd never known her mother to be quite so enthusiastic about a house, however perfect the architecture.

'Yes! In love with the house.' Her mother smiled mischievously. 'I hadn't met Andrew then, of course.'

'Mum?'

'I'm joking, of course. I'm just so happy that you're here, I've gone a little bit giddy.'

Her mother was indeed a bit giddy, Meg thought. It could have been the joy of driving a smart little car

5

through country roads lined with wild flowers on a hot spring afternoon, or it could have been happiness because she was reunited with her daughter whom she hadn't seen for a while, but somehow Meg thought there was more to it.

'Why did you apply for a new job? I thought you were happy as an assistant matron. You liked looking after the boys and the teachers were friendly, weren't they?' said Meg.

'It was a combination of things. I'd got bored with the school routine, counting sheets and dealing with lost property and it got a bit awkward eventually. Too many single men getting competitive.'

At just over forty, Meg's mother could be considered middle-aged but her lively, caring personality and her bright good looks meant that men were often attracted to her. She was medium height with a good figure, blonde hair, blue eyes and wonderful skin. This was one of the reasons that Meg was determined to earn enough money to buy a flat, so her mother didn't always have to take live-in jobs which sometimes made her vulnerable to unwelcome advances. Meg already had almost enough for a deposit if only they didn't need a man to support their application for a mortgage.

Her mother, on the other hand, felt that Meg should keep her savings for herself. It was a tricky subject which they avoided discussing.

'Before Andrew – your boss – went away and you had to deal with the chef, did you like the job?' asked Meg.

6

'Loved it! It's such a beautiful house – quite large – in an idyllic spot. Wait until you see it! And I liked doing something a bit different. I still have to count sheets and towels of course, but I deal with the guests, the staff, do the wages, look after the books. Anything that needs doing, in fact. And if I've got a spare after-noon, I do some decorating.'

'You've always enjoyed that.'

'It's because I so rarely get the chance to, always living in staff accommodation. But there are a couple of bedrooms that I can do up in my own time. Andrew let me choose the wallpaper and the paint. They're going to look lovely.'

'It sounds as if there's lots going on. Not the sleepy backwater I was imagining,' said Meg.

'Usually, it is a sleepy backwater, make no mistake. But at the moment, it's the scene of high drama!'

Meg laughed. 'This special lunch?'

Louise nodded. 'It's for fifty people, which is a lot for us.'

'Why are you so worried? If the hotel has done this lunch lots of times before?'

'But the chef hasn't. And he's sacked a lot of people, including a whole family, three generations, who'd worked for the hotel for years. He said he's organised agency staff, that it's more cost-effective to just get people in when you need them.'

'Well, obviously that's really sad but the agency staff may do a good job.'

'It's possible, but the guests have been coming to the lunch for years and they like being served by the daughters of the men who they've known forever. It's hard to explain, but Nightingale Woods is like a family, one that has been broken apart, and our guests will see that.'

'Oh, Mum!'

Louise sighed. 'I promised Andrew that I'd look after the hotel for him, and I feel I've failed already.'

'But how on earth are you managing without the staff?'

'It's only been a couple of days, so we've coped. I've been serving dinner.'

'And you can't take anyone new on?'

'Not officially, no. But while I may not be allowed to hire anybody, Geoff can't stop me inviting my daughter to stay! I asked Andrew before he left, in front of Geoff, and Andrew was positively encouraging.'

'Mum, I know I'm good – no point in being modest – but I'm not sure I could replace a whole team of people who've worked in the hotel for years!'

Meg had always been able to make her mother laugh even with the most feeble joke, and her mother obliged. Then she suddenly slowed down the car. 'Look, there's our permanent resident, Ambrosine. I'll see if she'd like a lift to the hotel.' She pulled up alongside an elderly lady in a hat that she had probably made herself and clothes that were either also home-made or came from a previous century. She was striding along with a basket on her arm. 'Ambrosine? Do you want a lift?'

'Oh, Louise, it's you! How kind. I've been to visit my friend the colonel. You could take my basket with pleasure, but I prefer to carry on walking.'

Louise opened her door and put the wicker basket on the back seat. 'This is my daughter, Meg. She's going to be staying with me for a little while.'

'How nice!' said Ambrosine, peering into the Mini. 'I look forward to meeting you properly later. But now I must get on and I expect you must too.'

'She is a true eccentric,' said Louise once they were driving again. 'She's over seventy but fit as a flea. Walks for miles every day. She'll outlive us all. That's what Andrew says.'

'So, she actually lives in the hotel all year round?' asked Meg.

'Yes. She has a couple of rooms in the old nurseries. She doesn't pay to live here. It's an arrangement made by Andrew's father, I think. The colonel is her gentleman friend who lives nearby and who is possibly even more elderly. Talking of elderly people, have you got any news of Clover? I miss that little dog.'

'Sad to say, I don't think she misses you. She loves living with Lizzie in the country, being doted on, and being taken for lots of walks in the woods.'

'I'd love another dog, I must confess. I'll ask Andrew about it when he gets back.'

'He may not like dogs,' Meg suggested.

'Of course he likes dogs! Would I like him if he didn't? His old dog died and he hasn't got round to getting another one.'

Meg was sorry she probably wouldn't meet Andrew. If her mother was keen on a man, and all the signs were there that she was, she needed to give him a thorough inspection.

'Look!' Louise slowed and then stopped the car and indicated a vista visible through a farm gate. 'There's the hotel, Nightingale Woods. Isn't it beautiful?'

It was. A perfect specimen of a Georgian house sat in extensive gardens. Everything was symmetrical, three rows of windows with dormers in the roof. There were chimney stacks at both ends. Behind the building was woodland and in front a valley with a river at the bottom. It had a magical quality, and could have been in a painting by an old master, it was so pleasing to the eye.

'It's gorgeous. I can see why you fell in love with it.'

'I know. Even in a very small black and white photograph it looked heavenly. I can't believe I'm lucky enough to work there. I was so happy before Geoff started throwing his weight around, sacking people and being so unpleasant.'

'That is such a shame. It's a really beautiful building in a heavenly spot.'

'I know. But, sadly, we're not nearly as busy as we ought to be.'

'Why on earth not? Surely people must absolutely love staying there.'

'They do, if they come, but there's another, newer hotel not far away that has more to offer – at least on paper.'

'What sort of things? What could this gem be lacking?'

Louise laughed at Meg's indignation. 'We don't have enough bathrooms, for one thing, and the other hotel has a swimming pool. I think it may even be heated. Younger people definitely want those things.'

'I suppose so,' said Meg, wondering if perhaps there could be changes made so this hotel, in this little patch of heaven, could attract younger visitors too.

'Come and see Nightingale Woods close up,' said Louise. 'I want to make Ambrosine's sandwiches while Geoff is on his break. Her colonel doesn't always feed her and I think she should keep her strength up with all the walking she does.' She started the car.

Meg couldn't help feeling excited as they drove to the beautiful house on the hill, but at the same time she wondered what on earth she was getting into.

Chapter Two

Once Meg had been shown the flat over the garages where her mother lived – two bedrooms, a sitting room, a tiny bathroom and a kitchenette, Louise said, 'Right. If you don't need or want to unpack or anything, I'll show you around the hotel.'

As Meg followed her, she realised just how much of her mother's heart was committed to Nightingale Woods.

It wasn't very different from the large, rambling, fairly grand family home it had been, although there were a few obvious differences. The black and white tiled hall contained a reception desk, for example, as well as a couple of small sofas, some chairs and a stand filled with leaflets about local places of interest.

'This is the hall, obviously,' said Louise, 'and that's the morning room, where guests go after breakfast if they're not going out. The sun streams in.' She paused as she and Meg inspected the room from the doorway.

'It's lovely,' said Meg, and she meant it, but she couldn't overlook the rather faded air it had about it.

'But it definitely needs to be redecorated,' Louise said, who obviously felt the same.

Although they agreed about this, Meg could tell her mother felt invested in the house and would take any criticism personally. She decided not to offer any opinions unless asked.

The ladies' drawing room, another of the many reception rooms, was at the side of the house and had a big bay window looking out on to the garden. The furniture was antique and beautiful and looked as if it had always been here. But the sofas and chairs were quite shabby and possibly no longer comfortable, the curtains were faded and the rugs were threadbare in places. There was a grand piano near the window, covered with silver framed photographs.

'Does the piano work?' asked Meg.

'Oh yes. It was tuned the other day, by a blind tuner. It's really quite good, apparently, although not by a famous maker.'

'I bet the new hotel doesn't have a room with a grand piano in it,' said Meg.

Louise rolled her eyes. 'It's probably got a Hammond organ that rises out of the floor! Now come and see the main drawing room. It's about the same as this really. Old-fashioned, really quite shabby but somehow elegant,' she said. 'Let me show you.'

'It's really lovely!' said Meg when they got there. This room looked out from the front of the house and the river could be seen glinting at the bottom of the valley. 'I love the wallpaper. It's like a mural, birds and flowers climbing up the walls. Faded, but all the more beautiful because of it.'

'I'm so glad you feel the same as I do,' said Louise. 'It just needs a lick of paint, and new curtains and cushions. It wouldn't take a lot of money. I'd make the curtains myself or even repair them. The carpets are ancient but genuine Persian so it doesn't matter if they're old.'

'It has a lovely light,' said Meg. 'It's like being in a picture from a book of fairy tales.'

Louise nodded. 'I know what you mean. But it's the dining room that makes us popular for weddings and larger events. Come and see.'

This room had been extended at some time in its history, the extension reaching out into the garden at the back of the house. It was far larger than the other rooms but light and welcoming and its decor was less tired.

'Andrew told me that one of the brides who married into the family brought money with her and she was insistent on having a room where they could have dances.'

'It looks as if it's been redecorated quite recently,' said Meg, admiring the beautifully painted cornices, pilasters and the huge ceiling rose from whence hung a huge chandelier.

'Yes. Andrew said he had to get out quite a large loan to do it as it needed a fair bit of repair as well as just decoration. But it's the room that earns the money.' She frowned suddenly. 'I wonder why no one has started to get it ready for the banquet. It takes a little while to get all the tables and chairs into place.'

'When is it?' asked Meg.

'Oh, didn't I tell you? It's tomorrow.'

'Yikes!' said Meg. 'That's very soon!'

'Let me show you the kitchen,' Louise said. 'Geoff is bound to be there prepping for the meal. I was so excited about you coming, I didn't ask him how things were going this morning.'

Meg sensed her mother appreciated having her there as moral support.

A stocky man in grubby chef's whites was talking loudly into a telephone. On the table was a box full of frozen chickens.

Meg looked around. It was a kitchen that had hardly changed, she reckoned, since it had been the engine room of the house, cooking for the family for generations. There was a large professional oven and one or two other more modern appliances but basically it was the same. A large wooden table, the surface ridged with decades of scrubbing, took up the middle of the room. A vast dresser covered nearly the whole of one wall, full of every kind of crockery, plate, dish, jug or jelly mould one could imagine. Two enormous sinks were located under the window and near these were huge plate racks. An old range, currently out of use, filled a fireplace big enough to roast an ox. It was a lovely room, Meg decided, but needed organising.

'Fuck off!' said Geoff and slammed down the receiver.

Meg instantly looked at her mother in shock. While Meg was quite accustomed to hearing such language in professional kitchens, she was horrified that her

15

mother should have been subjected to it. Louise caught her gaze, equally embarrassed.

'Geoff?' said Louise tentatively. 'This is my daughter, Meg, who's come to stay for a little while.'

'Bastard agency has let me down,' said Geoff, ignoring Meg. 'You'll have to go and see if you can round up a few waitresses from the local yokels.'

Louise gasped. 'Oh my goodness, that's terrible news! I knew it was a bad idea to sack them all.'

'Well, if you know everything, go and sort it out! Get them back!' said Geoff, directing his anger at her.

'I can't expect them to just come back at a moment's notice after the way they were treated,' Louise replied.

'You know what?' Geoff shot back. 'I don't care. I don't have to stay around and deal with this fiasco. I'm off.' He pushed past both women and left the room.

'Do you think he's been drinking?' said Louise, white with shock and visibly shaking.

'Going by the smell of his breath as he went past, yes,' said Meg. 'Do you think he's just gone to get a bit of a break? Or has he actually left?'

Louise put her hands on the big old table to steady herself. 'I don't know. I can't believe he's just walked out! It's so irresponsible. But I wouldn't put it past him. How on earth are we going to cope with the lunch tomorrow without him?'

Meg didn't hesitate. 'You go and see if the staff – the local ones you told me about – will come back. We'll need them even if Geoff hasn't left for good. If you explain what's happened, they may well take pity on you. We'll be so nice to the people who come, maybe the others will follow.'

'There aren't actually that many of them,' said Louise. 'Three permanent and a couple of extras for big occasions. But you're right. If I throw myself on their mercy and tell them Geoff has gone, they might relent. They won't want to miss doing the lunch as it's so important to everyone.'

'Then go!' Meg gave her mother a friendly push. 'But tell me the menu first. I'd better start dealing with these frozen chickens.'

Louise gave her daughter a sudden hug. 'I know I should be really upset about Geoff leaving, but in fact I just feel relief! He's made everyone's lives so miserable and difficult. But now you're here, and I don't need to worry any more.'

'Off you go, Mum,' said Meg, again. She wasn't quite as insouciant as her mother about the departing chef; she knew that she would have to take his place, and cooking for fifty with no notice to speak of wasn't going to be easy. 'But before you rush off, tell me what am I supposed to be cooking?'

'Oh, coronation chicken!' said Louise and fled.

Chapter Three

Meg really wanted to get changed out of the clothes she'd travelled down from London in but she remembered that her mother had locked the flat door and put the key in her pocket. Her means of getting in was currently travelling the country lanes with her mother, who was going door to door, begging for people willing to be waiting staff.

She found an apron to put on over her 'rather short' dress and set about sorting through the fridge. She could do this while thinking about the menu. She'd found a large quantity of slightly stale bread – there wasn't any fresher – and was inspecting it when Ambrosine came into the kitchen.

'Hello, my dear,' she said. 'I suggested to your mother that I came and gave you a hand. She said it was an excellent idea.'

Meg smiled. It was a sweet thought, but she did wonder what a woman in her seventies could do to help.

'I know you're wondering what I can do,' Ambrosine went on, 'but I can give you useful information. For a start, I know that your mother hides the egg mayonnaise – if she's had time to make some – behind the packets of margarine in the refrigerator.'

Meg put her hand to her mouth. 'Oh! Mum was going to make you sandwiches in case you hadn't had lunch. We both forgot all about it. I could easily make you some now.' She retrieved the bowl of egg mayonnaise. 'Do we know if we're expecting anyone for tea? It's too soon to make sandwiches but I could get a batch of scones on.'

'I don't think there are any guests booked in for tea. Local people have stopped coming recently. Tea and a selection of biscuits from a tin aren't very appealing.'

Meg was shocked. No wonder people didn't bother to come if that's all that was on offer. 'How many sandwiches would you like? And how many fillings? I think I saw some cheddar in the fridge and there may be a cucumber or a tomato to go with it?'

'Just one round of egg is all I require. I still find eggs rather a treat, after rationing in the war.'

As Ambrosine showed no signs of leaving the kitchen, even after the sandwich was made, Meg suggested she took a seat and put the sandwich on a plate for her. 'Then I can go on asking you things without feeling guilty about making you tired.'

'Thank you, dear,' said Ambrosine and pulled out a chair at the big table.

'Do you know anything about the lunch?' Meg asked.

'The locals tend to call it the banquet because to begin with it was a dinner.'

'My mother told me that it was originally for the tenants to celebrate the squire's birthday.'

19

'That's right. Now it's for the great and good of the neighbourhood. People look forward to coming all year. People see friends they don't see at other times, which makes it especially important.' Ambrosine paused and looked down at her plate for a second. 'This year is the first year that the colonel and I haven't been invited. The chef said we took up too much space in the dining room. And he's got a point. It's a lovely event but always a little cramped.'

'Well, I'm inviting you!' said Meg. 'If the chef could uninvite you, I can invite you. Now, I've got a menu here: vichyssoise, coronation chicken and chocolate mousse.'

'Not sure who chose that,' said Ambrosine. 'Cold soup isn't very popular with country folk, and chocolate mousse can be very indigestible.'

'What about the chicken? Do you like curry-flavoured mayonnaise with rice?'

'I do, as long as it's not too hot a curry. Although chicken can be a bit dry, can't it?'

'It can. But I know a way of cooking it which keeps it much more moist and I think if I'm careful I could get it going before it's defrosted. I've no idea how Geoff thought that he was going to get it all done in time.'

'He was expecting the food to be brought ready-made from the agency. Cherry, one of the girls, who I really hope will come back when your mother asks her to, told me she heard him ordering it. He was negotiating a very cheap price for what was going to be a very substandard meal.' Ambrosine raised an eyebrow. While enormously friendly, she had an aristocratic air about her, Meg thought.

'Even the chicken?'

'I suspect he had that in the freezer,' said Ambrosine. 'He was a great lover of the freezer and the packet. The vichyssoise was coming out of a packet. And the mousse.'

Meg shuddered.

'I know!' said Ambrosine. 'Absolutely frightful! He was doing the hotel no good at all, you know. Andrew – lovely man; his father was an old friend of mine – isn't very interested in food. Some people aren't, you know.'

'How can you run a hotel if you're not interested in food?' said Meg.

'You employ people who *are* interested,' said Ambrosine. 'So,' she said brightly. 'Now that dreadful man has left, what are we going to have for lunch tomorrow?'

'I'll have to stick to the menu we have, I think,' said Meg. 'Someone will have chosen it and be upset if they don't get it.'

'Never in life, my dear!' said Ambrosine. 'They won't remember, and if it's delicious, they won't mind anyway!'

Meg exhaled. 'I'm limited by my ingredients. I won't have time to go shopping.'

Ambrosine waved a hand. 'You have a garden full of vegetables.'

'Have I? I had no idea. My tour of the hotel didn't get as far as the garden. That's really useful.'

'Geoff got rid of the gardener but not very long ago and the vegetables will still be there.'

'So we could have vegetable soup?'

'Excellent idea!'

'Followed by the chicken. What would we like instead of the packet mousse?

'Almost anything would be an improvement.'

Meg thought of the stale bread she'd taken out of the fridge. 'I wonder . . .'

'You look as if you've had an idea.'

'It is a bit unusual for a formal event but what about bread-and-butter pudding?'

'I can't imagine anything nicer!' said Ambrosine.

'We would need an awful lot of bread, dried fruit, milk and cream, which might be difficult at short notice.'

'If you telephoned them now, you could order the bread from the local bakery. They'd sell you today's leftover loaves very cheaply.'

'But there might not be any leftover loaves!' protested Meg. 'Don't they have a good idea exactly how many they need to bake?'

'You can but ask, my dear,' said Ambrosine, who was obviously enjoying herself.

'What about the dried fruit, cream, milk and eggs?' said Meg.

'There'll be dried fruit left over from Christmas in that cupboard,' she indicated which one. 'It will be very dry though.'

'I'll soak it in brandy,' said Meg. 'What about the dairy products and eggs?'

'There's a very nice farm near here that always used to supply the house with all those things after we stopped having a home farm. I'm sure we could get everything we would need from them.'

'You seem to have all the answers, Ambrosine,' said Meg.

'I've lived here for over fifteen years. It has its advantages.'

'Then maybe you can answer another question. It's going to be quite hard to make bread-and-butter pudding look nice on a plate and we'd need some large dishes to serve things in.'

'Come with me,' said Ambrosine. 'I know where all the crockery is kept.'

Meg followed the old lady down a passage into a storeroom.

'*Voilà!*' said Ambrosine, indicating a small room, probably originally used to store meat, or game. There were shelves from wall to ceiling stacked with every sort of dish and tin.

'How do you know where everything is kept?' asked Meg, looking at the shelves with wonder. 'There's so much here!'

Ambrosine didn't answer this, pointing to the top shelves. 'Look, there are some pie dishes and there are the roasting tins from when we did Christmas lunch for everyone who worked for us at Nightingale's.'

'Well, I could certainly use those for the bread-and-butter pudding. Are you really sure the dairy will be able to supply us at such short notice?'

'I'll telephone them. I'll speak to the baker, too. Once I tell them what it's for, I'm sure they'll try their best to supply us. The banquet is important to all the local community – has been for years. Everyone will help out if they know there's a bit of an emergency. How much cream and how many eggs?

'My recipe book is in my suitcase,' said Meg, 'but I could make a rough guess.'

By the time Louise got back from her begging mission around the local farms and in the villages, Meg was a lot more familiar with her surroundings, not least because Ambrosine had given her a tour of all the many rooms adjoining the kitchen – cupboards, pantries, larders, stillrooms, as well as the servants' quarters – which in times gone by were felt necessary to support a big house.

She'd also been led into the walled garden which, although showing signs of recent neglect, was still full of vegetables, herbs and, potentially, soft fruit. And against the walls were apples, pears and plums. One wall could be warmed by a system of flues built into it. A fire would be lit in a little house at the end and the smoke going through made the wall what they called 'hot'. This wall supported a number of peach trees, apricots and a large fig tree.

'Are you a gardener yourself?' Meg asked Ambrosine as they were walking back to the kitchen, Meg holding quite a large bunch of herbs.

'Alas, no, my skills are a little more esoteric, but I love the house and want to keep its history known by the people who live in it. I'm writing a little booklet about it.'

'What a good idea!' said Meg, curious about Ambrosine's esoteric skills and hoping one day she'd be told about them. 'I'd love to read it when its finished.'

'Ambrosine was brilliant,' said Meg when Louise reappeared. 'She's shown me everything, told me everything, and has arranged for a supply of eggs, milk and cream to be delivered tomorrow morning, first thing. She telephoned the local bakery and they're happy to supply bread for the bread-and-butter pudding.'

Ambrosine, who was sitting at the kitchen table, nodded in agreement. 'I knew they'd all be happy to help when they knew what was at stake.'

'You certainly have been busy!' said Louise, looking at the many signs of activity.

'We changed the menu,' said Ambrosine. 'Except for the chicken. We're still having that.'

Seeing the chickens simmering in large pans on the stove, Louise said, 'Isn't it terribly dangerous to cook chickens when they're still frozen?'

'I'm fairly certain it's fine as long as I take them out as soon as they're cooked. And of course I'll check they're thoroughly done. You add half as much again to the cooking time.'

Louise was still worried. 'It would be so awful if we poisoned everyone. We could wipe out the great and the good of the whole community. It would be like the Black Death!'

'It'll be OK, Mum!' Meg was laughing. 'I waitressed for a woman who said she never had time to defrost the chicken and as long as you cook it fairly quickly and don't leave it hanging around in warm stock – the same for any bird – it'll be fine.'

'We're having hot soup to start, not that cold stuff that tastes like wallpaper paste,' said Ambrosine. 'Cold soup always seems wrong to me.'

'There are some lovely vegetables in the kitchen garden, including lots of herbs. If it all goes to plan every bowl will have a pinch of herbs and a swirl of cream,' said Meg, hoping her mother would approve of the menu changes.

'Think how much nicer it will be to have soup made with our own produce instead of those dreadful packets full of goodness-knows-what that Geoff was so fond of.' Ambrosine seemed very happy. 'And my favourite: bread-and-butter pudding to finish.'

'I think we're going to be fine tomorrow, Mum.' Meg took a breath. 'So, how did your mission to get us some staff go?'

'Well, Susan, who is – was – our main woman, took a lot of persuading to come back. She was so offended by Geoff's awful behaviour. But her daughter, Cherry, was there, and she was keen to serve at the lunch at least. Once they were on board, Susan telephoned her many local relations and people all agreed, although

I'm not sure many of them will stay after the banquet. But it's such a long-standing tradition and, I gather, fun to serve at, we've probably got enough people. Some are coming this evening to set up the room.' She frowned. 'I suppose I should check to see if we've got anyone booked for dinner tonight.'

Meg's heart lurched uncomfortably. 'If we have, they'll have to have omelettes.'

'Don't worry, dear,' said Ambrosine, 'the hotel never takes dinner bookings the night before the banquet. Anyone staying has to have something cold.' She smiled, and Meg suddenly thought what a beauty she must have been when young.

'Now everything is settled,' said Ambrosine, 'I'll pop upstairs and take off my hat.'

'I do hope I'm able to "pop upstairs", or indeed anywhere, when I'm her age,' said Louise. 'She's obviously had a wonderful time helping you.'

'At first I thought she might be a bit time-consuming but not a bit of it. She knows so much about the house, the garden, the hotel in its early days. She's writing a history. And better than that, she found a cupboard with some very useful ingredients in it, including a slightly rusting tin of tomato purée.'

'I haven't seen her looking so happy and stimulated since I got here,' said Louise. She sighed. 'Oh, darling, what would I have done without you?'

'I don't know, Mum, but like Ambrosine, I am hugely enjoying myself. I love solving a crisis and it's all going so well. Between us we can do anything!'

Chapter Four

Meg got up before dawn the following day. Apart from a lot of other preparations the previous evening, she had wanted to make sure that the chickens were all properly cooked and set to cool so had stayed up late to do that. Now she wanted to get the meat off the bones and start turning it into coronation chicken.

She was wearing her chef's whites and trousers. Yesterday she'd spent all day in the dress she'd travelled in but this morning she wanted to feel professional. She'd set up a deboning station on one of the tables at the edge of the room. She knew the big kitchen table would be in frequent use and there was a window she could look out of if she needed a break from chicken bones.

She was suddenly aware of a loud engine noise and out of the corner of her eye spotted a huge motorbike with a black-clad rider go past. It must be the milk and cream delivery, she realised. She was glad that it had all appeared so early. Time was rushing on, and she had a lot to do in order to be ready.

'Can you just put it on the table,' she said, turning round.

The tall, black-clad figure didn't have a couple of small milk churns with him. He was wearing a helmet and goggles and even without being able to see him properly, she could tell he was angry.

'Where the hell is Geoff?' he said, removing his headgear, revealing dark blond hair and steely grey eyes. He was in his early thirties. 'And who the hell are you?'

'Geoff left,' said Meg, bristling like an angry cat. 'And I'm Meg Sanderson.'

'And why are you here?' the man demanded.

Meg took a breath to answer but hesitated. If she just said she was Louise's daughter, would he know who Louise was? And her mother would certainly have mentioned it if she'd known such a large, spiky man was due to appear.

'Well?' He was impatient as well as hostile.

'I'm Louise's daughter,' she said reluctantly. 'I came to help out with the lunch today.'

'Well, you can go now. I'm here. And who the hell is Louise?'

Meg stood her ground. 'You haven't told me who you are.'

'Me? I'm Justin Nightingale.'

Meg went cold. This must be Andrew's son, the one her mother hadn't met, the one who had the say-so on who worked here and who didn't. But she mustn't show fear: bullies loved that. 'And you arrived this morning because?'

He widened his eyes in disbelief at her question. 'Because of the lunch! You do know about the lunch? And where is Geoff?'

'I told you. Geoff walked out. I've stepped into the breach!' Meg wondered if perhaps this was a bit melodramatic. It was a lunch, not a life-saving operation.

'Why did Geoff leave? Were you here at the time?'

'Yes.'

'And were you the reason he left?'

'Of course not! I was just here by chance.' It wasn't quite by chance. Her mother had been worried and invited her. She took a breath. 'He'd ordered most of the food for the banquet and all of the staff from an outside caterer. Not the chicken, he had bought frozen chickens for the main course. But everything else. And they let him down. So he walked out. I think he was drunk.'

'Why do you think that?'

'I can't tell you why he was drinking, but I know he was drunk because he smelt of alcohol when he pushed past me and there was an empty bottle of brandy in the rubbish.' Ambrosine had found that, but Meg felt mentioning her would only complicate matters.

Justin Nightingale didn't speak for a few seconds. 'He hasn't done that before as far as I know.'

'He's a friend of yours then?'

'I know him. I've worked with him. He's a half-decent chef.'

'Just not keen on his job,' said Meg.

'How would you know?' Justin demanded.

'He wouldn't have ordered in half the meal from outside caterers if he was interested in cooking.'

'He probably didn't have staff he could rely on.' Justin was trying to imply this was somehow Meg's fault, she realised.

'That's because he'd sacked them all.'

'But not you, apparently? And what's your job? You're wearing whites but you're not a chef, obviously.'

'Why obviously?'

'Geoff isn't a chef who'd tolerate a woman in his kitchen.'

Meg opened her mouth to speak but couldn't think of a suitably outraged reply.

'I'm not either,' he went on. 'So thanks for your help.' He gave her a patronising smile. 'I'm sure the waiting staff will be glad to have you.'

Meg took a deep breath. 'I have not got up at five in the morning to be dismissed by a man I've never seen before.'

'Why did you get up so early?'

'Isn't it obvious? I'm taking the meat off chickens so I can make coronation chicken for the lunch!'

'Coronation chicken? Dry and boring.'

'Your precious Geoff chose the menu! And besides, coronation chicken isn't dry the way I make it,' said Meg.

'How do you make it?' He seemed distracted from his tirade for a minute.

'It's a Rosemary Hume recipe. You simmer it in wine and stock. Keeps it moist.'

He seemed interested. 'And it works?'

'Yes. Ah! Here's the man from the dairy.'

A young man with a shock of dark hair and rosy cheeks came in with a small churn. 'Here's the cream. I'll get the milk and extra eggs now,' he said.

'What do you want all that cream for?'

'Bread-and-butter pudding.'

'That doesn't sound very suitable.'

'Everyone will love it and it's better than chocolate mousse made from a packet.'

'You decided to put on bread-and-butter pudding?'

Meg nodded, losing confidence but hoping it didn't show. 'We changed the menu.'

'Who are you to change the menu?' Their couple of moments' truce was over. Justin was being over-bearing again.

'What's going on?' Louise said, having appeared silently on bare feet. Her voice had a certain authority, which was spoilt by the fact she was wearing a very pretty dressing gown with a ruffle round the neck and down the front. She looked more like a film star than a woman in charge of a small hotel.

'Who the hell are you?' said Justin, more confused than angry.

'I'm Louise Sanderson. I'm the manager here.'

'Since when did this hotel need a manager?'

'Presumably since before I was offered the job. Now you know who I am, would you mind telling me who you are?' Louise hadn't worked in schools without picking up some of the authority of a schoolteacher. Meg felt proud of her.

'Justin Nightingale.'

'Oh.' Meg saw this was a shock for her mother. 'Andrew told me about you,' Louise went on, sounding very calm. Although her mother was perfectly polite, something about her manner told Meg that some of the things she'd heard about him were not good.

'On the other hand, my father told me nothing whatever about you.'

'Sorry to interrupt,' said Meg. 'But the hotel is hosting a lunch for fifty people in a few hours. I need to get on.'

Justin turned towards her. 'I said, I'm here now. You can go. I won't need you.'

'But if you didn't know Geoff had left, why did you come?'

Meg caught a flicker of something, possibly a concession that Geoff wasn't the efficient and experienced chef he'd implied he was. 'It's an important event for the hotel. I thought extra hands were needed,' he said haughtily.

'So why are you sending those hands – well, mine – away?' asked Meg, acutely disappointed to be dismissed when she'd done so much of the work already.

He looked at her coldly. 'I won't have women working in my kitchen.'

Meg was ready to explode with anger but she forced herself to stay in control. She knew that many other chefs refused to work with women. 'Don't you think that idea is rather old-fashioned?'

'Cooking is a serious business. It's not to do with fashion. It's hard work and tradition, learning skills, practising them in tough conditions.'

'And you think women can't do that?' Meg sensed her mother wanted to intervene, but she really didn't want her to.

Justin took a breath. 'Look, I don't want to be rude, but this lunch is very important to my father's hotel, to the community, to people in the area. It cannot be left to chance and people who dress up as chefs and think that gives them qualifications!'

'I don't want to be rude either,' said Meg. 'At least I do, but I'm making a real effort not to be. My mother knew that Geoff was a disaster. He sacked the staff, people who've worked here for years, several generations of the same family. And he tried to get the whole meal catered and served by an agency, who pulled out at the last moment, possibly because Geoff didn't offer them enough to cover their costs. Which is why my mother asked me to come down and help out.'

'Why did she – you' – he turned to Louise – 'think it would be useful to bring – what did you say your name was?'

'Meg.'

'Meg, who is obviously about seventeen years old? This lunch is a big event!'

Meg opened her mouth to defend herself but not quickly enough. Louise jumped in.

'Firstly, I know Meg looks very young, but she is twenty-two. Secondly, she's been working in kitchens for years now.' This was an exaggeration but Meg didn't correct her. 'She has a lot of experience and is very talented. Why else would a French chef, Michelin-starred, accept her as an apprentice?' Louise let this sink in. 'And your father left the hotel in my hands and I have done what I consider best for it!'

Meg broke in. 'And I have worked extremely hard sorting out this bloody lunch. I am not going to just walk away because you can't cope with the thought of working with a woman!'

Meg heard her voice crack and cleared her throat loudly. She was not going to cry. She was not someone who did that. At least, not in her professional life. In the time that she'd been working in kitchens she'd come across some very unpleasant individuals. None of them had ever reduced her to tears. It was the thought of the lunch being taken away from her that made her feel like crying now.

No one spoke for long minutes, the silence broken only by the ticking of the kitchen clock.

'OK, you can help,' said Justin, as if offering a great concession. 'But you must do as you're told and not get in my way.'

The desire to cry vanished. 'I can help? And not get in your way? Very generous of you! Feel free to over-look all the work I've done already. If you were starting from scratch now, you'd never get the lunch served on time.'

Meg could see Justin was about to respond when Louise stepped in. 'You've done a wonderful job up until now, Meggy, but Justin's here now. I think we can leave everything up to him.'

Meg wished her mother hadn't called her 'Meggy' as it made her sound so childlike. 'Everything? Doesn't he need any help at all?' She glared at him.

He glared right back.

'Darling,' said Louise after a moment's very tense silence, 'the main thing is the lunch being a success. Justin is obviously an experienced, professional chef—'

'The only thing that's obvious,' said Meg, 'is that he's a man and I'm a woman. That doesn't make him any better than me!'

Meg heard her voice crack again and walked out of the kitchen. If she started to cry now, no male chef would ever respect a female chef again. She had to get her emotions under control. She walked down the corridor and out into the kitchen garden. She stopped in front of an overgrown rosemary bush and took deep breaths, wishing she didn't suddenly feel so tired. She folded her arms and closed her eyes.

She was aware of someone coming up behind her. 'It's all right, Mum. I'm not going to let you down by making a fuss. I'm probably just very short of sleep. But for that man to swoop in on his motorbike and take over is just so frustrating. Why anyone should assume he's better than me just because he's a man is beyond me!'

She felt a hand on her shoulder and immediately realised it wasn't her mother standing behind her, it was the man on the motorbike. Now it was embarrassment that was crushing her.

'Listen,' Justin said firmly. 'I'm prepared to accept that in some people's eyes being a man doesn't necessarily make me a better chef than you, but years of experience almost certainly does. I've done the lunch before and I'm going to do it now. You can either help me, be part of it, or not. I don't care. But make up your mind because there's work to do.'

Turning to face him took an enormous effort of will. 'I'll stay,' Meg said. 'If only to make sure you don't mess up my coronation chicken.'

She gave a loud sniff and stalked back into the house. By the time he joined her in the kitchen she had blown her nose and was already back to taking the meat off the chicken bones.

To Meg's surprise, she and Justin worked well together. She refused to ask him anything unless she really couldn't help it but he seemed to accept what she did without question.

'Shall I start on the mayonnaise or do you want to do it?' she asked eventually.

'Can you make mayonnaise?' His raised eyebrow implied this was unlikely.

'Would I suggest it if I couldn't?'

'Do you always answer a question with a question? It's extremely irritating.'

'Just tell me! Please! Shall I make it? Or do you want to?'

'You do it,' he said after a couple of seconds' thought. 'I can always make it again if yours goes wrong.'

Meg had helped cater for a wedding once that involved gallons of mayonnaise. It wouldn't go wrong. She was almost totally confident. 'OK.'

She was separating eggs when he said, 'Tell me what experience you've had in catering. How often have you been in sole charge?'

Meg was terribly tempted to tell him she'd been a head chef somewhere or other, but she knew nothing would please him more than to catch her out. 'I've worked in a few kitchens as a temp. I'd go in as a kitchen porter, and the chefs didn't know why I was there so would give me any job that needed doing. With one job I was there for a few weeks and built up to doing desserts. No one else wanted to do them.'

'But you've never been in total charge?'

'No.'

'What made you think you could do a lunch for fifty people virtually single-handed?'

It was a fair question. 'Because the lunch is much more like the catering jobs I've also done. You often find yourself taking charge. And I had a plan. Cooking the same meal for fifty people is a lot easier than running a restaurant kitchen.' She paused. 'Also, there didn't seem to be an alternative.'

He nodded. He obviously couldn't bring himself to agree with her audibly.

Louise was in the kitchen when the staff began to arrive. Justin knew most of them and they knew him. They were delighted to see him.

'Justin! My, how you've grown!' said the most motherly of the women who came in, who Meg realised must be Susan. 'Where has the time gone since you were a little boy scrounging snacks?'

Justin smiled and shrugged, embarrassed but tolerant.

The woman turned to Meg. 'Now, who's this? Although no need to ask! You're Louise's daughter, aren't you? My, don't you look alike! Different colouring, but otherwise – peas in a pod, you are.'

Meg was flattered. She thought her mother was beautiful.

Louise laughed. 'Yes, this is my Meg, Susan. She's helping out. I asked her to come when Geoff started being so difficult. I knew I'd need someone I could rely on. And it's just as well considering he sacked everyone. And as she's my daughter and not really staff, no one could complain about her being here, could they?' Louise cast a quick look at Justin as if to check whether he was indeed going to complain.

'She looks very professional to me,' said Susan. 'Now, you know my Cherry – she and I will waitress.'

'I can waitress too, if you need me,' said Meg, suddenly thinking how much less stressful it would be. She knew she was a really good waitress. If she was in the kitchen she would be trying to impress a man who probably wouldn't be impressed if she announced she had a Michelin star.

'I'll need you with me,' said Justin.

'We know what we're doing,' said Susan, kindly but firmly putting Meg in her place. 'My sister's coming in later. Between the three of us we've got it all sorted.' She smiled. 'It's easier than having to tell someone else what to do.'

Meg was offended. She had worked at plenty of large functions, serving food over people's shoulders with two serving spoons. She had no trouble carrying several plates on her forearm at once. But Susan was not to know any of this and Meg wasn't going to tell her.

Instead, she forced herself to smile. When she'd dragged herself out of bed at five o'clock that morning, she had been in charge, with a plan, the saviour of a tricky situation. A few hours later she was assisting a chef who thought women didn't belong in kitchens and she wasn't even allowed to be a waitress. Soon, she knew, she'd laugh about this, but just now she wanted to scream.

Her mother came and put a hand on her shoulder, possibly reading her expression. 'Glad to see everyone is happy!' she said with a warm smile. 'I'm just going to get dressed and then supervise setting the table.'

Meg let out a small squeak, not intended to be heard.

A few hours later, even though she had done so much preparation, Meg realised that she wouldn't have managed the lunch on her own. Why, for example, had she changed the cold soup, which could have been put on the table while the guests were having their pre-lunch drinks, to hot soup, which was going to be a little harder? She'd made the soup already, but it still had to be heated. It was really annoying that Justin asked the same question, out loud.

'Why didn't you stick with having vichyssoise for the soup?' he asked.

'Geoff was going to make it from a packet and Ambrosine told me that lots of people didn't think cold soup was a proper thing to eat. Obviously, cold soup is easier to get to the table, but we have got a cold main course.' He was looking at her, his expression challenging, demanding, unrelenting. She knew she should just hold her head up high and stick by her decisions. 'I had planned to cook some frozen peas and put a few of them with a swirl of cream as a garnish.' She heard the words come out of her mouth and regretted them.

'Let's just stick with the swirl of cream, shall we?' said Justin, 'and hope no one thinks serving soup on a warm day is a bad idea.'

Secretly, just before service, Meg tasted the soup. It was delicious. The fresh herbs made it taste of summer and the good chicken stock base gave it substance. There was quite a lot of cream in it, which also helped.

Justin tasted it openly, when it was hot. He didn't say it was delicious, but he didn't add salt either, which Meg chose to interpret as meaning much the same.

Suddenly, the lunch had begun.

Chapter Five

Although to begin with they had all been a bit cliquey, the waiting staff began to unbend towards Meg as service went on. She and Justin were filling soup plates as fast as they could (and they were both efficient) and although there was only one door into the dining room, which slowed things down a bit, everyone was working well.

Meg was praying that the soup was hot enough. It was one thing people not liking cold soup, but they'd be really unhappy if it was only lukewarm.

'They liked the soup,' said one of the older women eventually. She was possibly Susan's sister, Meg thought. 'Men don't like cold soup really.'

'We just have to hope they like the chicken,' said another woman, delivering four empty soup bowls and taking three plates of coronation chicken. 'They'd have preferred a pie really. Men don't like salad.'

There was no time to argue about this. The kitchen wasn't designed to serve fifty people all at once, even if it had done so for many years.

However, the bread-and-butter pudding went down really well. It looked a mess on the plate, Justin said, but almost every plate came back empty.

Even with the door shut between the kitchen and the dining room, noise carried between them. It meant when the staff wanted to start on the washing-up, they had to be really quiet for the lengthy speeches to be finished.

Justin, as chef, didn't feel obliged to worry about the clearing up and went off into the office instead. Louise, who'd crept in to join everyone in the kitchen, whispered to Meg. 'I know everything is in order, but I'm not really responsible for the books. He might find some awful mistake made before I got here.'

At last, when all the guests had wandered out into the garden, where chairs, tables and umbrellas had been set up for their comfort – it being unseasonably warm – the washing-up could properly begin.

None of the guests seemed to want to go home. The waiting staff undertook to make tea and coffee for those who wanted, and the lads, sons and nephews of the head waitress took orders from the bar. Meg could see both what an important event this was for the locality and how fond they all were of 'the big house' even though it was now a hotel.

With Susan in charge, the washing-up got done surprisingly quickly, the women all chatting hard about the guests: which ones they were related to, what they were wearing and who had been sweet on whom years ago.

Meg slipped away into the kitchen garden. There was an old bench with a lovely view where she could sit, undisturbed. She was cautiously pleased with how the banquet had gone. It wasn't really her business, but she couldn't help feeling connected to the hotel now. She also knew that her mother felt very strongly about it. She thought she had done a good job for her.

In spite of the shade, Meg was hot. She unbuttoned her chef's jacket and was tempted to take it off completely. Under it she was wearing a boy's cotton vest over her bra. After a few moments, she shrugged off the jacket and closed her eyes. No one would find her here, behind the rhubarb.

She realised she'd dozed off when she opened her eyes and saw Justin looking down at her. She fought her instinct to pull on her jacket and tried to pretend her vest was really a sleeveless top and perfectly respectable.

'I'm sorry to wake you, but I need to go fairly soon,' he said, 'and I'd appreciate a word with you and your mother before I do. In the office.'

Then he walked away.

Meg pulled on her jacket, wondering how long he'd been watching her sleep, how undressed and sweaty she had actually looked, and what he was going to say.

She was relieved to see that Louise had already joined Justin in the office and had made tea. Meg took the last chair, squashed in behind the door, and took the cup her mother handed to her.

'I think I can report to my father that the lunch went well,' said Justin. 'Nightingale Woods can feel proud of itself on this at least.'

The way he said it told Meg he was going to follow this positive statement with a lot of negative ones.

'Mrs Sanderson, you must be aware by now that the hotel is losing money. It's not a situation that can be allowed to continue.'

'It's not something I can control,' said Louise. 'I'm just holding the fort—'

'I know. But unless my father can come back soon, I'm going to have to do something drastic,' he said.

'Are you going to take over here?' asked Meg, thinking she might be on her way to France sooner than she anticipated.

'I have a job already,' said Justin. 'I can't sort this place out too and obviously you won't be able to. It's a matter of just muddling along until something sensible can be done about the place.' He regarded Meg and her mother for a few doom-laden moments and then got to his feet. 'Louise, you're in charge of the office. Meg, you're the chef – temporarily.' He took a pen and wrote something down on a bit of paper. 'That's my number for when you get into difficulties and the salary I'm prepared to pay you, Meg. I've asked the staff who had left—'

'Been sacked,' muttered Meg.

'—to come back, and they've agreed to, for slightly higher wages.' Justin paused. 'Paying you instead of Geoff won't add to the overheads, but we will need to resign ourselves to having to wind down the hotel.'

'What about Ambrosine?' asked Louise.

Justin shrugged. 'That will be up to my father but I expect she'll have to find somewhere else to live when Nightingale Woods is closed.'

Meg instantly thought of how much Ambrosine loved the house and how helpful she'd been.

Justin stood up and put down his cup. 'I must get back.' He addressed Meg: 'But you did well – for a woman – hardly more than a girl really.' Was there a hint of a smile at the corner of his mouth and in his eyes? Yes there was, and there was also respect.

Meg suppressed her own smile in response. She couldn't help being pleased, even if he'd wrapped his compliment in derision.

Meg and Louise looked at each other when he'd gone.

'What a very unpleasant young man,' said Louise.

'Yes,' said Meg firmly. 'Let's see how much he thinks I should be paid.'

'That's nearly what we paid Geoff,' said Louise in utter surprise, when they'd looked at the scrap of paper.

'Quite right too,' said Meg, trying not to faint with shock.

Chapter Six

After the excitement of the lunch, Nightingale Woods settled down to its usual quiet self. With some of the staff back, Meg found she could easily manage doing the cooking and the guests they did have were extremely happy with the standard of food and level of service. To Louise's huge relief, Susan, who had been the most senior member of staff and in charge of them all, decided it would be better if her daughter Cherry came in daily to help clear up after breakfast and clean the rooms, and do anything else that was required. Susan's son also agreed to come in the evenings if a male presence was required – although everyone, including Susan, felt that they could manage perfectly well without a male presence for most of the time.

Louise and Meg did the rest, which included delivering the early-morning tea to the guests' bedrooms.

Everyone also agreed that the kitchen garden should be resurrected and money was set aside to pay for Susan's husband and her other son to do this.

'I'll tell you this, Louise, Bob's been that niggled, seeing all his good work disappear under the weeds he'd soon as do it for nothing.' Susan paused. 'Not that I'll be allowing that sort of nonsense.'

'Of course not, Susan!' said Louise, suitably horrified. 'We couldn't let him do it for nothing. Even if he begged to be allowed to.'

Susan laughed, as she was supposed to.

A few days later, Louise and Meg were in the office discussing whether they should do some advertising, even just locally, when the telephone rang. Meg answered it and then gave a small scream: it was Alexandra.

'Alexandra!' Meg couldn't contain her delight in hearing her friend's voice. 'How lovely that it's you!'

Alexandra was one of the two girls Meg had lived with in London. She was now living in a chateau in France, with her dashing French husband, who was, Meg felt, one of the kindest as well as one of the most attractive men she had ever met. She went on, 'If you've got my number, you must have got the postcard I sent you!'

'No, I didn't actually, but you'd told me the name of the hotel you were going to and I looked it up. I'm in London! I'm with David. There's a problem with the London house and we came over to sort it out. Well, I came to sort it out, he came to do an antiques market. His French stuff sells extremely well over here.'

'Just David? No Maxime?' Maxime was David's companion in France.

'No, he has to work,' said Alexandra. 'But he said that David and I should come on our own and get up to mischief.'

'It's so lovely to hear you! I really hope you don't have to go back to France just yet?' Although she hadn't intended to, Meg realised she sounded a little bit pathetic.

'No! Antoine is home and everything is fine at the chateau. We thought we'd come and visit you and Lizzie. Not at the same time, obviously. David will stay in a bed and breakfast when we see Lizzie, but we hoped you might have two rooms you could put us in.'

'We've got rather more than that,' said Meg. 'And we'd absolutely love to have you! As our guests, of course.' A second after she'd said this she realised it wasn't in her gift, really.

'Nonsense!' Alexandra said immediately. 'You know perfectly well I am not short of a bean or two and I've bought rather a dashing car so we'll swoop down in that. We'll visit Lizzie and Hugo first, as they're sort of on the way, and then we'll come on to see you!'

Lizzie was the other girl they'd lived with, who now lived in a little house in the woods with her husband and small daughter.

'Do you think Lizzie and Hugo could come for lunch or something? Or would it be too far?'

'I think it might be a bit far for that, but we'll work out something,' said Alexandra. 'And it would be nice if Vanessa could come too. She's living with her parents at the moment, who are driving her mad. Now that Hugo isn't there any more to dilute them, she says they're impossible.'

'Of course she can come,' said Meg, delighted to think the hotel would soon be filled with old friends.

'She told me she's at rather a loose end, waiting until she and Simon can get married.'

'Simon was Hugo's best man, wasn't he?' So much had happened since Lizzie's wedding, Meg took a moment to catch up. 'Remind me why they've been engaged so long?'

'It's not that long,' said Alexandra. 'Unlike with me and Antoine, they didn't get engaged immediately. Simon's brother is in Switzerland doing something important but is coming home for good in September, which is why they're waiting until then to have the wedding. Although preparations have begun, I gather.'

'Oh, OK. Well, when can you and David come to stay down here? Please make it soon!'

They made their arrangements and ended the call.

'That was Alexandra,' said Meg to Louise.

'I gathered that, darling. And she's coming to stay?'

Meg nodded. 'With David. Do you remember David?'

'Of course I remember David. He was so kind and helpful with our little dog. Do you want to finish telling me while I check the guest rooms that are booked for tonight?'

A few minutes later, Louise, deftly flicking a bedspread into place having inspected what was underneath, said, 'I don't think I met Alexandra, but you did tell me all about her wedding. She sounds wonderful.'

Meg watched her mother run her finger over the mirror, checking for dust like a caricature of a housekeeper. 'You wouldn't have forgotten if you had met her. She's beautiful, kind and funny and just a bit eccentric. I must work out a menu for when they are here. David and I loved cooking together. He taught me a lot.'

'When did you say they were coming?'

'This weekend. I hope there's room!' Meg suddenly worried that the wonderful reunion with her friends might be spoilt by too many visiting army types and their ladies, who would have to take precedence.

'I'm sure there will be, but we've got quite a few bookings for Sunday lunch. They're people who were at the banquet for the first time and are trying us out for another special meal.'

Meg smiled. 'That won't interfere with anything we might do for David and Alexandra. But I hope the Sunday lunchers will think we're as good when we're not serving cold food but a traditional roast.'

'As long as you've got really good gravy and crisp potatoes, it'll be fine.' Louise checked the washbasin by running her finger over it to make sure there was no trace of limescale which would make it look dull. 'You've always had a knack with gravy. I've only ever been able to do the Bisto kind.'

Meg remembered her mother's mahogany-coloured gravy, glossy and thick and tasting strongly of salt. It wasn't good. 'And Yorkshire pudding,' said Meg. 'Everyone loves that.'

'They'll love it all. We have good meat, maybe some home-grown cabbage or spinach, and the rest will follow.'

'But are they coming for Justin's cooking, or mine?' said Meg.

'You did the coronation chicken,' said her mother, obviously a bit surprised at Meg's lack of confidence.

'I just don't want them to be disappointed,' said Meg.

'Silly girl!' Louise dismissed Meg's fears. 'You did most of it for that lunch, you know you did. Now, what else do we need to do in here?' she said, looking round the room.

Meg realised if she wanted her mother's full attention and proper sympathy for her insecurities, she needed to ask for it when Louise wasn't inspecting guest bedrooms. She decided to stop worrying about her cooking.

'I'll just put a couple of flowers in a vase for the dressing table and that's it.' Louise gave the room a last critical look.

'You love all this!' said Meg. 'Making sure the rooms look pretty and are perfect.'

Louise nodded. 'I think I've finally found what I want to do when I'm grown up: work in a country hotel. I love the guests, I love getting it right, and I love working with lovely people like Susan and her family.'

Meg nodded. 'And I love Bob, their dad. He's so enjoyed getting the kitchen garden back into order. It was kind of Justin to get him back although it can't be all that cost-effective.' Meg was working on having positive feelings towards Justin. In her heart she resented him, swooping in, saving the situation, and swooping out again, while telling her she was just a girl.

'Bob is wonderful, isn't he? In fact, all of the hotel gardens remind me of *The Secret Garden*,' said Louise. 'I love the idea of it all being asleep—'

'Or just having a doze?'

'—and being woken by a gardener.'

'Although in the book it was Mary and Colin,' said Meg.

'I know it's not really like the book,' said Louise, who obviously felt Meg was splitting hairs, 'but the idea is the same.'

'I must say it would be wonderful if we can give Alexandra and David asparagus from the garden. There is some nearly ready.'

'As long as we can give it to everyone. Now, if you're happy here, let's get to the next room. And then I must check the bathrooms.' Louise frowned. 'I do wish we could have another one. It's rather a long walk down the corridor and there's that single bedroom . . .'

'Why don't you ask Andrew about it the next time he telephones you?' Meg's mind was now on new season's lamb for Alexandra and David, and beef for Sunday lunch, and she wanted an excuse to go and check on what was growing in the vegetable garden. 'I need to pick some parsley. There's a nice clump of it next to the greenhouses.'

Chapter Seven

It hadn't occurred to either Louise or Meg that Justin
would want to visit the hotel to see how things were
going and they were both extremely annoyed that he
chose the morning of Alexandra and David's arrival
to do it. Meg was in the kitchen garden gathering
herbs and Louise was picking flowers from the cutting
section so she could put them in the bedrooms. They
both jumped when he found them in the vegetable
garden, their hands full. Meg realised that Justin
couldn't have come on his motorbike or she'd have
heard his approach.

'Hello!' he called. 'Can we go inside and have a
chat? I see you're not busy.'

'I am busy,' said Meg. 'I'm picking herbs.'

'So am I,' said Louise. She held up her handful of
flowers. 'For the bedrooms.'

Justin sighed. 'I'll meet you both in the office. I
haven't got much time.'

'God, he's irritating. I could quite easily hate him!'
muttered Meg to her mother as they followed him
inside, both unable to carry on with their pleasant
tasks now he was here.

'Try not to, darling. Andrew thinks the world of him. Although he did say Justin could be difficult.'

'I should cocoa!' said Meg. Then she straightened her dress, the one deemed 'a bit short' when she first arrived in Dorset, and followed her mother into the office.

'You haven't many bookings, I see,' said Justin, looking up from the reservations book.

'We've a couple coming today who are staying for several days,' said Louise.

'A Frenchwoman?'

'She's a countess,' said Meg.

'She still only sleeps in one bed. Although I see there are two rooms booked.' He looked at Meg. 'Does this countess not share a bedroom with her husband?'

'It's none of your business!' said Meg indignantly. 'Anyway, she's not travelling with her husband.'

'They're friends of Meg's,' said Louise, sounding conciliatory. 'Very nice people.'

'It makes no difference what they're like,' Justin said. 'If bookings don't go up, we will have to close down sooner than I thought. We're not running a hotel for occasional blow-ins for Sunday lunch, one old lady and Meg's chums.'

'Has Andrew said this to you? About having to close down?' asked Louise.

'As you know, my father is away. I'm keeping an eye on things for him.'

'We're aware that we don't really have enough guests,' said Meg. 'But we have plans to improve that.'

'What plans?' asked Justin.

55

Meg's mouth had gone dry. 'I'm intending to write them all down and present them to Andrew.' This was the first she'd heard of these plans, but they sounded a good idea, even if she didn't yet know what they were.

'Present them to me. By the end of the week at the latest,' said Justin.

'You can have them when they're ready!' said Meg, now regretting her rash statement.

'Which will be by the end of the week,' said Justin. 'Now, Louise, can you talk me through the rest of the figures?'

'Of course, Justin!' said Louise, in a way that made Meg shudder with irritation.

'If you'll excuse me,' she said, and retreated to the kitchen.

Meg always felt calmer when she was in the kitchen. She felt at home there, and knew what she was doing.

Unlike many kitchens in large country houses, this one was full of light. The long scrubbed table meant there was plenty of space to work and she enjoyed using the old chopping boards worn down by generations of cooks. She loved putting her hand into the old salt pig and using the storage jars that were full of flour.

Now, she set about making pastry and, two hours later, she had made some quiches, a tray of little tart cases she planned to fill later, there was a roasting tin of tomatoes filled with peas, a flattened lamb joint that wouldn't take long to cook, and some scrubbed new potatoes. There was also a saucepan full of sliced vegetables, fresh from the garden, and a large pile of finely chopped parsley. Having this in abundance a few feet away from the kitchen never failed to give Meg a rush of pleasure.

Meg surveyed her preparations. If all went to plan, it would be wonderful. There was one other couple dining, so she and her mother would join Alexandra and David. Justin had disappeared, presumably having gone back to his usual job, wherever that was. Now she was ready, she allowed herself to get really excited about Alexandra and David's visit.

Louise took her up to a spot on the first floor which gave a good view of the entrance to the drive, where people slowed down to turn in.

'You've got time to be downstairs at the door, with your breath back, before they get here,' Louise explained. 'It's terribly useful. I like to know who's ringing the bell before they ring it.'

'I suppose that is nice. I've never had the luxury of being able to see people before they arrive before.'

'You get to like it,' said Louise and they settled in to wait.

'Did Justin say or do anything terrible after I left?' Meg asked. 'He didn't come and say goodbye.'

'No. He went and chatted to Ambrosine, who obviously adores him. He was so different when he talked to her. He wasn't patronising as so many people are when dealing with older people, he was just funny and kind. Although I'm convinced he thinks I'm a gold digger, after his father for all the wrong reasons, I was impressed by him.'

57

'If the hotel isn't making much money, and he made very sure we knew that, you could hardly be a gold digger.'

'But if Nightingale Woods stopped being a hotel, it would be a wonderful house!'

'But it's the hotel part you love,' said Meg.

'Oh yes! The people! I don't think I'd want to live here if it was just a house.'

'Just a house? A small stately home, rather.'

'You know what I mean,' said Louise, offended.

At last a car turned into the drive. Meg watched it for a few moments, checking it was the one she was waiting for. It was a large estate car and looked French. 'That's Alexandra!' she said gleefully, and galloped down the stairs to meet her.

Alexandra was out of the car and in Meg's arms in a blink. They hugged and jumped up and down. David got out more slowly and he and Louise greeted each other, observing with friendly amusement Meg and Alexandra's delight in seeing each other again.

They were all still in front of the house when Justin appeared. 'Good afternoon. Welcome to Nightingale Woods. You must be the Countess,' he said formally.

Meg suppressed a scream of surprise. She had been certain he was miles away. Why wasn't he safely back at his job? What on earth had he been doing all this time?

Alexandra held out an imperious hand to take his. 'Yes. I'm an old friend of Meg's. It's so nice to be able to visit her here. This is my friend David Campbell.'

'Nice car,' Justin said, having shaken David's hand. 'What is it?'

'A Citroën Safari,' said Alexandra, although Justin had addressed David. 'Perfect for large families and antiques dealers.'

'Which category are you?' asked Justin.

'Both.' Alexandra smiled, every inch the countess. 'Although I'm only a part-time antiques dealer these days.'

Meg was infuriated. It was outrageous, him encroaching on her precious time with Alexandra and David.

'Let me show you to your rooms,' she said, taking Alexandra's arm. 'Maybe Justin could take your bags?'

The look Justin gave her was both hugely satisfying and terrifying; he was sure to take his revenge. Meg didn't care. She was so angry with him. And as Alexandra obviously wanted to go into the hotel, they went up the shallow steps and into the hall.

'Isn't this lovely?' said Alexandra, looking round the hall with its smart black and white checked floor, antique furniture and welcoming atmosphere. Family portraits and old lithographs of the house decorated the yellow walls, and afternoon sun shone in through the front windows.

'It's all so pretty and comfortable,' Alexandra went on. 'I've just been in the London house—'

'Our old home,' said David, sounding nostalgic.

'Yes,' Alexandra agreed. 'And although we all loved it at the time, now it seems desperately gloomy and in need of repair and decoration. I was there to sort out the leaking roof – not personally, obviously – but really, the whole house is a disgrace.'

'Shall we go upstairs?' said Justin. 'I do have other things to do.'

Meg clamped her teeth on bitter words about why he wasn't doing them; she didn't want to spoil Alexandra's visit.

She wanted to snatch Alexandra's overnight bag from his hand but having more or less demanded that he take it upstairs, she couldn't do that now. 'I'll lead the way,' she said, trusting everyone would follow her.

Meg had so looked forward to showing Alexandra her room and she knew her mother felt the same. She walked up the stairs feeling angry and disappointed – all the more angry because it was entirely her fault. If she hadn't wanted to get at Justin he'd have been nowhere near them. Although he was so unpredictable he might have followed them anyway. She was desperate to know what he'd been doing all afternoon.

She opened the door to their best bedroom. It looked charming, she decided. The faded chintz wallpaper toned well with the cushions and bedspread. The dressing table had a very pretty antique dressing-table set in cut glass that included candlesticks and little vases – now filled with flowers. There was a small sofa near the window, perfect for curling up on with a good view, and a couple of small armchairs made it like a sitting room as well as somewhere to sleep. 'Here you are!'

Alexandra went straight to the large window that overlooked the front of the property and the parkland that surrounded it. 'This is just lovely!'

'This is the best bedroom?' asked Justin, questioningly.

'Yes,' said Louise firmly. 'It has the best view, a very comfortable bed and is near the bathroom.'

'But it's not a private bathroom?' Justin went on.

'No,' said Louise, sounding a bit sharp.

Justin left the room without saying any more.

'I'm so sorry about the bathroom not being private,' said Louise. 'I know they're starting to come in but there just isn't the money for putting bathrooms in all the bedrooms.'

'It's fine!' said Alexandra. 'Will I just be sharing a bathroom with David? We're used to that. It's a lovely room.'

Louise couldn't stop being apologetic. 'It needs doing up really. The wallpaper is very shabby in places.'

'I think it's perfect as it is!' said Alexandra, who had gone back to the window.

'David's room hasn't got such a good view,' said Meg, 'but it's still nice.'

'It is,' said David, coming up behind them. 'Justin showed me mine. What have you got against the poor man?'

Meg turned to him. 'Don't let's spoil your arrival by talking about him. And how did you know I don't like him?'

David shrugged expressively and then said, 'This is such a lovely house. Beautiful proportions and perfectly sited for the very best views.'

'Why don't you and Alexandra get settled in and then come down and have a grand tour?' suggested Meg.

'We'd love that,' said David. 'I can't wait to see it all. And please, show us all the below-stairs parts. I love seeing the butler's pantry, the housekeeper's room and, of course, all the larders and things.'

'We do still have a lot of those rooms,' said Louise, 'although I'm glad to say the game larder has been turned into a room to arrange flowers in.'

Alexandra and David would be very satisfactory people to show Nightingale Woods to, Meg decided. Louise probably felt the same. Meg went back to work, promising to organise tea on the lawn shortly.

'I do love our chateau,' said Alexandra a little later, when Meg had shown them every inch of Nightingale Woods. 'It's in beautiful Provence and it's home. But it's not pretty in the way this place is. The rose garden here is going to be glorious! I'd love a proper vegetable garden at the chateau too.'

'What I like best is the area behind the old tennis court. It's the perfect setting for a play. It's like a little amphitheatre,' said David.

'Sadly, it's a hotel, David, not a theatre,' said Meg.

'No reason why it couldn't be both, surely?' David said. 'I've a friend, an actor turned director, who puts on the *Dream* in a few special gardens every year. People love it! What can be more lovely than a fine summer night, a beautiful setting and a really romantic bit of Shakespeare?'

'Maybe I could put it on my list of ideas to make the hotel more profitable that I've got to make for Justin,' said Meg. 'I've been struggling to think of things.'

'Why is it down to you?' asked Alexandra. 'You don't even work here officially, do you?'

Meg sighed. 'I am on the payroll now and I think I've got emotionally involved. It's to do with Mum, I suppose. She loves Nightingale Woods, and I'm fairly sure she loves Justin's father, too. He's the current owner.'

'If Justin's father owns the hotel, why does he seem so . . .' Alexandra hesitated. 'Hostile?'

'He seems a perfectly nice chap to me,' said David.

'That's because he's sexist, and thinks women don't belong in kitchens,' said Meg. 'You're a man, and not working for him. It makes you safe.'

David sighed and smiled. 'He'll soon learn not to keep you out of a kitchen, Meggy.'

'To be fair, he did put me in charge of this one,' said Meg. 'I think he thinks it's just about allowable to have a female chef if there aren't any men who could possibly be given the job instead.'

Chapter Eight

The following day, Meg, David, Alexandra and Louise were enjoying a leisurely breakfast in the morning room when the front doorbell jangled loudly. Louise put down her coffee cup. 'I'll go. I'm not expecting anyone but it could be a delivery boy who doesn't know he should go round to the tradesmen's entrance.'

'I'll go, Mum,' said Meg, getting up. 'Your coffee will be cold otherwise.'

She pulled open the front door. It took her a moment to realise who she was looking at. 'Nessa! Gosh! How lovely to see you! Erm – were we expecting you?'

'No, you weren't,' said Nessa. 'I've run away from home.'

'Oh my goodness!'

'Well, I'm exaggerating a bit. But I had to get away. Mummy is driving me mad with the wedding. I'm not allowed any choice, but I have to keep telling her how wonderful she's being for organising it.'

'Oh, poor Nessa! Come in. You know Alexandra and David are here?'

'Yes. They told me they were coming and I was so jealous at the thought of you all being together when

64

I was stuck with Mummy writing thank-you letters for presents I don't want, I decided to run away.'

'I thought you weren't getting married until September,' said Meg, leading the way into the morning room.

'I'm not. But the presents are pouring in. I never want to see another box full of wood wool again.'

Meg laughed. 'But getting presents is supposed to be nice!'

'It's lovely if you only get one or two, but several every day just makes them an obligation.' Vanessa stopped and looked around her. 'This is all so pretty, isn't it?'

Meg nodded. 'We're all in the morning room. We have no outside guests at the moment so we've got the place to ourselves. Look who I found!' she said as they reached their destination.

'Do you mind me following you here?' Vanessa addressed Alexandra and David. 'I just had to get away from home for a bit. Why did no one tell me that getting married was such a nightmare?'

'Not actually a nightmare, surely? You love Simon, and you want to be married to him?' said Alexandra.

'Oh yes! In fact, I often think I wouldn't go through all this process if it wasn't for him at the end of it,' said Vanessa.

'On the other hand,' said David, 'if it wasn't for him, you wouldn't have to go through it at all.'

Vanessa shrugged. 'If it wasn't Simon, it would be someone else, I suppose. Eventually.'

'So it's just as well you're marrying someone you love,' said Louise firmly.

'What did you say to your mother when you left the house?' asked Alexandra. 'And did she mind?'

'I'm afraid I left a message with her maid. But I don't think she'll really mind. Although she will complain.' Vanessa paused. 'I'm being a brat, aren't I?'

'No. You're not being a brat at all,' said Meg instantly. 'You just need a break and to see some old friends. I'm utterly delighted!'

'Poor Meg has only had hotel guests and me for company recently,' said Louise. 'And when your mother is the youngest person next to you, the company of your own friends is especially welcome.'

Meg got up and gave her mother a hug as she went to the kitchen to make toast and tea for Vanessa.

'Did you find the hotel easily enough?' Louise was asking Vanessa when Meg came back. 'I sometimes wonder if we need more signs from the main road.'

'I found it easily, but I've been to this part of the world before. I came last year to help Mummy with her charity race-day event.'

'Oh?' said Louise.

'Yes. It's at the racecourse near Shroton? But we always stay at the hotel at Newton-cum-Hardy. It's quite new. Well, the building isn't but the hotel is. It's very swish. Mummy loves it.'

Meg and Louise exchanged glances. 'We need to know what that hotel offers,' said Meg.

'Why?' asked Vanessa.

'It's not far from here,' said Louise, 'and it could be taking business that should be ours. Tell us all about it, please.'

'The thing Mummy likes best is that several of the rooms have their own bathrooms,' said Vanessa.

'Which isn't something we can currently offer,' said Louise thoughtfully.

'But this is such a charming house,' said Alexandra. 'For Vanessa's mother, it would be like staying with friends – if she could be got here.'

'It is like someone's house,' said Vanessa, looking around.

'Someone who hasn't redecorated for a while,' said Meg.

'Years ago someone told me that really large houses are only redecorated about every forty years or so,' said Vanessa, 'and it must be true because our house hasn't had a lick of paint since I've been alive.'

'And you're only about twenty,' said Louise. 'So you'd have to wait another twenty years for it to be changed if you weren't keen on the wallpaper.'

'By that time it'll be so faded, no one could object to it,' said David, laughing.

After a moment, Meg said, 'Would you like more tea, Nessa? More toast? If not, would you like a tour of Nightingale Woods and the grounds? Alexandra and David have already had one—'

'We don't mind coming round again,' said David quickly. 'We're both extremely nosy.'

*

'What I think we should do,' said Alexandra when they'd inspected everything quite thoroughly and had gone back to the morning room to have some mid-morning coffee, 'is visit this other hotel in Newton-cum-Hardy. Nightingale Woods is such a pretty house, and the gardens are lovely even if they are a bit overgrown in places. It has "ton".'

'What?' said David.

'"Ton". I read about it in Georgette Heyer. It means class, really. That's something I bet the other hotel doesn't have.'

'We already know what it has instead – private bathrooms,' said Meg. '"Ton" is all very well, but it doesn't make the place any more comfortable.'

'It's perfectly comfortable,' said Alexandra. 'It's only the bathroom situation that could be improved.'

'I could put that on the list for Justin,' said Meg. 'In "Ideas for making the hotel attract more guests", but I don't know how we could do it.'

'There's a single room next to my bedroom,' said Alexandra. 'It was probably a dressing room. That could be a bathroom.'

'You have to forgive my friend Alexandra,' said David. 'She's spent a lot of time recently turning random agricultural buildings into holiday accommo-dation. If she sees a cupboard, she'll put a bathroom in it.'

'Only if it's quite a large cupboard,' Alexandra objected. 'It's not that there isn't room to put bath-rooms into the principal bedrooms, the problem is more likely to be money.'

'And taking away that single room would mean there's one less room available,' said Louise. 'When people with children come, we often put them in that room, so their child – or children: it can take another single bed – can be next door to them.'

'This is a family hotel, really,' said Meg. 'Mum told me that people come regularly, year after year, but in the summer holidays, mostly.'

'It's just people don't go on holiday much in May, although it's a lovely month. That's why you three are so welcome,' said Louise. 'But visiting the other hotel would be a good idea.'

'Maybe you three could go and inspect it for us? Go there for lunch, perhaps?' said Meg.

'Personally, I think a better idea would be if you came with us, Meg,' said David.

'Oh, I can't go!' said Meg. 'I might have to cook lunch if anyone comes, and I must prepare something for dinner.' Although, now he'd put the idea into her head, she did desperately want to see the other hotel for herself.

'I think you could safely leave me and Louise in charge of any lunch guests,' said David. 'And I can get dinner going, just as you can.'

'I think that's a brilliant idea, darling!' said Louise. 'You haven't had any time off since you've been here, and it would be fun for you girls to be together again.'

'We just need Lizzie!' said Vanessa.

'We'll have to tell her all about it, and suggest they come here for their holidays,' said Alexandra. 'But,

David, if you think you could stand in for Meg, it would be brilliant fun to go to the other hotel!'

'I wouldn't go so far as to say I taught Meggy all she knows,' said David. 'But I think I could step into her shoes if I had to.'

'If only your feet weren't so big,' said Alexandra dryly.

Louise gave Alexandra a look. 'Of course you could!' she said.

'Installing a few bathrooms and possibly turning some unused rooms into bedrooms would be such a lovely project. It's a shame I can't stay in England a bit longer,' said Alexandra. 'But the family needs me.'

Meg could tell that she needed her family too. 'Not to mention Antoine,' she said.

Alexandra tossed her head, trying to give the impression that she didn't care about her husband. Meg wasn't fooled for a second.

'So, where's this hotel then?' said Alexandra.

'The trouble is, I don't know exactly,' said Vanessa. 'Is this a problem?'

'It'll be on the Ordnance Survey map of the area,' said Louise. 'Or at least the village will be.'

David wrote down a list of villages to aim for while the others got ready for a day out. Meg felt giddy with joy at the thought. It was only now, when she had others to talk about it with, that she acknowledged to herself how much she'd been worrying about Nightingale Woods. It would be fairly easy to write down a list of things to do that might encourage visitor numbers, but actually having some concrete ideas, taken from seeing this rival hotel, would be far better.

She wouldn't have cared half as much if it weren't for her mother. The hotel was so close to Louise's heart, probably because its owner was also close to her heart. Having her mother securely settled would take away a worry that had hung over her, to a greater or lesser extent, ever since childhood. Although she saved every penny she could from her earnings, it would be a while longer before she had saved enough for a deposit on a house or flat. If her mother could be securely settled in a relationship that included a home, it should free Meg from her self-imposed obligation. Even so, Meg knew she would always want the safety net of her own savings, just in case anything went wrong.

Chapter Nine

They set off for the rival hotel in Alexandra's stately Citroën about half an hour later. Meg, who suffered from car sickness, sat in the front. Vanessa sat in the back with the map and David's list of places to aim for.

'This is so much fun!' said Vanessa. 'If only Lizzie were with us. Sorry, I know I keep saying that.'

'Do you remember when we had to get Lizzie home from a party at your house, Nessa? You helped us steal a car and Alexandra drove us all up to London,' said Meg. She gave a horrified laugh at the memory. 'And David helped us get the car back again, so no one ever knew.'

Alexandra also laughed. 'I don't know how I did it! But you'll be relieved to hear I'm a more experienced driver now and I have actually passed my driving test.'

'You were so brave!' said Meg.

'I just did what had to be done,' said Alexandra.

There was silence in the car for a few seconds. 'It's hard to take in that now you're a countess,' said Meg.

'I know!' Alexandra replied. 'With stepchildren! And hopefully some children of my own soon . . .'

*

A few wrong turnings, some confusing signposts and the fact that they had set off a bit later than they had intended, meant it was nearly two o'clock when Alexandra drove up the drive to the Newton-cum-Hardy hotel.

'I hope we're not too late to have lunch,' said Meg, who was not only hungry, but anxious lest their inadvertent tour of the back roads of Dorset meant they'd missed their chance to spy.

'It didn't say anything about mealtimes on the sign,' said Vanessa. 'It only said it was owned by Raoul de Dijon. I wonder if it's under new management. I'm not sure it said that when I was here before, with Mummy.'

'I've heard of him,' said Meg. 'He's getting a name for himself and has written a cookery book.' She sighed. Having someone people had heard of, at least in cooking circles in London, was something else Nightingale Woods, with its tired furnishings and shared bathrooms, couldn't match.

Alexandra drove up to the front of the house and looked around for somewhere to park.

'There's a sign to the car park round the back,' said Meg.

'But there's space here!' said Alexandra, sliding in next to a Jaguar, putting her car in a spot probably reserved for more important people.

'Shall we have lunch first? Or a look around?' asked Alexandra, leading the way into the hotel.

'Lunch first,' said Meg. 'The kitchen may be about to stop serving.'

Alexandra took the lead and got them a nice table by the window although they hadn't booked. The head waiter, who had moved swiftly across the room when he had seen her, was very attentive. He personally brought the menus and opened the bottle of champagne she ordered.

'It's a bit of a thank you for how you both got me through my wedding,' Alexandra said. 'Now, what shall we have? I think we should make sure we have different things, to test them out.'

'It's all very sophisticated,' said Meg, studying the menu. 'Lobster, crab soufflé, chicken liver parfait, crêpe Suzette. All the fancy things.'

'My mother likes that sort of food,' said Vanessa.

'It's about as different from what we serve as can be,' said Meg, feeling somewhat desperate. 'Basically, we do home cooking, using fresh and very local ingredients. We can't really compete with this sort of thing.' She paused. 'Although we could make an effort to get more fish. We're not far from the coast, after all.'

'I'll have the parfait,' said Alexandra. 'Followed by the chicken. I'll stick to the one bird.'

'Chicken à la king sounds rather American to me,' said Meg, feeling snippy because she'd lost confidence in Nightingale Woods being able to compete with this fashionable, prosperous establishment.

'I think it's quite popular with Americans,' said Vanessa. 'It's one of the things my mother doesn't approve of.' She sighed. 'She's such a snob.'

74

'So, do you think she could be lured away from the fleshpots of Newton-cum-Hardy and go to Nightingale Woods instead?' asked Alexandra.

Meg laughed. 'I'm not sure this place could really be described as "fleshpots", could it?'

'What I'm asking is, wouldn't Nessa's mother really prefer somewhere more English, restrained and classy?' Alexandra persisted.

'She probably would, really, if it wasn't for the bathroom thing,' said Vanessa. 'And there's a swimming pool here. Not that my mother uses it. Her hair wouldn't stand for it.' She rolled her eyes and sighed again.

'We can't possibly compete with a swimming pool,' said Meg. 'We'll have to concentrate on attracting parents of pupils at the local prep school, and people in the area celebrating their birthdays.' It didn't sound as if there would be anything like enough people to make their little hotel viable. 'I wonder if we could get in touch with the school, and offer their parents a discount if they stay with us?'

'Good idea,' said Alexandra, 'especially if you slightly increase your prices so you're not actually losing money.'

'That would be cheating,' said Meg and then blushed, aware her companions were looking at her as if she was mad.

'Well, offer them two nights for a slightly lower rate, or three, or whatever seems best,' said Alexandra.

'Actually,' said Meg, 'I think the headmaster came to this really big lunch we put on when I first arrived.'

'You didn't tell me about that,' said Vanessa.

'It was a sort of banquet,' said Meg. 'An event for local people who come year after year, and whose parents came before them. It's a tradition. But we – me and Justin – had to take over the cooking at very short notice. It was hugely successful.'

'Have you got a list of everyone who came?' asked Vanessa, interested. 'You could get in touch with them and offer them a special deal because they came to the banquet. People like to feel special.'

Meg nodded. 'They do all feel connected to the hotel already. So many of their relations worked there, or on the estate over the generations. They'd probably be thrilled, as if they were part of a club or something.'

'That sounds like a very good idea, Vanessa,' said Alexandra.

'I'm good at things like that,' said Vanessa, sounding wistful. 'Mummy always used to have people arranging parties at home and I used to hang around them, getting in the way. I learnt a lot.'

'You live in a stately home, Ness,' said Meg.

Vanessa didn't argue with this description. 'It's such a shame I can't stay with you and work on your advertising. If only I didn't have a wedding coming up. I wouldn't mind so much if I was allowed to organise it.'

She sounded very fed up, thought Meg. 'So your mother is doing it all?' she said. 'Golly! Remember Lizzie's mother? She was obsessed.'

Vanessa nodded. 'Whenever I make a suggestion, about the catering, the flowers, the photographs, or the cake, Mummy says, "We always use so-and-so," and that's that.'

'I thought everyone liked weddings,' said Alexandra.

Vanessa shook her head. 'I really like other people's weddings, like Lizzie's, and yours, but when it's your own, it's all a lot more worrying. And although Mummy is organising it all, I have to make sure she isn't doing something I really don't like. There's a perfectly ghastly tiara she thinks I should wear.'

'Grim,' said Alexandra.

'And Simon and I thought it would be nice for the guests who are staying with us, or nearby, to have a dance, after me and Simon have gone.'

'That sounds like a nice idea.'

'Mummy will only let us have the band we've always had. Do you remember at Hugo's engagement party? Most of the band are over seventy and only play waltzes and quicksteps.'

'But you won't be there,' said Alexandra. 'Does it matter?'

'Yes!' said Vanessa. 'It's my wedding!' She paused for a second as she spotted a couple of waiters coming across the room with two dome-covered dishes. 'At last! Our first course. The service isn't very good here, is it?'

All through the meal, Meg was aware that Alexandra and Vanessa were being disparaging about the food entirely for her sake. She herself could see it was excellent: modern, sophisticated and what everyone wanted to eat in London or other big cities. And apparently in rural Dorset.

They decided against the crêpes Suzette but had coffee in the lounge instead. It was while they were playing with the gold foil that had covered the chocolate peppermints that Alexandra said, 'We really need to have a look at one of the rooms. I'll arrange it.'

Meg looked in horror as her friend sashayed across the room and out into the reception area. 'I feel enough of a spy already,' she said to Vanessa, 'without looking at the rooms as well.'

'But you do need to do it really,' said Vanessa. 'How else will you know what your hotel is missing otherwise?'

Meg knew Vanessa was right, but even so, she crossed her fingers that Alexandra wouldn't be able to arrange it.

At last Alexandra could be seen on her way back to their table with a young woman smartly dressed in a black suit and black patent shoes with kitten heels. Meg hated her before she even spoke to her because she looked so perfect.

'Good afternoon, ladies,' said the woman. 'The Countess has explained you're checking to see if this hotel is suitable for your mother.' She looked at Vanessa. 'I'm Laura, I'll be happy to assist you in any way.'

Meg noticed that Laura was wearing a discreet badge with 'Laura Wilde, Reception', written on it. Should the staff at Nightingale Woods wear smart suits and badges? she wondered. She wasn't sure it was a look that would work for them.

They followed Laura up the thickly carpeted stairs to the first floor. 'I'm going to show you one of our deluxe rooms.' She unlocked a door. 'As you see, we have a large double bed. There is a dressing table, wardrobe and chair. All the furniture has been specially made for the hotel.'

To Meg's horror, Vanessa went over to the bed, pulled back the bedspread and rubbed the sheet between her fingers. 'My mother is very particular about her bed linen.'

Laura bowed respectfully. 'Of course. You will have noticed our linen is of the very best quality.'

'And everything matches,' said Alexandra. 'The curtains, the carpets, the bedspread.'

'Of course,' said Laura as if everything matching was an essential part of the service.

Meg could tell that Alexandra didn't really approve of this, and she preferred the decoration in Nightingale Woods too. Things went together, looked harmonious, but they weren't all the same.

'The bathroom is through here,' said Laura, opening a door. 'All very compact and convenient for our guests.'

'We'll go and see the grounds now,' said Alexandra. 'And we can manage on our own, thank you, Laura.'

'Oh.' Laura was put out. She'd obviously really enjoyed showing off the hotel. It was almost as if she owned it. 'You won't forget to see the swimming pool, will you? It's covered, and heated. Very pleasant when our English summers are so unreliable.'

'We wouldn't miss it for the world,' said Meg, eager to be rid of Laura and her annoying enthusiasm.

Reassuringly, the grounds weren't as nice or nearly as extensive as those at Nightingale Woods. The swimming pool and its attendant buildings took up a lot of space and the surrounding countryside wasn't as pretty. It didn't have the wonderful views down to the river, either.

'And there is absolutely nowhere where you could put on a play,' said Alexandra as they walked back to the car. 'And it's expensive.' She looked at a brochure she had in her hand.

'Did Laura give you that?' asked Meg.

'Of course. Do you have a brochure for Nightingale Woods?'

'Yes, but it's ancient,' said Meg. 'It goes on a lot about accommodation for nannies and how morning tea can't be served after ten o'clock in the morning.' She paused. 'Now, we'd serve morning tea in the rooms at any time if we could.'

'Add "rewrite the brochure" to your list of things for Justin,' said Alexandra. 'I am so sorry I won't be around to see all the changes.'

'You'll have to come if David's friend puts on a play,' said Meg, not sure this was likely.

'I'd definitely come to that – and bring the family. Félicité is brilliant at murals, as you know. She could paint scenery and Henri can play almost any musical instrument. Now hop in the car, you two. I wonder what David and Louise have been up to?'

Meg took a last look at the hotel as Alexandra sped away. It looked very imposing up there on the hill. She saw a figure come out of the side of the building and stand, possibly watching them leave. It was probably someone from the kitchen having a bit of a breather. What was it like to work there? she wondered. It would be very well organised, she decided, but not friendly. Nightingale Woods was like a family where everyone helped out.

The hotel felt very much like home to Meg now, and on their return they found David and Louise in high spirits.

'No bookings for dinner but a lovely young couple came up on spec. They wanted tea,' said Louise.

Meg gasped. 'Oh my goodness, what did you give them? There's only the perennial fruit cake we always have on the go.'

'We sent them round the garden,' said David. 'Louise set a little table just near where there'll be a play if I have anything to do with it . . .'

'Yes?'

'And I made scones,' David went on. 'So they had sandwiches, scones hot out of the oven, butter and home-made jam, and the fruit cake, cut into little square pieces. They were delighted.'

'We used one of the old tea sets from the cupboard,' said Louise. 'It was so charming. And the best bit is – they're coming for lunch on Sunday, with his mother.

They're newly married and also new to the area. I got the impression from the woman, Suzanne – not that we used her Christian name – that her mother-in-law is a bit of a tartar.'

'He – her son – said she had very high standards and that taking her out for lunch rather than trying to get it right at home would be a brilliant solution,' added David.

'And the mother-in-law is very high up in the local WI,' said Louise, 'so if we do a good job, she'll tell all her friends.'

'I'm only sorry I won't be here to supervise the roast lamb,' said David and then made a face at Meg so she knew he was teasing.

'We have always done teas, but not in the garden,' said Louise. 'We must do them again if the weather is nice.'

'You could advertise them in your new brochure,' said Vanessa. 'It would make you stand out from other hotels.'

'"Tea in the Garden",' said Meg. 'That would be brilliant. And, more importantly, wouldn't cost anything.'

She smiled, suddenly feeling much more positive about what Nightingale Woods could offer. It wasn't just a matter of spending a lot of money to make a hotel special. It was more to do with thought and care, and a lovely setting.

'Well done, Mum and David, for doing that.'

'We loved it!' they both said, more or less together.

Chapter Ten

❧

'It's so sad to see them go,' said Vanessa, standing on the hotel steps next to Meg and Louise the following day. 'Just being with you all makes me feel so much better about everything.'

'And between you, Nessa, and them, we now have so many really good ideas on how to improve things,' said Louise.

'I'm not quite so convinced by David's "singing round the piano" evenings,' said Meg, 'but all your ideas were brilliant, Ness.'

'We must make sure we do all the ones that don't cost major money,' said Louise.

'I'll add them to the list for Justin. He may be able to give us a small budget for the little things.'

'Although it's the big things, like private bathrooms, that will really make a difference,' said Louise.

'I wonder if I could talk my mother into coming here with her chums for the charity race day at Shroton? I certainly could if there were bathrooms,' said Vanessa. 'And if you put your prices up to what the other hotel is charging – even a bit less – you'd be quids in.'

Louise laughed. 'I'm not sure your mother would like you using expressions like "quids in".'

Vanessa joined in the laughter. 'But seriously, your gardens and grounds are so much nicer.'

'And we have a natural amphitheatre for outside entertainment,' said Meg. 'According to David.' She spent a few minutes imagining some wonderful performance in beautiful weather, the grounds thronging with people who were somehow bringing revenue to the hotel. 'I need to get in touch with all the people who came to the banquet. Vanessa thought we could offer them some sort of deal, for Sunday lunch.'

'What a good idea!' said Louise. 'I do have a list of people but that's a lot of letters to write.'

'I can do that,' said Vanessa eagerly. 'I did a shorthand and typing course. I'm not very good at shorthand but I was top of the class for typing.'

'Won't your mother be upset if you don't go home?' said Meg.

'Although of course we want to keep you,' said Louise.

'We really do!' confirmed Meg.

'I'll give her a ring, convince her I'm doing something ladylike and potentially useful. She won't really mind me not being there for a couple of days, as long as I keep up to date with my thank-you letters.'

'But how will you do that if you don't open the presents? You can't just write "thank you for the present" like the boys did at the school where I worked,' said Louise.

'Someone will open them and make a list and then I'll ring up and find out what the presents are. Simon and I made a wedding list, but people don't seem to stick to it much.' Vanessa shrugged. 'I don't really mind.'

'If you don't mind my asking, why are you getting presents so early? The wedding's not until September, I thought?' asked Louise.

Vanessa rolled her eyes. 'Another drama! Our vicar had to change the date after the invitations had gone out. Apparently most people got their present buying done early.' She paused. 'And I swear Mummy is using the extra time to invite a whole lot more people. I gather there's a secret "whose daughter has the biggest wedding competition" going on. It would be funny if it wasn't all such a strain.'

Meg felt her friend came from a different planet and patted her arm comfortingly. 'Well, if you can stay here – even for a little while – we'd be thrilled!'

Susan was on kitchen duty that evening. They had four people booked in for dinner and as this wasn't very challenging there was plenty of time to chat about her family, which was what she liked to do. 'Bob has taken up plumbing in his old age.'

'Oh, I do hope he won't give up on the garden,' said Meg, worried. 'His vegetables are vital. People always mention how delicious they are.'

'Fresh out of the ground, they're bound to be good,' said Susan, accepting the compliment about her husband's skills with a nod. 'But he's decided we need a bathroom upstairs. He says he's too old to traipse up and down stairs in the middle of the night.'

This made Meg look up from the profiteroles she was filling with cream. 'Is he good at plumbing?'

Louise also paused in her glass polishing. Meg knew her mother was thinking the same thing that she was.

'That remains to be seen,' said Susan. 'Is it just the one sweet on offer tonight?'

'No, we've also got chocolate mousse or crêpes Suzette,' said Meg.

'What's that when it's at home?'

'They served it at the other hotel,' said Vanessa.

'It's just pancakes with fancy liquor,' said Meg. 'I do it at the table. I found a chafing dish. It's all the rage in London, which is probably why they were serving it up the road.'

'London!' said Susan with a toss of her head.

'So tell us about the plumbing,' said Meg. 'We might need him to do some here. We may want to ask him to put in some extra bathrooms.'

'I'll let you know how it goes,' said Susan, 'although personally I think we've got quite enough bathrooms to keep clean.' She paused, enjoying being the centre of attention. 'But I think we should just serve what we do best. Good home cooking with fresh, local ingredients. It was good enough for my granny; it should be good enough for anyone.'

Meg and Louise exchanged worried glances: it was possible that Susan was right and they should forget their fancy plans for the hotel. But later, when dinner was over, Susan had gone home and they were sharing a drink, everyone agreed they must go forward with their new ideas.

'Change is always unsettling,' said Louise. 'But in this case, it's for the best.'

Vanessa had reluctantly gone home after a few days of helping with the hotel. She had written dozens of letters, drafted a brochure which Louise had taken to the printers, and helped them work out what sort of advantageous rates they could offer parents of the local prep school. She also suggested the hotel could offer special picnics, and tuck boxes full of home-made cakes and biscuits.

'You've been brilliant, Nessa!' said Meg, hugging her as her friend prepared to leave. 'I do wish you could stay forever!'

'Yes, you've been so helpful,' Louise agreed. 'I'm good at managing an office, but my typing is "hunt and peck" and takes me ages.'

'I've loved it,' said Vanessa. 'I'll come back whenever you need me – as long as my bloody wedding doesn't need me more!'

'I do hope you're joking,' said Louise. 'You do love your Simon?'

'Oh, Simon is wonderful; it's all that goes with him regarding the wedding day that's difficult. Anyway,' said Vanessa, finally getting into the car, 'I must get off!'

'Nice girl,' said Louise as she and Meg went back into the house.

'Yes. Her brother is lovely too. Which is surprising when you think how difficult her parents are.'

Meg was grateful that something had delayed Justin coming to see her plan for improvements, so, when he telephoned to say he was on his way, she was ready for him. It was a shame that Louise was in the local town for the day, so she would have to deal with him on her own. With luck, he would take the report and go.

'So, here's the plan,' she said, handing him the buff folder that Vanessa had insisted would make it look more professional. 'Of course, lots of the ideas to increase business would require fairly major changes to the house so would cost money.'

'As we have discussed, there's little or no money for alterations beyond a bit of paint,' said Justin immediately, before Meg had even finished getting her plan out of its cardboard folder.

Meg sighed. 'I've divided this into things that would cost nothing, or only a little.' The only thing that would cost nothing would be moving some tables out into the garden for afternoon tea on sunny days, but he'd realise that quite soon. 'And more major projects that would definitely increase bookings.'

'Tell me your plans.'

'Why don't you just read the report?' Meg felt grumpy because she was nervous and he was being so formal and unbending.

He sighed and now Meg noticed he looked tired. 'Just tell me. I can read the detail later.'

She took a deep breath. Here goes, she thought.

'Our problem is, we're quite old-fashioned. The locals know about us, but we can't survive on just local business and a few people who've spotted us in guidebooks that are several years old. We hadn't even got an up-to-date brochure, although we have had some printed. And we're not in any current guides.'

She hoped the seriousness of not being in guide-books would distract him from the fact they'd gone ahead with the new brochures without consulting him.

'Getting into guidebooks isn't a simple business, and it can be expensive,' said Justin.

'I know,' she said, although she hadn't been certain. 'As this is the case, we need to get in new business from other sources. So far, we've written to all the people who came to the banquet offering them special rates for Sunday lunch. We've had a few—'

'How few?' Justin interrupted.

'Three – but it's early days. And teas in the garden have been popular. But it's always the same people. It's good they're coming more, but as I said, we can't do it on local business alone.'

'Go on,' said Justin, looking more interested now.

'What we really need to do is to bring the hotel up to date a bit, without losing its country-house charm. That's one of the reasons people like it so much. But we need at least some bedrooms with their own bath-rooms.'

Justin stared at her but didn't comment.

'Vanessa – one of my friends who've just been staying – said her mother, Lady Lennox-Stanley, comes to a charity race day at Shroton every year and she brings people with her. Vanessa says her mother would come here if she had a private bathroom.'

'Where does she go at the moment?'

'The hotel in Newton-cum-Hardy, which is much more modern, has a lot of rooms with their own bathrooms, a swimming pool, is the same distance from the racecourse as we are, but is much more expensive.'

'Of course it's more expensive; it has a lot more to offer. And if Lady Lennox-Stanley can afford it, I don't see any reason why she wouldn't go on staying there.'

'But why would you want her to go elsewhere with her friends when they could come here? Where are your loyalties?' She'd meant this rhetorically but saw that his expression had subtly changed.

He looked at her directly, almost for the first time. 'Were you impressed with the hotel when you and your friends went to have lunch at the hotel last week?' he asked.

Everything fell into place. The smartly dressed young women who was so proud of the hotel and had shown them round had obviously told Justin they had been there.

'You work there, don't you? That's why you don't want this hotel to succeed, because you work there!' Meg found this terribly upsetting, far more upsetting than was logical, she knew. 'Did Laura Wilde tell you we'd been?'

He looked uncomfortable. 'Yes, I do work there, and yes, Laura did tell me about your visit. She was very impressed with the Countess.'

For a moment, Meg found herself close to tears and she didn't know why. She took a breath. 'Isn't that a conflict of interests? You're working for your father's hotel's main rival!' She didn't bother to hide her outrage.

'I don't think Nightingale Woods is a rival,' he said quietly. 'It's a charming, old-fashioned hotel.'

'And why not a rival?'

'Meg! You've been there – to the hotel where I work – you and your friends. It's new, it's owned by Raoul de Dijon . . .' He hesitated for a second as he realised this name hadn't got the reaction he was expecting. 'Who is, as you obviously don't know, the chef everyone in the business is talking about. He's launching a cookery book, and he's even going to be on television.'

'OK. I know quite enough about him,' said Meg, who had deliberately not reacted to the famous name. 'I still don't know why you're working for him, though, and not for your father's hotel.' A thought struck her. Maybe there was a personal reason for him working there. Maybe her name was Laura.

'My father can't afford to pay me – at least, not nearly enough.'

'Maybe if you worked at Nightingale Woods, more people could come, the prices could go up and we wouldn't be having these difficulties.'

Justin shook his head. 'You know that wouldn't work. People aren't going to come to a . . .'

'Very charming?'

'. . . hotel in a small corner of Dorset that no one's ever heard of because there's a new chef, who no one has ever heard of either.'

'What about word of mouth? We've got people who were at the lunch coming for meals. They're booking in for Sunday lunch, afternoon tea . . .' She realised she was repeating herself and sounding desperate.

'It won't be enough,' Justin said. 'Ultimately, the hotel will have to be sold.'

'Over my dead body!' The thought of the hotel she had come to love becoming the slick, soulless place she, Alexandra and Vanessa had had lunch at was horrible.

'Your body, dead or alive, won't have much to do with it,' said Justin. 'But I'll look at your ideas, and anything that doesn't cost money, you can do.'

Meg chewed her lip, wondering how to phrase what she intended to say next. 'No one's heard of me, I'm not even a classically trained chef, but people are coming.'

'Are you not trained at all, then?' Justin didn't seem to think this was possible.

Meg thought of the course she'd done with Mme Wilson. He would never consider that little cookery school in a Pimlico basement as training. 'Not formally, no. But in September I'm going to work with a chef in Provence.'

Justin laughed, not unkindly. 'You mean, you're being allowed to wash pots, for nothing, in a kitchen in Provence, while the chef shouts at you in a language you don't understand.'

Meg lifted her chin.

'I know. I've done it,' said Justin, 'and you're abso-lutely right to go. You'll learn so much. But you haven't learnt it yet. Although I have to admit, you are doing pretty well.'

Meg broke in. 'Supposing I said stop paying me. Keep my wage and invest it in the hotel.'

Justin stared at her as if she was a strange animal at risk of extinction. 'That's a ridiculous idea. Why would you do that when you have nothing to gain from it?'

'I do have things to gain from it, although nothing financial. My mother loves this hotel and I'd do it for her. I also love this hotel and I enjoy a challenge. There are such great ingredients available here. I know the locals probably don't want fancy food, like you produce, but they like good-quality plain food. Fresh vegetables and nursery puddings.' She paused. 'Though I might have to broaden people's horizons a bit there.'

'Don't you like cooking nursery puddings?'

'I like cooking what people want to eat but it would be more interesting to do other things too. I'm interested in becoming a pastry chef.' Meg paused. 'Not crêpes Suzette though. I'll leave that one to you.' She had cooked it a few days previously, but she felt it was showy. Susan, watching the process from the kitchen, called it 'all fur coat and no knickers'.

She took a breath, aware she was getting heated, which wouldn't be helpful. 'One of the reasons I want to go to France is so I can learn more about desserts.'

'You won't learn about that from a provincial restaurant, if you want to do more than crème caramel and îles flottantes.'

She knew this perfectly well. 'No, but while I'm there, I might be able to work in a pâtisserie.'

He studied her. 'You're serious about your cooking, aren't you?'

She nodded. 'Yes. Yes I am.'

'And you're prepared to sacrifice a summer's wages to improve a hotel you really don't have anything to do with.'

'I said, it's for my mother.'

Although giving up her wages would be a sacrifice, she was excited by the prospect of improving things at the hotel.

'How would your mother feel about you giving up your wages?'

Justin had put his finger on the weak spot. 'I'll convince her it's a perfectly good idea,' she said. Then she smiled. 'Tell me, what's the new favourite pudding of the smart people who eat at your hotel?'

He smiled back. 'Why should I tell you?'

'Because you owe this hotel something!'

'Fair enough. What they really like is the sweet trolley. You know, crème caramel, fruit salad for the dieters, an apple tart, profiteroles, Black Forest gateau, things like that. They're more likely to order a dessert if they can actually see it. We let people have a selection.'

'Isn't there a lot of wastage?'

'Some. You have to keep an eye on it. But it means people order something they hadn't intended to have.'

'Thank you,' said Meg, her mind full of puddings that she could put on the trolley.

'It's good if you can do desserts. So many chefs, me included, haven't got the patience for them.'

'I do like doing the fiddly stuff,' said Meg, forgetting that Justin was her enemy. 'I used to have to make trays and trays of canapés when I worked in London, for my evening job.'

'I can't imagine anything I'd like less. But good for you. It's an art.'

Meg thought how much she'd like to go on talking to Justin about food. Her mother was only partially interested, and Vanessa didn't really care about it at all, in spite of attending Mme Wilson's course. Not for the first time, she wished that David lived in England. He had always shared her passion.

Justin got up from his chair. 'Time I wasn't here. Look, I won't let you work for nothing, but I'll make the budget for making changes a bit bigger than I would have done.'

He walked out of the office and a few minutes later, Meg heard his motorbike roar away.

Chapter Eleven

Meg had contrived to take a look at the bathroom that Bob had put in his and Susan's house. It had turned out really well and Susan was proud of her husband's handiwork and had been only too keen to show it off. Meg decided she could ask Bob to do the work. But not without talking to her mother about it first.

She waited until she and Louise were both off duty and had taken a tray of tea and some cheese scones (her mother's favourite) into the office. She had poured the tea and her mother had just put some butter on a scone when the phone rang.

'Andrew!' said her mother delightedly. Since she turned away from Meg as she did this, Meg took the hint, and her tea, and left her mother to it.

'Andrew's coming back!' Louise said delightedly a little while later, joining Meg in the kitchen. 'He can't stay, but he needs the deeds to the hotel.' She paused, her eyes sparkling with excitement. 'I suggested I could post them but he said no, he wanted to come back.'

'To see you?' Meg suggested.

Her mother nodded, too happy to speak.

'I can't wait to meet him,' said Meg.

She had been using the time when she was waiting for Louise to make tiny meringue stars with egg whites left over from the crème caramel she'd prepared for the sweet trolley. Although the trolley was proving very popular, Meg was careful to make sure it wasn't too expensive. So two puddings from half a dozen eggs was satisfying.

'I know he's going to really like you,' said Louise. 'And you've done so much for the hotel.'

'I'd like to do more,' said Meg. 'I'd really like to ask Bob to create a couple of bathrooms. Well, three, actually, for the biggest bedrooms, which already have dressing rooms. Then maybe think about some others.'

'Those dressing rooms are now singles,' said Louise. 'We'd be losing that money if they were bathrooms.'

'We could charge so much more for the doubles though, Mum. And single rooms aren't used all that much, are they? We don't get travelling salesmen needing them.'

'We'll have to ask Andrew about it. We couldn't do anything like that without his knowledge and agreement.'

Meg realised that she hadn't made allowances for Andrew having a say in the matter. Because Justin had said she could go ahead, she felt this was permission enough. 'But I can ask Bob to quote for doing them?' she said. 'Then Andrew can make a decision having all the information he needs.'

Louise nodded in agreement, but it was obvious that her mind was not on en-suite bathrooms.

*

As the day of Andrew's arrival drew nearer, Meg could see that Louise was getting more and more excited.

Louise had given up trying to pretend that he was just the man she worked for and clearly wanted to make his homecoming special.

'Why don't we put a table in the library,' said Meg, 'just for the two of you?'

'No! You must eat with us or it might be awkward,' Louise said.

Meg realised her mother was nervous as well as excited. 'OK. But I'll just be in the way, you know.'

'No, you won't. He'll want to meet you, to get to know you properly. I'm very proud of my daughter and everything you've done for Nightingale Woods.'

'Well, that's lovely, but—'

'You can leave us alone when we have coffee if I give you the signal.'

'What signal should it be?' asked Meg, wondering if it was quite normal to be having a conversation like this with one's mother.

'I don't know. We'll think of something. Now I'm just going to change. What do you think I should wear?'

'Well . . .'

'Oh, don't worry, darling. I'll find something suitable. You were never very interested in clothes, were you?'

Meg considered this. 'No, not really.' As she went back to the kitchen to focus on what she had always been interested in, she concluded she'd never had anyone to dress up for. Justin floated into her mind and she gave a little laugh. Imagine wanting to dress up for him!

Andrew was just as nice as her mother had said he was, and relief flooded over Meg as she greeted this pleasant-looking, kindly man, who wasn't particularly dashing but had a beautiful speaking voice and obviously adored her mother.

'It's wonderful you were able to come down and help Louise when I had to dash off,' he said, taking the glass of sherry she handed him. 'I felt so guilty leaving her on her own with Geoff. Although he was always fine when I was here.'

Meg took a glass of sherry herself and sat down. 'I was thrilled to be able to come. I didn't much like the job I had in London. It had become very boring.'

'So, Andrew, do tell us how you're getting on in France,' said Louise, seating herself near him on the sofa. 'Is it lovely?'

'It's fine, I suppose,' said Andrew, 'but the estate is in a muddle and I missed being here.'

The 'with you' was silent, Meg realised, but still evident.

Meg went to put out the kipper pâté with Melba toast in the library, at a neat little table set for three. She was just taking the second batch of toast out of the oven, pleased that it had browned evenly and looked professional when she heard a motorbike. Oh God, she thought, Justin!

She didn't know what to do. Should she set another place? Or should Justin take her place? She wasn't a ditherer normally, but she found herself moving about the kitchen like a cat, unsure where to settle.

Justin came into the kitchen from the back door, nodded at her and then strode through to the main house, still wearing motorbike leathers.

Angry with herself for being so put out, Meg went to the door of the kitchen, trying to overhear what was going on in the drawing room.

'Justin!' Meg heard Andrew say.

'Dad,' said Justin.

'I didn't think you were going to be able to come over,' said Andrew.

'Raoul is taking my place on the pass tonight.'

'Would you like a glass of sherry, Justin?' Meg heard her mother say, her voice revealing how uncomfortable she obviously felt.

'No, thank you. Have you got any whisky?'

Meg ran back into the kitchen, trying to remember if the drinks cupboard was fully stocked. She ought to bring in some water. Was there ice? She pulled open the refrigerator and opened the bit at the top. There was a metal tray of ice in there. It took a bit of chipping with a knife but she got it out and was running hot water over it to release the cubes when her mother came in.

'It's Justin!' she said in a stage whisper.

'I know!' said Meg, also whispering. 'He came in through the kitchen. Did anyone know he was going to be here tonight?' she added in a normal voice.

'You mean Andrew? I don't think so.'

'Well, I'll carry on getting the meal out, you go back and take this ice and some water for his whisky. I eavesdropped,' she added.

'He's a bit unnerving in his motorbike leathers,' Louise said.

'Oh, Mum! Pull yourself together! He's only human,' said Meg.

'I'll take that as a compliment,' said Justin, striding into the room. 'You've got ice. Excellent. I am staying for dinner and you'll eat with us, Meg. Assuming you can get it on the table and eat it without dropping anything?'

He was being so rude that Meg just rolled her eyes. She wasn't going to reward his bad behaviour with a reaction. He was probably being overprotective of his father regarding Louise. It was natural, but annoying. 'I'll get you some water.'

'I don't need water.' Justin gave her one of the looks he had probably perfected over the years, so he could turn a kitchen porter into stone without having to raise his voice. 'But thank you for the ice.'

What should have been a quiet dinner for three, with the third rushing off as soon after pudding as she could, was suddenly fraught with tension: Justin wasn't happy.

As she watched him layer bits of melba toast with butter and pâté (she was glad she hadn't made butter curls, although she had been tempted), Meg saw there was antipathy between him and his father. The looks he sent towards her mother, who was trying to make polite conversation, were fairly savage too.

'Why didn't you tell me you were coming home, Dad?' he asked.

'I'm only here for a night,' said Andrew. 'I didn't think you'd be able to get away.' He paused. 'Did Colin tell you I was coming?'

'Yes,' said Justin.

'Colin is my brother,' said Andrew to Louise and Meg. 'I'm the executor of my father's will but, of course, he has an interest in it.'

'He doesn't feel that he has an interest,' said Justin.

'He's annoyed that he isn't an executor too,' said Andrew. 'Although I don't know why. It's a hell of a lot of work.'

'So why are you here, Dad?' asked Justin.

'I need the deeds to Nightingale Woods. There are some details that need clarifying.'

'I did say I could have posted them to you,' said Louise, obviously trying to be placatory.

'But that would have necessitated you knowing the combination to the safe,' said Justin. 'Which might not have been a good thing.'

Meg was outraged. Was Justin suggesting that if Louise knew the combination of the safe she might steal something?

Andrew frowned at his son. 'You don't have to be so rude, Justin. I wanted to check on things here so I decided to fetch them myself.' He gave Louise a rather obviously loving look.

Justin looked down at the table, scowling. Meg got up. 'I'm going to get the next course,' she said. 'No!' She held up a peremptory hand. 'I don't need help.'

In spite of this, Louise joined her in the kitchen. 'It's awful! Justin obviously hates me,' she said, whispering again, although there was no danger of them being overheard from two rooms and a large hall away.

'Take no notice. You know what he's like. Can you put a plate in the hot oven for me? I only warmed three.'

'Isn't that rather a lot of butter for the mashed potato?' said Louise, having obliged with the plate.

'No. It's a perfect amount!' Meg was getting tetchy. 'Now, is that everything?' She had a large tray laden with vegetable dishes.

'Why don't you serve it in here, and take the full plates through? Then there's less risk of spilling chicken chasseur on the tablecloth,' said Louise.

'Good idea, although I'm calling it hunter's chicken. I'll leave the fancy French names for the hotel in Newton-cum-Hardy with the fancy French owner and the grumpy chef,' said Meg.

'I'll take the tray with the veg,' said Louise.

'And I'll bring the plates. But only two at a time. I'll have to come back anyway. No need to show off how many plates I can carry on my arm.'

She wouldn't have admitted it to anyone, not even her mother, but Meg didn't trust her plate-balancing skills at that moment.

Had Meg known Justin was going to be at the meal, she'd have done something a bit more complicated than profiteroles, but they'd had a booking for afternoon tea and so she'd done eclairs for the visitors. After making a *croquembouche* for Alexandra's wedding she felt she could make choux pastry in her sleep. Now, although the profiteroles were piled up nicely in dishes, filled with cream and covered in a really good chocolate sauce, she felt embarrassed. If she was the good pastry chef she'd almost claimed to be, she should probably have been offering something a bit more elaborate, although she couldn't think what that might be. She brought them in on a tray, her head held high.

Justin gave her an inscrutable look, but didn't comment. Andrew and Louise both oohed and aahed obligingly.

'Would you like coffee in here or in the drawing room?' she asked the moment everyone had put down their spoons. She planned to dump the coffee and then flee.

She felt she'd got away with it: no one asked her if she wanted coffee, probably because she firmly said she didn't, and she had nearly finished the washing-up before Justin caught up with her in the kitchen.

'You're not a bad cook for an amateur,' he said, with just a hint of a twinkle.

'Couldn't you have said "gifted amateur"?' Meg replied.

To her surprise, he laughed. 'I suppose not even I can be that patronising. But considering you haven't been classically trained, you are very good.'

'I think Mme Wilson, who taught me in London, cared a lot about food. I only realised quite how high her standards were when I started getting catering jobs.'

'What sort of establishment was it?' Justin seemed curious.

'Most of her students were debutantes who were there to keep themselves busy in the mornings and to be made more attractive to aristocratic husbands. But we weren't all like that.'

'So you don't want an aristocratic husband?'

'I can't imagine anything worse!' Although saying this reminded her of Alexandra's Antoine, who was very aristocratic. But Antoine was different.

'What about your mother?'

Meg put down the saucepan she'd been scrubbing. 'What do you mean?'

Justin sighed. 'Does your mother want an aristocratic husband, or would one who is set to inherit a very beautiful old house do?'

'Are you implying my mother is after your father's money?'

'I'm hardly implying it, I'm saying it outright. Does your mother have a history of working for men she then tries to marry?'

There was so much that Meg wanted to say, to express her utter fury at the outrageousness of his suggestion that she took a deep breath and just said, 'No. It's usually the other way round. I've never known her to be remotely interested in any of the people she's worked for. She has to leave jobs because her employer begins to become a nuisance.'

'She doesn't seem to find my father a nuisance.'

'That's probably because he's not one. He just seems kind and considerate, a good employer, who doesn't make unwelcome advances.'

'Thank you for the testimonial.'

'The strange thing is that he has you for a son,' said Meg.

Justin laughed again, genuinely amused. 'At least you can't accuse me of making unwanted advances.'

'Well, not to me, you haven't, but maybe other women who work for you have had a different experience.' She looked him firmly in the eye and then suddenly thought of Laura Wilde who had shown them round: elegant, well-groomed and thin. They both worked at the hotel. But would advances from Justin be unwelcome? she wondered. Possibly not!

'I can assure you,' he said, still entertained, 'that I never make unwanted advances.'

'Good for you,' said Meg, wondering if she could nip round the kitchen table and escape, although it would be an extremely cowardly thing to do. 'And I'm sure you never bully anyone in the kitchens you run either.'

He found this even funnier. 'You are definitely lying. I know perfectly well you think I bully people who work under me.'

'I wouldn't suggest you bully the people who work for you any more than anyone else. You just bully everyone.' She sounded so brave, she thought. Alexandra, who was inclined to think that Meg didn't stand up for herself enough, would have been proud.

Justin frowned. 'I don't suffer fools gladly, that's true. But I wouldn't describe myself as a bully.'

'Bullies never do. It doesn't mean they don't bully people. You try to bully me, for example.'

'But you're strangely resistant,' he said.

'That's because you're not actually my boss. I'm good at my job and that means I don't have to take any notice of your nonsense.'

Justin looked a bit taken aback. 'You don't take any prisoners, do you?'

'No. And while I'm speaking truth to power, my mother is definitely not a gold digger and it's perfectly possible that your father is attracted to her just because she's . . .' Meg, who felt she'd been pretty eloquent up to this point, struggled for the right word. 'Nice,' she finished lamely.

'She is very attractive,' Justin said. 'One might almost say she takes after her daughter in more than just looks but that would be—'

'Ridiculous!' said Meg before he could get any further. 'Now I'm tired and I'm going to bed, if you'll excuse me.' Without waiting for a response, she left the kitchen, delighted to have had the last word for once.

Chapter Twelve

The next morning, Meg got up earlier than usual, pulling on a pair of slacks that were lying around and a handy Breton top that she had bought in France.

In the kitchen, she was surprised to find everything cleared away, although she'd gone to bed (or more accurately walked out in a huff) before it was finished. She took a pot of oats that had been soaking overnight and put it on the stove. Ambrosine loved porridge, with thick cream and brown sugar. Meg was fond of it too.

'Oh! Porridge!' said Andrew, coming in, looking freshly shaved and enthusiastic. 'I love porridge.'

'So does Ambrosine. We don't have it every day but I put the oats on to soak yesterday as we have some cream to go with it.' Meg paused. 'I hope you don't mind me giving the guests cream? I know Geoff—'

'Geoff was a horrible mistake,' said Andrew. 'Your mother told me all about him. And Ambrosine wrote to me. She was singing your praises.'

Meg relaxed a little. They could safely talk about Ambrosine and so, with luck, wouldn't run out of conversation.

'Ambrosine also told me how well you'd managed the lunch.'

'Justin came and we did it together, in the end.'

'And it was a brilliant success. I gather that people who went to it have come back? Sunday lunch and afternoon tea?'

'Yes. A friend of mine was staying for a few days and she typed letters to all those guests, offering them a bit of a bargain.'

'That was a very good idea. This hotel badly needs some fresh ideas. I hope when I've sorted out my father's estate – if that happy day ever dawns – we can make some changes.'

Meg felt a pang of disappointment. She'd wanted to make changes before then. She knew that it could take months and months to sort things out after someone had died.

'What we really need,' Andrew went on, 'is to get back into a guide. My father let that slip and somehow I've never put it right.'

'Maybe my mother and I could help you with that,' said Meg, aware she sounded rather formal. She liked Andrew but she didn't know him very well.

She busied herself with cooking: stirring porridge, slicing bread for toast and putting butter into a couple of dishes. Eventually, her mother appeared.

She looked different, Meg couldn't help noticing. She had that slightly sultry look of a woman who had been thoroughly made love to. Although Meg had no personal experience of this, she'd seen it on others. It was very unsettling to see her mother's familiar features looking softer and guessing the reason. But she also looked very happy, which warmed Meg's heart.

'Oh, you're here, Andrew,' Louise said. 'Meg, you must have got up very quietly.'

'I got up early because I knew I'd left the kitchen in a mess,' said Meg. 'Thank you for doing it for me, Mum. Unless it was you, Andrew.'

'Justin did it,' said Andrew. 'I came in last night to find him finishing up.'

'Very kind,' said Meg, blushing although she wasn't quite sure why.

There was an awkward silence. 'I've made porridge,' said Meg, stating the obvious as they all watched the pot on the stove giving the occasional glug.

'Look, darling—'

'Mum, I wonder—'

Louise and Meg spoke at the same time, laughed awkwardly, and then Louise said, 'I was going to say that I can do breakfast if you like. It's only us, Ambrosine, and the couple in the Yellow Room.'

'And I was going to ask if you could manage as I really want to . . .' Meg paused, not knowing how to say 'get out of your way' politely. 'Explore the countryside a bit, get to know my surroundings.'

'I've always loved the view from the top of May Hill,' said Andrew, helpfully. 'Especially at this time of day. The early-morning mist makes everything magical.'

'I'd love to see it!' said Meg.

'Take the Mini,' said Louise.

'If you're sure?' Meg looked at Andrew.

He nodded. 'It's insured for any driver.'

Meg left, taking a slice of bread and butter with her, wishing she'd given herself time for another cup of tea.

Meg took some time to get used to the car – she'd only driven it once before (carefully, as she hadn't been sure if it had been insured) – and then set off up the nearest hill. She had only the faintest notion where May Hill was, but going up seemed like a good start.

She drove slowly, giving herself time to look at the view of the Dorset countryside. It was wonderful, like a landscape painting. But although she enjoyed seeing the curved green fields, the hedgerows, dotted with white-flowering trees that reminded her of patchwork quilts, she was really thinking about her mother and Andrew. They did seem very smitten with each other.

Why was Justin so hostile to her mother? Meg wondered. Had his father been the object of predatory women in the past? Or was it not a logical feeling at all? If her mother and Andrew got together formally (she wasn't quite ready to imagine them married), would Justin always make her mother's life difficult?

The hill became very steep and as she rounded a bend at a snail's pace she was confronted with a machine she couldn't instantly identify, rearing up from one side of the road. Then she saw it was a motorbike. It was so unexpected that her heart gave a jerk. She stopped immediately and she saw Justin half lying, half sitting next to his bike in a ditch.

She pulled the car into the side of the road, only just finding space for it, and got out, running towards Justin.

'Are you all right?' she said, looking down at him.

'Mostly. I think.' He smiled up at her sheepishly.

Meg realised he was embarrassed. She wouldn't have thought he was capable of such an emotion. 'What on earth happened?'

'I wanted to clear my head and so got the bike out for a ride early, before I had to start on lunch. A car came round the corner too fast. I pulled over, out of his way. Went into the ditch.'

'And the car didn't stop?'

'Nope. I've done something to my leg, and I can't get the bike out of here on my own.'

'I'd better make sure you haven't broken anything and then I can go back and ask the local farm if they can send a tractor.' She paused. 'Where's your helmet?'

'I wasn't wearing it,' he said.

Meg pursed her lips but didn't comment, her mind full of 'what ifs'? that were frightening. Then, glad she was wearing slacks, she clambered down into the ditch. Too late she realised that it was deep and there was water running along the bottom. But the sides were too steep for her to pull herself out easily so she waded along to where Justin was sitting, her feet squelching in the mud.

'Where does it hurt?' she said to him.

'My ankle made a noise when I hit the ground,' he said.

'Painful,' said Meg. 'Which one?' He was a little above her so she was in a good position to investigate.

'Right.'

'I may not be able to tell through your boot.' She gently prodded.

'Ow!' he said.

'I wonder if it's broken or just sprained?' She was thinking aloud.

'You won't be strong enough to get me out of here to find out,' said Justin. 'You'll have to get help.'

Meg smiled sweetly at him. 'Let's try, shall we? I'll get myself out of this ditch first, though.'

Someone only had to suggest that she couldn't do something, and Meg was absolutely determined that she could.

Hanging on to a tree, she pulled herself out of the ditch, the old tennis shoes she was wearing so muddy they probably wouldn't survive. 'Right. I'll hold on here and lean across. You see if you can reach me and then I'll pull you out.'

'I really don't think—'

'Just try!' snapped Meg, nervous in case she was about to look like an idiot. She didn't usually mind about failing in front of other people, but Justin was a special case.

It took a little while and several attempts, but eventually Justin reached Meg's free arm and between them they managed to get him out of the ditch and on to the road. He then sat down and looked at his injured leg.

'You know you're not supposed to move people if they have an accident,' said Justin. Meg bit her lip in irritation. Surely he should have been thanking her fervently, not criticising her treatment of him.

'Too late. You're moved. How's the leg?'

'Is there any chance you could prod it again?'

'I still can't really tell what's going on inside your boot. Perhaps you should take it off?'

'No! I don't think so. It could be holding my foot on, for all I know.'

'I think you'd be in quite a lot of pain if your foot was that badly injured!' said Meg.

'I am in quite a lot of pain,' said Justin quietly.

It was his quietness that made Meg worry. 'I'd better find a phone box and get an ambulance.'

'No!' said Justin. 'I really need to get to the hotel as soon as possible—'

'You can't cook if you can't walk,' said Meg.

'I know, but I can reorganise the staff and find someone to rescue the bike. Can we get me to your car, do you think?'

He was definitely more subdued and Meg thought the pain was probably worse now. It took a lot of effort and a certain amount of swearing to get him to her car.

'Sorry about the bad language,' he said when at last she'd got him into the front seat.

'For goodness' sake! I've worked in professional kitchens. I know all the words,' Meg said, embarrassed by his apology.

'But still,' he said, 'my father would be appalled at me using language like that in front of a woman.'

'He'd probably be more appalled by you riding your bike without a helmet,' Meg pointed out. She walked round the car, got in and turned the ignition key.

Justin spent most of the journey with his eyes closed but when they reached the hotel he directed her round the back and she managed to find somewhere to park that was fairly near the door. 'I'm going to see if there's anyone to help,' she said.

'Good plan,' he said and closed his eyes again.

She was met at the door by Laura Wilde, no longer so svelte, in a dressing gown, looking panic-stricken. 'What are you doing here?' she demanded.

'I've got Justin—'

Laura didn't wait to hear more. 'Ever since I knew he'd gone out on his bike I've been worried sick! Where is he?'

'In the car. I think we need to call an ambulance.'

The amount of attention and urgency her words created gave Meg the impression that Justin was more than just a chef to Laura; maybe a lot more.

Chapter Thirteen

As Meg drove back to Nightingale Woods she found herself strangely put out by what had happened. She tried to analyse her feelings. She'd found Justin (whom she disliked) in a ditch. She'd done all she could to help him – she'd been a Good Samaritan. She'd driven him to the hotel where he worked, and his friends had taken over, leaving her free to go on her way. What was wrong with that?

When she got down to the root of her feelings she concluded it was Laura Wilde she found so irritating. She'd behaved as if she owned Justin, and Meg had felt almost blamed for his predicament.

She sighed deeply; she was put out because Laura was a very bossy woman. Bossy women could be irritating. That was it. No need to feel weird about it. It was all fine!

Meg found her mother in the kitchen when she got there. 'Oh, are you back already?' Louise said. 'But you're covered in mud! What happened?'

'I found Justin and his bike in a ditch on my way to May Hill.' She laughed ruefully. 'It's rather a long story. I'd better go and get changed before I tell you about it.'

'But he's all right, isn't he?' Louise sounded worried.

'Oh yes. He's going to be fine. He may have broken his ankle or something, but nothing life-threatening.'

'Thank goodness for that!' said Louise. 'I'd better tell Andrew. I never have trusted motorbikes.'

And I don't trust the men who ride them, Meg thought.

Once she was back in the flat, she realised she felt quite shaky, as if she'd been in the accident as well as Justin.

She got as clean as she could under the little shower, which gave out tepid water in a feeble trickle. Though there were probably streaks of mud in places she couldn't see, she put on her cleanest dress and sandals. Then she went back to the kitchen. It was where she felt happiest.

Her mother seemed a bit out of sorts, as if she'd had bad news since Meg had told her about Justin's accident.

'How did breakfast go?' Meg asked her now.

'Perfectly fine. It couldn't go wrong, really.'

'So what's up, Mum?'

Louise instantly pulled out a chair and sat down at the kitchen table. 'Andrew's going back first thing tomorrow. He should go today, really, but I persuaded him—'

Meg heard the crack in her mother's voice and realised she was near tears.

'Oh, I'm so sorry.' Meg put the kettle on. While a cup of tea wasn't the cure-all everyone expected it to be, it might help a bit. 'Where's Andrew now?

Her mother sniffed bravely. 'He's in the office, going through the safe, looking for the deeds to the hotel. He says the safe is absolutely full of old papers that people have stuffed in there over the years.'

'Why don't I do a tray of coffee and you can take it in, and help him look?'

'I could do that.' Louise lowered her voice. 'I didn't realise how much I'd mind him going back. He's been away for a while now and I've been fine. It's just . . .'

'What?' asked Meg gently.

'I didn't know quite how he felt about me before. And of course, after last night . . .'

Meg stiffened, willing her mother not to say any more. But Louise took a breath as if she was about to carry on.

Meg interrupted quickly. 'Look, I can do everything here. You go into the office now, so you can spend as much time together as possible. I'll bring the coffee.'

'Thank you, darling. That would be so kind.'

Louise cleared her throat, wiped her nose on her handkerchief and then went to the small mirror and adjusted her hair. 'I'd better put some lipstick on.'

'I'll sort out the drinks.'

A couple of days after Andrew had left for France, the telephone rang and as Meg happened to be passing the office, she answered it. It was Justin.

'Is that Meg?' he said.

'Yes.'

'I was wondering if I could ask you a favour?'

She tensed. The hotel had been a bit busier lately and she didn't want to be bothered with sorting out Justin's bike or whatever it was he wanted. Couldn't Laura do things like that for him? 'Ask away.'

He cleared his throat and Meg suddenly got the impression he was nervous. 'I need your help.'

'That's usually the case when you want to ask someone a favour.'

'You know I've sprained my ankle?'

This was better than if he'd broken it, Meg thought. 'I did find you in a ditch so I knew something was wrong. What is that to do with me?'

'Of course, well . . . it means I can't cook.' He sounded embarrassed, thought Meg. Possibly sensing Meg might give another sharp reply, he hurried on. 'I've had to put my pastry chef in the main kitchen which means I have no one to make desserts.'

Meg's interest was piqued. 'Bad luck,' she said, sounding disinterested.

'I would like you to supply desserts for the trolley. A few tarts, mousses, trifle, *pâtisserie* . . .'

'How are you going to manage the crêpes Suzette?'

'I've taken it off the menu. Can you help?'

'Why should I?'

'Because it would be a challenge and you can't resist a challenge.' Meg could tell he was smiling, confident he'd found her weak spot.

Annoying as his amusement might be, she wasn't going to turn the challenge down. 'The hotel has to gain from it in some way,' she said.

'I'd pay you, of course, and promise to send anyone we can't accommodate your way. We're often fully booked.' Justin paused. 'I would be deeply in your debt, and when you move on, I'll give you a reference.'

'How will I get the desserts to you?'

'Someone will collect them,' he said. 'Keep a note of everything you spend, plus your time.' He took a breath and his voice softened. 'I won't let you lose by it, Meg.'

Something suspiciously like tears rose up in her throat. It couldn't really be tears, she reasoned, but something about his deep voice, saying her name, using words that were kind, caused a moment of emotion.

'OK, tell me exactly: what do you need and when do you want them by?' she asked, hoping her voice sounded normal.

'I'd like half a dozen large desserts and as many individual desserts as you can manage. The day after tomorrow would be good.'

'I'll need dishes. Ramekins, things like that.'

'I'll get some to you,' he said and rang off.

Meg had always enjoyed making puddings, pastries and desserts. She enjoyed the delicate precision required and was good at piping. Now, she went into the kitchen and started a batch of pastry. Although she tried hard not to, she couldn't help feeling enormously flattered by this request. Justin was the head chef in a prestigious hotel and had a reputation to keep up. He might not have been personally responsible for the desserts, but it was up to him to make sure they were of the required standard. And he'd chosen her to produce them. He might not have had a huge choice of people who could do it, she realised, but she was confident he wouldn't have asked her if he didn't think she could produce food of a very high standard.

She was making *crème pâtissière* when her mother came in. 'Oh, that looks nice,' said Louise, observing the rows of pastry cases. 'Have we had another booking?'

'It's not for us,' said Meg, blushing and hoping her mother wouldn't notice. 'Justin rang to say he needs me to make desserts for their sweet trolley. He's paying, of course, and he says he'll put guests our way when they're full.' She took a breath. 'I thought as he was Andrew's son, I should be helpful.'

'Of course,' said Louise, but she sounded surprised.

'He can't cook because he's sprained his ankle so his pastry chef has taken over in the main kitchen,' she explained. 'I think we should charge quite a lot for the desserts. We're quite busy, after all. By the way, what did Andrew say about turning the singles into private bathrooms?'

Louise looked caught out. 'I completely forgot to ask him,' she admitted. 'It was so lovely to see him—'

'I understand,' Meg said hastily. 'Perhaps we could get on with the work and you could ask him next time he rings? He's unlikely to say no to you.' She smiled, pleased that the attention wasn't on her just at that moment.

'Yes, all right.'

'It shouldn't be very expensive. Bob would do it. Susan was saying that now he's started doing plumbing, he's really enjoying it.'

'Hasn't he got enough to do with the kitchen garden?'

'He's got a nephew doing that, apparently. One of Susan's sister's lads who needed a job.'

Louise laughed. 'People might say this hotel is run entirely on people who are related to other members of staff. Mostly Susan.'

'Well, it is! And that includes me!' said Meg, giving her mother a sideways hug.

Justin appeared in the early afternoon. He limped into the kitchen with a huge box.

'What's that?' asked Susan, who was decanting home-made jam into glass bowls.

'It's everything you could ever need for making desserts, little cakes, tarts, anything you can think of,' said Justin, depositing the box on a side table.

'Oh!' said Meg, longing to stop icing tiny eclairs and investigate the box.

'What are you doing, Susan?' said Justin. 'Is that clotted cream? Where did you get that?'

Susan nodded proudly. 'I made it myself, overnight on the range, just as my mother did.'

Justin seemed disappointed it didn't come from a shop, but then went on: 'I need to have a look in the safe. My father rang to say he doesn't think the deeds of the house are in the bundle he took back.'

'My mother is in the office,' said Meg, starting to unpack the box. Why did Andrew ask Justin about the deeds? Why not ask her mother, who was on the spot? She and Andrew seemed to speak on the phone often enough.

Justin back came into the kitchen a few minutes later. As he wasn't holding anything, Meg assumed he hadn't found the deeds either. 'Would it be possible for you to drive me back to the hotel? Louise says it's all right for you to take the car.'

'You go on, Meg,' said Susan before Meg could save herself. 'I can manage the teas. If not, I'll ask Cherry to come up. She's got nothing better to do. And Louise is always happy to lend a hand.'

Deprived of her excuse to say no, Meg took off her apron and washed her hands. 'Come on then.'

As they walked slowly to the car, Justin limping quite badly, Meg realised she was about to be trapped in a car with someone she didn't like and didn't know what to say to. Fifteen minutes of awkwardness stretched ahead of her.

Soon after they'd set off, Justin said, 'I'm not used to being driven by a woman.'

Meg was tempted to say that she wasn't used to driving grumpy chefs with sprained ankles around the lanes of Dorset but decided it was more dignified to stay silent. The silence lasted a few moments but then she had to speak.

'It's all right. You probably don't need to hold on to the handbrake like that. I have passed my driving test.'

Justin didn't let go.

'And I learnt to drive in London, which is a lot more challenging than these charming country lanes.'

Justin put his hand back in his lap. 'Sorry.'

This apology surprised her.

'I expect you're wondering why my father sent me to find the deeds when he could have asked your mother,' he said at last.

'A bit. After all, you're injured, even if you did need to bring me the bowls and things. And if you're not cooking, you must have extra responsibilities to make sure the kitchen is up to standard.' Meg was pleased with this. It made her sound as if she really understood from personal experience how large, busy hotel kitchens worked.

Justin nodded. 'That's true. But it wasn't my father who asked me to look. I said it was, for convenience sake, but it was my uncle Colin, his brother.'

'Oh,' said Meg, surprised.

'Although he's not an executor of my grandfather's will, he wants to see the deeds of the hotel too, and it appears my father may not have brought the right ones with him back to France.'

Meg glanced across at Justin as she pulled up at a crossroads. The route involved a maze of little lanes criss-crossing each other and she needed to concentrate. Although she'd made the journey a few times, she had been distracted by what Justin had been saying. Now she wanted to remember the way herself and not have to ask Justin for directions.

'The thing is, there's conflict between Dad and Uncle Colin,' Justin went on. 'Dad loves the hotel and wants to keep it. Uncle Colin wants to sell.'

'Who was it left to?'

'To both of them, I think.'

'So if Andrew wants to keep Nightingale Woods, he might have to buy his brother's half?'

'I don't know the details of the will, and I don't know how things have been left, but that's quite probable.' Justin paused. 'It's unlikely the hotel will earn enough to support any sort of loan from a bank so I doubt my father could raise enough money to pay off my uncle.'

Meg felt a sudden gulp emerging and coughed. She was glad of another crossroads she had to stop at. She realised she'd lost track of where she needed to go. 'Which way here?'

Justin frowned, implying she should know. 'Straight on.'

'I was distracted.'

He didn't need to ask why. 'I know you feel very fond of Nightingale Woods. It has a lot of charm, but it isn't really a going concern, is it?' he said.

'It can be made one,' said Meg firmly.

Justin sighed. 'It doesn't have enough guest rooms currently. More would need to be done up. It's very old-fashioned and it doesn't provide what people want any more.'

Meg didn't reply. The first two things could be changed, but the last would take money, quite a lot of it. She thought of Alexandra, how in France she had turned all sorts of different buildings into accommodation. Surely there'd be scope for that at Nightingale Woods?

Chapter Fourteen

A couple of days later, Meg returned to the hotel at Newton-cum-Hardy, this time with the back of the car full of desserts. When he heard they were ready, Justin offered to come and collect them but Meg wanted to make sure everything arrived in as good a condition as possible. Besides, if she went to his hotel, she could leave when she wanted. If Justin came to Nightingale Woods, she was stuck with him until he chose to go.

She pulled up to the service area and opened the double doors at the back of the Mini Traveller. All the desserts were in wicker baskets and cardboard boxes, often with greaseproof paper as extra protection. A brief glance told her there had been no disasters.

Just as she was about to go to the kitchen to find people to help her unload, Justin arrived, with a couple of young men. He peered in. 'They look good,' he said.

'No need to sound surprised,' said Meg, secretly pleased. 'You asked me to do them *because* I'm good.'

'I just didn't realise you were quite as skilled as that,' he said with a smile.

Meg leant into the back of the Mini: ostensibly to retrieve some fruit tarts; in fact to hide her blushes.

'Would you like to come in and have a look round the kitchens?' Justin asked. 'Have a cup of coffee?'

Meg hesitated. She'd have loved that, but somehow it seemed disloyal to her too-small, too-old-fashioned place of work.

'Go on,' Justin said. 'It'll be good for you to see a proper professional kitchen in action.'

'I've seen plenty of professional kitchens, thank you,' she said stiffly, hoping she hadn't done herself out of the tour.

'Well, have a look at this one too. It would be handy for you to know how we do things in case you ever get offered a job working here.'

'I thought you didn't approve of women in kitchens,' she said, delighted to be able to catch him out.

'If you were offered a job, I wouldn't be here,' he said, 'and some of these younger chefs aren't so old-fashioned.'

'Old-fashioned,' she murmured. 'Yes.'

He laughed and opened the door to the hotel. 'If you think about where you work, you are in no position to mock anything for being old-fashioned.'

'It's one thing working in an old house that hasn't been changed much from when it was a family home and another having outdated ideas. It's quite easy to change the decor. Apparently, it's harder to change a mind.' She gave herself a mental cheer.

Justin wasn't impressed. 'My mind is fine as it is, thank you. Now, here's the beating heart of the hotel.'

It was hard not to envy this kitchen, with its sleek, purpose-built spaces, full of the best ovens, gadgets and equipment. She particularly coveted the cold kitchen, separate from the hot kitchen, where cold dishes, very often desserts, could be created in a chilled environment so gelatine wouldn't melt, and cream would hold its shape. Just the size of the mixer, capable of beating dozens of egg whites into a cloud of potential meringue, made her realise how much her wrist and arm ached when she beat eggs with her balloon whisk.

By the time the tour was over she was determined to buy a professional mixer, even if she had to use her own money. She could take it with her when she left Nightingale Woods. She might also see if she could convert one of the many larders and still rooms into a separate space for making desserts.

The tour over, they went together to the back door. 'Here's some money for the desserts,' said Justin. 'I know we didn't talk about how much you were charging for your labour, but I think this is fair.'

He handed Meg an envelope which seemed to be stuffed with notes. She took it without looking at it, let alone counting it.

'Aren't you going to check how much I've given you?' said Justin.

Meg wanted to lie, to be able to say something that wouldn't reveal her ignorance about what her work was worth, but she knew she wouldn't get away with it even if she tried.

'I don't know how much I should be paid for making them. I'm just hoping you're not cheating me or the hotel.'

'That's very honest of you, Meg. And I promise you I'm not doing you out of anything. I've paid the going rate.' He smiled. 'I'll need you to make some more desserts when these are gone. That's OK, isn't it?'

'Oh yes,' said Meg breezily, ignoring the insanely early mornings when she'd started long before dawn in order to get the desserts made while it was quiet and cool. Now she remembered all the things she hadn't done that morning, in order that she could do the desserts. 'I'd better go now. I hope your foot gets better soon.'

Just then, the door to the kitchens swung open and Laura rushed in. 'Justin! You're not supposed to be on that foot, and you know it! I could have paid . . .' Laura hesitated, obviously searching for a name. 'Meg. Or she should have just sent an invoice like a proper business would have done.' She smiled at Meg. 'It was very kind of you to make the cakes and things. I don't suppose we'll need your services again.'

Meg smiled but didn't say that Justin had just told her the contrary.

'After all,' Laura went on, also smiling, 'the home-made thing is all very charming but we like a more professional look here.'

Meg smiled harder. Only the imagined vision of Laura's carefully made-up face deep in a cream cake kept her from saying something waspish.

'I'll walk you to your car,' said Justin.

'No need, Jussy!' said Laura. 'I can do that. Although I'm sure Meg is perfectly capable of getting to her car on her own.'

'Yes, I am,' said Meg, and turned to go. But curiosity about how Justin would handle this situation kept her there.

'I said I'd walk her out,' said Justin. 'I've one or two things to say to her about Nightingale Woods. Thank you, Laura,' he added, dismissing her.

When they got to Meg's car, she turned to him. 'Jussy?' she murmured.

He pursed his lips, suppressing either a smile of embarrassment or an outburst of anger, Meg couldn't tell. 'No one calls me that.'

'Except Laura,' said Meg.

'Get in the car!' said Justin huffily. 'I'll be in touch.'

Meg was a good driver, she knew, but she didn't like being watched if she was making tricky manoeuvres. However, she managed the reversing without having to go back and forth too often and escaped. She didn't wonder why Justin hadn't said anything to her about Nightingale Woods; she knew perfectly well he'd only said that for Laura's benefit.

Once she was a little way away from the hotel, she pulled into a lay-by and inspected the money he had given her. It might not buy a mixer on its own, but it was definitely a step in the right direction. 'No offence, Justin,' said Meg to herself. 'But don't feel obliged to get back to work too soon. The longer your pastry chef is doing your job, the sooner I can buy some things that will make my life a bit easier.'

It was lunchtime when she got back and Susan and Cherry were both on duty. As it was still unseasonably warm, Meg had poached a salmon and made mayonnaise early; now it just had to be served with a cucumber salad and new potatoes from the hotel kitchen garden. Luckily everything had been picked earlier as it had come on to rain, really quite hard.

'We needed the rain,' said Susan. 'But we don't need you, Meg. Why don't you take some time off? You've been working long hours making those fancy folderols for that other hotel.'

Meg didn't even consider arguing. She made herself a sandwich and took it into the office. Her mother was there, looking rather glum.

'I think it's the first time we've had proper rain since I've been here,' said Meg.

'We needed the rain,' said Louise, but without the brisk fortitude that Susan had showed when she said the same thing.

'But it's not the rain that's making you so gloomy?' Meg said.

Louise shook her head, and Meg observed that her mother hadn't been her usual cheery self since Andrew left.

'I'm all right, although I do miss Andrew. I know it's silly. I'm not a teenager.'

'No. But it's a shame he has to be away.'

'And God knows how long sorting out his father's estate will take.'

Meg rejected the idea of telling her mother that Andrew's brother, Colin, was also keen on finding the deeds. He didn't like the hotel and wanted to sell his half if he could. The thought of Nightingale Woods being sold was so depressing.

'Why don't we try to find the deeds ourselves?' she suggested now. 'Susan and Cherry are doing lunch; we could empty the safe and sort through everything.'

'Oh, Meg, I couldn't! That would be so wrong. Besides, I haven't got the combination,' said Louise.

'Damn!' said Meg. Irritated by her mother's scruples and being denied entry to the safe, she pulled at the handle of the safe. To her surprise, it swung open. She and her mother exchanged shocked looks.

'Justin mustn't have closed it properly,' said Louise. 'Like everything else in this hotel, it's a bit broken and doesn't really work.'

'If he didn't make a big effort to make sure the door was shut – or indeed any effort – there can't be anything very private or confidential in it,' said Meg.

'True,' said Louise.

'Which means there's no real reason why we shouldn't look for the deeds,' said Meg.

Her mother swallowed. The idea of rummaging about in someone else's safe without express permission was clearly anathema to her. Then Louise took a breath. 'I'm going to do it!'

Coming over to join Meg on the floor, Louise opened the door to the safe wider and together they looked inside. As expected, it was completely stuffed with papers.

'You don't think it would be like reading someone's diary?' said Louise, despite having sounded so certain before.

'No,' said Meg. 'More like reading someone's shopping list. If it's so full of private things, Justin should have jolly well shut the door properly.' She paused.

'And if we found the deeds we could tell Andrew, and maybe Justin. Then it's up to them. If they tell us off – if they tell *me* off; Justin will know that it was me who put you up to it . . . well, it doesn't matter. We won't steal anything or do anything with any information we discover.'

'OK, then,' said Louise, still looking anxious. 'Let's get on with it.'

Louise was deep into her task when the telephone rang. It was David for Meg.

After an exchange of news (he was very impressed by her making desserts for the posh new hotel), he said, 'Now, Meggy, do you remember when we went round the garden of your hotel I said how perfect it would be for an open-air play?'

'Yes,' said Meg slowly; so much had happened since David mentioned it.

'Well, my friend is wild to put on the *Dream* there.'

'Sorry, David . . .' Meg felt very confused.

'*A Midsummer Night's Dream*. Think how perfect it would be with that setting and that backdrop?'

'Your friend wants to put on a Shakespeare play in the garden of Nightingale Woods?' said Meg. It sounded an extraordinary idea.

'Yes! I want to bring him down to see the garden to make sure it's suitable.'

So many reasons why this wasn't a good idea tumbled around in her head. Then she looked out of the window. Rain was streaming down as if a monsoon had arrived in Dorset. 'But, David, what if it rains!' she said.

'Don't worry about that. It's all taken into account. Now, I want to come with my friend in a few days' time.'

'I'm really not sure about this, David. It's not my hotel. It's not easy to get in touch with the owner, and we couldn't possibly put on a play without permission.' There were a few things Meg was willing to do off her own bat but a full-blown production of a Shakespeare play wasn't on the list.

David tutted briefly. 'Really, Meggy, if you want that charming but outdated architectural gem of a house to become a going concern as a hotel you have to do something radical. I know you know that because we talked about it.'

'But how would having a play in the garden help? If you can convince me, I can get Mum to ask Andrew about it.'

'Well, the actors would need to be put up, although of course you wouldn't want them in the best bedrooms. But if you could find lesser spaces – attics, things like that – that would earn money. Any local people willing to put up actors in their spare rooms would earn money from it too. And of course, you'd get the great and the good coming from all over to watch. My friend is very well respected in the business and there's talk he might get Miriam Twycross to play Titania. She loves outdoor theatre.'

Meg gasped. 'Miriam Twycross?' Even she had heard of her.

'Yes!' said David, obviously pleased to get the right reaction at last. 'And although some would say she's a little old to be playing Titania, you really don't notice her age when she's on the stage. It's one of her favourite roles.'

'She won't be on a stage,' said Meg. 'She'll be on a lawn.'

'That's a technicality and, of course, she may not come at all. But imagine if she did?'

'That would be nice,' said Meg, still sounding doubtful.

'And think of this,' said David, who had presumably anticipated Meg's reluctance. 'The play is likely to be reviewed in the national newspapers. It's publicity you couldn't pay for!'

'That does sound good.'

'If I come down, would there be room for Nessa?' asked David. 'I know she'll want to come too.'

'I'm sure we'll squash her in somehow,' said Meg, laughing. 'She was so helpful last time she was here.'

'You need to take a leaf out of Alexandra's book and convert some outbuildings for extra accommodation.'

Meg laughed again. 'Hah! I've been wondering about that already. But Lexi and I are hardly in the same position. She's married to the owner of all the outbuildings. I'm not.'

'The principle holds,' said David. 'Now, when can we come?'

'Why don't you find out when Nessa and your friend are free and we'll fit you in?'

'If you run out of rooms, we can always go and stay at that smart hotel in Newton-cum-Hardy.' Meg could picture David's teasing expression when he said this.

There was a tiny pause while Meg tried to think of something cutting to say. 'You only said that because you're too far away for me to throw something at you,' she managed.

David laughed, and shortly afterwards said goodbye.

It took quite a long time to explain the telephone call to her mother, although she'd been in the room all the while, sorting through the contents of the safe.

'Are there any unused rooms we could make suitable fairly quickly?' Meg said, when she'd finally got her mother to fully understand David's preposterous suggestion.

'There may be one or two. And there are dozens of rooms in the attic. I don't think the children or their many attendants were ever expected to come downstairs. And there's definitely an unoccupied gardener's cottage. Bob has always had his own house with Susan, as you know. There might be other cottages too. There'd have been a gamekeeper when the estate was in its prime,' said Louise. 'And I think there are rooms over the stables, the ones that weren't turned into garages in the twenties. Goodness knows what sort of condition they'd be in. If they weren't too far gone, we could make them habitable.' She sighed. 'But it would all cost money.'

'Distemper isn't very expensive,' said Meg. 'And they may just need a thorough clean. We could ask

Susan and Cherry to help. They might enjoy the challenge.'

Louise nodded. 'They would appreciate any efforts
that would make their jobs secure, that's for sure.'

'We could pay them out of the money I earn for the
puddings,' said Meg. 'And if we were desperate, we
could break into my savings. If it all works, I could
claim back the money.' Thinking about this money
reminded her how much she wanted an electric mixer
and she suddenly decided to get one. It would make
her life so much easier.

'Tell you what, when I've finished here, let's explore
and see where else we could put people,' said Louise,
obviously cheered by the prospect of finding places
to do up and decorate.

'I've got a better idea,' said Meg. 'Let's just shove
everything back into the safe and go and explore now!'

Louise contemplated the piles of old accounts books,
envelopes, folders, letters and other detritus strewn
around her. 'I'll do another twenty minutes, while you
go and make me a cup of tea, and then put everything
back. But it's going back in tidily!'

When Meg came back with the tea, she found her
mother sitting on the floor with a battered brown
envelope in her hands and a stunned expression on
her face.

'I've found them,' Louise said. 'They were wedged
under the flap of something else. That was probably
why Andrew couldn't see them. What on earth do we
do now?'

Chapter Fifteen

'We must tell Andrew,' said Meg. 'And, I suppose, Justin?' She really wasn't keen on this idea. He definitely wouldn't take the news calmly.

Louise's expression told Meg she wasn't keen on telling him either. 'He's bound to be furious. We've interfered in his family's private papers.'

'He will be angry. But I'll make sure he isn't angry with you.' Meg smiled. 'I'm used to him shouting. It's what chefs do. Now, let's have our tea, put the deeds back in the safe and then go and poke our noses into other private bits of this family. By which I mean bits of the property we've never seen before and they've probably forgotten all about.' She paused. 'I've just checked with Susan and Cherry. They're very happy to do tea.'

'And I've never seen anyone slice bread as thinly as Susan does,' said Louise happily. 'With the loaf tucked in the curve of her arm, in the old-fashioned way.'

'I suppose it's a skill one could learn,' said Meg. 'Like carrying plates all up your arms.' She passed a plate to her mother. 'Have a broken Linzer biscuit. I made them with leftover pastry for the torte I made for Justin. They're delicious, just very crumbly. Perhaps we should come clean and tell him about the deeds now?'

Louise thought for a moment. 'No. I need to think a bit. The deeds are back in the safe and I've made sure the door is properly shut. Let's go and explore. We can decide when to tell Justin later.'

'He won't mind about the deeds being found, I'm sure,' said Meg. 'But we did have to do a little safe-breaking to do it. That's the difficult part.'

'This time we've got keys,' said Louise as they collected various rings of them from the board that hung in the passage on the way to the garden.

'Not that we need keys,' said Meg. 'We have the special powers to make doors open at just a touch!'

'Let's go to the gardener's cottage first,' said Louise as they stepped outside. 'I've wanted to get my nose in there ever since I arrived.'

'I wish you could see Lizzie's cottage. I think they may have extended it a bit, but it's so sweet,' said Meg, a little later, as they approached the gardener's cottage. 'It's in the woods but gets the sun. She's made it so pretty with curtains and cushions and clever things.'

'We can make this cottage sweet too, if it isn't in a dire condition,' said Louise. 'You can do a lot with some bright curtains and a coat or two of whitewash.'

She led the way down the path to the front door, a large bunch of keys held purposefully in her hand. It took a couple of tries before the right key was found and the door opened.

Inside it was terribly dusty, but didn't smell damp although the smokey aroma of years of open fires pervaded. The two women stepped warily at first but as no bats flew out and the floorboards seemed solid, they went about with more confidence.

The house was one room deep and they had gone straight into the main living room. There was a large fireplace with a mantel above it on which a clock sat, silent and proud. Next to the clock were flat-backed figurines, ornamental jugs and candlesticks. Next to the fireplace was a wooden settle. Beams ran from back to front and large hooks were visible. Old lamps and various metal items that could have been traps hung from some of the hooks and old pictures decorated the faded wallpaper.

'It's all very quaint,' said Louise, 'but I understand why Susan didn't want to bring her children up here.'

'Where was the kitchen?' asked Meg.

'Originally it would have just been the one room but I'm fairly sure there's an added-on kitchen at the back now.' Louise opened the door to what was little more than a scullery. A large sink stood under the window on which were large flower pots, an ancient soap dish and some jam jars, most of which contained dead spiders.

'It seems more or less OK, doesn't it?' said Meg. 'Old-fashioned, but just needs a good clean.' She turned on the tap. There was a lot of gurgling and spluttering but eventually water came out. 'Running water, at least.'

'Not exactly running,' Louise said, 'and it's a funny colour, but it's probably OK. Nothing to cook on though.'

'There'd need to be some sort of stove if it was going to be rented out,' said Meg. 'But there's room for it here. Let's go upstairs. I expect the bathroom is up there.'

Louise was doubtful. 'I don't expect there was a bathroom, darling.'

Meg shuddered. 'It's hard to imagine that whole families would have lived in here.'

'No wonder Bob didn't want to but went to live with Susan in the village. Let's go up.'

The stairs were behind a door and were very steep and twisty. At the top were two bedrooms, small but adequate.

'The lack of a bathroom is a bit of a problem,' said Meg.

'There'll be a privy in the garden and probably a tin bath hanging up somewhere,' said Louise.

'Could you rent out a house without a bathroom?' asked Meg.

'Not to paying guests,' said Louise, 'but if it was all clean and comfortable some hardy non-paying types might be happy to stay here.'

'Let's go and see the privy.' Meg shuddered at the thought of what they might find there. 'I'm not awfully good with spiders.'

But to their surprise and delight they found a small wash house attached to the cottage and the privy, which was a perfectly functioning lavatory, was next to this.

'That could be a bathroom,' said Meg. 'Eventually.'

'If there was a bathroom, this little cottage could be a darling place to stay!' said Louise. 'I bet there are chests full of old curtains and things up in the attics of the main house. Families who owned houses like this never threw anything away.'

'Is the family interesting? I know Ambrosine is writing a history of the family and the house. It would be wonderful to have a leaflet to put in all the bedrooms,' said Meg. 'We might as well exploit the grand past of Nightingale Woods. They didn't have anything like that in Justin's hotel.'

'That's a good idea, darling. Now, let's carry on our explorations. It would be wonderful if Nightingale Woods could have enough accommodation to actually be profitable.' Louise sighed. 'Come on! I'm hoping that communing with spiders and patches of mildew, damp and anything else old houses can provide will help me decide what to do about those deeds.'

They found that the space over the old stables could make a neat little flat, there were a few more bedrooms in the house that could be made nice, and they saw a path that Susan said led to the old gamekeeper's cottage. They decided not to follow the path. They didn't know how far away the cottage was and they were getting tired.

As they walked back to the hotel, Louise said, 'I still don't know what to do about finding those deeds. I'm not at all sure saying that the safe door just swinging open is quite a good enough reason for us to have delved inside. It's really another version of "it came off in my hand".'

'We could do what I suggested and shove it all back in and make sure the safe door is properly closed,' suggested Meg.

'That would be silly. The right answer will come to me. Now let's go and see the stables that haven't been turned into garages. It's possible a flat like ours could be built over them.' By the time they got back to the house, they were filthy but convinced they could put up quite a large number of people who didn't mind roughing it a bit. They were both feeling very positive about it all and discussing paint colours and curtains when they reached the house.

'I need a gin and tonic,' said Meg. 'Let's go and get one. There's no one in for dinner.' Then she looked down at herself. 'Gosh, I'm filthy. I'll just go and wash. Shall I find ice? Or not bother?'

'Not bother. Although a slice or two of lemon would be nice.'

Before getting herself clean, Meg went into the kitchen. Susan and her daughter were there, clearing up after tea.

'Why don't you take the rest of that home,' said Meg, seeing three-quarters of a Victoria jam sponge on a plate. 'I'll make another for tomorrow.'

'We'd get another day out of it,' said Susan.

'But Dad loves Meg's sponge cakes,' said Cherry. 'Thank you, Meg.'

Meg smiled. 'Do take it. You've earned it.'

'Then I will,' said Susan, picking up the plate and putting it in her basket. 'By the way, young Justin's just arrived.'

'What?' All Meg's contentment vanished.

Susan nodded. 'He came in here and said hello and that he was going to the office. Had a slice of cake first, mind.'

Meg fled from the kitchen and across the hallway like a startled hare to where her mother was standing in front of the office door, her arms outstretched as if forbidding entry to a sacred space.

Justin, a piece of cake in his hand, was looking confused and angry as he loomed over her. 'Don't be ridiculous! Let me in! I need to get into the safe.'

'You can't,' said Louise dramatically.

'Why the hell not?' demanded Justin.

'What my mother means,' said Meg, loudly, so Justin would stop unnerving Louise, 'is that there's something I need to tell you before you do.'

Justin turned to her and Meg saw her mother's posture relax.

'What?' said Justin, obviously more confused than ever.

Louise started to speak but Meg put up a hand. 'Things in there aren't as you left them.'

'What do you mean? Did the ceiling fall in? Did someone let a bath overflow?'

'Nothing like that,' said Meg. 'Mum? Why don't you get us all some drinks? There's tonic in the fridge. I'm going to explain everything to Justin.'

Louise moved away from the door and Meg went in, Justin following closely behind.

Meg spoke quickly, knowing it wouldn't be long before Justin would start being loud and while she certainly wasn't afraid of him – absolutely not – she wanted to take the initiative.

'I discovered the door to the safe wasn't properly closed.' She saw Justin look shocked and she hurried on. 'I know we shouldn't have – *I* shouldn't have – but we opened it and looked for the deeds. And found them.'

'You found the deeds?' Justin said at normal volume but obviously surprised. 'My father and I both looked exhaustively.'

'I know. But everything was so jumbled up. My mother—' Too late, Meg forgot to take full responsibility. 'She sorted everything out and found them tucked under something else.'

'Can you give them to me?' said Justin.

'Er – no. We closed the door properly after we found the deeds.'

He made an irritated sound as he turned the dial on the safe, finding the numbers. Then the door opened. 'Good Lord! It's tidy!'

'That's my mother. But I take full responsibility for opening the safe,' Meg said firmly. 'Look, the deeds are on the top there,' she added, spotting them.

Justin took them out and then opened the envelope. 'These are the ones.' He looked up. 'What did you say happened to the door of the safe?

At that moment, Louise came in with a tray. She had glasses with gin in them, a dish of lemon slices, a bowl of ice and two bottles of tonic. 'You'll have a drink, Justin?' she said. 'Meggy and I promised ourselves a gin.'

'I'll get nibbles,' said Meg, knowing her mother poured strong drinks.

She ran through to the kitchen. Susan was just buttoning up her cardigan, ready to go home. 'Have we got anything I can serve with drinks?'

'There are some broken vol-au-vent cases in the tin,' Susan replied. 'Do you want me to stay and help?'

'No, no,' said Meg automatically. 'I'll manage.'

The top oven in the range was hot and it didn't take her long to grate cheese and sprinkle it over the cases, cut into suitably sized pieces. A bit of cayenne and the baking tray was in the oven. She drummed her fingers on the table, willing time to pass.

'Are you sure you don't want me to stay? You seem all of a jitter.' Susan and Cherry regarded her curiously.

'I'll be fine. I'll explain everything later. Tomorrow!' said Meg. Why was she so jumpy? Justin didn't seem that bothered about them opening the safe although she would have to think of some sort of explanation.

Shortly afterwards she set off with her tray to find that Louise and Justin had gone into the sitting room. Justin had a drink in his hands and was sitting on the sofa, his legs stretched out in front of him.

'Justin's staying for supper,' said Louise as Meg set down her emergency cheese straws and a bowl of olives on a table near him.

Meg took a restorative gulp of her drink, forgetting how strong her mother made them. 'How did you get here?' she said to Justin.

'Someone gave me a lift,' he said.

Was it Laura? Meg wondered, putting down her glass, resigned to driving him back again. No, if Laura had been with him, she'd have stayed, no question. But maybe, considering she had been so proprietorial about him when she'd delivered him to the hotel after his accident, Laura could come and collect him?

'Did you come over to look for the deeds?' asked Louise.

'No,' said Justin. 'I came to ask Meg if she could make me a Black Forest gateau for a birthday tomorrow. I could have just telephoned but as I'm asking quite a big favour, I thought it better to do it in person.'

'I haven't any cherries,' said Meg, pleased to be able to get out of the task without feeling churlish.

'I thought you might not have. I brought a couple of jars of them. And some kirsch, also some half-decent chocolate. You do make such good cakes,' he added. 'I just had a slice of your Victoria sponge.'

'You're flattering me, so I'll say yes,' she said bluntly, and sensed her mother's look of disapproval. 'But I'd make better cakes – or at least I'd make a Black Forest quicker if I had a mixer.'

'You haven't got an electric mixer here?' Justin frowned.

'A wooden spoon and a balloon whisk only,' said Meg.

'Very traditional and old-fashioned,' said Justin. 'I'll arrange for a mixer to be delivered.' He gave a reluctant laugh. 'I know my hotel is better, and yours is stuck in the nineteenth century, when Mrs Beeton ruled with the only cookery book anyone had, but you do need a stand mixer. We have a couple spare.'

Meg tried to stop herself smiling back. 'Good.'

'And I'll tell the client they can't have a Black Forest gateau,' said Justin. 'I couldn't get the mixer to you in time.'

'No, don't cancel it,' said Meg. 'I'll make one by hand.'

Justin considered this. 'You could come up to my kitchen and use my equipment. It would save transporting a fragile cake in the back of a car.'

'That sounds like a good idea, darling,' said Louise, who was halfway through her drink and obviously feeling far more relaxed. 'No one is coming until teatime tomorrow.'

'No, thank you. I can do other things in between processes if I make it here,' said Meg quickly. Then she tried to think of a process that gave her time to do anything. 'While it's cooking,' she finished lamely.

'Do come and make it up at the hotel,' said Justin.

Something about the way he said it implied that Nightingale Woods was not a place for professional cooking. 'No, really. I'll be fine doing it here, thank you,' she said stiffly.

She picked up her glass and took another gulp. 'Have a bit of broken vol au vent,' she said to Justin, offering the plate.

'Delicious,' he said. Meg could feel him studying her as he ate it.

She took a bit herself before passing the plate to her mother. 'Right!' said Louise a few moments later, getting to her feet. 'I'm going to make omelettes for our supper.'

'I thought it was Meg who made such good ones,' said Justin.

'She does make excellent omelettes,' said Louise. 'But I taught her how.'

Neither Meg nor Justin spoke for several minutes. She refused to make polite conversation just because her mother had put her in this awkward position and Justin obviously didn't feel the need to make polite anything.

Meg broke first. 'Will you take the deeds to your father?'

'Yes. The sooner this estate is sorted out the better. Everyone needs to get on with their lives and they can't when they don't know if they'll have money to do it or not.'

'You mean your father and his brother?'

Justin nodded. 'My uncle has – things – he needs to settle.'

'By "things", do you mean debts?' asked Meg.

Justin laughed ruefully. 'Yes. It was very indiscreet of me to say that.'

'But your grandfather will have left things equally between his two sons, surely?'

Justin shrugged. 'I didn't know him well but he was fairly eccentric. If he didn't want the hotel sold, he might easily have willed the hotel to my father, and any leftover cash to Colin.'

'Would that be an equal way to divide the money?

'No, and Uncle Colin would feel very bitter about it. So I must get the deeds to my dad as soon as possible. I'm still out of action anyway, so it's a good time for me to go to France.'

'Let my mother go instead,' said Meg, surprising herself. She had no idea where that thought had come from but now it had, she knew it was right. 'She'd love to see your father and you're busier than she is.'

'Are you pushing her and my father together?' Justin sounded suspicious.

'No,' said Meg. 'We both know they are together already. It would give my mother a chance to see him, and him her. Imagine how lovely it would be for them in France, in early summer.' Then she realised it was possible that Justin had no imagination.

'That's a ridiculous idea,' he said dismissively. 'You couldn't do all the cooking and the office work – even in a hotel as quiet as this one.'

'Of course I could!' said Meg, who hated to be told she couldn't do things.

Justin sighed. 'I'm not sure I'm as keen as you are about your mother and my father getting together.'

'Why?'

'My father has been chased by women before. It hasn't turned out well for him.'

'My mother does not "chase" men, as you so delicately put it. They are mutually attracted to each other.'

'And would Louise be so attracted if my father didn't come with a very nice country house attached?'

Meg was clenching her teeth now. 'I know you can't help being rude, it seems to be your predominant characteristic, but considering you hardly know my mother at all, that is an outrageous thing to say – to suggest! Anyway, depending on your grandfather's will, the country house may not be attached as firmly as all that.'

Justin laughed, startling Meg. 'You're absolutely right. And if Dad and Louise still love each other if and when Nightingale Woods has to be sold, I'll give their union my blessing.'

'I don't think it's up to you to bless it or not!' Meg was indignant.

'You seem to have given it your blessing. Why is it different for me?'

It was Meg's turn to sigh. 'It's just been the two of us for as long as I can remember, and we both feel protective of each other. My mother is entitled to love, to security, and not to be lonely. I've wanted that for her for a long time.' She didn't add that every penny she could spare she saved, gathering together enough money for somewhere her mother could live that was theirs.

'Would you like another drink?' she said.

'I'll do it,' he said, starting to get up.

Meg was quicker. 'I insist. I'll just get some more tonic.' She left the room as quickly as she could without running.

Her mother had lit the fire in the drawing room and laid two places at a table drawn up near the fire. 'I thought it was a bit bleak, and having a fire in the summer always seems a bit decadent and so special.'

'Why only two places, Mum?' said Meg pointedly. 'You're not abandoning me now!'

'I just thought Justin would prefer to have you on his own.'

'For one, you're quite wrong, and for another, I don't care! I'm getting us more drinks.'

Justin was in the sitting room, by the fire, with a large gin and tonic by the time Meg came down from delivering supper to Ambrosine. There was always a bit of chat involved and Justin's presence downstairs involved a bit of teasing and some raised eyebrows about his intentions.

She was relieved to see that her mother had laid a place for herself at the table.

'Come and join me,' said Justin. 'I must say, this room is quite cosy.'

'It has class,' said Meg, accepting the drink, deciding that how Justin was going to get back to his hotel wasn't her problem. 'And so appeals to the more discerning guest who wants to stay somewhere that feels like it's a stately home.'

Justin laughed. 'You're wasted in the kitchen. You should be writing advertisements.'

'Have you thought any more about letting Mum go to France with the deeds?'

'After one and a half stiff drinks I think I can agree to that.'

He smiled at her, genuinely. It was like the sun coming out from behind a storm cloud, Meg felt. Then she pressed on. 'While you're in the mood to grant favours, can we have permission to turn the small single next to the best bedroom into a bathroom? It was the dressing room so there's already a connecting door. I'd ask Bob – you know? Susan's husband?'

'I've known Bob half my life. Has he given up gardening?'

'Not entirely but he's recently taken up plumbing. It would make so much difference to us, having even one bedroom with its own bathroom.' She paused. 'Although you may not want to have the competition for the hotel where you work.'

He hung on to his good mood. 'I'm not afraid of the competition and it shouldn't cost too much. I'll say yes.'

'Oh, thank you!' said Meg, aware too late that she didn't need to be grateful. He wasn't granting her a personal favour; he was allowing a sound bit of investment. 'There are four principal bedrooms with singles next to them that could be converted.'

'Do them all. Why not?'

Meg felt the atmosphere between them had changed. Before they had been combative – rivals; or rather, Justin had been the Goliath and she was a little David, doing her best with her five stones and a slingshot. Just now, they were more like allies. She knew better than to think anything had basically changed but it was restful not to have to be on her mettle all the time.

153

'Omelettes are ready!' said her mother, coming into the room with plates. 'Meggy? I've found a bottle of wine if you'd like to fetch it, and can you take the potatoes out of the oven?'

Justin caught Meg's eye as she put her hand on her glass. 'I know you don't like to drive if you've had alcohol,' he said. 'I can ask Laura to come and collect me. She won't mind.'

Although this was the ideal solution for Meg, for some reason her good mood melted. But she smiled firmly. 'So, when do you want this gateau?'

'Tomorrow evening? Short notice, I know, but it's what our guests expect. This is a really delicious omelette, Mrs Sanderson.'

'Louise, please.'

'Louise. Meg tells me you might be willing to go to France and take the hotel deeds to my father? Please don't feel obliged, but it would be a great favour it you could.'

'Oh, I'd love that!' said Louise enthusiastically. 'It would be a real treat! But I can't go. Meg couldn't run the office and do all the cooking.'

'I thought I'd ask Vanessa to come and help,' said Meg. 'She'd love an excuse to get away for a few days and spend some time somewhere she's in charge. At home, with her mother planning her wedding, her opinion counts for nothing, she told me. All she's allowed to do is write thank-you letters for the wedding presents which are in coming in lorryloads.'

'Getting presents should be such fun!' said Louise.

'I think you can have too much of a good thing,' said Meg.

Justin got to his feet. 'Well, it was delicious, thank you, Louise. But now I should be getting off. I'll use the telephone in the office, if that's all right.'

Although Meg felt strange about Laura coming to collect him, she was a bit put out when her mother offered to drive Justin home instead. 'It'll give me a glimpse of your fancy hotel and save someone being disturbed,' she said.

'That would be very kind,' said Justin. 'If it's not a nuisance.'

'Certainly not. I'll get the car keys.' Louise smiled benignly.

As Meg watched her mother and Justin go out of the back door together, towards the Mini, she remembered to be pleased he'd agreed to her mother going to France instead of him. Maybe he wasn't entirely horrible, only about 95 per cent.

Chapter Sixteen

Meg got up at dawn the following day. She'd had a very broken night and felt she might as well get on with her day rather than lie in bed trying to get back to sleep.

She went into the kitchen where, to her surprise, there was a stand mixer on the table. Her mother must have brought it back with her after she'd taken Justin home. She was delighted. Now all she needed was a recipe.

She put the kettle on for tea and then investigated the mixer. She was glad to see it had a very long flex. She wondered where the nearest socket was and for a moment wished she'd opted to make the gateau in Justin's kitchen. That would have plenty of electric sockets; it was modern.

Louise came in. 'You're up early! Couldn't you sleep?'

'No. I was worrying about the Black Forest gateau.' Meg paused. 'I found this.' She indicated the mixer.

Louise laughed. 'Justin insisted I took it back with me. He made that poor girl – Laura, is it? – go and find it although it was quite late.' She became thoughtful. 'I think she was waiting up for him.'

'Really? How odd!' But as Meg didn't want to reflect on this oddness, she went on: 'I wish I had a recipe for this gateau. All of the books here are too old and too English to have Black Forest gateau in them.'

Louise pursed her lips. 'It was very kind of Justin to find you the mixer, though, wasn't it?'

Meg was aware she was being subtly told off for not being grateful. 'It was. But of course, it is for his benefit, the mixer. Although, thank you, Mum, for bringing it back.'

'I just think that underneath the swagger, Justin is a nice man.'

'I'm sure he is. And I'm sure Laura thinks so too.' Meg realised her feelings about Laura were not logical and nor were her feelings for Justin. She would just make the gateau and stop thinking about him. 'Now, where can I plug in this mixer?'

'In the old dairy. There's a spare fridge in there.' Her mother looked at her as if she had a screw loose, needing to be reminded about this. 'Remember?'

'I had forgotten. That's good!'

'And give Justin a ring for the recipe. He'll have one or he wouldn't offer Black Forest gateau.'

'Oh, it's OK. I've eaten it a few times. I can work it out. Do you think a fatless sponge? Maybe that's too fiddly. I think a good chocolate cake recipe with lots of ground almonds and good cocoa powder. I had one from Fortnum's once and it had a pastry base.'

'Are you OK? You haven't got a headache?'

'I'm fine, really! It's just this bloody cake.'

Louise frowned. 'You were flattered because Justin asked you to do it and now you're regretting it.'

Meg relaxed a little and smiled. 'That's it exactly.'

'Don't worry. You'll do a brilliant job. And he told me on the way to his hotel yesterday that he's happy for us to do anything in the way of updating or repairs, as long as they're not too expensive.'

Meg gave her mother a rather vague smile. 'So can you and Susan do the breakfasts then? I need to learn how to use this mixer.'

The stand electric mixer was a joy, Meg decided, and its joyfulness didn't make her feelings about Justin any easier.

She had made three layers of a light chocolate sponge cake which were now cooling. Later she would divide them and turn them into a tower of chocolate, cream and cherries. She could keep back a layer for their own sweet trolley. She could cut the layer in half vertically not horizontally and make sure it was full of cream and fruit to tempt their diners.

While she had the mixer, she made meringues, a chocolate mousse, a couple of meringue cases, and a vacherin using an old recipe that Mme Wilson had shown them: broken meringues layered with cream and fruit and frozen.

Eventually the Black Forest gateau, complete with the pastry layer, was ready. While all the layers of sponge (moistened with kirsch), cream, cherries and chocolate were assembled, Meg wrote a note saying that someone should whip more cream before serving, for the sides of the cake and add chocolate shavings. She'd have done it herself only she didn't see how she could pack the cake and get it to the other hotel unharmed if she did.

Louise came in to see how she was getting on. 'That is brilliant, darling!' she said. 'It looks absolutely delicious! Like something you'd see in a French *pâtisserie*.'

'I wouldn't go that far,' said Meg, 'but it tastes fairly good. It didn't seem right to send off a dessert and not know what it tasted like.'

'True,' said her mother. 'I'll have mine after supper. Now, how are you getting it to Justin?'

'We haven't made a plan, but maybe you could run it up there for me? You know the way now.' Meg knew perfectly well she should ring Justin and he could make the arrangements, but she really didn't want to.

'You know we've got guests coming. I'll have to be here to welcome them,' said Louise.

'I'll have to be here to cook for them.'

'Ring Justin and he can decide what he thinks is best,' said Louise firmly, possibly reading Meg's mind, and realising how she felt about ringing him.

Meg chose her moment. She waited until the lunch-time service would have been at full throttle and left a message at reception of the Newton-cum-Hardy Hotel. She added the bit that the cake needed finishing off. Then she put it out of her mind and turned her attention to making cakes for afternoon tea and to dinner.

That was the plan, anyway. But she jumped whenever anyone came into the kitchen in case they were Justin.

Meg had just sent Susan off to the dining room with the last of the main courses for an unexpectedly busy dinner service when Justin and Laura appeared.

'Justin wanted to make sure the cake was up to standard,' said Laura. 'So I brought him over. It would have been far more convenient if you'd telephoned earlier, Meg. Although maybe you've only just finished it. I did think it would be too much for Meg, didn't I, Justin?'

Justin nodded.

'His leg is bothering him,' Laura went on. 'I could have done the cake myself; I am properly trained. And I thought you probably wouldn't be able to find a recipe but Justin felt this little place could do with the business!' She paused. 'So where's the gateau?'

'Through here,' said Meg, leading the way to the old dairy. 'Thank you for the mixer. I'll just wash it and you can take it back with you.'

'You can keep it. We don't need it,' said Justin.

'Thank you so much,' said Meg. 'That will be really helpful.' She forced herself to say this. She didn't want to feel beholden but she didn't want to give him back the mixer either.

'Are you sure we don't need it?' said Laura.

'Quite sure,' said Justin quietly. 'Now, Laura? If you take the cake back to the hotel, I have to stay on here for a bit.'

For a split second, Laura looked mutinous, as if she might refuse this request. 'Fine. I can make the cake look presentable, put on some finishing touches.' She smiled at Meg. 'I did a course in cake decoration. Call

160

me when you want to be picked up, Jussy – Justin!' she said, and left.

'I need to discuss Louise's travel arrangements to France and then I'd like to see the rooms you want upgraded. Make sure we wouldn't be throwing good money after bad,' he said.

'I don't think any money has been thrown at those rooms for years, good or bad,' said Meg.

He nodded. 'But it may not be worth trying to modernise the rooms. The house may well have to be sold anyway.'

Meg knew this, in her heart, but she tried to put it out of her mind as much as possible. She hated the thought of this lovely house belonging to people who might not love it as much as its current inhabitants. She thought of Susan, Bob and their children, who all contributed to the running of Nightingale Woods with affection and loyalty as well as because their family had been part of the household for years. Would a new owner understand that? They'd get rid of Ambrosine, for a start.

'I'll show you the rooms. You may need someone with imagination and creative flare with you when you look.'

'You don't think I have those qualities?' he asked.

'Not when it comes to this hotel, no.' Then she wished she hadn't qualified it and just denied he had creative flare at all. But she was a very fair person and couldn't.

'The rooms are going to have guests in them tonight but I expect they've been done already. Susan runs it all very well. She's out of the dining room and up to the bedrooms with hardly time for tea and a biscuit.'

They walked up the stairs and Meg led him into the best bedroom. This was the one with the stunning views over the gardens, the ha-ha and the fields beyond. It had beautiful wallpaper, almost like a mural, with a pattern of flowers and birds. The furniture was antique and now smelt of beeswax polish. It was desperately in need of paint, new curtains, cushions, and perhaps the chair should be reupholstered. But it had immense charm. Meg could picture the lady of the manor lying in bed, her breakfast on a tray on her lap, reading her letters, deciding on which invitations to accept and whom she should invite to her next dinner party. She didn't say any of this to Justin, of course.

Instead, she said, 'I love this painting. A young girl with woods behind her, and her spaniel playing at her feet.'

'Those are Nightingale Woods,' he said. 'They used to be much more extensive in those days. They've gradually been cleared to create more farmland and now they're quite small in comparison.'

Convinced she could feel his breath on the back of her neck, and this making it hard for her to breathe normally, Meg moved away a little.

'I think this room is like a beautiful old painting,' she said, 'which needs cleaning and maybe a new frame, but is still beautiful.'

'That's a very poetic way of putting it for such a practical person, Meg,' he said.

'I am practical,' she said firmly, to convince herself as much as anything. 'I think life has meant I've had to be, but it doesn't mean I can't be poetic as well.' Then she regretted confiding in him. Her innermost soul was nothing whatever to do with him.

'I agree with you about this room. It is lovely. I hardly ever came in here when I was growing up, it being a guest bedroom, but it has a lot of charm. Now, where did the door to the dressing room used to be?'

'Behind this big mirror,' said Meg. 'The door hasn't been very well blocked up at all.'

'Let's go and see what's on the other side.'

Once they were in the single bedroom, he said, 'This room isn't huge but it's bigger than a bathroom, surely.'

'Bigger than the private bathrooms in your hotel, you mean.'

He laughed briefly, acknowledging her dig. 'I suppose I do.'

'But your hotel is much more utilitarian in general than this one, isn't it?' said Meg. 'Let's go and look at the other bedrooms. It would be good to get Bob working on getting at least one of them done quite soon.' She was thinking about the play that might be put on in the garden and wondered if she should ask Justin about that.

'What's on your mind?' he said as they walked along to the next principal bedroom.

Annoyed that he could tell there was something on her mind, Meg decided she hated keeping secrets and she might as well tell Justin everything. 'David – you remember? – has a friend who might want to put on *A Midsummer Night's Dream* in the garden. It would fill the hotel but we'd want the bedrooms to be perfect.' She paused. 'It's possible Dame Miriam Twycross might appear.'

Justin appeared to be impressed. 'Gosh. I'm a complete philistine when it comes to the theatre but I know my father is a big fan of hers.' He paused. 'Why would she want to appear in a play in someone's garden though?'

'It's outdoor theatre! Practically Glyndebourne! But even if she didn't come it would be a great thing for the hotel. Publicity you couldn't pay for. We might get reviewed in the national press! We could do picnic hampers, dinners . . .'

'But supposing it rains?'

'It's all taken into account,' she said, quoting David, possibly word for word. 'Anyway, if the play was likely to happen it would be awful to have to turn down the opportunity because Miriam Twycross couldn't have a bedroom with its own bathroom, wouldn't it?'

He laughed. 'You are very persuasive. OK, you get Bob on to it as soon as he's got time. Now, I must find Louise and talk to her about travel.'

'She's in the office. Or if not, she'll be in the garden, picking flowers to put in the bedrooms.'

'Fresh flowers in the bedrooms?'

Meg nodded. 'From the garden. So much nicer than carnations that last forever and a bit of that white fluffy stuff,' she said, describing the arrangements she'd seen in his hotel.

'And free,' said Justin.

'We know how to make every penny count in Nightingale Woods,' she said.

He took a breath. 'By the way, you'll have noticed that my ankle is better and so I'm back in the kitchen and can ride my motorbike again from tomorrow. Although Raoul was very impressed by your desserts, he said our pastry chef had to go back to doing them.'

'Oh,' she said, 'that's good.' But some part of her felt disappointed, as if she'd miss his visits. What was wrong with her?

She was following him down the stairs when at the bottom he suddenly stopped, and she nearly bumped into him. He caught her arms and steadied her. 'But he said that your profiteroles were streets ahead of the pastry chef's.'

Standing on the bottom step made her the same height as him. They were eye to eye and Meg was certain that he wanted to kiss her. She wanted to kiss him. But there was Laura. Laura had a pet name for him, and was obviously more than a receptionist.

Meg swallowed and looked away. He moved and the moment was over.

Long after he'd seen Louise to discuss travel, and had been driven back to his hotel by Susan's nephew, Cyril, Meg wondered what would have happened if she hadn't remembered Laura. The thought bothered her for a long time.

Chapter Seventeen

Meg couldn't help feeling a bit felt lonely when, a few days later, she'd waved off her mother who was being driven to the station in the Mini by Bob's nephew, Cyril, who was now the official driver to the hotel and regularly collected guests from the station. When not doing that he was the gardener.

Meg knew she would be fine. She had Susan's whole family to help and not very many visitors booked in. Bob was starting on the new bathrooms that day. And she'd been in touch with Vanessa, who'd said she would be here tomorrow.

Meg had managed to do breakfast with Susan's help, take the money and send the night's guests on their way, full of praise for the food and the 'quaint' decor. Meg didn't much like the word 'quaint' though – it meant 'olde worlde tea shoppes' and fake antiquities to her and it felt like damning with faint praise.

But she knew she couldn't really argue. Quaint could mean frayed at the edges and this was indeed the case where Nightingale Woods was concerned.

Susan had sent her out of the kitchen so Meg was in the office when the phone rang. It was Vanessa, who, going by the various noises, was calling from a telephone box.

'Please don't say you're not coming!' said Meg.

'No, no, I'm on my way, but I've got my mother with me. She's got friends in the area she wants to visit and she may want to stay at Nightingale Woods!' Vanessa paused, during which time Meg panicked, before adding, 'It'll only be for one night though, if she stays at all.'

This was a disaster. They were nowhere near ready for a guest such as Lady Lennox-Stanley. 'But Bob is only just starting on the bathroom in the best bedroom!' Meg wailed.

'I'm so sorry, Meg! I tried to stop her but I think she wants to get away from Daddy, who's making such a fuss about the wedding bills, even though he can afford to pay them perfectly well.'

'OK. So, when do you think you'll arrive?' In other words, how much time did she have to make a bedroom ready?

'Oh, not for hours!' said Vanessa breezily, unaware of the anxiety this caused Meg. 'Mummy wants to have coffee with one lot of friends and lunch with another. But I'll try to ring when we're quite near, to give you some warning. We'll definitely be with you for supper.'

'What about tea? Should I make some eclairs?'

Vanessa paused. 'What she really likes are meringues.'

'I'll do them then. Thank you for warning me, Nessa. I really appreciate it.'

'Oh, I nearly forgot! David rang me last night. He and his director friend are coming today too.'

'My goodness! Why didn't he ring me and tell me that?'

'Apparently he did, but there was no answer, which is why he rang me. I'm just so sorry to – Oh, got to go! See you soon.'

And Vanessa was gone.

Meg was in a state of shock when she went into the kitchen. Susan was scrubbing the kitchen table and looked up.

'You look as if someone walked over your grave,' she said.

Meg laughed reluctantly. 'I think several people are going to! Vanessa, my friend, who was coming to help me while Mum is in France—'

'I've met her.'

'Well, she just telephoned to say her mother is coming with her. I really need to impress her mother. It's mostly because of her that we're having bathrooms. But she won't have a private bathroom if she comes now. Bob's only just started work, as you know.'

'Sit down, Meg, and stop looking as if this is an emergency,' said Susan, moving the kettle on to the hot part of the range.

'And my other friend, David, the one who thought this would be a good place to put on a play, is also coming, with his director friend. I need to impress

168

him, too!' Her mother had only been gone a few hours and already she was panicking.

'Don't be silly. What you need to do is book Vanessa's mother a "just-in-case" room at that big hotel where Justin works. Then if she is too grand to stay with us, she can go and stay up there. In the meantime, we can suggest her ladyship tries the Yellow Room, which is right next door to a bathroom, and give her exclusive use of it, and see if she's happy there.' Susan still called the rooms after what they were called on the bell indicator, although no one had rung the bells for a while. 'The two chaps will have to go where we put them. And I'll see how Bob is getting on. We may need to send Cyril to the builder's merchants with a list.'

'And maybe hire a plumber.'

Susan didn't speak for several anxious seconds. 'Maybe it'll come to that.' Then she pulled herself together. 'Now, have you had breakfast? Tea and toast for you, young lady, unless I can interest you in a boiled egg? Everything seems better when you've had breakfast.'

Cherry, who had come in from clearing the dining room and drawn up another seat at the table, was told the story and nodded. 'I've got a little lace cap I could wear,' she said. 'Ambrosine gave it to me. She'd found it in one of the attic rooms. It's ever so pretty. Vanessa's mother might like that, if she's a "lady".'

'Lady Lennox-Stanley is very old-fashioned so she probably would appreciate a lace cap,' said Meg, feeling more cheerful now she was on her second piece of toast.

'It'll be nice to see David again,' Cherry went on. 'He was very charming. I expect his director friend will be too.'

'Do you think I should book a room for him at Justin's hotel, as well as Lady Lennox-Stanley?' said Meg.

Susan shrugged. 'Men aren't so obsessed with bathrooms as women are, in my experience.'

'Just the one room then,' said Meg. 'We wouldn't want to find ourselves having to pay for it, after all. I'll go and do that then.'

'And I'll have a word with Bob,' said Susan. 'Tell him it's urgent. Cherry? You make a start on the Yellow Room. It's not as nice as the Blue Bedroom, where the bathroom's going to be, but it'll have to do. Meg will pick flowers for it later.'

Meg halted on her way to the kitchen door. 'My mother always does the flowers.'

'You'll have to do them today, Meg! Now put your best foot forward. We'll get through this, you know we will. We can think what to serve for dinner later. I can ask Sam what he's got that's special. We'll want something nice for David. He appreciates his food.'

Sam was the butcher, and, like almost everyone in the area, related to Susan. 'Run along now,' she said to Meg, making a shooing gesture. 'Book the room, pick the flowers and we'll do the rest. Until it's time to start cooking, of course.'

Meg poached a very fine salmon that Sam the butcher provided as well as some pork loin which he had turned into escalopes. Meg knew that while David would enjoy a hearty beef stew at any time of year, Vanessa's mother almost definitely wouldn't. There were some new potatoes in the garden which would go beautifully with both.

Everyone worked very hard at getting things ready. Cyril was roped in to help. He dug potatoes, fetched and carried for Bob, collected a lavatory from the builder's merchants, and generally earned himself the accolade 'good lad' from Susan. It made him turn a bit pink.

Meg didn't stop. She managed to pick and arrange a few vases of flowers for some strategic places and, aided by the electric mixer, made meringues and a chocolate mousse for pudding. She was still behind on her list of things to do when she heard a car. Her heart sank. The thought of having to deal with Vanessa's mother as well as finish preparations for dinner made her heart sink.

She was surprised when Justin marched into the kitchen. Part of her was relieved, but the other part was terrified she was going to make a huge blunder and show herself up an amateur. A part she didn't want to acknowledge was excited.

'What are you doing here?' she asked. She was slicing cucumbers to make fake scales for the salmon.

'I wondered why you'd booked a room at the hotel. Laura told me about it.' He seemed curious.

'Vanessa's mother is coming to stay unexpectedly,' Meg explained. 'She wants a private bathroom and we haven't got one yet, only a building site. The room at your place is in case she won't stay here.'

'Goodness. And have you got a lot of guests in? That's a very large salmon.'

'We have got a few. David and his friend who puts on plays in the open air, as well as Vanessa and her mother.'

'That is a lot at such short notice, especially when Louise is away. Do you need a hand? I'll dress your salmon if you like. Give you time to get on with something else?'

Meg opened her mouth to refuse but just then Cherry came in. 'Hello, Justin! Have you come to help? We could do with it, couldn't we, Meg?'

'Yes,' said Meg, although admitting it nearly killed her.

Susan appeared just then and was even friendlier to Justin than Cherry was being. Meg wondered if she should announce, in a loud voice, that he had nearly kissed her, just to see if it changed their attitude to him. Except that he had held back. Nor did she want to reveal that he wanted to sell the hotel, so she didn't do either of those things.

After Susan had joked with Justin for a few moments she turned to Meg. 'I've ironed the sheets again, now they're on the bed. I don't think your flowers are quite good enough though. Otherwise, the room looks very nice.'

Where was Lizzie when you needed her? Meg thought, turning her mind to one of her dearest friends, who was a genius with flowers, among other things. 'Cherry? Are you any good with flowers?'

'No, but Ambrosine is,' said Cherry. 'Why don't you ask her?'

'Good idea,' said Meg and left the room swiftly. A few words with Ambrosine would make everything seem better.

Ambrosine was more than happy to do the flowers for Lady Lennox-Stanley's bedroom when Meg offered to bring them to her. She also agreed to come to dinner and invite her colonel. 'Not only will it look as if we have a few more guests than we do actually have,' Meg explained, 'but Vanessa's snooty mother will see she isn't the only grande dame we have in the place!'

Ambrosine laughed. 'I'll be my very grandest, I promise,' she said.

'My old friend David is coming too, with a director friend. They want to put on *A Midsummer's Night's Dream* in the garden.'

'I met him when he was here before. Delightful chap. But good Lord, Meg! Shakespeare in the garden? Whatever next? Still, it's a lovely idea. Now you run and get me the flowers and I'll see what I can do. But before you go – can I suggest you put a dress on? You don't want to be greeting your grand guests in those scruffy checked trousers and a chef's jacket.'

Meg did as she was told and then went into the garden to find some more white flowers at Ambrosine's request. She hadn't found very many when she came round the corner to see David's car pull up in the drive.

She was so happy and relieved to see him that she flung the few bits of a shrub she'd picked into the hedge and ran up the drive to greet him.

He got out of the car and took her into his arms. 'Meggy! What's all this?'

He hugged her tightly and Meg closed her eyes, knowing that here was a true ally, who would make everything all right. When she opened her eyes again, she saw Justin looking coldly at her. David released her.

'Let me introduce you,' Meg said. 'Justin, this is David, my old friend from London who now lives in France.'

'We've met,' said Justin.

Meg could have kicked herself for forgetting.

'And let me introduce you to Russell,' said David as his passenger got out of the car. 'Russ, this is Meggy, who I've told you about. Russell wants to put a play on in the garden.'

Russell laughed. He was handsome and well dressed and very self-assured. 'Meg, I'm delighted to meet you. David has told me – at length – what a good cook you are.' He turned his attention to Justin.

It was like looking at dogs deciding whether or not to fight, thought Meg. Justin was still looking bad-tempered and Russell seemed not to care. It was only a matter of seconds before they shook hands and greeted each other but Meg couldn't help wondering why Justin was being quite so frosty.

'Do come inside, everyone,' said Meg, wishing her mother was here but so glad she wouldn't have to cope with Lady Lennox-Stanley on her own.

'Is it too early for a drink?' asked David. 'I bought some Monbazillac on the ferry and I'm dying to try it.'

'It's four o'clock, David,' said Meg. 'But if you can't wait until six o'clock for a drink, like a civilized human

174

being, don't let me stop you. You'd better be quick, though, as Vanessa and Lady Lennox-Stanley will be here soon.'

'I'd better go,' said Justin. 'My presence is obviously surplus to requirements.'

'What do you mean?' asked Meg. She didn't want him to stay, his presence felt a bit awkward, but she wanted to find out why he was being so huffy – even for him.

'I've dressed the salmon and you've got your friends to assist you.' Then he relaxed a little. 'Although I admit I'm curious to see this Lady What's-her-name.'

'She may well turn up at your hotel,' said Meg.

'And I really ought to get back. Raoul is there at the moment and wanted the kitchen to himself for a while,' said Justin.

'He doesn't want you stealing his secret recipes,' said Meg solemnly.

Justin laughed, as he was supposed to. 'That will be it. I'll be off then.'

As he set off round the house to where he'd parked his car, Meg noted that he was still limping just a little bit.

Chapter Eighteen

'Tell me,' Russell asked. 'Why was that Justin chap so on his guard?' They were in the drawing room which, Meg was delighted to see, was looking particularly lovely. Evening sunshine came through the French doors, filling the room with watery light and reflecting off the polished floor and the furniture. The smell of the wisteria that climbed up the outside of the house wafted through the open windows, adding to the fragrance of a large arrangement of flowers that someone – it must have been Ambrosine – had put on a table.

Meg sighed. 'I don't really know. But if he had his way, the hotel would be sold. But he has been really helpful lately so I don't know. He's naturally bad-tempered, of course. So many chefs are.' But when he wasn't being grumpy he could be very kind – and there had been that moment which haunted her dreams when he'd almost kissed her.

'Present company absolutely excepted with regard to bad-tempered chefs,' said David, going to the drinks tray on the hunt for glasses. He poured from the bottle he'd brought with him. 'Now tell me if that isn't liquid honey!'

Everyone took a sip. 'That is delicious!' said Meg. 'I wonder if you could make jelly with it? Is it too sweet for a syllabub, I wonder?' Seeing David look at her questioningly, she went on, 'I was doing the puddings and desserts for Justin's hotel. He told me about dessert trolleys. I knew about them, of course, but I hadn't thought of doing one for here, but they're fun.'

She got up. 'Now, can I leave you chaps to look after yourselves? I need to see what's going on in the kitchen before Vanessa and her ladyship arrive.'

'I think we should take our drinks into the garden,' said Russell. 'I want to look at where we might put on the play.'

'Good idea!' said David. 'I'll bring the bottle.'

'I have to say that young Justin has turned into a very helpful person,' said Susan as soon as Meg arrived. 'He's made all the escalopes or whatever you call those bits of pork dipped in egg and breadcrumbs and also whipped a large bowl of cream so you can fill those tiny meringues you made. Dolly-sized, I reckon.'

'I'm glad he made himself useful,' said Meg, feeling pleased, but also a bit on edge. 'David and his friend Russell, who seems very nice but quite actorish, if you know what I mean, are going round the garden to look for where the play might be put on.'

'Plays in the garden? Whatever next!' said Susan. 'Mind you, I think there are old photos of the family doing theatricals in the garden. More pageants than plays, really. You should talk to Ambrosine. She found out all about it when she was writing her little book about the house.'

'Oh, really?' Meg was heartened by this; if it had been done in the old days, perhaps it wasn't such a silly idea after all.

Teatime was now definitely over and Meg was wondering if she should add the little meringues to the dessert trolley or if they would be soggy by dinnertime when she heard another car. Lady Lennox-Stanley and Vanessa – it must be them!

She almost ran into the hall, opened the front door and was joined by David, who was approaching from the garden. There was no sign of Russell. It wasn't much of a reception, there were no uniformed staff in a line, but Meg hoped that Lady Lennox-Stanley wouldn't feel it was a shabby greeting.

David had gone out to open the car door but as Lady Lennox-Stanley exited from it, Meg heard her say, 'I can't believe we're finally here!' She wasn't saying it in an excited way, but as one who felt they had been hard done by. Meg remembered this woman was her friend Lizzie's mother-in-law. Poor girl!

Lady Lennox-Stanley was wearing a very elegant suit that had probably been made for her in Paris, and with it a matching hat which included a veil.

In spite of David's accompanying arm, and Vanessa's soothing mutterings, Lady Lennox-Stanley was obviously not in a good mood.

Meg took a breath and put her shoulders back. She stepped forward. 'How lovely to see you, Lady

Lennox-Stanley. Did you have a wretched journey? Do come in.

'Vanessa,' she added quietly, 'so glad you're here.'

Vanessa made an apologetic face out of her mother's vision.

'Nessa, do you think your mother would like to visit the powder room?' said Meg, thinking of the least explicit name she could think of.

'If you mean, do I need the lavatory, I wish you'd say so,' Lady Lennox-Stanley snapped. 'And yes, I do!' She glared at Meg from under her veil.

'Follow me,' said Meg, ushering her ladyship into the ladies' room on the ground floor. Susan had found linen towels, a cake of soap from Floris and Ambrosine had put some flowers in an antique vase in there. Meg knew this small room had never looked grander.

'I'm sorry she's so grumpy!' wailed Vanessa. 'She's been ghastly ever since we had lunch with her friend who said something that really got her goat. Oh, David, I'm so glad Meggy's got you! My mother would eat her alive otherwise.'

What little confidence Meg had in herself to deal with this situation melted. 'Just tell me, Nessa, tea or alcohol?'

'Both,' said Vanessa and David as one. 'I bloody well deserve a drink,' Vanessa added.

'Strong G and Ts coming up!' said David.

'No!' Meg put up a hand. 'I'll do it. I've got everything ready. You look after Nessa's mother.'

She almost didn't recognise Cherry, who was wearing the lace cap. Meg did wonder if she looked like a maid in a French farce but decided it didn't matter.

'Vanessa's mother is a nightmare!' she said quickly to Cherry and Susan. 'She's in the loo now. We want drinks and tea.'

'The tea's all ready,' said Susan calmly. 'Cherry and me will take that in on the trolley. There are cold tonics in the fridge, and ice and lemon, so you bring those. There are already glasses and drinks on the tray in the drawing room. There's a new bottle of Armadillo sherry, Spanish, none of that Cyprus rubbish – and everything else you might need.'

'Susan, I don't know what I'd do without you. Thank you so much!' Meg had instantly decided it didn't matter what Susan called the sherry; she was a life-saver.

Susan looked pleased. 'Come along, Cherry. Let's show the gentry that us country bumpkins know how things are done.'

Having noted Cherry's lace cap with approval, Lady Lennox-Stanley accepted a cup of tea from her. Cherry bobbed a curtsey as she handed it over, risking slopping it into the saucer. Lady Lennox-Stanley also accepted the offer of a drink.

'Can I suggest a gin and tonic?' said David. 'Ice and lemon?'

'Thank you, but no ice. I'm not American.'

The amount of disdain Lady Lennox-Stanley managed to get into this declaration was astounding, thought Meg as she mixed the drinks. She put a lot of gin in the glass before adding a splash of tonic and a slice of lemon. Cherry put the drink and the rest of the little bottle of tonic on a tray and took it to her ladyship.

'Where is Russell when you need him?' David murmured while Meg was mixing a drink for Vanessa. 'He's brilliant with snooty old women.'

Meg suppressed a smile. Thinking of Lady Lennox-Stanley as a snooty old woman, instead of someone she was desperate to impress, took the sting out of her a little.

'Ah! I think I can spot him through the window,' said David. 'Do those doors open?' Without waiting for a reply he strode across the room and unlocked the French windows. 'Russell? Come in and have a drink!'

Meg was watching Lady Lennox-Stanley, who, she had decided, wouldn't be welcome in the hotel again if she could guarantee them full bookings for the rest of the year. As Russell entered the drawing room, very much like a character in a play, Lady Lennox-Stanley's expressions changed. Her hand went up to her mouth and her eyes opened wide.

'Let me introduce you,' said David. 'Lady Lennox-Stanley, Russell Rook—'

'I know who Russell Rook is,' she said in a faint voice. 'I saw you in *Present Laughter* when I was in my twenties!'

Russell laughed. 'I was in my twenties then myself, although you don't look very much older than that now!'

Seeing how utterly thrilled her terrifying guest was, Meg felt free to leave the room. No one noticed. She went back into the kitchen where Susan and Cherry were ready to welcome her.

'How is it going?' asked Susan. 'Here, have a sherry. We're having one.'

'Well, it was awful! She's a dragon.' Meg didn't need to specify which 'she' was being referred to. 'But then Russell – the chap who wants to put a play on in the garden – came in and she sort of melted! Apparently, she saw him in a play and she obviously fell in love with him. They're much the same age, although Lady L-S seems older because she's so snooty.' Meg took the glass she was handed and sipped it. It was delicious.

'So, are they drinking tea or alcohol?'

'Both. They're drinking gin but they're eating cake as well. Maybe I'd better get out the cheese straws,' said Meg.

'To go with the tea they're not drinking?' said Cherry.

'I think your cap is making you frivolous,' said Meg. 'We can't have that.'

Susan shook her head. 'This is no time for joking now, Meg. And can I suggest you run a comb through your hair and maybe put on a little lipstick? That dress is pretty – I recognise it from when your mother last wore it – but you're still looking a little like a tomboy.'

When she'd availed herself of the spotted mirror in the lavatory the staff used, in which her mother kept a lipstick, Meg went back to the kitchen. 'Will I pass?'

Susan nodded grudgingly.

'Then I'd better go back in and find out what time they want dinner,' said Meg. 'And also find out if Lady Lennox-Stanley will stay with us or go up to the other hotel.'

When Meg went back into the drawing room she found it very serene.

'She's almost literally eating out of his hand!' muttered David out of the corner of his mouth. 'Look! They're sharing a plate of cake. He is bloody marvellous, that man.'

'I just need to know when she wants to eat,' said Meg. 'Then I can go back to the kitchen and arrange it. Oh, and find out where she'd like to sleep. I'll go and have a word with Nessa.'

Vanessa, who was sitting nearby, was apparently almost as charmed by Russell as her mother was. Meg made nodding movements which Vanessa correctly interpreted as her friend's need for a private word.

'When would your mother like dinner?' Meg said. 'And where do you think she'd like to sleep? She will have her own bathroom, but it's down the hall a bit, so not attached.'

'Is Russell Rook sleeping here?' asked Vanessa.

'I imagine so. There are rooms ready for him and David.'

'Then I'm sure she'll want to stay.' Vanessa paused. 'But what's the alternative if she says no?'

'I've booked her room at the hotel in Newton-cum-Hardy – where she usually stays.' Meg felt a little smug about this, considering it was all at such short notice.

'We need to show her the room,' said Vanessa, 'but how we're going to get her away from Russell Rook I have no idea.'

'Let's get David on to it,' said Meg. 'I've never been in a hole he hasn't been able to get me out of.'

'And this is hardly a hole,' said Vanessa primly. 'It's a very nice hotel.'

Meg dug her in the ribs and caught David's eye.

Having checked that Lady Lennox-Stanley's glass was replenished, David addressed her and Russell. 'Meg is wondering what time we'd like to eat? And also if you'd like to see your room, Lady Lennox-Stanley?'

Russell, who took the hint, stood up immediately. 'Let's do it together, Lady Lennox-Stanley. Did you have lunch on the road? We found a charming little pub that provided us with bread and cheese and a glass of ale but you may not have fared so well.'

Meg knew she had to do her mother's job and make sure the guests were happy with their rooms and as she followed the party upstairs she amused herself by picturing Lady Lennox-Stanley being offered a lump of cheese and a pickled onion for her lunch. It did present an entertaining picture.

Everyone was gathered on the galleried landing and Meg sidled her way to the front. 'Do follow me. This is the Yellow Bedroom,' she said. 'All the rooms are called after the names on the bell indicator in the kitchen. Although,' she added hurriedly, 'they're no longer operational.'

She actually had no idea if the bells worked or not, but she wasn't risking Lady Lennox-Stanley ringing one at all hours of the day or night. She opened the door of the room.

'There's just a small chance the room was named after the colour of the wallpaper,' said David.

Meg gave him a look. The wallpaper was beautiful; it was pale yellow with exotic birds and creepers climbing up it. It was faded but possibly nicer because of it.

Lady Lennox-Stanley went in. All the furniture was antique and the curtains were also yellow though rather faded.

'It's a lovely room, Mummy!' said Vanessa encouragingly.

'Where's the bathroom?' asked Lady Lennox-Stanley imperiously.

'Here,' said Meg, leading the way. 'It's not directly adjoining but it is for your exclusive use. The hotel isn't busy at the moment.'

'Not surprising if you can't offer bathrooms with the rooms,' said Lady Lennox-Stanley, glancing at the large old-fashioned bath, the elegant washbasin and the lavatory with a varnished wooden seat. She didn't seem to notice the array of towels, the flowers or the selection of soaps and bath salts.

'We're currently installing bathrooms into some of the rooms,' said Meg. 'If you should come again, they would certainly be available to you.' She paused and swallowed. 'However, if this accommodation isn't up to your high standards, there is a room available for you at the other hotel which is nearby. They have bathrooms "en suite".'

'As they say in France,' said David.

'Oh, do stay here, darling Lady Lennox-Stanley,' said Russell. 'It'll be such fun to have you!'

Lady Lennox-Stanley laughed in a way that could only be described as girlish. 'You must call me Amanda! And of course I'll stay. The room will be perfectly adequate.'

Meg caught Vanessa making an apologetic face at her. The Yellow Bedroom was lovely and would be extremely comfortable, her face said. But 'adequate' probably represented high praise.

'I can see you're longing to get back into the kitchen, Meg,' said Vanessa. 'Shall we find our own rooms? Meet you downstairs later? What time did we say we wanted dinner?' She looked at her mother.

'Eight o'clock,' said Lady Lennox-Stanley.

'Eight o'clock it is,' said Russell quickly. 'I'm sharp set, as my father used to say.'

'What about your luggage?' asked Meg, suddenly aware that her mother's job entailed far more than she realised.

'We'll sort that out,' said David. 'You go and see to dinner.' He smiled sympathetically. He knew dealing with the likes of Lady Lennox-Stanley would be hard for Meg and she'd far rather rustle up a four-course meal for twenty.

Chapter Nineteen

Meg had just finished shelling eggs so she could halve them with a delicious sauce involving cream and sherry and a little curry powder when Vanessa came in.

'Hello, Meg. Thank you so much for making every-thing so lovely for my mother.'

'You must thank Susan and Cherry for that,' said Meg. 'You ironed the sheets again once they were on the bed, didn't you, Susan?'

'I did. I have my pride. I'm glad her ladyship was satisfied.' Susan was still a bit suspicious of Vanessa, but Meg hoped once Vanessa had been here for a couple of days, she'd be treated as part of the family.

'It's all simply smashing,' said Vanessa. 'Flowers in the bathroom was a particularly nice touch.'

'Ambrosine did those,' said Meg.

'Is there anything I can do now?' Vanessa went on. 'It's such fun to be working. I'm finding home very difficult to live in at the moment.'

'You could write out the menu. We don't usually offer a choice but we thought – I thought – it would be good to offer a bit more. If we're trying to impress your mother.'

'I've written so many thank-you letters for wedding presents, my handwriting is now really good, but it'll seem strange you not eating with us,' said Vanessa.

'Obviously, I'd love to, but I'm cooking.'

Vanessa laughed. 'You know perfectly well you're delighted you're cooking and not having to make polite conversation with my mother.'

'You could nip in and out,' suggested Susan. 'The starters are cold anyway.' There was a mischievous twinkle in her eye when she said this, Meg noticed.

'I have to fry the escalopes freshly. They can't hang around,' Meg said firmly.

'Keep them warm in the oven?' suggested Susan.

'Or you could join us when you've served the escalopes?' said Vanessa. 'You know David would love you to be there and I'm sure there are things Russell needs to talk to you about.'

'I may join you for coffee in the drawing room,' said Meg. 'And should we light the fire in there? I know it's not really cold but—'

'Bob's still here,' said Susan. 'I'll get him to see to it before he goes off home. That room can be a little damp sometimes.'

'There was extra, so I've made Bob something to eat,' said Meg.

'That's kind, Meg. Although to be fair to him, he's not one of those men who can't feed themselves.' She paused. 'I suppose you want the butter putting into curls?'

Meg nodded. Dinner was almost ready; it was time for the fine-tuning.

Although she had thought she had plenty of time, Meg found it melted away and, before she knew it, she was taking Melba toast out of the oven and piling it on to silver dishes to serve with the pâté, should anyone order that. She took a couple of the dishes through so she could check the dining room.

Susan had done a very good job. The best linen, and polished silver candlesticks with new candles in them. (Despite the fact that, as Susan said, once candles were lit no one could tell if they were new or not, and she couldn't abide waste.) But her economical instincts had been set aside and the dining room looked splendid.

All the tables had flowers and candles and a menu, even though only the two tables set for four would be used.

She glanced into the drawing room just to check no one needed more tonic, or, heaven forbid, more ice.

Ambrosine, spotting Meg in the doorway, waved, but obviously didn't expect Meg to come in. She would have felt embarrassed in her chef's whites among so much elegance. Lady Lennox-Stanley still wasn't down although Bob had already been in and lit the fire.

Meg waved back and returned to the kitchen.

'Can you go and announce that dinner is ready, Cherry?' asked Meg. Lady Lennox-Stanley had been down late and it was already nearly eight thirty.

Having adjusted her cap so she could actually see, Cherry duly went. She came back a few minutes later, looking flustered. 'We need to lay another place. Justin is here.'

'Justin?' said Meg and Susan together.

'Did he tell you he was coming?' Susan asked.

'No! And I've no idea why he's here,' said Meg. 'There should be room on Lady Lennox-Stanley's table. Put a place for him there.'

'Lady Lennox-Stanley has obviously taken a fancy to him,' said Susan. 'She seems well away, I must say. I think that David must have been plying her with drinks in the short time she's been down.'

In spite of her anxiety, Meg couldn't help laughing. It would be just like David to keep Lady Lennox-Stanley sweet by topping up her gin and tonics, and she wasn't surprised she'd taken a shine to Justin, too. But what Justin was doing here, she had no idea. Luckily, she had plenty of food.

Meg had managed to put Justin's presence in the dining room out of her mind until, just as she was in the middle of frying escalopes, he arrived in the kitchen.

'Lady Lennox-Stanley wants to know if the escalopes are veal,' he said.

'What's the right answer?' said Meg, hardly looking up from her task.

'Yes.'

'Then say yes. Actually, they're local pork but I'm sure she won't know the difference.'

'I agree with you: she won't.'

Justin looked very different and very smart in a suit. In spite of herself Meg was aware of being short of breath. 'Why are you here?' she asked.

'I came in case your grand guest might need a lift to the hotel.'

'Very kind,' said Meg, 'but she's staying with us. I did telephone and cancel the room.'

'She's enjoying the company, I can see that,' said Justin.

Acutely aware of his presence, Meg stepped around him so she could get plates out of the oven.

'How well do you know David?' he asked after a short pause.

'Very well. We used to live together in London. I thought you knew that from last time.'

'Isn't there rather an age gap?'

It dawned on Meg that Justin had misunderstood her and thought that she and David were having some sort of relationship. If she hadn't been in the middle of service, she'd have laughed. 'Only the same gap as Alexandra and her count, roughly,' she said. 'Now can you please go and sit down?'

Justin wandered grumpily away.

Even though the situation made her anxious, Meg couldn't help smiling when she went into the drawing room for coffee and saw Ambrosine and her colonel in their best clothes. Ambrosine was wearing some exotic jewellery and the colonel not only had all his medals stretched across his chest, but wore a monocle too. They could have been characters in a play.

Russell Rook was sitting with them and Lady Lennox-Stanley was on the outside of the group. When Ambrosine saw Meg, she raised her hand.

'Meggy, do come and sit down and have a drink. That was a splendid meal!'

Meg pulled up a pouffe and joined them.

'Lady Lennox-Stanley has been telling us all about the charity race day she runs at Shroton racecourse. Such fun! I think we'll all go, won't we?' said Ambrosine. 'And Russell here has been telling us about putting on a play in the grounds. I remember doing that when I was a girl in the house I grew up in, but it was pageants, not quite so ambitious.'

'But Russell is a very experienced director,' said Lady Lennox-Stanley. 'A play would be easy for him.'

'I wouldn't say easy,' said Russell, patting Lady Lennox-Stanley's hand. 'But possible. And I'm rather hoping Dame Miriam Twycross might play Titania.'

'Isn't she a bit long in the tooth for that sort of thing now?' asked the colonel.

'On paper, she's nearly sixty,' said Russell, 'but I promise you, once she's on stage, the years fall away and she's as lovely as ever.'

This news caused Ambrosine to look a little sceptical. 'I daresay they can do wonders with make-up, these days.'

'I saw her in *Saint Joan*, years ago,' said Lady Lennox-Stanley. 'She was enchanting! It's such a shame that my husband doesn't share my love of theatre. I don't get to go nearly as much as I'd like to.'

Meg wondered why she couldn't just go with a friend. They had a London house, after all.

David came over. 'Now, can I get you a drink, Meggy? And how is everyone else getting on?'

'I'd love another snifter of port,' said the colonel. 'I'll regret it in the night, but now, I'd love it.'

Meg was glad she couldn't see Justin's face. He'd probably be terribly disapproving of her giving away the vintage port. But he was deep in conversation with Vanessa and Russell, so he didn't notice.

Some time later, Meg was giving the kitchen a final wipe when Vanessa came in.

'You look tired, Meggy. Go to bed. Everyone else seems to want to stay up drinking, but why don't you slip off?'

Staying up drinking was the very last thing Meg wanted to do but she wondered if it was her duty.

Possibly because Meg didn't answer, Vanessa went on, 'You know that Justin fancies you, don't you?'

This woke Meg up. 'No he doesn't! Don't be ridiculous.'

Vanessa shrugged. 'I could be wrong, I suppose.'

'I'm sure you are wrong!' said Meg. 'And I can't go to bed. Supposing someone wants something?' she asked, meaning Lady Lennox-Stanley.

'I'll see to it,' said Vanessa, understanding what Meg meant. 'She's my mother. And I'm practically a member of staff now!'

Chapter Twenty

Breakfast the following day went better than Meg could have hoped for. Lady Lennox-Stanley's grapefruit was juicy and perfect, her boiled egg (supposedly so easy, but in Meg's opinion, a sort of Russian roulette) was cooked just as she liked it. And the toast was the perfect colour too. Although she really didn't want to, Meg put on a clean apron and went to ask her ladyship about it after she had finished.

Lady Lennox-Stanley was flanked by David and Russell Rook, with Vanessa next to David.

'Good morning,' Meg said, trying to smile and look confident. 'Did you all have a good night?'

'Positively splendid!' said Russell. 'Perfect sheets and such comfortable pillows. So quiet, and such a charming view! I woke this morning and flung back the curtains and drank in the glory of the garden. I can't wait to put on the *Dream* here! The setting is so perfect.'

'It was jolly comfy, Meg,' said David, giving her a supportive smile.

Lady Lennox-Stanley also smiled, but it was a stretching of the lips and nod of the head, lasting the shortest possible time. Then she spoke.

Meg had known that by asking Lady Lennox-Stanley how she'd passed the night she was making herself a hostage to fortune. Lady Lennox-Stanley, Meg was convinced, was honour-bound to relate everything that was wrong with it. She braced herself for bad news.

'Of course it was very inconvenient not having a bathroom attached to the room,' said Lady Lennox-Stanley, 'but otherwise, as I said yesterday, it was all perfectly adequate.'

Vanessa rolled her eyes at Meg. 'It was lovely!' she said, obviously embarrassed but not surprised by her mother's faint praise. 'You slept really well, didn't you, Mummy?'

'I never have an unbroken night's sleep,' Lady Lennox-Stanley explained, 'but while I was lying awake in the night, I was comfortable.'

'Bingo!' said David. 'I mean, jolly good.'

'And in other good news,' said Russell, 'it seems that David and I can give Amanda a lift back, so Vanessa can stay here and help you, Meg.'

Lady Lennox-Stanley frowned. 'The young are so selfish,' she said, 'but fortunately, Russell and David are practically passing my door.'

Meg's sense of geography wasn't very good but she was fairly certain this wasn't true; however, she was extremely grateful to the two men for convincing her ladyship this was the case.

'Isn't it splendid?' said Russell. 'Now, who's for a last turn round the garden? Let's see what, if anything, needs to be done to make it into a proper open-air theatre.'

Vanessa came to see Meg in the kitchen while this was going on. 'I can't be spared to help you for more than a couple of weeks, I'm afraid.'

'My mother will be home by then, I'm sure. To have any help in the office will be brilliant, so thank you.'

Cherry, who had entered the kitchen with a full tray, put her burden down. 'I'd be happy to help in the office, when Vanessa has to go, if you like.'

'And how am I supposed to manage without you in the kitchen?' said Susan.

'We could get someone else to do my job. Mary, for instance. She'd be fine and Auntie Kath would be delighted if she had a bit of work,' said Cherry. 'I want to improve myself. If I worked in the office here, I could tell people I have office experience.'

Susan sighed. 'In my day a young woman was perfectly happy to work in a nice hotel; she didn't want to "improve herself".'

'Times are changing, Mother,' said Cherry. Having emptied the tray, she went back to the dining room.

'It would be a great help to me, Susan, if you didn't mind,' said Meg.

'Bless you, deary! If it helps you to have young Cherry to answer the telephone and welcome the guests, it's fine by me.'

'I'd be very happy to train her,' said Vanessa, 'just as soon as I've learnt what to do myself.'

The farewells that afternoon were long and effusive. When they were finally over, they all retired to the kitchen.

'Thank goodness that's over!' said Meg. 'It was fun but very hard work.'

'I wouldn't like to say your mother was a difficult guest,' said Susan, obviously feeling the complete opposite, 'but—'

'At home the staff call her Lady Fussy-Knickers,' said Vanessa.

'That about sums it up,' said Cherry. 'Now, shall I put the kettle on?'

For the next couple of weeks, the hotel was a hive of busyness, and although Meg fell into bed exhausted every night, she loved the sense of purpose and achievement.

Bob, Susan's husband, and various nephews, god-sons and sons of old friends got the bathrooms in and decorated the rooms. There was a lot of 'making good' required, and the hotel bacon was saved by Ambrosine finding several rolls of wallpaper that had originally matched the wallpaper in the bedrooms. It no longer matched but the pattern was the same, just in much brighter colours. When there were four bedrooms with bathrooms attached, Susan sent the gang to do up the gardener's cottage and any other suitable outbuilding.

'Bob's never been happier,' she explained to Meg one lunchtime. 'He loves the gardening, always has, but this plumbing's got him really excited. And of course it's more money. Longer hours.'

'I'm so glad to hear that he's happy,' said Meg, hoping Justin would be as happy paying for the longer hours.

197

There were more hotel guests, too. People who had been for Sunday lunch or afternoon tea told their visitors about Nightingale Woods, and Vanessa and Cherry were kept busy finding rooms for them.

Louise telephoned from France the night before Vanessa was due to go home.

'Well,' Meg told her mother with satisfaction. 'We've been going great guns. We have four bedrooms with their own bathrooms now, and they're working on the gardener's cottage.'

'Who is "they"?' asked Louise, obviously intrigued.

'Various connections of Susan's,' said Meg. 'She's like Rabbit in *Winnie-the-Pooh* – she has a lot of friends and relations.'

'Useful!' said Louise.

'Extremely.' Meg drew a breath, about to ask Louise when she'd be home and did she need meeting at the station when Louise forestalled her.

'Darling, would it be a frightful nuisance if we stayed a bit longer? It turns out that Andrew's father had to have two wills, an English one and a French one. The French one is a nightmare. Apparently, he went round his farm saying, "Have this field, *mon brave!*" without giving a thought to the legal side of it.'

Meg wasn't much interested in the legal side of it, she was overcome with disappointment that her mother wasn't coming home. 'Oh.' She swallowed hard, wanting to hide her feelings from Louise.

'You'll be OK? You've got Vanessa?'

'For a little while; she has to go home soon.' Meg paused, hoping she didn't sound too pathetic. 'And the charity race day is coming up.'

There was a pause in which Meg waited for her mother to say, 'Then of course I'll come home immediately.' Instead, Louise just said, 'But Cherry's helping in the office now? You'll be all right?'

Meg had never been the sort of daughter to make demands on her mother's time – it had never been possible. So now she just said, 'Of course.' Then she added, 'So do you have any idea when you and Andrew might be back?'

'Not a clue, darling. But it seems to me you're doing an absolutely brilliant job of running Nightingale Woods. Is Justin being helpful?'

'Yes,' said Meg, feeling even more bleak. 'He's paying to have the alterations done.'

'Well, Andrew's given him money to do that. But is he being helpful in other ways?'

'We're all busy, Mum! Now I'd better go. I've got something in the oven.'

Yet another of Susan's relatives was now employed full time in the kitchen and dining room with Cherry spending all her time in the office. Cherry had also learnt to arrange flowers from Ambrosine and was willing to turn her hand to anything.

'Not sure where all this will get her,' said Susan, cutting the crusts off sandwiches one teatime. 'But Cherry's happy as a lark working here now. Strange to think not long ago we all thought the hotel would have to be sold because we had so few guests. Look at us now!'

'I reckon it's all down to you and Bob,' said Meg, hoping that they were doing enough to stop the hotel being sold. 'None of it would have happened without you.'

'None of it would have happened without you, Meggy!' said Susan. 'Now run along and get some time off before dinner. There's eight in tonight!'

Chapter Twenty-One

The day before the charity race day, the hotel was as near perfect as it could be, Meg thought. All the rooms were booked, mostly for Lady Lennox-Stanley and her friends. New bed linen had been bought after one guest had put their foot through an ancient linen sheet. There were toiletries in the attached bathrooms – Floris for Lady Fussy-Knickers, as she would be called forever. There were vases of freshly picked flowers in buckets in the cool larder, waiting for Ambrosine to turn them into posies for the bedrooms. The wine cellar had been investigated thoroughly by Ambrosine's colonel and a new wine list written. Justin had visited just long enough to add the prices, which were eye-wateringly high.

There were a couple of things that were worrying Meg, however. One was the fact that the lock on Lady Lennox-Stanley's door was a bit dodgy and Bob hadn't had time to fix it, and the other was the rain. On and on it rained, and there was even talk that the race day might have to be cancelled.

Meg would have felt happier about it all if Vanessa had been with her for moral support, but she'd had to go home. She would be with her mother for the race day – in fact they were arriving today – but from Meg's point of view, that was a bit too late.

It was mid-morning; Meg, Susan and Ambrosine were in the drawing room. The room had been thoroughly dusted and swept, now they were checking on final details. The pouring rain was the subject of conversation yet again.

'If they did cancel the race day, it would be for the first time,' said Susan. She was lighting a fire because although it was mid-June, everyone thought the room felt a little damp.

'And if it isn't cancelled, it'll be very muddy,' said Ambrosine, tweaking a bit of Daphne, especially chosen for its fragrance. 'And not all horses like to run around in it. Don't much like mud myself.'

'It's going to make the hotel very difficult to keep clean,' said Susan, sitting back on her heels and admiring the fire, which was finally going well. 'But we'll manage,' she added, possibly seeing Meg's stricken expression.

Meg forced a smile. 'The weather forecast is quite good,' she said.

Ambrosine and Susan looked at her sadly. 'When have you ever known one of them things to be right?' said Susan.

Meg took a breath to give an example, couldn't think of one, and breathed out again. It was depressing; it was so important for Nightingale Woods that the race day should be a success.

'I'm going to make up the beds now,' she said.

'Young Sally's up there to help you. She's young but a good worker.'

Sally appeared to be about twelve, Meg thought, although she was very adept at hospital corners.

'Hello, Sally, I'm Meg.'

Sally smiled. 'Auntie Susan told me. She's not actually an aunt, but I can't remember how we're related.'

'Well, thank you for coming to help, Sally.'

'I like helping. I don't like school much.'

'Well, you can always come and work in this hotel in your spare time if your aunt lets you, while I'm in charge anyway,' said Meg. 'Would you like to smooth that pillow a bit? A woman your aunt calls Lady Fussy-Knickers is going to sleep here.'

Sally giggled. Meg did too. Who cared about the weather? They couldn't do anything about it, after all.

'I think that's perfect,' said Meg a few minutes later. 'And the flowers look beautiful, and we've got all the best towels. Let's move on to the next room.'

Sally gave the counterpane a final twitch and then agreed.

A couple of hours later Meg had retreated to the kitchen to think whether there were enough desserts for the trolley. This was something she could control, she had decided. There was no point in worrying about things that she couldn't, like the mud, or if the lock on Lady Fussy-Knickers' door was wonky.

Justin found her there. She hadn't heard a motorbike so assumed he must have driven. His sudden presence made her jump.

'What are you doing here?' she asked.

'I came to see if you needed any help. You've got a big day coming up tomorrow and my father and your mother are still away. Is there anything I can do for you?'

He was looking at her in a way Meg couldn't interpret. Was he was watching for signs that she was going to refuse help, even if she needed it? This wasn't unreasonable; he knew how she liked to solve her own problems. Or was it something else? Vanessa's ridiculous suggestion that he fancied her floated into her mind. Her mouth went dry, she coughed and moved away. She couldn't take the intensity of his look any longer.

'Actually—' she began.

And then Laura came into the room. 'Here you are, Jussy – Justin!' she corrected herself hurriedly and gave Meg a coy look. 'I suppose he knew he'd find you here, Meg. You are pretty much always in the kitchen, aren't you? We've come to help. The race day is a big one for local hotels and we knew you were here on your own.'

'I do have Susan and her team,' said Meg, indignant on their behalf. 'And Vanessa is coming today with her mother, Lady Lennox-Stanley.'

'Oh, her!' said Laura. 'Our hotel is still talking about how difficult she was when she stayed last year. Isn't that right, Justin?'

Justin made a non-committal gesture. 'What was it you said needed doing, Meg?'

'The lock on Lady Lennox-Stanley's door is a bit tricky. I asked Bob to sort it out, but he's been so busy—'

'I'll go and have a look,' said Justin.

'Her room is the one—' Meg began, but he was halfway out of the door.

'I know which one it is,' he said.

'Justin is so kind, isn't he?' said Laura, sitting on the table as if settling in for a chat. 'I knew he'd say yes the moment I suggested we came over to help. But couples do that, don't they? They know what the other is thinking.'

Laura showed no signs of moving and Meg didn't quite feel she could ask her to. She put some scattered utensils in a tidy row, hoping to give Laura the hint that she was sitting on a work surface. 'Are you and Justin engaged then?' she asked as casually as she could.

Laura shrugged and giggled. 'As good as! I think he's just waiting for the right moment to propose. Or he may be having a ring made. It's just the sort of thing he'd do, don't you think?'

'I couldn't say,' said Meg, wanting to run out of the room and scream.

'Well, take it from me, it is.'

Having rearranged her wooden spoon, paring knife, pastry crimper and, randomly, a pair of secateurs for the second time, Meg was at a bit of a loss. She wanted to ask if Laura and Justin were sleeping together. She wanted to know and she also wanted to shock Laura, who was so smug and complacent it was all Meg could do not to push her off the table.

'Now, Meg,' Laura began in a low, caring voice, 'I want you to be completely honest with me: are you really enjoying working here at Nightingale Woods? I know you're not professionally trained but I'm sure you can manage the sort of simple fare the clientele here would be happy with. But don't you want to stretch your wings a bit? You could learn so much if you went somewhere else? In London, maybe?'

Just for a minute, Meg wondered if she was being warned off; Laura was telling her to leave the hotel and go as far from it as she could. It was certainly one way of interpreting her words.

No, Meg decided. Laura was far too sure of her standing with Justin to think even for a moment that Meg might be a threat. It was a fairly laughable thought, after all. Laura was so svelte and confident and she, Meg, was always in her chef's whites and checked trousers. She was very confident about her cooking, but not so much about her physical appearance.

Justin came in. 'The lock works fine now. It just needed a drop of oil,' he said. 'Laura? Are you ready to go?'

Laura jumped off the table. 'Of course, darling – Justin!' she hastily corrected herself. 'No endearments at work, although strictly speaking' – she sent Justin a look from under her eyelashes – 'we're not at work, are we?'

'Come on,' said Justin briskly. 'It's lunchtime; we need to get back.'

Laura hurried after him.

Meg didn't bother with lunch. Once she'd scrubbed the kitchen table, getting rid of any germs Laura might have left on it, Meg made a trifle for the dessert trolley and then a couple of cakes. While these were out of the oven and cooling, Meg wrote a detailed list of things she needed to do. She had found Laura's visit very unsettling, and annoyingly it had knocked her confidence; a good list would help.

Meg was just wondering if she was hungry when Ambrosine came into the kitchen. She was wearing a pair of galoshes over the sensible lace-ups she wore for walking and had the colonel with her. He was dressed in ancient, much-darned tweed shooting apparel and was carrying a flat wicker basket.

'Oh, hello!' said Meg, feeling guilty. 'Do you want lunch?'

'We had bread and cheese at the pub,' said the colonel. 'And a very good drop of ale.'

'I've just popped in because I think I left my secateurs here,' said Ambrosine. 'Bertie is kindly going to help me pick flowers for a big arrangement in the hall. We're going to bring the garden into the house in the fine tradition of Constance Spry!'

'That would be wonderful, Ambrosine. I'm so grateful,' said Meg.

'We must have everything perfect for Lady Fussy-Knickers!' said Ambrosine, twinkling.

Meg's hand flew to her mouth. 'I didn't realise other people knew of that nickname,' she said, remembering too late that she'd said it to Sally that morning.

'As long as the guests don't hear us calling anyone that, all will be well,' said Ambrosine. 'Now, have you enough cakes for tea? Some people go mad for cake.'

'Now you're making me worry, Ambrosine,' said Meg. 'I'll make a batch of butterfly cakes as well. They don't take long to cook and Susan can help me ice them.'

'I'm sure they'll be delicious,' said the colonel, who was one of the people who loved cake.

Soon after they'd left, Susan and Cherry, who'd been home for lunch, came in.

'Are we absolutely sure how many people Lady Fussy – Lady Lennox-Stanley is bringing?' Susan asked.

'I meant to ring Vanessa yesterday to check,' said Meg, 'but never got round to it. I did ring this morning but they'd already left.'

Cherry, who had the guestbook tucked under her arm, took it out and studied it. 'It's just Lady Lennox-Stanley, her two friends who are a couple, and Vanessa. Plus the other guests, of course.'

'Should be fine,' said Meg, trying to sound optimistic but failing. She knew she'd feel better when Vanessa got here. She could tell her all about Laura sitting on the kitchen table and bragging about Justin.

Tea was over and Meg was in the entrance hall, admiring Ambrosine's floral arrangement, when a car pulled up on the gravel outside. Vanessa came tearing into the hotel. 'My bloody mother! I swear to God she does it on purpose! I am so sorry!'

Meg suppressed the jolt of anxiety this caused. 'Don't worry, Nessa. I'm sure whatever your mother has done can be managed. Where is she?'

'Her new friend is parking the car. They wouldn't let me stop on the way to telephone and warn you, but I made them let me come in now.'

'We knew your mother was bringing two friends,' said Cherry soothingly. 'We just thought they were arriving separately. No need to panic.'

'It's not those friends! They *are* coming separately. It's Basil.'

'Basil?' said Meg bemused.

'A man my mother has only just met. He heard we were coming to Nightingale Woods for the race day and he said he was desperate to come too. So my mother – who has never made a spontaneous gesture before in her life, I swear – said, "That would be such fun. You can help Vanessa with the driving."'

Meg put on a smile. 'Don't worry, Ness. We can find room for a single gentleman.'

'Yes!' agreed Cherry. 'We made up an extra room for just this emergency – although of course it isn't one really.'

'Oh, it is really!' said Vanessa. 'Do you still keep a bottle of sherry in the kitchen?'

'Of course,' said Meg.

'You take her through,' said Susan. 'We can deal with Lady L-S and this Basil she's brought with her.'

Once in the kitchen, Meg could see that Vanessa was genuinely flustered, and poured her a teacup full of sherry.

'I'd better not drink all of this,' said Vanessa, looking at what Meg had just handed to her.

'It's a very dainty cup,' said Meg. 'It doesn't hold much. Now what's really the matter?'

Vanessa took a desperate sip from the teacup. 'I haven't told you everything. Basil is close friends with Russell Rook and so he has invited him to come too! I know you've converted at least three single rooms into bathrooms, so where on earth are you going to put everybody?'

Meg and Susan exchanged glances. The situation was a little more serious that it had at first seemed. 'Well, you're not a problem, Nessa,' said Meg. 'You can share my little flat.'

'That sounds fun!' Vanessa was definitely calmer now.

'And Russell and Basil are friends?' asked Meg, to make sure.

'So we put them in a twin?' suggested Susan.

Vanessa's eyes widened in shock at the thought. 'Definitely not.'

'OK,' said Meg. 'We'll put Russell in your single as he's almost a friend now, and then find somewhere for this Basil person.'

'He's called Basil Knott-Dean. Going on how Mummy was treating him, he may be quite important,' said Vanessa.

'You leave it all to me,' said Susan calmly. 'Meg? Going by the sounds coming from the hall, you're needed there.'

The hall was full of people. Lady Lennox-Stanley was in the middle, surrounded by luggage and two large gentlemen, one of whom was Russell Rook.

'Good afternoon, everyone,' said Meg, trying to be like her mother, who would have been gracious and helpful but not obsequious. 'Welcome to Nightingale Woods. I do hope you all had good journeys?'

'Meg, darling,' said Russell, 'I've brought my old chum with me. He's heard good things about your hotel and was mad to come.'

'Basil Knott-Dean,' said Russell's chum, putting his hand into Meg's. He was tall and well spoken and seemed to have perfect manners. 'I'm that annoying thing, a last-minute guest on what's probably a busy night. Can you help? I can always go away again if you haven't got room.'

'How do you do?' said Meg, shaking his hand. 'And of course we can accommodate you.' Meg wasn't at all certain of this but she knew the gods of hotel-keeping would strike her down if she sent away a potential guest. 'Can I suggest everyone goes into the drawing room and has a drink? Lady Lennox-Stanley? We can get your cases into your room and find some-where comfortable for Mr Knott-Dean.'

'I can pour drinks,' said Russell, earning Meg's eternal gratitude. 'Amanda,' he said to Lady Lennox-Stanley, 'let me mix you a gin and ver. I have the knack.'

Lady Lennox-Stanley was two drinks down when Meg showed her and Vanessa to her room. Sadly, alcohol did not seem to have softened Lady Fussy-Knickers very much and it was Vanessa who provided the enthusiasm.

'Oh, Mummy!' she said delightedly. 'Isn't it all smart now? And look! Your own private bathroom through this door. This is so pretty. And so much more like a proper home than that other hotel on the hill. Don't you think so, Mummy?'

'As everyone else seems very happy with their rooms I suppose I must be too.' She gave one of her freezing smiles. 'Did Vanessa order picnics for to-morrow? There will be lunch laid on at the racecourse, but some people – my friends in particular – prefer a picnic.'

Vanessa looked at Meg in total horror. She'd obviously never heard of this requirement before either.

'If you're quite happy in your room, Lady Lennox-Stanley,' said Meg smoothly, 'Vanessa and I can just check on the details.'

Vanessa started apologising the moment they were out of the room. 'Meg, I had no idea she'd want picnics! I don't think she's ever wanted them before.'

'It's fine, Nessa,' said Meg, who was not nearly as calm as she was pretending. 'We can sort it out. We have time. Although it will have to be after dinner now.'

As they entered the kitchen a strange sound like a rusty door hinge emerged from the corner of the room.

'What's that noise?' asked Meg, looking at Susan.

Susan sucked her teeth. 'Look up there,' she said, pointing to the bell indicator box. One of the little flags was flapping.

'Oh my goodness,' said Vanessa. 'Don't let my mother see that – she'll never stop demanding things!'

'We could pretend it doesn't work,' said Susan. 'No one expects things like that to work any more, do they?'

'No, we can't do that,' said Meg. 'We'll just make sure they don't work after this visit.' She paused. Who could answer this imperious demand? Sally, the most junior member of the team, was away doing something else. Meg sighed. 'I'll go.'

'Your legs are younger than mine,' said Susan, inarguably.

Meg made a face at her and left the room at a lick.

'Oh, excellent service!' said Basil Knott-Dean when she arrived. 'Is it always so efficient? Often one waits hours for anyone to come.'

'How can I help you?' asked Meg, trying not to audibly pant.

'A tray of drinks? Whisky, water, some little eats for later?'

Meg wanted to tell this demanding guest that he'd had plenty to drink and that dinner would be more than adequate, he wouldn't need 'little eats for later', but she did want to make the guests happy. She nodded and smiled and was about to leave when he stopped her. 'Yes?'

'You can charge extra for meals served in the rooms, you know.'

Meg gave him a genuine smile this time and left the room.

Dinner had gone relatively smoothly, pronounced by everyone to have been delicious, except by Lady Lennox-Stanley who complained it was 'rather filling'.

Meg was making quiches for the picnic baskets when Justin came in, as if he owned the place, Meg thought. Her heart gave a little leap of excitement to see him before she remembered her conversation with Laura and it subsided a little. She cleared her throat.

'Hello!' he said. 'What are you doing?'

'Rolling out pastry,' she said. 'It's a technique often seen in kitchens.'

Justin tutted and she looked away. She didn't want to meet his eyes and was aware this probably made her look grumpy.

'I came to see if you needed anything,' said Justin. 'More linen perhaps?'

'You're a saviour,' said Susan, bustling in with a tray full of dirty coffee cups. 'The hotel is full and we've used every sheet we have. If I know anything,

Lady Fussy-Knickers will want clean linen tomorrow and we haven't got any. Cup of tea?'

Susan was looking at Justin as if his second name was Lancelot. For some reason this made Meg genuinely grumpy instead of just looking that way.

'Yes, please,' said Justin.

Susan poured his tea and went to collect more dirty dishes.

'Now, Meg, what's rattled your cage?'

Meg had a sudden urge to tell him all her problems. She sighed. 'Just tired. Lady Lennox-Stanley brought unexpected guests, and out of the blue wants me to make picnics to take to the races. There's catering laid on there, of course, but if Lady Fussy-Knickers wants picnics, picnics is what she gets.' She managed a smile.

'So, what are you going to put the picnics in?' asked Justin. 'Have you a supply of wicker baskets?'

'No,' said Meg. 'Currently I'm planning to wrap them in large red and white spotted napkins and tie them on to sticks. Who says you don't learn anything from pantomimes?'

He laughed. 'Poor Meggy! And I'm not surprised you're tired. I can't lend you picnic hampers, but the hotel does have a supply of white cardboard boxes used for big cakes. I reckon they'd be perfect. I'll get them to you early tomorrow.'

This was the ideal solution. 'Well, thank you, Lancelot,' she said, hiding her gratitude under sarcasm.

'What's that you called me?'

Meg shrugged, feeling more cheerful. 'Nothing.'

He gave her a look that was decidedly unnerving. It was one thing teasing him as if he was a lion in a cage, but suddenly the lion was the other side of the bars. Her heart beat faster. If only he wasn't with Laura, she may well have looked at him back, and taken the risk that he might kiss her. But she couldn't.

She was very glad that Susan returned at that moment, breaking the tension.

A little later, when he'd gone, Susan said, 'Justin likes to keep an eye on things, doesn't he?'

'I know!' said Meg, hoping for a chance for a good old grumble about him as she piped filling into frangipane tarts for the sweet trolley. 'It's as if he doesn't trust us to run things on our own!'

'Maybe it's not "things" he's keeping an eye on,' said Susan. 'Maybe it's you!'

Chapter Twenty-Two

Breakfast the following morning was a bit of a scramble, with everyone wanting to leave at the same time. But between Meg, Susan, Cherry (back in her role as waitress), Sally and Bob's apprentice, who could turn his hand to waiting if called upon, everyone got what they wanted in reasonable time. But the best thing was that the rain had stopped, the sun had come out and the world looked freshly washed (if not dried). It was going to be a beautiful day.

When everyone had left, in pre-booked cars for those without them, cardboard picnic baskets with those who requested them, the hotel staff breathed a collective sigh of relief. Cherry was sent back to the office as the telephone kept ringing and the others set to work on the washing-up which was enlivened by a good dissection of the guests, their clothes, and anything else they could think of.

Susan, Sally and Meg were all sitting in the kitchen having finally cleared up, and drunk more tea than Meg thought possible, when Cherry came in, looking very excited.

'You'll never guess what!' she said.

'No, we won't,' agreed her mother. 'Why don't you just tell us?'

'Well, Mr Knott-Dean – Basil?' she added, as everyone looked blank.

'Oh yes,' said Meg.

'Well, I thought he'd gone to the races with everyone else. But no!'

'Get to the point, love, some of us have got beds to make,' said Susan.

'He asked if he could use the telephone and I said yes and showed him to the office,' said Cherry, apparently now resigned to delivering her story without theatrical pauses. 'As I had the bills to prepare – everyone is going tomorrow – I took my folder into the hall and carried on working on them.' She checked to see that everyone was paying attention. 'I could hear every word he said!'

'What did he say?' asked Susan.

'He asked for a London number!'

'There's a shock,' said Susan, refusing to be impressed. 'Man from London telephones a number in London.'

'It was a newspaper. He's a restaurant critic. When he came out of the office, he said he was phoning in his copy!'

No one really understood what this meant. 'You mean he rang the newspaper he works for, telling them what he wants to write?' Meg said.

'I think so,' said Cherry. 'And it was very complimentary!'

'Well, isn't that nice!' said Meg. 'Can you remember what he said exactly?'

'Not really, but he did use the word quirky,' said Cherry.

'That doesn't sound good,' said Susan. 'It sounds as if we're a bit coggly.'

'I'm sure he didn't mean it as a bad thing,' Cherry said, obviously a bit deflated.

'You did really well, listening in,' said Meg. 'Even if you weren't able to catch every word.'

It was only later that she realised praising people for eavesdropping probably wasn't morally right.

Meg had gone out into her favourite spot in the garden, behind the walled garden, in a seat covered by an arch of roses. She had been chased there by Susan who said she needed a break. She closed her eyes and listened to the birds, trying to keep her thoughts away from the hotel and the endless meals. She even considered going to get her book. The trouble was, while she needed a mental break from cooking, her thoughts strayed to Justin however hard she tried to stop them. That was not in the least helpful. She closed her eyes.

'Meg?' a kindly male voice made her open them again. It was Basil.

'Oh, hello!'

'Meg, dear – may I call you Meg? I hope so because I've just done it three times in quick succession.'

Meg laughed. 'It's perfectly all right.'

'I'm so glad. And I'm here because I know perfectly well that the delightful Cherry overheard me dictate my review to my paper – she was meant to overhear! I want you all to know how good I think you are. But what she can't have overheard, because I didn't mention it, was that I also write for *Excellent Hotels and Restaurants*, which you may know is where all the best hotels in the United Kingdom are listed.' He paused, waiting for a reaction.

Meg obliged. 'Oh my goodness!' She had heard of the guide and it was definitely the best one to get into.

'And I want Nightingale Woods in that guide!'

'I don't know what to say!' Meg was stunned.

'My friend Russell had mentioned that Nightingale Woods was rather special so when I met Lady Lennox-Stanley and she told me she was on her way here, of course I expressed interest. Then she suggested I came along.' He paused and smiled confidingly at Meg. 'Part of me wanted to test how the hotel would cope when presented with a last-minute guest, and I'm happy to say you dealt with it perfectly!'

'I'm so glad.' Fancy Lady Fussy-Knickers inviting a restaurant critic to the hotel on the spur of the moment! Her mother, David – and Andrew – would be so thrilled. She couldn't wait to tell them. But although Cherry thought his review had been good when she overheard it, maybe she'd got it wrong. What then?

Basil patted her hand. 'I can see that now you're worried. No need. I'm going to give you what I've written so you can see for yourself. There will be small alterations, of course. I'm often told I have a rather . . .' He paused. 'Flowery writing style, but basically, here's what I think. I won't stay to watch you read it. I'm going to take a turn about the garden and enjoy the peace and quiet.'

When he'd gone, Meg picked up the paper and read.

If you search the hidden hills and dales of Dorset you may be lucky enough to chance upon the charming Nightingale Woods. It is a gem!

I have said before in print that good service is as important as good food and accommodation and sometimes you get one or the other. Here you have all three. The beautiful old house welcomes you like a friend, and while there are definitely rooms that need redecorating, there are now some rooms with private bathrooms. If the welcome is warm, the food of a very high standard, and the staff excellent, dealing with a demanding clientele with efficiency and charm, worn-out upholstery and chipped paint fades into insignificance. Do visit this quirkily original hotel if you possibly can. It's somewhere really very special.

When she'd had a few moments to take in the review, Meg went to find Basil in the garden. 'I'm overwhelmed,' she said. 'This is such a lovely review. Of course, I only work here, it's not my hotel, but it's so nice to hear it so praised.'

'I realise you don't own Nightingale Woods, but who does?' said Basil, who had patted the space on the bench next to him so Meg would sit and talk.

'Well, currently it's being run by Andrew Nightingale, but his father, the owner, has died so Andrew is sorting out his will. My mother is with him. She's why I'm here.'

'But you fit in so well!'

Meg smiled. 'It's my first experience of working in a hotel, and the first time I've been in charge on my own in a kitchen. But with Susan and everyone to help I've found I can manage it, and I love it.'

'Your style of cuisine—' He began and then stopped. 'What? What have I said to make you laugh?'

'I hope I didn't seem rude. I didn't realise I had a "style of cuisine". It sounds so grand.'

Basil laughed. 'You do have a style! It's simple food, from really excellent ingredients—'

'All local, all from friends and relations of Susan's.'

'Put together with care and attention and no fussy bits. Don't get me wrong: I appreciate food as theatre as much as the next man – more than many – but that's not what you're doing here. And your puddings make strong men weep!'

Meg was really giggling now. 'But how do you know?'

Basil tossed his head. 'A strong man – well, Russell actually – confessed to me last night how much your lemon meringue pie moved him. You may laugh, but a simple dessert, beautifully made, is a rare and joyful thing.'

'I love doing desserts. Lots of chefs don't, but I don't mind how much fiddling I have to do to make things look pretty. I don't like puddings like lemon meringue to look fussy – the woman who taught me cooking in London was very against anything piped – but when I make little fruit tartlets or mille-feuille, anything dainty, I do get very obsessed.'

Just then, Meg heard the sound of a motorbike. 'Oh, that's Justin. I wonder what he wants.'

'Who's he?' asked Basil.

'He's the son of Andrew, which makes him the grandson of the dead owner. He's a chef at the hotel in Newton-cum-Hardy, which is quite near here.'

A few moments later Justin came striding into view. 'Hello! Taking the weight off, Meg?' Then he smiled at Basil in a way that made Meg feel obliged to introduce them.

'So,' said Basil when this had been done. 'You're the nearest thing we have to an owner in the vicinity?'

'I like to keep an eye on my father's investment,' Justin said.

Privately, Meg stored this away. She'd let Susan know as soon as she could think of a sensible way to do it that Justin had made it absolutely clear he came to see the hotel, not her.

'I wonder if you should show him my entry for the guidebook?' said Basil.

'Hand it over,' said Justin, in no doubt. He read it very quickly. 'This is really very good!' he said a couple of minutes later. 'My father will be delighted when he reads it.'

'I'm delighted already,' said Meg.

'Meg is a very talented chef,' said Basil. 'I'm not sure if you're aware.'

'Those are very flattering words coming from you,' said Justin. To Meg's ears, he somehow managed to convey polite disbelief.

'This little hotel is a potential gold mine. Currently your prices are far too modest,' Basil went on.

'But the place is quite shabby in places,' Justin pointed out.

Meg had been about to say this herself but resented Justin saying it. 'Basil doesn't think that matters.'

Basil held up a hand. 'I didn't say that precisely. Some redecoration is necessary but the knocks and scuffs of life the hotel has won't interfere with the guests' enjoyment. Now, if I were to ring to find out about lunch, are you the only person here? In which case the bell would be like a tree falling in a forest.'

Meg laughed. She was getting used to his manner and it didn't worry her. 'I'm sure Susan is in the kitchen, but if you'd like lunch we can certainly do that for you. What would you like and where would you like it?' He didn't answer immediately. 'May I suggest a chicken salad in the garden with a nice glass of rosé from Provence? My friend has a chateau there.'

'That sounds perfect! Constantly eating rich food plays havoc with the waistline. A nice salad would be just the ticket.'

'I'll see to it right away.'

'Neatly done, Meg,' said Justin when they were on their own. 'You made him feel he wanted to eat what you wanted to give him. And I loved the "my friend has a chateau in Provence" – it made it seem the rosé was from her vineyards.'

'It is from right next door,' said Meg, blushing, 'and I think the vineyards did belong to the chateau at one time, so not a serious untruth.' She sighed. 'I'd better go and make the salad. You'll have guessed I already have cold chicken. I'll add some fresh herbs for extra flavour.'

'What else will you put in it?'

As he seemed genuinely interested, Meg said, 'Oh, you know, the usual: bit of celery, bit of onion, grapes, toasted almonds, mayonnaise – I'm sure you know!'

'I'll chop the almonds for you if you like,' he said. 'Will you put them under the grill or fry them in butter?'

'Grill,' said Meg. 'It's all quite rich already.'

They set off towards the house together and had nearly reached the kitchen door when Justin put his hand on her arm. 'Meggy—'

This made her jump. 'Who said you could call me Meggy? Only my closest friends and my mother call me that!' The moment the words were out of her mouth she wished she'd kept quiet. It wasn't really important what he called her, after all. But she felt he was taking an intimacy she hadn't granted him. They couldn't be intimate; he was with Laura.

'I'm sorry,' he said. 'I just – Never mind. I'll try not to do it any more. But, Meg, I feel I should warn you. My uncle Colin is coming over later. He wants to have a close look at the hotel. He hasn't been near it for years as he has no interest in it, but, as you know, my grandfather has died and Colin is due to inherit half of it. Although I suppose if there's other money there might be enough to make things equal so my father can have the hotel outright.'

Meg looked up at him. 'Of course I don't know anything about this, but don't you think, if there was a lot of money sloshing around, your father wouldn't have persuaded your grandfather to keep the place up a bit?'

Justin inclined his head. 'I agree with you. If there was spare money, things would be in better repair.'

'And if there isn't money to make it fair between the brothers?'

He nodded. 'The hotel will have to be sold.'

'You know how I feel about Nightingale Woods. Selling it would be awfully sad.'

'Going in the guide with that really good review is going to make a big difference though,' said Justin. 'Basil said your prices are too low, and they'll have to go up a lot to cope with the increased demand. You've done that, Meggy – Meg!' he corrected himself hurriedly.

'No, I haven't. Not really. I've just been part of the team.'

'To quote the great Basil Knott-Dean, you're "a very talented chef".'

Meg snorted. 'You don't believe that any more than I do.'

'Actually, I think I believe it more than you do, but let's not argue about it.' He paused. 'My uncle is due to come at half past ten tomorrow. Will that suit you?'

'Why does it need to suit me?'

Justin hesitated as if he didn't know how to put it. 'I think you need to know what my uncle may be planning. If you're with us, to show us round, it'll give you some idea. I've telephoned Dad. He's trying to get back as soon as possible. With your mother, naturally.'

Something about the way Justin said this sent Meg's hackles up. 'You seem unhappy that our parents are apparently a couple now.'

'I'm not unhappy, but I don't know your mother really, and as I've said before, anyone would be charmed by Nightingale Woods. Maybe that's what she wants: a house in the country, as well as my father.'

'I can assure you, as I have also done before, that my mother is not a gold digger. But as it seems likely the hotel will have to be sold, it's not relevant.' She took a quick breath. 'Now, I need to make a chicken salad. No need for you to help me. I can chop my own almonds.'

Chapter Twenty-Three

⚜

The guests took a long time to depart the following morning. Fortunately, Lady Lennox-Stanley had a luncheon appointment, which meant she didn't delay too long. Vanessa, who'd come to the kitchen to collect a breakfast tray for her mother, relayed that, so far, she'd had a 'very pleasant stay, considering the hotel was really rather shabby'.

'I probably shouldn't have told you that,' said Vanessa. 'But I thought you might as well know the worst.'

Meg laughed. 'In my eyes, your mother can do no wrong! She brought Basil Knott-Dean with her, and he has just given us a wonderful review.' She paused. 'And in parts, the hotel is rather shabby. Now, does your mother prefer thick-cut marmalade or thin-cut?'

'I can't believe you offer a choice!' said Vanessa.

'I wouldn't, but we've bought it from two different connections of Susan's. One is more painstaking than the other. Some guests say they don't like peel so prefer thick-cut. Easier to pick it out.'

'I'm afraid I don't know which she likes. She never comes down to breakfast,' said Vanessa.

'Let's give her a dish of each,' said Meg. 'Now, are you sure you can manage the tray? Why don't you let Ted carry it?' Meg smiled at this helpful young man who'd appeared in the kitchen at that moment.

Saying goodbye to Russell and Basil seemed like saying goodbye to old friends. 'Of course, I'll be back before you know it,' said Russell, kissing Meg firmly. 'And I'll probably bring this old darling, if he's not too busy to come to my little entertainment at the end of the summer.'

Basil pushed his friend's shoulder in a friendly way. 'Your "little entertainment" that happens to include one of the greatest stars of the current theatrical firmament?'

'You mean Dame Miriam?'

Basil nodded. 'And of course I'll come if I possibly can.'

'Lovely,' said Meg weakly, hoping the hotel could find space for all these big names who had even bigger personalities.

Basil and Russell both put fat white envelopes down on the desk. 'A little something for the staff,' said Basil, who'd come with Lady Lennox-Stanley and now settled down in the hall to wait for her.

Somehow it was no surprise to anyone that while most of the guests left generous tips for the staff, Lady Lennox-Stanley gave less than was considered usual.

Vanessa, acutely embarrassed, explained. 'She thinks that service is included in the bill. The staff are just doing their jobs, and they shouldn't expect extra.'

229

'She has a point,' said Meg, who never included herself when sharing out the gratuities, 'and everyone else was very lavish. Please don't worry!'

The last car was driving away just as Justin and his uncle pulled up at the front of the hotel. Meg, who happened to be in the hall saying goodbye to the last guests, went down the steps to greet them.

Meg couldn't decide if Colin Nightingale was younger or older than his brother Andrew. He was dressed in a sheepskin jacket, a checked Viyella shirt, casual trousers and suede shoes. He seemed to Meg like a picture in an advertisement, promoting cigarettes or fast cars. He was the epitome of easy camaraderie.

'You must be Meg,' he said, coming towards her with his hand outstretched. 'Colin Nightingale. I've heard such a lot about you.'

Meg took it and Colin rubbed her hand with his free one.

'Can't believe a pretty girl like you wants to be stuck away in a kitchen all day!' he went on. 'Surely you should be front of house, where you can charm the guests?'

'Meg takes her work as a chef very seriously,' said Justin, sounding irritated.

'And you're awfully young to be a chef,' said Colin, who was still massaging Meg's hand.

Meg was about to say 'I'm twenty-two' when she realised this was not quite what Colin was implying. 'I manage,' she said and, with a sharp tug, withdrew her hand.

'Meg is being modest. She does far more than manage, Uncle Colin,' said Justin. 'She's been praised by Basil Knott-Dean.'

'Oh, really?' said Colin, obviously completely au fait with the name. 'You mean the one who's the main contributor to that guide? The one all the really smart places are mentioned in?'

'That's the one,' Justin confirmed. 'This hotel is going to have an entry.'

Colin gave a hearty laugh. 'Oh, well done! That's absolutely splendid!'

Justin exchanged looks with Meg. 'Let's go in,' he said.

'I'll organise some coffee,' she said, keen to escape.

She carried the tray through to the sitting room, which was still in some disarray from the evening before. But Colin and Justin didn't seem to notice. They'd made themselves comfortable in the window embrasure, looking out into the garden.

'There are some pastries to go with the coffee,' said Meg. After she had put down the tray she made to go back into the kitchen, where she felt most comfortable, but Justin put a hand on her arm.

'You should stay, Meg. You can answer Colin's questions when I can't.'

'Please stay, lovely girl,' said Colin, giving her a smile which may well have charmed birds off trees but did nothing for Meg.

She sat, and as she'd put three cups on the tray, accepted a cup of coffee when Justin handed her one.

Cherry came in from the office, looking flushed and excited. 'Meg? Sorry, I didn't mean to interrupt.'

Meg leapt up. 'It's fine. Do you need me?' How she hoped the answer was yes!

'It looks as if you've got good news,' said Justin.

'I think I have!' said Cherry. 'Apparently the review that I heard Basil ringing his newspaper about has been published. Already! And everyone and their wives wants to book before the hotel gets well known.'

'You have remembered not to accept anything while the play is on?' asked Meg, suddenly anxious.

Cherry smiled reassuringly. 'Don't worry. I've blocked out all that time. Are you sure all the rooms will be taken by the theatre people? There's the head groom's cottage. It's got three bedrooms, which is unusual, but will my dad have put in the bathroom in time for the play, do you reckon?'

'I hope so. We'll need all the cottages.' Meg shot a glance at Justin and his uncle. Colin was looking at her as if she was some sort of child film star, and Justin was as inscrutable as ever. 'I did wonder about converting some of the farm buildings that are no longer used. My friend in Provence—'

'The one with the chateau,' added Justin.

'—has converted farm buildings with great success,' finished Meg, giving Justin a stern look. Was she always mentioning that Alexandra had a chateau? When it wasn't relevant? She must make sure she didn't.

'This all sounds really interesting. You've made enormous improvements now my conservative brother is out of the way. Can I have a guided tour when we've finished our coffee?' Colin asked.

'Of course,' said Meg, feeling unable to say anything else.

Cherry went back to answering the telephone.

'Who'd have thought a woman could have such entrepreneurial skills, eh, Justin?'

Meg was so cross she didn't know how to respond. She had had ideas on her own but her partners in the scheme had also been women. How could he be so blind and so stupid?

'These pastries are good,' said Colin, apparently assuming that Meg was basking in his compliments.

'Meg's pastry is famous,' said Justin firmly. 'She's an excellent pastry chef, better than many men I've worked with.'

Meg blushed as she looked at him. He'd said this almost as if he was proud of her.

Colin seemed very impressed with all the improvements and Meg found herself warming to him as they walked round.

'And this is where there's going to be a production of *A Midsummer's Night's Dream*,' she said when they were in the garden. 'Apparently, it's perfect, a natural amphitheatre. Ambrosine has found old photographs of pageants being put on here.'

'What if it rains?'

'Provision will be made,' said Meg.

'Does my brother know about all this?' Colin asked.

'I keep Dad fully up to date with what's going on,' said Justin. 'The play will be a gold mine if it's successful. But with Dame Miriam Twycross as Titania, it can hardly fail.'

'Well,' said Colin. 'It's all extremely encouraging. You've done wonders with the old place, you two. Now all we need to do is get it valued – taking the huge increase in bookings into consideration.'

Meg's heart plummeted. She could overlook the assumption that the improvements were all Justin's idea – people would always assume there had to be a man behind every plan – but everyone had worked so hard on making improvements, encouraging more visitors, and although they were on their way to doing that, it now seemed likely that Nightingale Woods would be sold after all. Everyone might lose their jobs. It was all extremely depressing.

'Excuse me,' she said. 'I must go and see about lunch.' They had no lunch guests, but she wanted a private weep.

Ambrosine found her in the kitchen a few moments after she arrived. 'Come now, Meg dear, this is not like you! What's the matter?'

'I'm just tired, I think,' said Meg, blowing her nose. Ambrosine stood over her in a way that made her go on. 'And Colin is here – Andrew's brother—'

'I know perfectly well who Colin is, dear, but I don't know what he can have done to make you cry.' She frowned. 'I shall go and investigate.'

'Please don't!' said Meg, but it was too late.

Meg watched her leave the kitchen wondering if she could have stopped her. But few people were able to stop Ambrosine when she was on a mission.

Although they hadn't any hotel guests booked in for lunch, Meg thought she ought to make something for the staff anyway. They deserved something nice; everyone had worked so hard for the race day.

She was chopping carrots when Justin came in.

'Colin is getting in an estate agent to have the place valued. I've rung my father. They're can't get here until the day after tomorrow. Colin wants the estate agent to go round with just him.'

Meg's mouth went dry. This was bad news.

'He's seen so much potential for expansion, as he calls it,' Justin went on. 'Realising that the workers' cottages could be used for renting has given him big ideas.'

'But I thought he wasn't interested in the hotel,' said Meg.

'Oh, he's interested. He wants to develop Nightingale Woods in order to sell it. Half of a much bigger operation will be quite a lot of money.'

Meg cleared her throat and sniffed, determined not to cry. But she was tired from the race day, still emotional and becoming more and more upset. 'What about Ambrosine?' she asked, the catch in her voice annoyingly obvious.

'Of course she'll have to go. Colin wants to put in a lift so all the old nurseries can become guest accommodation.'

'But isn't there a moral obligation to give Ambrosine a home? There must have been at some time or she wouldn't be here now.'

Justin shrugged. 'There won't have been any kind of legal contract. No, make the soup – we're going to need it.' His smile was rueful and kind and Meg suddenly wanted . . . wanted to go to him, and feel his arms around her. She wanted to hold his warm body and feel it next to hers.

Suddenly, she realised she had fallen in love with him. It was a shock and yet it seemed like something she had always known. She had fought so hard not to become friends with him, she never noticed love creeping up like a vine that entwined itself around her heart and now couldn't be cut away.

Chapter Twenty-Four

After lunch, which Meg served but wouldn't share, pleading a need to go to her bedroom and do something feminine as an excuse, she found herself crossing the hall to overhear Colin being grumpy on the telephone. The office door was open and Colin was sitting in the typist's chair with his feet on the desk.

'I need someone urgently. I can't believe you can't send someone tomorrow if not today.'

Meg waited, out of sight, unashamed to be eavesdropping. There was a silence while someone on the other end of the telephone was speaking.

'Listen! I need someone who can be discreet and give me a valuation of the property. God damn it! The commission on a place like this would be huge!'

More silence.

'Then I'll go elsewhere!' said Colin and slammed the receiver down.

Meg moved away quickly. She wished she had someone to talk about it all to, and yearned for the days when she and her friends all lived in Alexandra's house in London. But even Justin had gone back to

Newton-cum-Hardy and, presumably, Laura. And she knew she couldn't bother Susan or any of the other members of staff with her worries about Colin. She wished that Andrew and her mother would hurry up and come back.

'Meg, sweetie, I should have said earlier, but is it OK if I put my things in Andrew's room? I need to stay the night here.' Colin had on his most charming smile as he joined Meg in the kitchen.

'Oh, no, not Andrew's room!' she said hurriedly. She didn't want to mention that this was also her mother's room in case he didn't know and it caused problems. 'But we're not often full during the week. I'll ask Cherry to put you in the nicest room that's available. Ah, here she is!'

Meg guessed that Cherry had seen Colin pursue her to the kitchen and, like the loyal friend she was, had followed to rescue her. None of the women cared for Colin. They didn't talk about it, but they had all experienced his casual touching, patronising manner and general sense that he could do what he liked and it was their job to put up with it.

Cherry put him in the room that Basil had had. 'I said that the hotel critic had stayed there and he knew what a good review he'd given us. I did mention that the bell didn't work. If he knew it did, he'd having us running up and down the stairs like we had nothing else to do!'

'Well done, Cherry. You're doing such a brilliant job.'

238

They exchanged anxious smiles. 'Let's hope it hasn't all been a waste of time,' said Cherry, 'and the hotel has to be sold after all.'

'It won't be a waste of time,' said Meg firmly. 'We're going to finish the summer season flying high. We'll have the play. Every bed will be slept in and paid for. All the actors and audience and other people here will enjoy themselves. It'll be utterly exhausting—'

'But we'll love doing it!' Cherry finished for her.

'We will!' said Meg, wishing she could be more certain about the future of Nightingale Woods.

It was lovely to see her mother two days later. Meg had watched from the upstairs window to see when the car was winding up the hill through the morning mist and was there on the doorstep when it arrived. It was still early and there were a few breakfast guests, but Susan and Cherry had undertaken to deal with them, so Meg was free to greet her mother.

'You'll have missed your mum,' Susan had said. 'A lot has gone on since she and Mr Nightingale went to France.

Mother and daughter embraced on the steps of the hotel until Andrew hustled them inside. 'I know you two are pleased to see each other, but can we get through the door first?'

Meg and Louise continued their hug in the hall. 'Are you OK, sweetie?' Louise murmured. 'This isn't like you!'

'I'm fine!' Meg murmured back, very close to tears. 'It's just been really busy, that's all.' She swallowed and let go of her mother. 'Now, let me get you some coffee or something. Have you had breakfast? Did you sleep all right on the ferry? Was it a calm crossing?'

'We'd love coffee,' said Andrew. 'We had a continental breakfast on the ferry, but I wouldn't say no to something more substantial. Is the drawing room free? Could we have it in there?'

Colin joined them at the same time that Meg brought in their breakfast. She had been hoping to hear how they'd been getting on, but seeing Colin come into the room changed her mind.

'Could you get me some coffee?' asked Colin. 'Oh, and some toast? Thank you.'

As Meg turned to go, she asked herself why she was so offended by his manner. Looking after people was her job. She shouldn't mind if they asked her for things.

'I couldn't beg a pot of tea, could I?' asked her mother. 'It know it's an awful cliché but really, you can't get a decent pot of tea in France. And bring a cup for yourself, please.'

When Meg came back with the tea, Cherry having brought in the coffee and toast for Colin, she said, 'Why don't we take this up to your room, Mum? We can drink it there and you can tell me everything.'

They sat together at the little table in the window in Andrew's room, and after Louise had exclaimed at the flowers, the perfectly ironed bed linen and the matching linen towels that had been hiding in an airing cupboard for many years, she poured the tea.

'Darling,' she said, studying her daughter. 'Are you all right? You don't seem your usual calm self.'

Meg exhaled. 'It's just that so much has been going on and Colin is behaving as if he owns the place.'

'Well, he doesn't. No one does yet. And Andrew is still in charge. Don't worry.'

'There have been changes – you and Andrew do know about them – but Colin seems very excited by them.'

'Is that bad?'

'Mum, how well do you know him?'

'We've only just met—'

'He's *horrible*,' said Meg. 'He's touchy-feely, he only seems to think about money and he wants to get the hotel valued so he can sell it.'

'It can't be sold until the will is sorted out and who knows how long that will take,' said Louise. 'There's a third person in the will who can't be traced. I think they'll have to be declared dead or something before anything changes, and that could take years.'

Meg sipped her tea and felt a bit calmer. 'Are you sure?'

'Quite sure. It must have been very worrying for you with all this happening, but we're here now, and I'm sure Andrew will be able to sort everything out and explain it all to Colin.'

'I do hope so. But apart from that, we have been amazingly busy.'

'Andrew told me. There are now rooms with bathrooms, and you're doing up all those workers' cottages – who'd have thought of that?'

'Well, Alexandra is doing it in France and having the play here means we need as much accommodation as we can sort out. Of course, not everyone has to stay with us, but it's all extra income.'

'How will guests manage about meals if they're in the cottages?' asked Louise.

'We thought – Susan and me, that is – that guests could book in for meals at the hotel – it'll probably just be dinner, or possibly tea – and have their other meals in the cottages. We could do breakfast hampers if required. A continental breakfast of course. Not bacon and eggs.'

'Oh, Meggy, you have been such a breath of fresh air for the hotel. I am so glad I asked you to come!'

'I've loved it,' Meg said. 'I just hope it doesn't all have to be sold.'

'No need to worry about that just yet!' said Louise triumphantly. 'Until we find this third person in the will – and no one has ever heard of them – nothing can be sold. And as I said, it could take years.'

While this was something of a relief, Meg's conscience pricked her. 'But what will happen to Colin? Is that really fair to him?'

Louise frowned. 'I gathered from Andrew – more from what he hasn't said than from what he has – that his relationship with Colin is sticky. Colin is older, but Andrew is the executor. Colin has never been good with money. Andrew hinted he may have been a gambler. That's probably why Andrew's father left Andrew in charge. And because Andrew loves the hotel, of course.'

Meg felt emotional all over again. She didn't know how to reply, so instead she said, 'Do come down when you're ready. Everyone is dying to see you. Do you want me to help you unpack?'

'Darling! I've been doing my own unpacking since I was six.'

Meg laughed. 'I have had to unpack for guests sometimes. I've added it to the list of things I have experience of.'

'Good for you. Go and tell Susan I'll be down shortly. I have missed you all!'

It was decided, by everyone except Meg, that Justin would cook dinner that evening. Louise insisted that Meg put on a dress, brush her hair and even consider wearing a bit of mascara and eyeliner. And having decided that she would, Meg found herself cheering up. Although the kitchen was where she felt at home, coming out of it, being a girl and not a cooking machine, was pleasant.

Or so she tried to tell herself. In fact, she felt somewhat disenfranchised. She'd been the pivot around which Nightingale Woods spun, and now, suddenly, the owner was back, her mother was back and she was just Louise's helpful daughter, who currently had nothing to do.

She decided to have a walk in the garden, otherwise she might have to make polite conversation and she wasn't in the mood. She was too emotionally attached to Nightingale Woods, she felt. She should be able to see it as just another job, something to write on her

CV, but she knew it would always be more than that. And not just because she had apparently – inexplicably – fallen in love with the son of the owner. There was some other link that made her feel connected to it all.

She had reached the part of the garden where the play was to be put on. It was at the far end of the vast walled garden at the opposite end to the house. It had possibly been a tennis court in past times and although the surface was all weeds now, it was still level. There was a fig tree growing against the wall behind the old tennis court and now its emergent leaves reached like little green hands towards the sky. There was a seat that faced the view where now she sat down.

It was a lovely spot and Meg was imagining the play being performed with the old wall as a backdrop. She was wondering why the fig tree was outside the walled garden and not in when someone called her name. It was Ambrosine.

'Hello, Meg dear. You've found one of my favourite spots.'

Meg got up hastily. 'Do you want to sit here? Have some time on your own?'

'By no means. Please don't move. We can sit together.'

Meg sat down again and Ambrosine sat next to her.

Neither of them felt the need to speak for a few moments; then Meg said, 'Can you imagine a play being put on here?'

'I rather think I can,' said Ambrosine. 'This is where I come when I want to think about things that aren't logical and probably aren't possible, but are desirable, nevertheless.'

'I usually just sit by the back door if I want a break, but it's even nicer here,' said Meg.

'It's nicer because being a little bit away from the house people are unlikely to find you – although, of course, I found you,' Ambrosine added with a laugh.

'I was pleased to be found,' said Meg.

'And what were you thinking about, if I may ask?'

'I was thinking – or rather wondering – why I feel so connected to Nightingale Woods. It's not my family home or anything, it should just be another job. But it's more than that and I don't know why.'

'I think it has a certain magic that gets under your skin,' said Ambrosine, who didn't seem at all surprised at what Meg had said. 'I felt it the moment I came here.' She paused. 'Did you know that if you come at the right time of year you can hear nightingales sing? Of course the wood used to be much bigger, but the nightingales still come.'

'I'd love to hear them.'

'You've missed your chance for this year,' said Ambrosine, 'but next year, if you're here in April or May, then you'll hear them. They don't only sing at night, you know,' she went on, 'but because not many other birds sing at night, they're more audible.' She laughed. 'And of course, a lot more romantic! Titania speaks of them in *A Midsummer Night's Dream*, you know. "Philomel with melody, sing in our sweet lullaby."'

Meg cleared her throat, horridly aware that she was near tears again. 'I don't think I will be here next year,' she said bleakly.

Ambrosine took a breath. 'Then we must arrange it so that you are!' she said briskly. 'Now I'd better go. I'm meeting my colonel and he's tiresomely punctual.'

Meg was seated next to Andrew at the dining-room table that evening. Justin was in the kitchen (her kitchen) cooking dinner and had summoned them to the table and then gone to fetch the starter. Susan and Cherry had gone home and Meg was desperate to go and see what Justin was up to but she'd been ordered to sit down and stay still.

Andrew and Colin were also seated, arguing gently over a childhood memory.

Louise said, 'It's a shame Ambrosine couldn't be here. She's so much part of the family.'

Colin looked up. 'Oh, the old lady who lives here? Sweet of you to see her like that, Louise.' He obviously didn't find it sweet; irritating, rather.

'She's having dinner with her colonel,' said Meg. 'Do you think they're courting? Or are they "just good friends"?'

Before anyone had time to answer, the door opened and Laura came in. She was looking lovely, thought Meg. Her hair was done up and her cheeks were slightly flushed. She was wearing a simple sheath dress that showed off her slim figure. Meg couldn't help noticing, though, that her arms were just a bit stringy and her knees were a little knobbly.

The two men got up instantly.

'So sorry I'm late!' Laura said gaily. 'Couldn't get away. Now, where am I sitting?'

Meg had laid the table and had no idea she was coming. She got up now. 'Why don't you sit here? I'll get another place setting.'

'Oh no. I think Justin will expect me to be at his side!' She gave a tinkling laugh. 'You know what you men are like!'

Her coy look was received with a knowing laugh from Colin and an inscrutable raise of the eyebrows from Andrew.

Justin came in with a tray. 'Oh. Laura? You're here!'

'Yes! So sorry I'm late. I couldn't get away. I'm going to tuck myself in here, next to you. Meg? If you could get another place setting?'

Laura managed to make it sound as if she hadn't already offered to do that, thought Meg, getting up and going to the sideboard. Really it was easier when she was just the cook and not a guest; she knew where she was then.

Having cooked a delicious, simple dinner without apparently breaking a sweat, Justin came and joined the party when they moved to the sitting room. Andrew produced a bottle of cognac and Louise found suitable glasses. Every time Meg had got up to do anything, she was flapped at by her mother until she sat back down again.

Colin lit up a large cigar and Meg and Louise exchanged a glance, conveying concern about how they'd get the smell out of the curtains afterwards. 'That was an excellent bit of grub,' he said to Justin. 'You can do a bit of cooking, I gather.'

Laura gave her tinkling laugh but Meg could tell that Colin's remark had obviously made her a bit anxious for some reason. 'I'm sure you know, Colin – you don't mind if I call you that? We're practically family! – Justin is a very well-regarded chef. Raoul de Dijon picked him to be his chef. Although Justin heads a team, which means he is more than just an employee.'

'It's OK, Laura,' said Justin, eyeing her crossly. 'I think my uncle was joking. Glad you enjoyed it!'

'Well, in that case . . .' She glanced around the table, making sure everyone was looking at her. 'This might be the moment to tell everyone our plan?' Laura was obviously excited at the prospect.

'Erm . . .' Justin began but Laura ignored him.

'Now the hotel is doing so much better,' she began, 'and I think we all know why that is?' She sent Justin an adoring look under her fluttering eyelashes. 'We thought it's time for us to leave Newton-cum-Hardy and take over the kitchen here. Just can still help Raoul if he needs it. It's so handy the two hotels being so close to each other.'

Meg stared at her, wondering what on earth she was saying.

'Justin will do the all the main cooking and I will take over the dessert side of things. For those of you that don't know . . .'

Which was almost everyone, thought Meg.

'. . . I'm a trained pastry chef. So I'll do that and Meg – lovely Meg who we all value so much – will have a very special role making the cakes and scones and sandwiches and things for the afternoon teas.'

'Lovely idea, Laura my dear,' said Colin. 'But have you given any thought to the cost? Nightingale Woods is scraping along the bottom on one chef. It could never afford to pay for three. Isn't that right, Andrew?'

'I'm afraid it is. Justin, have you costed any of this?' asked Andrew.

Justin looked at Laura as if unsure what to say.

Meg couldn't bear it. The thought of working alongside the man she loved and his glamorous, 'trained pastry chef' girlfriend was too painful. 'It's all right, everyone. I have a plan of my own. I won't be available to make cakes for the hotel.'

'Why ever not?' asked Laura.

'I'm going to France. I'm going to work in a restaurant and learn my trade,' she said.

'As a waitress?' suggested Colin. 'Can you speak French?'

'Not as a waitress. In the kitchen. It's what's called doing a *stage*,' Meg explained.

'What's a *stage*?' asked Laura. 'I don't understand.' She was obviously a bit put out.

'A *stage* is when a young chef, someone who wants to learn, works in a professional kitchen,' Justin explained. 'They're not usually paid and they are worked to the bone.' He paused. 'That said, there's no better way to learn, and if Meg has managed to persuade a chef to take her on, she should absolutely

249

do it. She's far too talented a chef to waste her skills making Victoria jam sponges,' he finished.

'Could you get a French chef to let you work in his kitchen?' asked Andrew. 'I thought the French were terribly conventional about things like that?'

'I wouldn't have thought that a restaurant kitchen is a suitable place for a lovely young girl like you,' said Colin. 'They're terrible places. Isn't that right, Justin?'

'Meg is a talented and experienced chef. She has worked in professional kitchens before. This is a great opportunity for her. She should definitely take it,' Justin said firmly.

'But that means I'd have to make all the cakes!' Meg heard Laura whisper to Justin.

'Yes,' said Meg. 'And apart from making Victoria jam sponges, a fresh one every day, you'll need to make a good Dundee cake, ginger cakes, coffee cakes, chocolate cakes, flapjacks, shortbread and, of course, scones.' Meg smiled. 'But for a professionally trained pastry chef, that will be – literally – a piece of cake!'

Laura continued to address Justin from behind her hand but at a lower volume this time. 'We didn't do any of those things in Switzerland.'

Meg got up. 'Now, if everyone will excuse me, I'd better go and pack.'

'When are you going, darling?' asked Louise, anxious.

'Tomorrow,' said Meg. 'It's for the best.'

She left the dining room with her head held high but once in her room she sat on the bed and stared into space. She felt utterly shocked and bereft. She was too upset to cry.

A little later Louise came in. She was carrying two mugs of hot chocolate and a pile of broken, home-made biscuits. 'Are you all right, darling?'

She put her arms round her daughter and it was only then that Meg allowed herself to burst into tears.

Chapter Twenty-Five

Sadly for Meg's pride, she couldn't disappear from Nightingale Woods just like that. She had to arrange her journey to France, apart from cooking until Justin took over. However much she yearned to leave the hotel and not face anyone the following morning, she found that she couldn't let the hotel down.

Andrew came into the kitchen early, while Meg was planning what to cook for dinner and lunch, should anyone be in. Breakfasts were simple and could easily be managed by Susan and Cherry, especially as Louise was back looking after the office side of things, so Cherry could be in the kitchen.

'Meg,' he said, 'Louise tells me you really do want to leave to go to France.' He paused. 'Is there anything I can do to change your mind? You've done so much for Nightingale Woods – I really don't want you to go.'

Meg was very touched and realised she felt tearful again, although she thought she'd wept all the tears in the world the previous night. 'Justin is a brilliant chef. It'll be fine. And Laura – I'm sure her desserts will be amazing.'

Andrew frowned. 'Laura – hmm. Do you know how close she and Justin are?'

Meg took a breath. 'They're practically engaged. Laura told me.'

'Ah,' said Andrew after a few moments. 'So perhaps it is best for everyone if you do go.'

'I'm going for the sake of my career!' Meg insisted. 'No other reason.'

Andrew smiled and shook his head. 'That may be why you're going, of course, but I wonder if that's the only reason that Justin was so keen for you to go to France.'

Meg longed to ask him what he meant but didn't feel she knew him well enough.

It was extremely hard telling Susan, Cherry and the others that she was leaving Nightingale Woods. They'd been through so much together and were such a good team.

'So that little madam is going to be in here making fancy desserts, is she?' said Susan, her mouth in a hard line and her eyes narrowed. 'And how will the guests feel about that, I'd like to know!'

'They may like it a lot,' said Meg, trying to placate her. 'She's professionally trained, so—'

'Professionally trained she may be,' said Susan, still bristling with indignation, 'but she doesn't know how to treat people, not like you do, Meggy.'

Susan didn't often call Meg by her pet name and she realised Susan was really upset. 'I'm so sorry, but I can't stay. Laura would only have let me bake cakes and make scones and learning to cook in France will be very good experience.'

'Then perhaps when you've done that, you can come back to Nightingale Woods!' said Susan, cheered by this thought.

Meg smiled and shook her head. As long as Justin was there, she would never be able to come back to Nightingale Woods and the thought made her desperately sad.

Later, when Meg had escaped with a cup of tea to her favourite spot in the garden, Ambrosine found her. She was also holding a mug of something and sat down next to Meg.

'So, darling, you're leaving us, I gather,' Ambrosine said.

Meg gave a long sigh. 'I really don't want to, but I don't have any alternative. Justin is going to cook and Laura is going to do desserts. She's professionally trained and they are practically engaged, and so there wouldn't be room in the kitchen for both of us.'

'Louise told me Laura wanted you to stay and make cakes.'

Meg made a dismissive noise. 'That's all I'm capable of, it seems.'

'It's possible that Laura doesn't feel confident making them,' Ambrosine suggested.

'I still can't stay! And working in a French restaurant will be amazingly good for my cooking.' She paused as a flash of anxiety about what she was about to undertake hit her. 'Although it will be very difficult.'

'You're very good at "difficult", if I may say so,' said Ambrosine. 'But Nightingale Woods is going to miss you.'

'Not nearly as much as I'm going to miss Nightingale Woods, Ambrosine! I've loved being here so much. And yes, some of it has been difficult, but so rewarding! It's been a privilege to work in such a beautiful place, with such wonderful people around me.' Meg gave Ambrosine a shy smile. 'Like you.'

Ambrosine laughed. 'Silly girl! And remember, what's *for* you won't go *by* you, so cheer up!'

Meg managed a laugh in reply. 'I'll do my best.'

Later that day she rang Alexandra and told her about her rapid need to vacate Nightingale Woods.

Alexandra was reassuringly quick on the uptake and didn't need details of Meg's feelings.

'Don't worry. David is in London selling his *brocante* to the English. I'll get in touch and ask him to ring you. You can travel here with him. He's got a big old Peugeot now and it'll be fun.' She paused. 'It's going to be so lovely to have you here. I can't wait!'

Chapter Twenty-Six

Meg didn't relax until they were well on their way to Provence, in David's enormous Peugeot 403 estate.

'The last time I was in France, headed south, I was on the train going to Alexandra's wedding!' she said. 'I was a bit nervous about making her wedding cake.'

'And you did that amazing *croquembouche*, which turned out wonderfully, as I recall,' said David. 'What a day that was!'

As Meg thought back to that golden day, full of friends, food and French glamour, she felt tears gather in her throat. With her being in love with Justin, and Justin being promised to Laura, if not yet officially engaged, she doubted she would ever have a wedding day like that.

'Are you all right, chook?' David asked, shooting her a quick glance.

'I'm fine! I just got a bit of dust in my eyes. And I'm worried that I haven't brought enough clothes.' Too late she remembered the rule that if you are going to lie, it's better to just stick to one untruth, or it looks suspicious.

David, who obviously saw straight through her attempt to pretend she wasn't having a moment of sadness, patted her knee.

'Oh, don't worry about that. Alexandra will take you to the market and get you all kitted out.'

'I've got my working gear, which is the most important thing,' said Meg. She looked out of the window. 'It's lovely to be back in France. It's so different from Dorset.' She gave a shuddering sigh.

'You're tired,' David said. 'Why don't you shut your eyes and get some sleep?'

Meg felt she would never sleep but shutting her eyes would mean she didn't have to make conversation. Although David was a relaxing presence, he did worry about her; hiding her broken heart was an effort. No doubt it would all come out when she got to Alexandra's, but for now, she wanted to appear as if everything was fine.

She did doze a bit and was ready for lunch when David pulled up in front of a small restaurant in a little market town.

'This place is always very good,' said David. 'Do you feel a bit better now?'

'I do, actually,' said Meg. 'Quite a lot better.'

When they were established at a table with their *plat du jour* on its way, she said, 'I feel bad that you're doing all the driving, David. I should take a turn.'

He brushed her offer aside. 'I've done the journey many times since moving to France,' he said. 'The car knows its way without me. I just switch her on and point her in the right direction. There's a spot where I get an hour's nap, and on I go.'

Meg laughed. 'You love living in France, don't you?'

'I certainly do!' He broke off a piece of bread and ate it before going on. 'Are you thinking you might stay over here, too?'

She shrugged. 'If I survive my *stage* and get a job, I could. The world is my oyster, after all.'

'Such a shame they're not in season. You've put the idea into my head now.'

Meg was genuinely amused. She gave David a playful tap on the wrist. 'Oh, David!' she said.

'I know!' he said. 'Now tuck in. This is our last meal until Provence.'

At last, the big old car was headed down the drive towards the chateau. Meg could see Alexandra standing in the open doorway. Next to her was a large dog and two cats as well as a couple of teenagers. Meg remembered them all from Alexandra's wedding and was thrilled to think she'd be with them in a matter of moments.

'Welcome!' Alexandra said when the car had pulled up in front of the chateau and Meg had got out. She swept Meg into her arms. 'We are all so thrilled to have you here! Stéphie is just decorating the table outside. Let me show you the bathroom and then we'll go and have a drink in the garden.'

The table in the garden was beautiful. Meg couldn't imagine that the set designers of *A Midsummer Night's Dream* could possibly create anything as lovely. Stéphie had threaded jasmine, roses and honeysuckle together and woven the garland round the dishes, jugs, glasses and carafes that covered most of the surface. The fragrance was heady.

David was already holding a glass of wine next to a very handsome man whom she recognised as Maxime; she'd met him at Alexandra's wedding. Meg was inclined to be a bit shy of Antoine and Maxime, both glamorous Frenchmen who seemed very sophisticated to her. But she soon relaxed under the influence of food and wine and kindness.

'Are you sure you've had enough to eat?' asked Alexandra a little later. 'You wouldn't like some cheese?'

'I can't wait to try all the cheeses when I'm not so full or so tired,' she said.

Alexandra got up from the table. 'Come on, let's get you up to bed. You're not starting at the restaurant tomorrow, are you?'

'No, I certainly hope not. I think I start on Monday?' Meg looked across at Antoine, who nodded.

'So, you've got the weekend to relax,' said Alexandra.

'Yes,' said Antoine. 'And after tonight, we must speak to Meg in French all the time, so she gets used to it. Pierre – he's the chef – agreed this would be a good idea.'

'Luckily a lot of the language of the kitchen is in French, so I'll know those things,' said Meg.

'No need to be anxious,' said David. 'As I've said before, many times, you're going to be fine.'

Somehow this heartfelt assurance didn't make Meg feel very much better.

Antoine had found a little car for Meg to use so she could get herself to and from the restaurant, and the next morning, she and Alexandra did a trial run to the small market town and identified somewhere she could park.

'It's an easy journey and there won't be much traffic at seven in the morning,' said Alexandra.

'Yes. It's so kind of Antoine to get me a car. I'll have to sort out an international driving licence.'

'Antoine will help you with that.'

'And it's so kind of you to make sure I have plenty of whites and trousers. And neckerchiefs. I never wore them in London. I never worked anywhere that bothered with them.'

'The chef, Pierre, is very traditional, I gather. But don't worry, he has strict instructions not to make you cry.' Alexandra paused. 'How long will be you working in the restaurant, do you know?'

'I suppose until Pierre either gets fed up with me or takes me on as part of the team. We'll have to see.' Meg smiled bravely, but she knew come Monday, she'd be shaking in her chef's shoes.

Although it was only 7 a.m. there were a few people buying bread for breakfast in the little town the next morning and the café on the corner was sending out wonderful coffee smells. Meg was almost tempted to have one before starting her day but Alexandra had got up very early to make her coffee already; she didn't really need more.

She knocked on the side door of the restaurant, as instructed, and after an anxious few moments, it was opened. Pierre, the chef-patron, was there to greet her in a torrent of French Meg couldn't understand. She picked up a few words including *jolie* meaning pretty and *très très jeune* which she knew meant very young.

Let's hope it means they'll make allowances for me, she thought, following Pierre down a narrow passage to the kitchen.

Strangely, the kitchen made her feel at home immediately. She'd been in lots of restaurant kitchens and they were all different but also the same. There always seemed to be a very tall young man with spots and a prominent Adam's apple whom everyone was rude to but who didn't seem to mind. There was always an older man who was obviously much respected, and there was always a chef.

The atmosphere in the kitchen was currently calm but everyone looked at her as she came in and started commenting. She was glad she couldn't understand much French but was relieved that Mme Wilson had insisted on using French culinary terms: she should be able to recognise those, even if they were spoken in a strong Provençal accent.

What was worrying her most was her lack of her own knives. It had been explained to Pierre and he had agreed to lend her a set, but it made her look unprofessional, she felt. While she had worked in professional kitchens it had always been as part of a team who had been brought in to make desserts for a special event. She'd never been a permanent member of staff.

Still, during her weekend at the chateau she had sharpened all Alexandra's knives so that she could sever a tomato in two with one long stroke. She had also done a lot of chopping, dicing, and slicing very, very thinly. It had been supposed to distract her from thoughts of Nightingale Woods but she couldn't help wondering how everyone was getting on without her. They were probably managing brilliantly.

Now, Pierre put her in front of a chopping board and said in English, 'Wait here. I will fetch your knives.'

There was a fair amount of staring and commenting while Pierre was gone but Meg looked straight ahead, wishing she wasn't blushing, glad she didn't know quite how rude they were being about her.

'*Et voilà!*' said Pierre, putting a knife-roll on her bench. 'Now be careful! These knives are sharp!'

'*Oui, Chef,*' said Meg.

Then he put a crate of potatoes down. 'Wash and peel these and turn them into spheres, all the same size. Bigger than a marble, smaller than a golf ball.'

'*Oui, Chef,*' she said again.

She wished when Pierre had said 'turn them into spheres' he had meant there was a trick to it. But Meg knew that 'turn' meant carving the potatoes so they were perfect balls. She was grateful she didn't have to dig them out with a melon baller. They'd learnt how to do that at Mme Wilson's. It created blisters on your hand if you had to do too many.

She was expecting to be bullied and harassed as she knew this was not uncommon in kitchens but she discovered that the atmosphere wasn't unkind at all. The tall boy with acne showed her where to scrub her potatoes and later on, when she was carving them and saving the parings for soup, he brought her a mug of coffee. She smiled gratefully and said, 'Merci,' in her very best French accent. She realised she was not the only one who blushed as he acknowledged her response.

Her feet felt as if they were no longer attached to her body, her back ached and her hands were operating automatically, and this was before lunchtime service.

She had washed, dried and picked the parsley off the stalks, had been told off for bruising it and was shown how to make a chiffonade so as to make as few cuts as possible but still end up with fine parsley. She had picked the leaves of thyme, no stalks permitted this time. She had chopped the tarragon for a traditional sauce béarnaise – a sauce she would have been making herself if she was still at the hotel.

The advantage of working so hard, under challenging circumstances, meant that, in theory at least, she didn't think about Justin, or about everything she'd left behind. And the hard work did help. By the time Pierre took her knife out of her hand and led her to where she'd put her outdoor things and pushed her out of the door, her brain was a maelstrom of everything she'd done that day. There hadn't been much time to think about the past.

Alexandra and one of the estate workers were waiting for her. 'I'm going to drive you home and Bruno here is going to drive your car.'

Meg was so relieved not to have to drive, she just got into the front seat of Alexandra's car, although not before she'd got into the driver's seat by mistake.

'I am so tired,' said Meg. 'How am I going to do all that again tomorrow?'

'A hot bath, a good meal, a lot of wine and then straight to bed. I'm sure you'll get used to it.' Then Alexandra laughed. 'Of course I'm not speaking from experience, but it surely can't hurt!'

Chapter Twenty-Seven

Alexandra was right; Meg did get used to it. As gruelling day passed gruelling day, Meg was given more interesting tasks and she no longer considered driving herself to and from the restaurant difficult. She got used to the temperature of the kitchen which meant that perspiration running down her back was normal. Her feet, which still ached at the end of the day, returned to normal by morning.

And she realised she had become the kitchen pet. Everyone loved her, teased her, flirted with her and generally made her feel she belonged. She was still the dogsbody, given all the time-consuming, fiddly tasks she was so good at, but she was appreciated.

By Bastille Day, 14 July, it was so busy for everyone in the kitchen, Meg found herself doing things that a couple of weeks previously she would not have been allowed.

Seeing how things were going, she put herself next to the pastry chef and the moment he discovered she had a swift and steady hand with a piping bag she was on to it.

Later, Pierre complained that his commis had been stolen but by this time Meg's French was good enough to suggest that she was only his assistant commis, so hardly worth considering. Much laughter all round.

When she finally got home, she'd done a twelve-hour shift in the kitchen. She had made choux buns, eclairs, little tart cases, *crème pâtissière* and had filled and decorated hundreds of tiny, time-consuming little items. Many of the things she had previously made for Nightingale Woods but, she realised, at about a quarter of the speed she could now knock them out. She never mentioned to anyone that she'd made lots of these cakes before, she just got on and worked.

Pierre announced he was closing the restaurant for four days following this epic effort and Meg went home to sleep.

She managed to sleep until eight o'clock the next morning but by then was wide awake, and so got up and then went downstairs to find herself a cup of coffee. Alexandra was delighted to see her.

'I know it's breakfast time, but could you manage with just a cup of coffee for now?'

Alexandra looked a bit shifty and, as they then heard a car, Meg suddenly panicked.

'You haven't invited Justin or anything crazy like that, have you? You know he's practically engaged to Laura? I told you! And I never want to see him again. I'll go and hide—'

Alexandra put out a calming hand. 'Meg, relax. I'd never do anything like that to you. I know how you feel about Justin. Just see who it is! I promise you'll be pleased.'

Alexandra led them to the front door and opened it. There, coming up the steps, looking ridiculously excited, was her mother, closely followed by Andrew.

'Meg, darling!' said Louise, enfolding her daughter in her arms. 'I didn't think you'd be here! I thought you'd be at the restaurant and we'd have to wait all day to see you!'

To begin with, Meg couldn't say anything, she was so thrilled. 'The chef closed the restaurant after Bastille Day for four days,' she said at last. 'It's so lovely to see you!'

'We've brought breakfast,' said Andrew, holding a clutch of paper bags. 'I do miss the *boulangeries*, however much I appreciate Susan's home-made bread.'

'Oh, brilliant! Thank you so much,' said Alexandra. 'Now come into the kitchen and I'll make coffee. Or maybe we could have breakfast outside?'

'Keeping the croissant crumbs out of the house is a good idea,' said Andrew.

Antoine and Stéphie appeared while Meg was putting out plates. Antoine had been up early, working. Stéphie explained that she had been helping him.

'I don't know what I'll do when my assistant has to go back to school,' he said after he had greeted Louise and Andrew.

Only when everyone had eaten a pastry or some bread and butter did Meg say what she had been longing to ask.

'Are you just here for a holiday?' asked Meg. 'Why didn't you tell me?'

'We're not just here for a holiday, although Alexandra and Antoine have kindly insisted we stay for a few days,' said Louise.

'Your mother has something to tell you, and she's getting all embarrassed about it,' said Andrew.

'We're engaged,' said Louise, holding out her left hand, which had a very pretty ring on it. 'We wanted to tell you in person. And the wedding is in September, at Nightingale Woods. Will you come home for it?'

While Meg was genuinely pleased, she couldn't help wondering how Justin had taken this news. And could she really go back to Nightingale Woods? But she didn't say any of this. Her mother looked so happy, and so did Andrew.

'Oh, Mum!' said Meg, hugging Louise. 'Of course I'll come!'

Louise hugged Meg again. 'I'm so relieved. I wasn't sure how you'd feel about your old mum getting married.'

'Well, I'd obviously hate if it was to anyone but Andrew!' She sent him a warm smile. 'I'm thrilled.'

After a lot more hugging and many congratulations, Meg said, 'I'd love to make your wedding cake, if you'd like that.'

'I can't think of anything nicer!' said Louise.

'She made ours,' said Alexandra. 'The most delicious *croquembouche*.'

'Oh,' said Meg quickly. 'That's traditionally French. You'd probably rather have a rich fruit cake.'

'That *croquembouche* was one of the best I've ever eaten,' said Antoine. 'In fact, it was when I told Pierre about it that he agreed to you doing a *stage* at his restaurant.'

'But it's more something that Laura should make,' Meg said, partly wanting to know how she was getting on at Nightingale Woods without asking directly. 'She's a classically trained pastry chef.'

'I think a *croquembouche* sounds delightful and different,' said Andrew. 'And I think I speak for us both when I say I'd like you to do it, Meg.'

Meg blushed and felt emotional all over again.

'Meg,' said Alexandra. 'Why don't you go upstairs with Louise and make sure she's got everything she needs? It'll give you a chance to have a bit of a mother-and-daughter chat.'

'I'd love that!' said Louise.

Meg took hold of her hand. 'Come on, Mum. Which room, Lexi?'

'The one with the mural. It's our best,' said Alexandra. 'And the bathroom is just next door.'

It wasn't long before Meg and Louise were sitting on the bed together. 'There are two things I'm dying to know,' said Meg.

'Go on then, ask me.'

Meg decided to ask the easy one first, the question where she wasn't emotionally involved with the answer. 'Has Andrew managed to discover who the third person in the will is?'

'No!' said Louise. 'We've drawn a complete blank. Colin and Andrew can't seem to find any trace of her. They've placed advertisements in the local papers in France – with a French name they decided there was no point in doing that in England, but nothing! Colin is looking into seeing how long they have to search for this Frenchwoman whose name I keep forgetting before her share can revert to him and Andrew.'

'That's a bit frustrating for everyone,' said Meg. 'Is Colin being very grumpy about it?'

'Rather,' said Louise, 'but then he puts on the charm again.' She sighed. 'I just wish he wouldn't pat Cherry and Sally. I had to speak to him about it. It was really awkward.'

'I can imagine! Poor Mum! You're probably better with schoolboys when it comes to that sort of thing.'

Louise gave a little laugh. 'To be honest, I said more or less the same things I would have said to sixth formers who were inappropriate with the assistant matrons. But I hated having to do it.'

'So how are things going otherwise? What is it like at Nightingale Woods now?'

'You really want to know how Laura is working out?' Louise smiled at Meg understandingly.

'Yes! I do! And I feel mean about it.'

'Well, don't feel mean. I'm happy to tell you that she's not very popular.'

'Why not?' Meg felt she knew the answer to this question.

'I'm sure you can guess. She's so bossy for a start. She thinks she can tell everyone how to do their jobs, including me. She was some sort of a receptionist at the other hotel, which of course makes her an expert.'

Louise was very fed up about all this, obviously. 'Does she try to boss Susan about?'

'She did. Got short shrift, as you can imagine. Then, when she couldn't get Susan to do what she wanted, she tried to get her sacked! I spoke to Andrew about it before Laura could say anything to him. I told him what a nightmare it was without Susan when he first went to France.' She took a breath. 'So how are you really, Meggy darling?'

'Oh, I'm fine,' said Meg. 'I'm doing really well at the restaurant. Considering I'm English, the lowest of the low, and very young, everyone is extremely kind to me.' She hurried on, before her mother could comment. 'What are Laura's puddings like?'

'They're fine except she's so *slow*. She can't keep the dessert trolley filled. I've had to do my family trifle recipe a few times.'

'With no jelly and fresh raspberries?' Meg loved this version of the traditional English pudding herself.

'That's the one. It's so quick! I don't even always use custard. I just slather whipped cream on to the sponges and mushed-up jam and fruit. The flaked almonds always make it look OK.'

'I love that!'

'But the worst thing is, Laura managed to persuade everyone it's a bad idea to have the play, so it's been cancelled.'

'What? But who cancelled it? Russell or Laura?'

'Laura gave us the impression it was her.'

Meg flinched. This really felt like a blow. 'That is so sad. And think how much business it was generating! I can't believe it was allowed to happen.'

'I know. But Laura nagged everyone so much about it, it seemed easier to just give in.' Louise sighed deeply. 'And we are really quite busy without it since the review and the guide coming out, which was Laura's argument.'

Just then, there was a knock on the door. It was Stéphie. 'Lexi says, although it's early, it's not too early to have a glass of champagne. We're having it in the garden.'

'Oh, thank you, Stéphie,' said Louise. 'I think champagne is a brilliant idea. And it is nearly eleven o'clock, after all!'

They found Alexandra, Antoine and Andrew in the garden, sipping champagne and nibbling olives.

'Well, Meg,' said Andrew. 'What are your plans for when you've finished your time at the restaurant?'

Meg hesitated.

'There'd always be a place for you at Nightingale Woods,' Andrew went on.

'Yes,' said Louise. 'Guests are still asking for you, and Susan, Cherry and Ambrosine miss you terribly. Although, of course, Justin is a very good chef.'

'I don't really know,' Meg began. She didn't really have any plans. Work in the kitchen had been so demanding she just thought about getting to the end of each day without there being a disaster.

Antoine said, 'I have to tell you here that my old friend Pierre, who took Meg on as a favour to me—'

'So kind of him,' Meg interrupted.

'—is now thanking me from the bottom of his heart,' Antoine went on. 'She has made a great difference to his kitchen. I think he may be about to offer her a job.'

'Goodness!' said Meg. 'It never occurred to me that would happen.'

'How exciting!' said Alexandra, clapping her hands in delight. 'You could stay with us here – or have one of the gîtes when they're no longer booked.'

'Or I could find a little apartment in the town,' said Meg. 'I could have half an hour longer in bed in the morning.'

'You'd settle in France?' asked Louise, sounding surprised.

'That would be all right, wouldn't it?' asked Meg. She said this more to herself than to her mother.

'Of course, darling! You must do whatever you need to do in your life.' Louise smiled and squeezed Andrew's hand. 'I'll have my wonderful husband by my side now.'

'And I'll have you,' said Andrew, looking at Louise with adoration.

'And we'd love to have you, Meg,' said Alexandra. 'Near, if not actually living here. And I know David would be delighted.'

'For a moment I'd forgotten David lived nearby,' said Louise. 'In which case, I'd be very happy for you to live here. We could come and visit.'

Everyone seemed so enthusiastic at the thought of Meg moving to France permanently, she supposed it must be a good idea. Yet she knew her heart was in a little corner of Dorset where, at the right time of year, the nightingales sang.

'As long as you're back for the wedding,' said Andrew. 'No substitutes accepted.'

Chapter Twenty-Eight

Until Meg had actually been offered a job at the restaurant, she and Alexandra decided it was better for Meg to stay living in the chateau. In fact, Meg wasn't in a hurry to be independent. She loved all the family and they seemed to love her. She set off each morning in her car and came back each evening, delighted to see the chateau at the end of the drive, welcoming her home.

It was early August when Pierre came into the kitchen when they were clearing up after the lunch-time service. He went over to Meg and nodded his head towards the restaurant. '*P'tite*, you're wanted out front.'

It was Justin. And he looked ghastly. Meg's mouth went dry. It must be bad news but he didn't speak when he saw her.

'Is everything all right? My mother? Ambrosine?'

'Both fighting fit. Can we talk?'

Pierre, who had come out to witness the meeting, nodded. 'A man in love. You'd better hear him out, *p'tite*.'

Meg gave her boss a look which was as near to rolling her eyes as was polite, hoping to convey that he was quite wrong about this, but she didn't wait to explain more fully. 'There's a café next door. We'll go there.'

They found an outside table and she ordered two coffees and some cognac for Justin. 'Now drink this and tell me calmly what the problem is. You look terrible!'

He sipped the coffee and then laughed. 'You don't look terrible. Anything but!'

She suddenly became aware of how she must look, in her little cap and chef's whites. She pulled off the cap and her hair fell round her face. She knew it needed cutting but she hadn't had time. She also knew she'd picked up a bit of a tan recently, although right now she was probably bright red in the face. She pushed a lock of hair out of her eyes and tucked it behind her ear.

'Why are you here, Justin? There must be something very wrong for you to come all this way.'

He took a deep breath, looked at her intently, but still didn't speak.

'Has something happened to Nightingale Woods? I wish you'd tell me because I'm now imagining that it's burnt to the ground.' Suddenly this seemed like a likely explanation. 'Oh God—'

'It's not that – it's nothing life-threatening.'

'Then what is it?'

He exhaled deeply. 'Nightingale Woods, which one day I will own part of, isn't the same without you.'

'Really?' She felt a little breathless. She hadn't expected this.

'Yes. It doesn't work in the same way without you in the kitchen.'

'I find that very difficult to believe. You're a professional chef. I've never been more than a . . . gifted amateur.'

'I don't expect being a gifted amateur makes you welcome in a restaurant like this.' He indicated the restaurant next door to the café. 'I looked it up. It has a very good reputation.'

She sat up straighter. 'It has. I'm proud to work in its kitchen.' She took a sip of coffee to give herself time to think of something else to say.

Justin caught the hand that had just put down the coffee cup and held it. 'Meggy, I've come all this way – I came the long way round – to talk to you – to tell you – about how we all need you at Nightingale Woods!'

Something didn't make sense. 'My mother and Andrew were here, not long ago . . .'

Thinking about it, Meg remembered that her mother had said that Laura wasn't working out very well. Meg had assumed she just hadn't settled in properly and that it would all be working well by now.

'No, well . . .' said Justin. 'It wasn't so bad when they came over. It's got worse since.'

She tried to move her hand but it was still enveloped in his much larger one. She couldn't reply so she swallowed instead.

He cleared his throat. 'Superficially, things are going smoothly, but the guests aren't happy. They write very half-hearted things in the Visitors' Book and we're losing bookings. Of course, it was a bad mistake, Laura cancelling the play.' He paused. 'In short, we're lacking what made the hotel special.'

'But surely Laura can put things right? So it all works properly and people are happier?'

'Laura has left Nightingale Woods. It wasn't her sort of place. She made very good macarons – although it took all day to do it – but she never got the hang of the nursery puddings everyone loves. And while she was efficient she had no . . .' He paused, looking for the word. 'Heart.'

How did Justin feel about this? He was giving no sign. 'But you were practically engaged!'

Justin sighed. 'Only in her mind. It's true we were a couple for a while, but we broke up quite quickly after she came to Nightingale Woods. She didn't like being buried in the country, as she put it. She didn't get on with Ambrosine . . .'

'Did that matter?' Meg asked softly.

'Yes,' said Justin firmly. 'Yes, it did. Ambrosine represents the spirit of Nightingale Woods. She's charming, a little bit eccentric, but she knows what she wants and can be a bit demanding from time to time.' He sighed. 'Laura didn't get the charming and eccentric bit. She was happy to give the guests bought biscuits in little packets instead of the home-made ones you always provided.'

'It's the attention to detail that makes all the difference,' she said, thinking about Nightingale Woods and all the effort everyone had put in to making it special.

She was sad and angry to think that all that effort wasn't being kept up.

Justin put down her hand as if he'd forgotten he'd been holding it. 'I know it's really annoying of me, coming here when you're working, but I had to tell you. You not knowing felt all wrong somehow.'

He was looking at her so intently that she had to look away. It was so bizarre, sitting in a French café, just after lunch, when a few moments ago she was wiping down surfaces. She shook her head to clear the thought. 'I still don't really know why you're here.'

He raised his hand for the waiter, who was hovering, apparently fascinated by the young woman dressed as a chef and the man who looked as if he had been travelling all night.

'Cognac for *mademoiselle*, please,' he said in French.

When it came, Meg took a sip, hoping it might help her clarify her feelings. While the news about her beloved hotel was so bad, she was ridiculously pleased to see him. She didn't know what to think, what to say.

'I would never ask you to give this up, Meggy.' Justin's gesture indicated the bustling town around them. 'I know you've wanted to do this *stage* for a long time. It's important to you. But could you ever see yourself coming back to Nightingale Woods . . .?'

She took a few more sips of cognac, knowing it was a bad idea when she had to think clearly. Had Justin really come all this way, and arrived looking as if he hadn't slept, just to ask her to go back to the hotel? And what would going back mean? If he just wanted her back in the kitchen, and thus giving Nightingale

Woods back its heart, would that be enough for her? Could she go back if he wasn't going to be there too?

'I would need to think about it.' She looked at him across the café table. 'Where are you staying?'

'I telephoned Alexandra on the way here. So with her – with you – at the chateau. Do you mind?'

Meg shook her head. 'Did you come to France on your motorbike?'

He shook his head. 'No, I brought the car. Just in case I could persuade you to come back with me.'

She took a breath and then looked at her watch. 'I need to get back to work now.'

'Of course. But, Meg, can I see you later?'

Meg sighed. 'Of course.' Maybe by the end of her working day she would have thought of what to do. She needed to work out if she should give up the promise of a new life in France for a small hotel in Dorset. One thing she did know was that if Justin would be there and wanted her as more than a good cook, she'd go in a heartbeat. But how did he feel about her?

'So, *p'tite*,' said Pierre, who had obviously been awaiting her return with interest. 'Did the young man propose to you? Are you now affianced?'

'No! Nothing like that! He just wanted to talk about the hotel where I worked before. He says it isn't thriving without me and has asked me to go back.'

Pierre thought this was highly amusing. 'He came all the way here from England to ask you to go back to the small hotel in the country that you told me about? Do they not have chefs in England?'

'Of course they do! Justin is a very good one.'

He made a large gesture as if Meg was lacking in comprehension. '*Exactement!* He wasn't talking about you going there to cook. He loves you!'

'I'm not even sure he likes me very much sometimes.'

'*Voilà!* That proves it. He came here because he loves you. You must go home *immédiatement!*'

Meg stayed at work long enough for Justin to arrive at the chateau and settle in, and then did what Pierre told her and went home. She had not known before what a romantic soul he was.

But she drove back with trepidation. Justin didn't like to be kept waiting and he might demand a decision before she was ready to make one. That said, the Justin who had arrived at the restaurant had a very different demeanour to the man who had roared up to the hotel on his motorbike when she'd first arrived at Nightingale Woods.

Alexandra met her at the front door of the chateau. 'You're early! How nice! Antoine is showing Justin round the farm and the buildings we rent out. Come in and let's take some wine into the garden. I need to know everything.'

'Just let me wash my hands and I'll tell you all I know,' said Meg.

'I'll have a glass of rosé poured for you,' said Alexandra, obviously hoping for some exciting news.

As Meg splashed water and dried her hands she realised she didn't feel as if she knew or understood anything.

There was a jug of rosé and a plate of charcuterie waiting on the big wooden table when Meg joined her friend. Alexandra knew that Meg didn't usually eat much at the restaurant.

'So?' said Alexandra when Meg had taken a few sips of wine and eaten some salami.

Meg didn't instantly reply so Alexandra pressed on. 'Justin told us that he was trying to talk you into going back to the hotel. But it can't be just that, can it? Did he tell you he loved you?'

'No! Of course not! I mean, Pierre is convinced that's what he meant, but he only said how the hotel isn't the same without me. Laura – his girlfriend – has left Nightingale Woods. I gather she's left him as well as the hotel. And now the hotel wants me back.' She ate an olive. 'I mean, the hotel is functioning – Justin is cooking, my mother and Andrew are doing the front of house – but apparently it needs me as well.'

Alexandra nodded wisely. 'There's definitely more to it than just that. It would be crazy to travel all this way to ask you to come back when he could have just rung you up.' She paused. 'So do you know what you want to do?'

'Not yet. I'm doing well at the restaurant. Pierre trusts me now; he's teaching me things.'

'So? If you didn't care about Justin that would be your decision. You'd stay, continue to learn.'

Meg sighed. 'I've got to go back for Mum's wedding in September. That would be the logical time to go back.'

'Can you wait that long? Do you want to?'

'I don't know, Lexi,' whispered Meg as they heard Antoine, Justin and Stéphie approaching.

Soon they were all sitting outside under the pergola, drinking rosé and picking at bits of salami.

'Thank you so much for the tour, Antoine,' said Justin. 'Seeing how many buildings you've managed to turn into accommodation is really useful. Obviously, we're not doing quite the same thing at Nightingale Woods, so people cater for themselves, but would come to the hotel for some of their meals, we hope. But in order to make a proper profit we need more rooms.' He looked at Meg. 'The hotel's fortunes were really turned around by Meg here.'

Meg blushed. 'It was just luck,' she protested. 'David knew Russell who wanted to put on a play in the grounds. And – and Nessa's mother, Lady Lennox-Stanley – or Lady Fussy-Knickers as we called her – met Basil Knott-Dean, the restaurant critic, and brought him to the hotel.' She paused, remembering. 'I can't believe that terrifying woman is Lizzie's mother-in-law.'

Everyone laughed at her horrified expression.

'But didn't you make the guests feel welcome and comfortable and cook them lovely meals that they enjoyed?' asked Alexandra, one eyebrow raised, obviously determined not to let Meg throw off the praise that Justin had given her.

'Well . . .'

'Of course she did,' said Justin firmly.

'Talking of which, is this supper? Or just a snack?' asked Antoine.

'A snack. David and Maxime are coming to dinner,' said Alexandra. 'And I think the older children are bringing friends.'

'Oh, good!' said Stéphie.

'You must let me help you—' Meg began.

'No,' said Alexandra very firmly. 'Certainly not. You must rest. You've been working.'

'Then you must let me help,' said Justin. 'I haven't been working in a kitchen all day, like Meg.'

Alexandra considered his offer. 'You've been travelling though – for two days in fact.'

He shrugged.

'How did you get here, Justin?' asked Antoine.

'I took the ferry from Southampton and drove down through the Auvergne. I stopped on the way, though – I'm perfectly fit enough to cook for a few people.'

Alexandra nodded. 'In which case, that would be wonderful. But you must have a siesta, Meg.'

Meg realised this was Alexandra's code for saying she should lie down and think about her future.

To her surprise, once in her cool room, with the shutters closed, Meg fell asleep. She'd just wanted to rest her feet for a bit and think about things but instead she had drifted off. It was after six o'clock when Stéphie went into her room.

'Time to wake up! We're eating outside. I've been helping Justin. Henri and Félicité have both got friends

283

with them. David and Maxime are arriving any minute. Everyone is drinking *crémant* which isn't champagne.'

'I'll just change,' said Meg. 'But I'll be really quick, I promise.'

'Are you going to put make-up on?' asked Stéphie, obviously not considering her job was done.

'I don't wear much make-up.'

'Nor does Lexi, except sometimes,' said Stéphie. 'You could borrow hers if you wanted.'

Meg thought for a moment. 'I won't bother with the make-up.' It was too late for that; Justin had seen her too many times without it. 'But if Lexi has got any perfume you don't think she'd mind me borrowing, I'd love that.'

'Her favourite is Bien-être but Papa says it's not proper perfume because it comes in such large bottles. I think you should borrow her Miss Dior – that's my favourite.'

'Whatever you think is best. And then, when I've put it on, would you come down with me?'

'Of course!' Stéphie frowned. 'Are you feeling nervous? It's just us, really. I found out that Lexi felt nervous when she first came to us as our nanny, but you would never have guessed.'

'Lexi is very brave,' Meg agreed. 'I'm not.'

'I expect you're brave in a different way,' said Stéphie kindly. 'I'll go and get the perfume.'

If Alexandra had been trying to send a message to Meg that Provence was the place to be, she couldn't have done a better job. Outside there were jam jars with candles in them hanging from the trees as well as all up the centre of the long wooden table, now covered with a linen cloth.

A little way away from the table, Henri was playing a guitar. A few young people were gathered round and a teenage party was going on.

Nearer the dining table stood a small table and chairs. David, Maxime and Antoine were sitting, drinking wine and chatting. A faint smell of Gauloises cigarettes mingled with the scents of the evening. There were bowls of olives and nuts scattered around and it reminded Meg of a picture in a magazine: beautiful people and a perfect setting with a chateau as a backdrop. She wondered if she could create something similar at Nightingale Woods and then remembered that she might not be going back.

Alexandra emerged from the kitchen, large platters in either hand. '*À table!*' she said, setting down her dishes on which sat two huge quiches surrounded by lettuce leaves.

Justin followed with jugs of wine and a knife with which he divided the quiches.

David was there to pass the plates down the table and the others followed to take their places.

Not sure how it happened, considering she was making sure it didn't, Meg ended up sitting next to Justin. But he was on his best behaviour and just smiled at her in a friendly way. This was a bit unnerving, but Meg could hardly complain. She smiled back, knowing she must look awkward. Being in a group and behaving normally together was unusual for them. It was a sign they shouldn't be together, thought Meg. But she didn't think she could move when Justin got up to deal with the main course.

Justin had served chicken garnished with little onions, tomatoes and artichokes before he turned to her, obviously about to speak.

Meg said, quickly, 'This is so lovely, isn't it? Eating under the trees, the candles, the long table, everyone together.'

'It is,' Justin agreed. 'So French. We could reproduce it at the hotel, although we don't often have the right weather.'

Meg swallowed quickly. This was exactly what she had been thinking. 'But if we did – and we do get heatwaves in summer sometimes, even in England – we could set up some tables outside, put candles in jam jars, just like Alexandra has.' Too late Meg realised she should have answered in a non-committal way or not at all. She hadn't decided what she wanted to do. Talking about the hotel might give Justin the impression that she had.

'We could build a pergola and grow roses up it – Ambrosine would like that – and as long as it was wide enough so people didn't catch their clothes on the thorns it could be really romantic,' said Justin.

'You don't worry about things being romantic, do you, Justin?' Meg said, surprised.

'I've changed,' he said. 'People can.'

'I'll get the pudding,' said Alexandra. 'No, stay there, Justin. I can manage.'

'I'll give you a hand,' said Antoine, getting to his feet.

'I'm going to help too,' said Stéphie.

'Well, Meg,' said David. 'It seems you have some hard decisions to make. England or France. I chose France, but I lived in London, which doesn't seem so far away.' He looked at Maxime who was sitting opposite him. 'And there were other reasons.'

'Dorset seems a very long way away,' Justin agreed. 'France is such an enormous country.'

'You had a very long journey,' said Meg with a rush of guilt.

'All because of you,' said Justin, smiling. 'It shows how devoted I am to Nightingale Woods. I want the best for it.'

'Are you sure that's all you're devoted to, old man?' said David.

Colour rushed to Meg's cheeks and she could have happily killed David at that moment.

She was spared having to think how to do this when Stéphie rushed out. 'There's a telephone call from England. For you, Justin!'

'Have another glass of wine,' said David, filling Meg's glass as Justin went into the chateau. 'Sweetie, he's obviously in love with you. You need to decide if you want him or not.'

'Don't be so pragmatic, David,' said Maxime. 'It's not an easy decision. She might want him but also want to stay in France.'

To Meg's huge relief, Henri and Félicité and their friends decided they wanted to go and play records and dance in the orangery and the attention was no longer on her. Permission had to be sought from Antoine, who was helping Alexandra with the pudding. Félicité went in, and soon came out again, smiling. The young things all left the table.

'I think I just want to enjoy this lovely evening and not make any big decisions,' said Meg, who'd thought of this while there was to-ing and fro-ing with the young people.

Maxime smiled at her. 'Well said, Meg.'

Alexandra and Antoine came out carrying trays of desserts. '*Chérie,*' said Antoine to Stéphie, 'could you be very kind and go and tell your brother and sister and their friends that dessert is here? If they wish to collect it and take it back to the orangery, that is permitted.'

'Who called?' Meg asked Alexandra, while various tarts and gateaux, all bought from the *pâtisserie* in town, were put on the table and cut into.

'I think it was Justin's father but annoyingly you can't eavesdrop from the kitchen.'

'What on earth can it be about?' said Meg.

'I'm sure we'll find out soon enough,' said Alexandra. 'Look at all these puddings. I think maybe I bought too many. They just look so tempting.'

'Don't worry, *chérie,*' said Antoine, 'the young people will eat everything we leave, I assure you.'

'We had better make our decision as to what we would all like quickly,' said Maxime. He looked at Meg and smiled. 'You don't have to be quick with *your* decision.'

Meg had eaten half a portion of a delicious raspberry mousse and spread the other half about her plate when, finally, Justin appeared. He came straight over to her.

'Meggy? It's Ambrosine. She's had an accident. She's broken her hip. But – No, don't worry, she hasn't died. But she is in hospital and she's asking for you.'

'Then I must go to her!' Meg stood up, flustered, her knees suddenly weak.

'Well, if you're sure about that,' said Justin. 'It's a very long journey; we can set off really early tomorrow morning and get as far as we can. I'd already booked the car on to the ferry but I can change the booking. We'll be in England the day after tomorrow. Ambrosine is doing well, I'm told.' He paused. 'We probably don't need to rush—'

'No.' For once Meg was certain. 'We must get there as soon as we can.' She turned to Antoine. 'Can you explain to Pierre what has happened? And how sorry I am to be leaving the restaurant?'

The discussion quickly became about the best route across France. Maxime took Meg aside. 'It looks as if you now know what you're doing. The toughest decisions often do make themselves, in a strange way.'

Meg didn't reply. Maxime seemed to have a lot more wisdom than his youth and good looks would suggest. Perhaps it was because he was a lawyer.

Chapter Twenty-Nine

When the knock on the door she'd been waiting for finally came it was so quiet, she was aware that she wouldn't have heard it if she hadn't been waiting for it. It was very early in the morning.

'Did I wake you?' Justin whispered when Meg opened the door.

'I've been waking every hour since two a.m.,' said Meg. 'And I'm all ready. Let's go! I hope we don't wake Milou and he starts to bark.'

'It'll be fine,' said Justin. *'En avant!'*

Outside, the dawn was breaking and it was cool. Later the temperature would rise and it would become uncomfortably hot, but now, it was perfect. The chateau looked golden in the early sunshine and although they were in a hurry, Meg couldn't resist a last look at the place where she'd been so welcomed by Alexandra and Antoine and their children.

'Can I drive to begin with?' Meg asked. 'I have the right licence and everything to drive in France but I don't suppose I'm insured to drive your car. I should drive when we're unlikely to get stopped.'

Justin took a second to absorb this but then nodded. 'It makes sense. As much as I'd like to tell you that women don't belong behind the wheel of a car' – he gave her a quick smile so that she knew he was joking – 'it's a very long way for one person to drive, even in two days.'

'Exactly.'

They didn't speak much. It was such a beautiful early morning and soon they were surrounded by fields of purple lavender stretching over the hills into the distance. They had the car windows open and the fragrance was almost overpowering.

'It makes you long for a sports car,' said Justin.

'It does. Although it wouldn't get us there any faster, I don't suppose.'

'Think of the wind in your hair . . .' he said.

'. . . turning it to wire wool,' Meg finished for him, laughing. If it weren't for the anxiety about Ambrosine, she would have been loving this drive with Justin. She might have been undecided about her feelings but the scenery was beautiful, the roads empty, she was enjoying driving Justin's powerful car – it was nearly heaven.

'If only we weren't in a hurry,' said Justin as if he were reading her mind. 'We could stop for a long lunch somewhere. Have a siesta, then go on.'

'We might need a siesta anyway,' said Meg. 'I didn't sleep much and will be tired later. Although it is so lovely now.'

'Yes. Antoine told me that the beautiful poplar trees, which Napoleon insisted on to give his troops shade, often get crashed into if people go off the road because they're drunk or tired.'

'Well, we'll make sure we're neither of those things,' said Meg. 'I wish you hadn't told me that!'

They stopped in a village and bought baguettes, butter, ham and tomatoes – everything they would need for a picnic. Then they found a quiet spot and Justin filled the baguettes with butter and ham.

'One day I'll take you to Paris and we'll have *jambon-beurre* from a little place that only sells that. Sometimes they add some cornichons.'

The thought of Justin wanting to take her to Paris made her heart give a little skip. To disguise it, Meg finished her mouthful. 'Ham and butter is a wonderful combination. Do you know Paris well?'

'I was a student there for a time.' He handed her a bottle of Perrier water. 'Here. I think when we've finished lunch, we should have a nap for half an hour. It's getting hot.'

Meg thought she would never be able to doze off where she was in the car, hot and not relaxed, in spite of being tired. But somehow her eyes closed and she slept until Justin woke her.

'We need to press on. I'll drive now.'

Meg pulled her cheesecloth shirt away from where it was sticking to her body and agreed.

They had decided to avoid Paris and, when they felt they should think about stopping for the night, searched for a convenient place. They were in a small town which should have been promising but several hotels they tried were either closed or full. The patron of the last one gave Justin an address where his aunt had a small *chambre d'hôte*.

'It's a little way away out of town,' said Justin, studying the map which was spread out over the front of the car.

'If it has a roof and a bed, it'll be fine,' said Meg. 'I just don't want to have to sleep in the car.'

'I hope I can look after you a little better than that,' said Justin, more sternly than her light-hearted remark required, she thought.

At last they found the address but the aunt had just one room. Justin looked at Meg questioningly. 'It's fine,' she said and smiled. She had been beginning to fear that sleeping in the car was a real possibility, so having a proper bed was luxury enough and she felt she could ignore the fact that she had to share it.

'Would you like dinner?' Madame asked.

'Yes, please,' said Meg and Justin together.

When they were in the room, which was spacious, clean and comfortable, Justin said, 'We may have been able to find a wonderful little restaurant mentioned in the Michelin Guide, but equally we might not.'

'I totally agree. We might have to go miles and I'm so tired that the thought of eating and going straight upstairs to bed is too tempting to ignore, even if the food is a bit simpler.'

'Sleeping is all we're going to do in this bed,' said Justin pointedly. 'I want you to feel completely safe. If you'd rather I slept on the chair . . .?'

293

'That would be ridiculous,' said Meg. 'Now I'm going to tidy myself a little. Shall I meet you downstairs?'

As she tried to get a comb through her hair and laid her nightie on the bed, she felt a pang of regret that Justin had promised she'd be safe. She wasn't sure she wanted to be safe any longer. She was still very young, she knew this, but wouldn't losing your virginity to a man you felt you loved be a good thing? Or was it the high road to heartbreak?

They were the only ones in the dining room and ate the simple meal, served with local red wine, without talking much. Meg was grateful she didn't need to make conversation. They didn't need to talk just for the sake of it.

'This is very good,' said Justin, having been eating the slow-cooked lamb for several minutes.

'You almost always eat well in France, don't you?' said Meg. 'We could do this at home, with Dorset lamb.'

'It's obviously been cooked for a very long time,' said Justin. 'With the potatoes added to the liquid later.'

Meg sipped her wine and laughed. 'Honestly, here we are, on a mercy dash to England, and we're speculating on how the lamb has been cooked.'

Justin smiled and shrugged. 'We're chefs. We can't stop thinking about food.'

Meg looked across the table at him and realised she'd rather lost interest in what she was eating.

The temperature in the little dining room seemed to get hotter and hotter as they ate. Madame came and took away their plates and said there was thunder in the air. 'It will be a relief,' she said. 'It gets very hot here in the summer.'

Meg didn't like thunder. She prided herself on being mature and grown up, but her childish fear of thunder had never left her. Fear that there might be a huge storm as well as the heat meant she could only get through half of her *tarte aux myrtilles*.

'It's too hot to eat, really,' she said. 'Although I know I'll regret not eating it one day when I'm really hungry.'

'A storm would clear the air,' Justin said.

'I suppose so,' said Meg, still hoping there wouldn't be one.

Justin regarded her seriously. 'Have you decided what to do? Will you come back to Nightingale Woods? Or is your heart in France?' He smiled, possibly aware his question was a tough one. 'I mean when Ambrosine is discovered to be fit and well again?'

'I really hope she is,' said Meg, who didn't know how to reply to his question. 'I feel very close to her – as if she's my grandmother or something.'

Justin was still looking at her. 'You haven't answered my question.'

Meg considered. France had welcomed her when she'd thought her heart was broken. Her *stage* had filled her time, taken her energy so she had no time to brood. Eventually she said, 'I've loved it – but no, my heart isn't here.'

'I'm sure that everyone at Nightingale Woods hotel will be delighted.'

Meg smiled, relieved that the awkwardness had passed. She didn't want to tell him the main reason for her heart not being in France.

'So where is your heart?' said Justin, reading her thoughts, as he so often seemed to do.

Just then there was a flash of lightning and Meg nearly fell off her chair in fright.

'Are you all right?' Justin asked, concerned.

'Fine! It just made me jump, that's all.' Meg would never confess to being frightened of thunder, especially not to Justin. 'Unless you disagree, I'm not sure I want any more of that verbena liqueur.'

He nodded. 'I'll settle up.'

He came back to their table a few minutes later and held out his hand. 'Let's go to bed.'

Meg's stomach had flipped. Just hearing him say the words drove away her fear, although she knew perfectly well he meant that they should retire for the night, nothing more. But the gathering heat, the effects of the wine and just being near him all day was making Meg long for more than a chaste night, in her white cotton nightie, between French linen sheets.

'I think we'd better,' she said. 'We've had a long day and there'll be another tomorrow.'

She didn't add that they might be woken by a storm and she knew she would lie awake in terror, trying to pretend it was only the noise that disturbed her.

In spite of her best efforts to appear calm and practical about the sleeping arrangements, Meg's nerves were at full stretch.

'They don't worry so much about bathrooms in France as we do in England, or at least at Nightingale Woods,' she said cheerily when she came back to the room having visited it. 'Lady Fussy-Knickers would have a fit if she had to manage with one several yards down the hall, and the loo several yards further.'

'Will you manage?' asked Justin.

'Of course!' Just for a moment Meg let herself imagine having to get up to go to the loo in the middle of a thunderstorm, having to walk down that long corridor with lightning threatening to strike her at every step. 'It's perfectly all right. Very clean. What are you worried about?'

'Honestly? That we have to share a bed.'

'I knew from the moment Madame said she only had one room that we'd have to share. But it's quite a big bed, don't you think? 'She sounded really calm, she thought, pleased with herself.

'So? Window open for coolness? Or shut against mosquitoes?' he asked.

'Let's have the window open but close the shutters. That limits the way in for the mosquitoes.' And it might keep out some of the lightning, she added silently.

'Get in, then,' said Justin.

She lay down, the sheet pulled up to her chin, knowing she would never sleep. Her eyes were tight shut against the lightning. She felt him get into bed beside her. Part of her desperately wanted him to kiss her and part of her wanted to become unconscious so she could wake up in the morning, unaware of any storm that may have broken overnight.

'Do you snore?' she said, to break the tension.

He laughed gently. 'You'll find out!'

She laughed too, but she still felt like a corpse laid out on a mortuary slab, completely incapable of moving. She sensed the heat coming off his body but didn't know if it was real or her imagination.

She tried to breathe deeply, telling herself that she was bound to fall asleep eventually. However tense she was, she wouldn't stay awake all night.

She could hear Justin's breathing and could tell he wasn't asleep either, or even near it.

Eventually she did find herself getting drowsy and might have actually been asleep when there was a crack of thunder so loud it was deafening and a flash of lightning lit the entire room.

She screamed and sat bolt upright.

'What's the matter?' Justin sat up too, obviously startled. 'Are you all right?'

She gave a little sob. 'I'm just so frightened of thunder!'

He had his arms around her before she'd stopped speaking.

The feel of his warm skin and being held was instantly comforting. His chest was bare and she laid her head on it, hearing his heart beat comfortingly slowly. Although it was so hot, she felt soothed by his warmth. She closed her eyes.

To begin with, he just held her and then he gently stroked her back. A little murmur escaped her and then his mouth was on hers, kissing her as if he would never stop. She didn't want him to.

But he did stop. He was panting slightly. 'Meg! Darling! We've got to think. Is this what you want? You have to be sure.'

'Yes,' said Meg, knowing she was sure, that she would face any repercussions. Just at this moment she was about to make love with the man who had filled her heart and mind for so long. It was the right thing to do.

There was no more thunder and lightning that night, only the storm of passion they made together.

They stole out of the house before dawn, keen not to awake Madame who might insist they ate the breakfast they had paid for. The sound of the car doors shutting sounded very loud but no one stirred. They were back on the road again, anxious to catch the ferry that evening.

Although it felt as if it was all she could think about, Meg didn't want to talk about the previous night. Her body held the memory of what had happened and she knew her heart always would. She had no regrets.

By hardly stopping and driving as fast as they dared (Meg was still sharing the driving, no longer worrying about insurance), they just caught the last ferry back to England.

After the scramble to collect their tickets and get on the boat, they decided to go to the bar.

'I think we should celebrate!' said Meg. 'Getting here on time!'

'Good idea. What would you like? Have a brandy before dinner?'

'Yes. At least I'm not worried about imminent thunderstorms tonight.' She realised what she'd said and felt instantly embarrassed.

'Meg . . .' Justin reached out his hand.

'It's fine, Justin,' she said as cheerfully as she could manage. 'More than fine. I just want to make sure that Ambrosine is all right now. I'm not sure why she was asking for me, but she can tell me.' She paused. 'I imagine it's about flowers for her funeral. She's very particular.'

Still holding her hands, Justin laughed and ordered brandy for both of them.

The cabin had two narrow single bunks and at half past nine, when they got into them, all Meg wanted to do was sleep.

She did.

Chapter Thirty

Because they had been one of the last to get on the ferry, they were among the first off. At half past seven on a bright summer morning they were on their way again.

'Unless you're starving now,' said Justin. 'I suggest we get to the hospital and find a greasy spoon for breakfast near it. Then we can settle until they let us see Ambrosine. It won't be visiting hours but they might let you see her because she's asked for you.'

'I am starving now but I'm happy to wait,' said Meg. 'The last forty-eight hours or so feel like about a year. It seems so strange to be back in England. As if France was a dream!'

'A happy one, I do hope,' said Justin, looking at the road ahead.

'A very happy one, thank you,' said Meg.

Having slept so well and had time to think about what had happened between them meant that Meg no longer feared the conversation that surely must take place between them. She knew now, without doubt, that she loved Justin, and given the tenderness and care he had shown her when they made love, she was fairly sure that he loved her too. She knew everyone in France was certain that he did but she needed to have it spelt out for her. Laura had thought she had been engaged to Justin, but she'd been wrong. Meg didn't want to make the same mistake. And for now, she would focus on Ambrosine.

They found the perfect café with condensation running down the windows and a thick fog of cigarette smoke filling the air.

'The tea will be very strong and the bacon very salty and I imagine there'll be several thick slices of bread and butter to go with it all,' said Justin, ushering Meg to a free table.

They ordered everything that a proper breakfast offered, including fried bread, toast and baked beans.

They didn't speak as they ate. They were both ravenous, having not had much to eat the night before.

'Well, that was utterly delicious!' said Meg at last. 'Should we add baked beans to the breakfast we do at the hotel? I am joking!' she added hurriedly. 'I really don't think Lady Fussy-Knickers would like it.'

The proprietor of the café came up. 'More tea? Toast? Anything?'

Meg shook her head. 'But that was perfect! Thank you so much!'

The man was obviously unaccustomed to being thanked so profusely but when Justin asked if Meg could sit there while he went to the hospital to see if they could visit a relative, he nodded readily.

'I'll bring you another tea anyway,' he said. 'Just in case you change your mind.'

Meg was not at all surprised that when Justin came back it was to announce that they could visit Ambrosine immediately, even though the hospital had a very strict matron and it was hours before visiting time.

Nor was she surprised to be ushered into a side ward by a nurse with 'Sister Judy Ellwood' on her badge. Ambrosine was obviously getting the very best attention. She had a room on her own, with a large window and a view of the garden.

'Darling!' said Ambrosine as Meg and Justin approached. Meg had a huge bunch of flowers bought from a greengrocer whom they'd caught opening up and Justin held an equivalently large box of chocolates that he'd bought on the ferry. 'How very kind of you to come!'

'We're rather grubby from the ferry,' said Meg, putting down the flowers and kissing her friend's cheek.

In spite of her expansive manner, Ambrosine looked small and frail in the hospital bed and Meg felt a sudden rush of emotion to see her there. A broken hip was serious and while Ambrosine would probably recover, she realised, she was still elderly and couldn't last forever. The thought of losing her was heart-breaking.

'I'll find someone to get me a vase for these,' said Justin from the door, obviously wanting to leave Meg and Ambrosine alone to talk.

'No! Come back, Justin dear,' said Ambrosine. 'I want to talk to Meg but I think you should hear what I've got to say too.' She regarded Meg, who had pulled up a chair. 'I've always thought that you two should be together, so he may as well know now things he'll find out later.'

Meg blushed. 'Anything you told me in confidence would always stay a secret.'

Ambrosine made a dismissive gesture. 'I'm too old for secrets now, which is why I asked you to come. It's all part of history, and history shouldn't be forgotten, or it will die with its participants.' She gestured to Justin. 'Get a chair, dear boy, and listen. Oh, maybe open the chocolates first. I think I could manage a coffee cream.'

Once the box was open and Ambrosine had fortified herself with a couple of soft centres, she began to talk.

'I haven't always lived in England, you know. I was in France during the war, married to a Frenchman who turned out to be very unpleasant. Of course I just had to put up with his nastiness – there was no choice – but I did lead as separate a life as I could. But when the country was invaded, my husband became a collaborator, and it all became a little more complicated.'

'I can imagine,' said Meg, shocked by what Ambrosine must have been through.

'I had to entertain German officers in my house. Be pleasant to them. Although to be fair, not all of them were unpleasant.' Ambrosine sighed wistfully, as if remembering something.

'Can I ask what your husband's name was?' said Justin.

'He was a count. Guillaume Fauré-Dubois,' said Ambrosine. 'He was a rat, but of course I didn't find that out until after I'd married him.'

Something in Justin's expression told Meg that this name meant something to him. 'Go on,' he said.

'Because I had my own circle of friends before the war, when it started, it turned out I knew several people in the Resistance.' She paused. 'Eventually – it took a long time for them to trust me; Guillaume was a factory owner who made concrete for the Germans – eventually they turned to me to help.'

'What did you do?' asked Meg when Ambrosine had sipped some water and eaten another chocolate.

Ambrosine took a breath as if about to explain something a bit complicated. 'Have you heard of the SOE?' she asked.

'No,' said Meg.

'Weren't they people dropped into France to act as spies and to help the Resistance?' said Justin.

'More or less. What many of them did was to radio any information about the Germans they could discover back to London. Their radios made them terribly vulnerable. The Germans could find out where they were within about half an hour. Having a radio was dangerous.' Ambrosine stopped speaking, lost in the past for a moment.

Meg cleared her throat, thinking about Ambrosine's enormous courage.

'We lived in a very large house in Nantes. There were attics, cellars, servants' quarters – although very few servants. There was a lot of space. But because we allowed the larger rooms to be used for meetings for the Germans, and gave dinner parties for them, and generally were terribly nice to them' – she gave a little laugh – 'they didn't search the house!'

'I can't imagine how awful it must have been, living in occupied France,' said Meg.

'Indeed. But I was able to hide a number of British people, men and women, who needed to lie low. I kept their radios down behind the back fascia of the house and I hid British spies wherever there was space. My difficulty was that I had to keep them hidden from my husband, too. He was very unlikely to visit the attics or the cellars or the outbuildings, but it was still a risk.'

Ambrosine turned to Justin suddenly. 'One of the spies – the man in charge – was your grandfather, Justin. I don't suppose you knew that because we were trained to keep silent about our goings-on.'

'But you managed to keep your husband away from where you were hiding radios and people?' Meg asked.

'For a while, yes,' said Ambrosine, 'but he found out eventually. It was inevitable. Once I realised he knew, I was scooped up by the last lot of SOE types to travel back to England. I spent the rest of the war working in a canteen, staying with an old school friend.

'Luckily, I had a little money of my own and then, after I heard that Guillaume had been killed, I got married again. Sadly, he didn't live very long. And then, a while later, when my money had pretty much run out, your grandfather, Teddy, who turned out to be one of the chaps I'd helped escape, got in touch with me asking if I wanted a home in Nightingale Woods. I didn't really know him, the chaps were never with us for very long and I don't know how he came to find me, but I visited Nightingale Woods, it was all very pleasant, and I accepted gratefully.' She folded her hands, indicating her tale was over.

'That's an amazing story, Ambrosine,' said Meg. 'Thank you so much for telling us.'

She shrugged. 'It's time these things were more generally known, I think. When I had my accident, I realised that the things I'd done in the war would die with me. I wanted to tell someone and I thought you were the perfect person.' She paused. 'You love Nightingale Woods as much as I do and it seemed fitting.'

Meg swallowed hard. 'Would you like us to keep it a secret?' she asked, knowing she'd find it very hard to do so.

'Certainly not! Keeping secrets is very wearing, darling,' said Ambrosine.

'Are you very tired?' asked Justin.

'At my age one is always tired,' said Ambrosine. 'Why do you ask?'

'Because I can add a bit to your story that you may not know. But I can tell you tomorrow, if you'd rather.'

'My dear young man, it's hardly worth me ordering tomorrow's copy of *The Times* in case I'm not there to read it.' She had brightened up. 'Tell me now!'

'Well, you know my father is looking for a mystery Frenchwoman, whose name no one recognised? No? Well, he is! Because my grandfather left you a third of the hotel in his will.'

Meg stared at Justin. 'So Ambrosine is the missing person?'

Justin nodded. 'Mme Fauré-Dubois.'

'Heavens to Betsy!' said Ambrosine. 'What a very strange thing! Why would he do that?'

'It's not at all strange. My grandfather wanted you to be secure for the rest of your life. He wrote a letter. It was among his papers. It didn't mean anything to anyone because until now, no one knew who he was talking about.'

'But he knew I'd got married again,' said Ambrosine.

'I gather from my father that my grandfather was getting rather vague towards the end. I suppose he'd known you longest as the woman married to Count Fauré-Dubois.'

'That would explain it. My second marriage was very short,' said Ambrosine. She gave a sudden shuddering yawn. 'Now I think I might need to rest,' she said. 'Would you mind . . .?'

'Of course!' Meg and Justin got to their feet. Ambrosine had closed her eyes and on impulse, Meg went over to her and kissed her cheek. It was wet with tears.

They were in the town having driven away from the hospital and found somewhere to park. They had agreed they needed time to think about what they had heard before they went back to Nightingale Woods.

'Is it too early for a drink?' said Justin, glancing at his watch. 'The pubs should be open now. I'd like to talk it all over, digest it a bit. That was all quite a shock.'

'I agree,' said Meg. 'I know people did amazing things during the war but imagine having Nazis for dinner when you've got secret agents in your attic. What a nerve!'

'But if anyone could do it, Ambrosine was the one,' said Justin.

They approached a teashop, apparently full of ladies halfway through their morning's shopping. 'What about in here?'

He shook his head. 'I know a pub where we can talk privately. I don't want to be overheard.'

The King's Head had the characteristic smell of stale beer and cigarette smoke that pubs always have when they first open. It felt chilly and unhospitable. Justin found them a table and then went to get drinks and just for a few minutes Meg missed French cafés which would have smelt of fresh coffee and would already be bustling. But they weren't here to absorb the atmosphere, they were here to help each other understand what Ambrosine had done before she was an eccentric old lady living as a resident in a small country hotel.

'I'm so touched she chose us to tell her story to,' said Meg, sipping her lime juice.

'It was you she wanted to tell. I was just there,' said Justin.

'It was just as well you were there. I wouldn't have known she was the third person in the will.'

'Odd that she didn't know either,' said Justin.

Meg shrugged. 'She hadn't seen the will and no one had any idea that she'd once been married to a French count.'

'One thing is certain, my uncle Colin won't be happy about Ambrosine being the third person.'

'Why not? He's known for a while that the hotel is to be split three ways.'

'He hasn't accepted it,' said Justin. He was drinking lime juice too. 'I think he was hoping that the mystery woman could be declared dead, and he doesn't get on with Ambrosine. Also, he'll be worried about who she'll leave her share to when she does shuffle off her mortal coil. It could be a favourite nephew, or a cat's home.'

In spite of everything, Meg couldn't help laughing. 'I'm really hoping it's the cat's home,' she said, 'although of course I'm sorry for the hypothetical favourite nephew.' She sighed. 'Seeing Ambrosine in that big white bed was a bit of a shock. She looked so frail. I'm used to seeing her marching around the garden with a trug on her arm and a strange hat on her head looking like someone in a play.'

'Any particular play?'

Meg shook her head. 'Just one of those where people keep coming in and out of French windows talking about croquet.'

Justin smiled. 'Do you mind if we get everyone together for a meeting before we share her news, and explain who she is? It's your story really.'

'But you who realised about her share in the hotel,' Meg interrupted. 'And I agree, it would be best if everyone heard the news at the same time.' She paused. 'I don't think she told us half of what she went through to do all that.'

'Nor do I.' He looked at her intently. 'And we will have to talk about what happened in France between us some time.'

'I know. But please, not today.'

Despite his very loving behaviour towards her in France, Justin still hadn't told her he loved her. The fact that he'd made love to her was no guarantee that he did. And now she was dreading having to hear Justin explain that she was a lovely girl and one day she would find the man who would make her very happy. But although he was obviously very attracted to her, that man was not him. She could almost hear him say it in his low, attractive voice.

Chapter Thirty-One

❧

Meg was extremely touched by their welcome at Nightingale Woods. Someone had obviously spotted the car and so everyone was on the steps to greet them. Louise, Andrew, Susan, Bob and Cherry all stood in a row. They waved wildly as the car pulled up and Sally appeared with a bunch of flowers which she presented as soon as Meg was on the step.

'It's so kind of you to all come out and meet us,' said Meg.

'Nightingale Woods has missed you, girl,' said Susan gruffly. 'We're all pleased to have you back.'

Cherry and Sally allowed Meg to hug them but Susan obviously felt she had said quite enough on the subject and withdrew to the kitchen, although Meg could tell she was delighted. Bob, Susan's husband, gave Meg a nod. 'The garden's full of herbs for you, Meg. I've made sure of it.'

Meg remembered that Bob was doing more plumbing and carpentry than gardening these days and was touched that he'd made time to keep the herb garden going.

'How was Ambrosine?' asked Louise when she, Andrew and Justin were settled in a sunny corner of the library.

'She's fairly comfortable, I think,' said Meg tentatively.

'And do you know why she wanted you so particularly?' asked Andrew. 'I know she's very fond of you, but we were a little surprised when she asked for you specially like that.'

'Actually, Dad,' said Justin. 'It's probably better if we wait until Uncle Colin is here so we can tell all of you everything at the same time. It's quite a long story.'

Andrew seemed surprised. 'Oh! Are you sure?'

'If he can't be here for days we'll tell you now,' said Justin, relenting. 'But otherwise . . .'

'He's coming this afternoon,' said Andrew. 'He's still hoping for a better valuation.'

'In which case, I may go and unpack and get changed,' said Meg. 'I feel really grubby.'

'Me too,' said Justin.

'OK. Susan is doing lunch for one thirty,' said Andrew.

'I'll come and help you,' said Louise.

Meg nodded and smiled, knowing perfectly well that her mother didn't want to help her unpack her very small suitcase, but rather to hear how her relationship with Justin was going.

'Well?' said Louise when Meg had had a shower and washed her hair. 'Everyone at the hotel is convinced that Justin is madly in love with you. Is he?'

Meg put the only dress that was hanging in her cupboard on the bed. 'I'm not exactly sure.'

Louise seemed delighted. 'You're not saying no, definitely not, never in a million years, then?'

'No, I'm not saying that.'

Meg looked at her mother, who appeared to be waiting for some sort of news. Did she have any? She was fairly sure her mother wouldn't die of shock if she told her that she and Justin had slept together, but she might not approve if she knew that they weren't committed to each other. She had to say something!

'I don't know, Mum,' she began, rubbing her wet hair with a towel. She intended to censor her story just a bit. 'We had to share a room on our way back from Provence—'

'And a bed?'

'It would have been OK if there hadn't been a thunderstorm.'

Louise smiled. 'Oh, darling, are you still scared of thunder?'

Meg nodded, all thought of protecting her mother from the truth disappearing. 'Yes. I yelped. He took me into his arms and one thing led to another.' She sighed.

'At least I can tell that part all went well,' said Louise calmly.

'Yes.'

'And afterwards?'

'We were focused on Ambrosine, her story – it's so amazing – I know we said we'd tell everyone all at the same time—'

'Tell me now, darling, or at least some of it. I can't bear to have to wait for Colin, who's being so difficult and unpleasant.'

Hardly aware that she was doing it, Meg related everything that Ambrosine had told them. She managed not to mention what Justin had known and said about Ambrosine being the third person in the will. That was the tricky part.

'That is amazing,' said Louse. 'And it explains a lot. I was never sure why she was here in the hotel, although she's always been a huge asset.'

'She has, hasn't she? I just hope Colin sees it like that.'

'Why does it matter what he thinks?'

'If you can just hang on, Mum, you'll be told every-thing, very soon!'

Colin arrived after his visit to yet another estate agent, so Justin decided there was time for a quick meeting before evening service. There weren't many guests, the meal was simple and Susan and Cherry were fully capable of seeing to it all.

Possibly anticipating trouble, Justin poured every-one lavish glasses of sherry. He had told Meg that he'd already told his father, but didn't want Colin to realise he was the last to know. He was resentful enough about everything without there being family secrets.

Andrew and Louise were sitting next to each other, the backs of their hands touching, as if they were going to hold hands at any minute.

'So, what's this meeting about,' said Colin. 'I haven't time for all this!' He looked at his watch, implying he was busier than everyone else.

'It won't take long,' said Justin.

'I hope not,' said Meg, 'I've left Susan in charge of dinner.' Susan had been so pleased to see Meg, but Meg couldn't help noticing that she had lost confidence a bit. Had Laura done that? If so, it was unforgiveable. Susan was a plain cook, but what she produced was very good. Just because it wasn't fancy didn't mean it was inferior.

She also wanted to encourage the opinion that she didn't know what Justin was going to say.

'You know that Ambrosine asked for Meg when she went to hospital so Meg came back from France?'

Colin mumbled something inaudible and possibly vaguely insulting.

'When we went to the hospital, Ambrosine insisted that I stayed as well as Meg, and she told us her story. She said she'd kept what she'd done in the war a secret for too long, and that she wanted people to know now.'

Justin went on to relate how, married to a collaborator, Ambrosine had entertained Nazis at the same time as hiding Special Operations Executive officers and their equipment.

When everyone had exclaimed in surprise and admiration, Justin continued: 'My grandfather was one of those she rescued and he made a point of finding her after the war to make sure she was all right. She'd married again and was fine until she was widowed once more and ran out of money. That's when he said she could live at the hotel for the rest of her life.'

'Well done, Dad,' said Colin. 'Can we go now?'

'Not yet,' said Justin. 'There was something she didn't know that I could tell her, and now I can tell you.'

Colin gave an exaggerated sigh. 'Just spit it out, can't you?'

'Ambrosine told us her married name and I recognised it. She's the mysterious Countess Fauré-Dubois. She is the third person in the will. It's brilliant news as it means we can now get everything sorted out and apply for probate.'

Colin did not look like someone who had just received brilliant news. 'What? That old woman owns part of the hotel? That's outrageous! She's not a member of the family! She's just some random old biddy—'

'Who saved our father's life!' said Andrew.

But Colin wasn't having this. 'No. It's not right. I'll see a solicitor. I'm going to dispute the will!' He rose from his chair.

'Where are you rushing off to?' said Andrew.

'To see a man about a dog,' said Colin. He left the room leaving the cloud of irritation his behaviour had created behind him.

Justin rolled his eyes. 'I'd better go after him.'

When he came back, he said to Meg, 'Can I have a word?'

'Is everything all right?' she asked. 'You were gone a long time.'

'Colin is fine; he's just being grumpy. But I found a message for me in the office. It's from someone who rents a property I own in London. I need to see to it immediately.' He paused. 'I'm so sorry, Meggy. I hate to leave you just now, but this man's lavatory has broken and is leaking. If it's not sorted soon, it'll take the ceilings out of three other flats. For some reason he can't get a plumber. I'll be back as soon as I can.'

He pulled her into his arms and kissed her, holding her as if he would never let her go.

Meg was so sad to see him leave, but her heart had lifted: surely he wouldn't have hugged her like that unless he really loved her?

The following morning, Meg bravely telephoned Russell and asked him, tactfully, if it might be possible to put the play on at the hotel after all, and if there was anything she could do to encourage him.

'It was that Laura person!' said Russell, obviously with lots of pent-up frustration to express. 'She refused to do anything to accommodate us and just said no to every request. I had to pull us out. We were all so disappointed.'

'I am so sorry, Russell, that's awful!' said Meg, secretly relieved that this had been the reason. 'If I told you that Laura is no longer with us – with the hotel I mean; she hasn't died – and said we would do anything in our power to make whatever you want happen, might you be able to change your mind?'

There was a long, worrying pause and then a long sigh. 'We could tag you on to the end of the season.

We'll need a couple of rehearsals, but not too many as we know the play backwards by now. But knowing you, Meg, knowing how much trouble you went to, to look after your guests, we'd be thrilled. I'll just have to check with Dame Miriam. She may have another engagement. Or she may just be tired.'

'Russell, I can't tell you how delighted I am! We're longing to have you all!'

Meg put the phone down, triumphant that the *Dream* would be put on at Nightingale Woods after all. She ran to find Louise and Andrew, excited to be able to tell them the good news.

Chapter Thirty-Two

Early the next morning, Meg stood in the kitchen at Nightingale Woods. It felt so strange and yet so familiar. In some ways it was as if she'd never been away and in others she felt like a completely different person. The last time she had been in this kitchen she had hated Justin, now she loved him and felt, although didn't know for certain, that he loved her.

'It's like a novel,' she said out loud, to the surprise of Susan who walked in at just that moment.

'What's that, Meg dear? Anything I need to pay attention to?'

'No,' said Meg quickly. 'I was just thinking how different this kitchen is from the one I left in France. It's lovely and calm here. The French one was so hot, noisy and very busy.'

Susan looked askance. 'You'll be glad to get back to civilisation, no doubt.'

Meg laughed. 'Absolutely!'

The hotel suddenly became almost as busy as the French kitchen Meg had left. Everyone agreed (except for Colin, who wasn't consulted) that Ambrosine could no longer live in the attic – there were far too many stairs. They settled on a little room on the ground floor that opened directly out into the garden. There was room for a bathroom next door and although it was small, Louise and Meg felt it could be made nice for Ambrosine and Louise took on the challenge. Bob went in with his pencil behind his ear and worked out the plumbing.

There were two things that prevented Meg from being entirely happy (being desperately busy and possibly overworked was what she liked). One was Justin's continued absence. He did telephone her sometimes, but it was never very satisfactory talking to him when neither he nor she were alone.

The other thing was Ambrosine. Although she was improving, her recovery was slow. Meg visited as often as she could, bringing flowers from the garden, titbits from the kitchen and whatever gossip she could come up with. Ambrosine knew that Justin was away and was sympathetic but, of course, even she couldn't make him come back any sooner.

But at last, Ambrosine's hip was declared properly mended. They were told that in three days, Ambrosine could come home. Meg, who was present when the doctor declared this, hugged her friend. 'I can't wait for you to see your new room, Ambrosine. It's lovely!'

Shortly afterwards she rushed back to Nightingale Woods to tell Louise, so they could make sure that it was indeed lovely. Luckily, there was nobody in for afternoon tea and Meg and her mother could focus their attention on Ambrosine's room. They were just wondering if the bed should go right near the French doors or a little way back when Cherry came in.

'Meg? Russell's on the phone; he needs to talk to you.'

Meg's heart sank. It had to be about the play. 'Did he say what about?'

Cherry shook her head. 'But it's never good news when people telephone, is it?'

Really hoping that Cherry was wrong, Meg left the room.

'I am so sorry, Meg love,' said Russell. 'But we can't put you on to the end of the season like I thought. Dame Miriam has a holiday booked.'

'Oh no!' said Meg. 'That's very sad. Everyone will be so disappointed.'

'Well, don't despair,' said Russell. 'We *can* fit you in. But next Saturday – that's only five days' time, which is very short notice, and probably too short. We'd come to Nightingale Woods on Thursday.'

Meg gulped. This was the same day that Ambrosine was due to come out of hospital, but that needn't affect the theatre people. And there wasn't time to consult everyone else about this. They only had three days to arrange things anyway, and couldn't afford to spend two of them wondering if the hotel could manage it or not.

She took a bracing breath. 'OK. Next Saturday it is,' she said quickly. 'It will be too late for us to publicise the play though. I'm so sorry about this. It would be an awful shame if everyone went to all the trouble of putting it on and nobody came to watch it.'

Russell laughed. 'Don't you worry about that! We have a mailing list. People will travel miles to see Dame Miriam. We'll get a mailshot out today. We're never short of bums on seats.'

'That's wonderful then, Russell. Thank you so much for managing to squeeze us in.'

'We really wanted to come,' said Russell. 'So! We'll see you sometime on Thursday afternoon.'

Meg went to break the news to Andrew and Louise.

'You mean Ambrosine is coming home and the theatre company are coming here on the same day?' said Louise.

'I'm afraid so. It's either that or the theatre company don't come at all.' Meg looked apologetically at her mother and Andrew. 'I didn't think we could miss the opportunity of a full hotel for several nights.' She paused. 'Although I can ring him back and say we can't do it.'

'No, no,' said Andrew. 'Nightingale Woods will come up trumps, I'm sure. We can get Ambrosine settled in her new room in the morning.'

'I've got the list of how many rooms Russell's troupe need somewhere,' said Louise. 'It's a lot. And while they are getting a special rate, as arranged before they cancelled, it's a good amount. Meals are extra.'

'Have we got enough really good bedrooms?' asked Meg.

'If we haven't now, we will have by Thursday!' said Louise brightly. 'We'll all just have to work extra hard.'

Chapter Thirty-Three

Running a hotel and a building site had its difficulties, Meg thought, but nothing was impossible if you just put your mind to it. By the Thursday the hotel was as ready as it could be for twenty or so extra guests and Ambrosine's room was looking beautiful. Meg had got up extra early to get ahead with the meals and the baking. It was just a shame it was raining, Meg thought, praying that it would clear up before the actual performance in two days' time.

The previous evening Justin had rung her and they'd managed to have a long, private conversation. He told her that he had repaired the leaking toilet, but while he was in London, he'd come across problems with other property he apparently owned. He was really hoping to be able to come back down to Nightingale Woods to see Ambrosine, even if he couldn't stay down for long. It had been lovely to talk to him, Meg thought, even if the conversation had mostly involved plaster, brickwork and the difficulty of getting various tradesmen to turn up on time.

'We're lucky having Susan,' Meg had said. 'As almost everyone who works here is related to her in some way or another, none of them dare slack on the job.'

Justin had laughed. Then there was an awkward pause, filled with unspoken declarations. Then he said, 'Goodbye, Meggie,' and Meg's heart overflowed with love.

Now, while she was flattening escalopes of pork (nice and quick to cook), Louise came in.

'Big day today!' she said. 'You're well ahead, I see. Tea?'

Meg had already had about three cups of tea but didn't decline.

'Now, remind me of the plan,' said Louise, having poured tea for everyone, who now included Susan and Cherry.

'I'm going to collect Ambrosine at nine,' said Meg. 'We'll come back here and have a brief welcoming party. Justin is going to try to be here but how he'll manage that, coming from London, I don't know.'

'He'll come,' said Susan. 'He'll come down on that noisy motorbike of his, you'll see.'

Meg smiled at her gratefully. 'Well, if he's late, it doesn't matter. I've made a coffee cake, Ambrosine's favourite. When she's properly settled in, we can concentrate on the theatre party.'

'Colin's here already,' said Louise. 'He arrived late last night, after you'd gone to bed, Meg.'

Susan harrumphed. 'Trust him to come when we could have done with having his room for the theatricals.'

Although Meg knew Louise completely agreed with this statement, she said, 'Well, Nightingale Woods is his as much as it's Andrew's. He has a perfect right to be here.'

Susan's expression spoke for them all; none of them liked Colin.

They went to collect Ambrosine immediately after breakfast. They were given strict instructions about her medication, which seemed to take ages, but at last she was safely loaded into the front of Andrew's car. Meg was driving it and felt her responsibility keenly. She would have preferred Andrew, or even her mother, to carry out this delicate task, but Ambrosine had wanted Meg, and so Meg it was.

'It's so sweet of you to collect me,' said Ambrosine as they left the little town.

'It's sweet of you to trust me when I'm driving Andrew's big car. I'm used to the Mini, which is perfect for the lanes,' said Meg.

'I have complete confidence in your ability to do anything you choose to.'

Meg laughed. 'When I think of what you've done in your life, nothing I do – or have done – really compares.'

'We all have different rows to hoe, my dear. And you are hoeing yours very well.' Ambrosine patted Meg's knee. 'Now, when I'm back I'd like to gather everyone together for a little meeting. I know I'll need to go to bed for a while today, but before I do, there are things I need to tell people.'

Meg took a breath to tell Ambrosine that she didn't need to tell anyone anything today, that there would be plenty of time to do that when she was properly settled in and completely herself again. But she kept silent; Ambrosine knew what she wanted and wouldn't be persuaded otherwise. Besides, once the theatricals arrived (everyone referred to the theatre party in this way now), every minute would be spoken for.

'I'm sure we can do that,' said Meg. 'Justin is hoping to be there to greet you, but it will be quite an early start for him, coming from London.

'If he says he'll be there, he will,' said Ambrosine. 'I know he can be a bit bossy and overbearing, but at heart, he's a very good man.'

Meg laughed. 'Only a bit bossy and overbearing?' she said. 'More than just a bit, I think.'

Ambrosine joined in the laughter but shook her head. 'He's wrapped round your little finger, if you did but know it.'

Andrew, Louise, Susan, Bob and Cherry were all waiting for them on the steps of Nightingale Woods. There were hugs, a few discreet tears, a lot of carrying of cases and eventually Ambrosine was ensconced in the drawing room.

'You're really sure you don't want to go to your room straight away?' asked Louise, not for the first time.

'Quite sure,' said Ambrosine. 'When I've said my piece, I'll retire to my room, but not until.' She said this with a firmness that left no one in any doubt of her intentions.

Soon, everyone was assembled except Justin. While she was not really expecting him and had already resigned herself to his absence, Meg couldn't help feeling disappointed.

Colin was the last to appear. He sat on a chair next to Meg (the one she had been saving for Justin) and said to the room, 'Where's Justin?'

'He's in London,' said Meg, looking firmly ahead.

'Oh,' said Colin. 'Probably seeing that Laura. She was a nice girl.'

Meg pursed her lips and said nothing.

Then, when Andrew had filled glasses with sherry and Louise had poured coffee and handed out cake, a familiar sound reached Meg's ears. It was the roar of a motorbike.

Moments later, Justin came in, dressed in black leather and looking particularly dangerous and sexy. He came over to Meg and pulled her up out of her chair, put his arms around her and kissed her until she was dizzy.

'Well, I think that deserves a round of applause,' said Andrew, grinning.

Ambrosine was also amused. 'Now sit down, Justin. I've got something to say and I haven't got much energy. I'll need a nap in precisely five minutes.'

'We're all listening, Ambrosine,' said Justin, who'd moved to a sofa with Meg, who was so happy she forgot to be embarrassed by his kissing her so publicly.

Sitting next to him, her leg lightly touching his (although she knew he wouldn't feel it through his motorbiking gear), she couldn't help looking forward to the evening, after the play, when she'd be able to invite him back to her room in the little flat.

'And so,' Ambrosine was saying when Meg finally got her mind back to the meeting, 'as my name means "Immortal", which means I'll live forever' – she looked at Colin, to make sure he got the point – 'I've decided to make over my share of Nightingale Woods to Meg.'

'Oh!' said Louise. 'How lovely!'

Because she'd been distracted at the beginning, Meg wasn't absolutely certain about what she'd heard. Ambrosine was going to make over her share of the hotel to her?

'I'm sorry,' she said. 'Ambrosine, would you mind very much saying that again?'

Ambrosine obliged, and then added, 'Meg, darling, you will be the very best person to have my share. You love Nightingale Woods and you are good for it. You can follow your dreams here.'

Meg suddenly needed to clear her throat. She didn't want to cry in front of people but she was very touched by Ambrosine's words.

'Hang on! A non-family member giving all that valuable property to another chit of a girl who just happens to be working in the hotel?' said Colin. 'It's outrageous. I'm not even sure why Ambrosine was in the will anyway!'

'I thought I'd explained,' said Andrew, sounding frustrated. 'Without Ambrosine, there wouldn't be a family. Our father wouldn't have survived the war!'

'I never knew what he did in the war,' said Colin, subsiding a little.

'That was because he never told us,' said Andrew.

'It was ingrained in us not to tell anyone anything,' said Ambrosine. 'And it would have been more important for your father. He'd signed the Official Secrets Act. I was just an amateur.'

'Ambrosine told us about her war while she was in hospital,' said Justin. 'But to reiterate' – he looked at Colin – 'she was incredibly brave and helped people in the SOE – Special Operations Executive. Saboteurs and information-gatherers, basically.'

Ambrosine sat forward in her chair. 'Edward, your father – Teddy, as I knew him' – she nodded to Colin – 'was particularly valuable to the SOE because he'd spent a lot of his childhood in France. His French was perfect, and his work in the mines, before the war, meant he had knowledge of explosives. That came in very handy, I can tell you.'

Meg couldn't help smiling at Ambrosine's under-statement, in spite of the serious nature of her story.

'You were both extremely brave, you and my grand-father,' said Justin. He turned to Colin. 'And I hope you now understand why he wanted Ambrosine to have a home for life.'

'I suppose I do,' said Colin resentfully. 'But I still don't think Ambrosine should be allowed to make her share of the hotel over to – to . . .' He searched for her name. 'Meg. I'm sure it isn't legal.'

'It will be legal when everything is sorted out,' said Ambrosine firmly. 'The colonel's son is a lawyer and he's been advising me.'

'I think that's a wonderful idea, Ambrosine,' said Justin.

'So do I,' said Andrew. He gave Louise a fond glance.

Colin shook his head. 'I shall fight it! I'm not going to listen to the opinions of a teenager—'

'She's twenty-two!' said Louise.

'That's still very young!' said Colin.

'Colin,' Justin interrupted. 'Listen to me for a moment. Would you like to sell your share of the hotel?'

'Stupid question!' Colin replied. 'Of course I'd like to sell it. But unless everyone agrees to sell the bloody place, I'm stuck with it. Which is why I'm so annoyed at this ridiculous decision.'

He glared at Ambrosine, who seemed amused. 'Colin, dear,' she said. 'You wouldn't've much liked having to listen to the opinions of a very old lady. At least Meg knows what she's talking about.'

'If I bought you out,' Justin persisted, 'you could walk away from Nightingale Woods and—'

'—only come back as a guest!' said Louise, obviously anticipating that Justin was going to say something inflammatory.

Colin was paying attention to Justin now. 'Could you afford to buy me out?'

'We'd have to get the hotel valued—' Justin began.

'Oh, I've done that. It's worth approximately . . .' He named an eye-watering figure.

Justin nodded. 'So as long as my valuer reached roughly the same figure, I could certainly buy you out.'

'Where on earth did you get that kind of money?' Colin asked.

Meg felt uncomfortable at the thought that Justin was going to have to discuss his finances in a room full of people. Louise got up, obviously feeling the same. 'This is a private matter.'

'It's all right,' said Justin. 'I'm perfectly happy to talk about it. And it's a reasonable question. I did get the money honestly and I can afford to buy Colin out.' He paused, and then became aware that everyone was looking at him.

'Well . . .?' demanded Colin.

'I bought a flat very very cheaply when I was a young chef. It was in a really bad part of London. It has since become a very good part of London, but before then I'd bought the whole house and the one next door. I was lucky; I got some good bonuses. And recently, I've sold them, which will give me enough money to be able to buy you out.'

'Well done, Justin,' said Andrew. 'I knew about the property, of course, but I didn't know they'd gone up in value so much.'

'But, Justin—' Meg began.

He gave her a reassuring look. 'It's all right. Originally, I wanted to buy a restaurant in London, but I realise now I can fulfil all my dreams at Nightingale Woods.'

'Well, I'm absolutely delighted!' said Ambrosine. 'Now the future of the hotel is assured with you young people having a stake in it.'

Meg was blushing again as she realised that Ambrosine had seen a future in which she and Justin were together. She was very pleased when Susan came in. 'People are arriving!'

Meg went over to Ambrosine. 'I can never, ever thank you enough,' she said.

'You being you is all the thanks I need,' said Ambrosine, patting Meg's hand. 'Now, I think I need to lie down for a bit.'

Chapter Thirty-Four

Leaving Louise and Andrew to help Ambrosine to her new quarters, Meg went to the reception area and gasped in shock. David and Vanessa were there, neither of whom she was expecting.

'I begged Russell to make me part of the team for this venue only and, bless him, he did,' said David, kissing Meg's cheek. 'Alexandra and family are coming if they possibly can, but she said don't save rooms for them. They'll manage if they can make it.'

'And I've cancelled my wedding and run away from home,' said Vanessa. She smiled but she looked as if she'd done a lot of crying recently.

'I found her just outside of the town. She'd run out of petrol,' said David. He gave Meg a significant look that told her that Vanessa was very distressed.

'Well, it's a lovely surprise to see you both!' said Meg, giving Vanessa a long hug. 'But I'm not sure where I'm going to put you.' She paused. 'You can come in with me, of course, Nessa.' It cost her a pang to have to cancel her dream of spending the night with Justin but she didn't have a choice.

'I can sleep under the grand piano, if all else fails,' said David. 'I've done it before!'

'I can't imagine how that would work,' said Meg, 'but I've just remembered that Ambrosine's old room is available. Oh, here's my mother!'

'David! Vanessa?' said Louise. 'Are you OK?' she said to Vanessa.

'I've cancelled my wedding,' said Vanessa, her voice suddenly clogged with tears. 'I couldn't stand all the arrangements, the presents, everyone telling me what I had to do. None of the choices were mine. So I had to call it off and—' She gulped. 'That means I had to write to Simon and . . .' There was a long pause. Then Vanessa cleared her throat with determination. 'I suppose I've broken it off with him.'

'Oh, you poor love!' said Louise. 'Come into the kitchen. I'll make us a cuppa.'

Justin and Colin appeared at that moment, Andrew just behind them, looking content.

'David! Hello!' said Justin.

'Turning up like the proverbial bad penny,' said David. 'I hope you don't mind.'

'Delighted!' said Justin. He turned to Meg. 'I'm terribly sorry, darling, but I can't stay long today. I've got a few loose ends to tie up. But I'll come back as soon as I can, and help with the cooking.'

'You'll be here tomorrow?' Meg asked, aware she sounded plaintive.

He nodded. 'I really hope so.' Then he kissed her. 'One day we won't spend all the time saying goodbye to each other.'

Meg managed a laugh and watched him walk out of the front door.

There was a faint whistle from David. 'You look as if you are a proper solid couple now.'

'Well, I think we are.' Meg hesitated. Should she tell David about Ambrosine giving her a third of the hotel? She decided not. It wouldn't happen for a while, anyway, and would take so much explaining.

'I'll help you in the kitchen when I can,' said David.

'That's so kind of you, but you're here for the play, and it's not for long.' She paused. 'I'll go and see how Vanessa is.'

Before she could, Cherry emerged from the office, almost as pleased to see David as Meg had been. 'Did you hear that Dame Miriam wants to be put in a cottage instead of the main hotel?' Cherry said when they had greeted each other.

'Russell told me,' said David. 'Apparently she's convinced she wants a sweet little cottage in a wood.'

Meg nodded. 'We've made the head groom's cottage as nice as we possibly can. Mum has worked her home-making magic, but we're fully prepared for Dame Miriam to change her mind when she sees it. Our good rooms are lovely now but there aren't many of them.' She paused, then added, sotto voce, 'Should I ring Lizzie and tell her Nessa is here safe?'

David nodded. 'But I'll do it if you like. You're so busy. Then Hugo can deal with his parents.'

Meg shuddered at the thought of dealing with Lady Lennox-Stanley and her tyrannical husband. No wonder Vanessa had run away from home!

'Cherry? If Vanessa's sister-in-law, Lizzie, comes to stay – and I promise she is lovely! She's married to Vanessa's brother, who is such a nice man. They are neither of them like their parents, who are truly awful. Well, you know Lady Lennox-Stanley—'

'Yes?' Cherry interrupted, possibly keen for Meg to get to the point.

'Would we have room for them? I expect it'll only be Lizzie and her little girl. Lizzie will be here to support Vanessa.'

Cherry considered. 'There are the attics. I thought your friend from France could go there if she managed to come—'

'Perfect!' said Meg. 'Lizzie and Alexandra – the Countess – were both my housemates in London.' She paused, mentally counting guest numbers. 'So there'll be room for everyone?'

'Alexandra's older stepchildren are teenagers,' said David. 'They could camp with the stage crew in the scout tent in the field. They'll love it!' he added. 'Don't you worry about a thing, Meggy. It's all going to be fine!'

Cherry smiled. 'There are four bedrooms in the attic, near to a bathroom and with a lovely view out of the window. When it's not raining, of course.'

'The rain is due to clear up later,' said Meg, wishing she felt more confident about this. 'Bob told me. Some old countryman's lore.' She turned to David. 'Do you know when Russell is likely to arrive? We've spoken on the phone several times but I've never managed to pin him down. Also, Dame Miriam?'

337

David shook his head. 'They won't arrive together and it won't be until mid-afternoon, I believe.'

'We've got a cold collation planned for lunch,' said Meg. 'So it can be served at any time.'

David nodded. 'I'm going to say hello to Susan.'

Cherry looked at Meg. 'That David: he turns up out of the blue but the moment he's through the door, we're depending on him!'

Meg laughed. 'And he always comes up trumps!'

'Meg!' said Louise, while they were slicing hard-boiled eggs in half for the collation. 'Why don't you take Nessa over to your flat so she can make herself tidy?'

'Her case is in my car,' said David, who'd just come into the kitchen. 'Although it's not very big.'

Meg interpreted this as him saying Vanessa didn't have enough clothes. As Meg didn't have many clothes herself, Louise's wardrobe might have to be raided.

Vanessa's luggage collected (basically, a vanity case), they set off for Meg's little flat. 'It's a perfectly nice flat,' she said as they walked through the mizzle. 'But not exactly luxurious. It has a shower but you have to run around under it to catch the drops of water.'

'Don't worry,' said Vanessa, who seemed to be cheering up. 'At boarding school we had to have strip washes except for once a week when we were allowed a bath. And coming from the gentry, I'm used to spartan living.'

Meg laughed. When she had first met Vanessa at the little cookery school in London, she had thought she was like many of the other girls, posh and a bit stuck-up. She soon discovered that, actually, Vanessa was huge fun and had just been shy when they first met.

When Meg's abode had been examined and declared 'Absolutely fine!' by Vanessa, Meg said, 'Do you want to tell me about calling off your wedding? Or have you had enough of that?'

'I told Louise most of it,' said Vanessa. 'Your mother's so kind, isn't she? Runs in the family! The wedding just became too much for me. And the parents are so absolutely livid with me. I can never go home again.' She was smiling, as if making a joke, but Meg could tell she genuinely believed this.

'But what about Simon? Don't you love him any more?' This seemed very unlikely, somehow.

Vanessa shook her head. 'I don't know how I feel about him. I try to imagine hearing that he's ill or something and I can't feel anything. That's terrible of me, isn't it? But I seem to have lost the ability to feel anything except miserable.' She smiled to imply she was joking, but she obviously wasn't.

'How did he take the news that you'd called off the wedding?' asked Meg. 'Was he devastated?'

Vanessa gave a dramatic shrug. 'I don't know. I just wrote him a letter and haven't heard from him since.'

Meg didn't know what to make of this, so changed the subject. 'You do know your mother is coming here for the play? Now it's been rescheduled, Russell made a point of getting her to come.'

Vanessa nodded. 'I'll find somewhere to hide while she's here.' Then she frowned a little. 'You know, it's really quite freeing to think I might never have to put up with my grumpy father or snobbish, bossy mother ever again.'

Meg didn't think she should openly agree with Vanessa's summing up of her parents, although she did, completely. 'Come on, let me give you a peek at where Dame Miriam will be staying, unless she changes her mind and wants to come back into the house. I think the rain has nearly stopped. Shall we go out and see?'

The cottage was a short walk away through the stable yard. It was one of the largest of the staff cottages and at one time would have housed the head groom and two under grooms.

'What do you think?' asked Meg, having unlocked the back door and led Vanessa through to the main room.

'Oh my goodness!' Vanessa clapped her hands. 'It's wonderful!'

Meg was pleased. 'Mum worked very hard on it, getting the right textiles, so it looks in keeping but is cosy and comfortable.'

'What about the bathroom?'

'There were three quite large rooms upstairs, so Bob – you remember, Susan's husband – has stolen a little bit from two of them to make space for a bathroom. It's small but should be OK.'

'Let's go and see.'

Vanessa looked round the bedroom. There was a large, comfortable-looking bed, a small wardrobe and a little dressing table with an antique dressing-table set consisting of little trays, candlesticks and small bowls. On the wide windowsill was a matching ewer and washing bowl. The bedspread was faded cotton and bits of the same fabric edged the new curtains and cushions.

'This is all so pretty!'

'When the play was going to be on earlier, and before she fell over and broke her hip, Ambrosine found some bedspreads in a chest in the nursery. This is the best one. It's very faded, of course, and fragile, but still pretty. The dressing-table set and jug and bowl had all been shoved in an attic. But of course Ambrosine knew where it all was.'

'I think Dame Miriam is going to absolutely love it.'

Meg smiled and shrugged. 'I'd prefer Dame Miriam to love being in the main house where it will be so much easier to get meals to her, but she must have what she wants.'

'What will she do about meals?'

'Someone will bring round baskets with food in them, like Little Red Riding Hood.'

Vanessa laughed. 'This is so adorable. Old-fashioned but perfect.'

'Ambrosine is going to fill the jug with flowers if she's up to it. In fact, I'll take the jug to her room so she can do it sitting down if she wants to. Dame Miriam could arrive at any moment! But hang on, let's nip into the bathroom, then I can say I've checked it, if Russell asks me.'

The bath was small and there was a footstool leading up to it. 'This is really sweet too,' said Vanessa.

'The bathrooms in the house are better but Bob was very clever squeezing in a bathroom here at all. I'm not quite sure where the grooms who used to live here washed. In basins with jugs of water, I expect. There's a privy in the garden.'

'Are all the cottages as good as this?'

'Not quite. This was Mum's special project. She'd have made the others as lovely if she'd had time.'

Vanessa looked a little awkward. 'Your mother told me she and Andrew are getting married. How do you feel about that? Is it a bit weird?'

'I'm quite used to the idea,' said Meg. 'And I'm delighted. I've never seen Mum so keen on anyone before. I think marriage is the right thing for her.' Meg thought about their lives before her mother had come to Nightingale Woods. 'I've always felt obliged to look after her – not in a day-to-day way – but I've always wanted her to have a home that's hers, and not attached to a job.'

She laughed at herself suddenly. 'Of course, this home is completely tied up with her job, but she'll have a say in what goes on. No one can fire her – or make it so she has to leave, just like that. She should never be homeless again.' Meg stopped, realising that the same would soon apply to her: she was about to own a third of Nightingale Woods.

*

An hour later, a very smart red Mini shot up the drive through the drizzle to the front of the hotel and out came a young man who looked as if he would be very charming were he not so hot and flustered. 'Dame Miriam is coming just behind me!' he announced urgently when he reached the front desk. 'Her chauffeur is driving. I'm just here to check the accommodation.'

'Would you like a drink of water first?' said Meg, who'd seen the car drive up and had gone into the hall to greet him.

'Actually, that would be fab! My name is Inigo.' He gulped the water that Meg brought him. 'Can I see where you're putting the jewel in the crown of the London stage?'

Meg laughed, immediately taking a liking to this young man. 'We were informed she wanted a cottage and we've got one we hope she'll like but we all feel – people from the hotel, I mean – that she'd be more comfortable in one of our luxury rooms.'

'You're probably right but she's got her heart set on something rustic, to fit in with the play. Let's have a look.'

But when Inigo saw the head groom's cottage he relaxed. 'I genuinely do think she'll be comfortable here,' he said when he'd inspected all the rooms. 'She might want me to sleep in the other bedroom, in case she needs anything in the night.' He exhaled. 'Looking after one of the finest – if not the finest – actresses of our age is such an honour, but it is, frankly, exhausting!'

343

'Is she difficult?' asked Meg, pleased that the cottage everyone – her mother in particular – had worked so hard on passed muster.

'Not at all, but because of who she is, we all think we have to check she's not just being accommodating and really wants whatever it is she's said she wants.' He took another breath. 'Is there any chance I can grab a sandwich before she gets here?'

They went back to the kitchen where Susan, who was indulgent towards handsome young men with lovely manners, was obviously charmed by him.

'We've got chicken salad – my best coronation recipe which makes sure the chicken is really moist,' said Meg.

'You could have that in a sandwich if you liked,' said Susan, although she knew it had been specially prepared for Dame Miriam.

'Or there's local crab, which we got for our special guests,' said Meg, who didn't mind about the chicken because there was plenty. 'We tried to get lobster but there was none available.'

'Or there's ham,' said Susan, still focused on feeding the good-looking young man. 'From our butcher who specialises in pork. Best there is. Now, what sort of sandwich do you really want?'

Inigo said everything sounded perfect but opted for ham and had eaten two sturdy doorsteps before a car was heard and he shot out of the kitchen to receive Dame Miriam.

Not wanting to miss the arrival of this prestigious guest, everyone else in the kitchen followed him.

Meg, who couldn't rid herself of the notion that a theatrical dame must look similar to a pantomime dame, took a breath as she watched Inigo help her from the car.

Dame Miriam looked as if she'd stepped out of a painting by Renoir, only fairy-sized. She was extremely pretty in her matching dress and coat and large picture hat. She was smiling in a way that spread sunshine through the greyness. It was, Meg realised, very easy to imagine her playing Titania. Inigo was carrying an enormous handbag, which was obviously too big and heavy for Dame Miriam to carry herself.

Inigo and the chauffeur led her up the steps to the hotel, and as she came nearer, the lines became visible and her true age more apparent.

'Darlings!' she announced in the foyer. 'Isn't this just heaven! I thought Russell must be exaggerating when he said how lovely it is here, but I see that he didn't at all!'

Meg stepped forward, wishing her mother would emerge from wherever she'd disappeared to. 'Good afternoon, Dame Miriam. I'm Meg. It's such an honour for us to have you here.' She hadn't prepared a speech, although now she felt she should have done.

'Dear child! It's always a joy to work with Russell and I love the *Dream* so much. Inigo, darling, can you pass me by bag?' She rummaged in it for a few moments and eventually produced a lace handkerchief. 'I know it's silly but ever since I was in *The Importance of Being Earnest*, I've felt obliged to have a

345

bag big enough to keep a baby in. Luckily, I've got this darling boy to carry it around for me.'

'There's a charming little cottage for you to stay in,' said Inigo. 'Would you like to see it now?'

'Maybe a restorative cup of tea first?' asked Dame Miriam. 'If that's not too much trouble?'

'Of course,' said Meg, aware of Susan flying back to the kitchen. 'Can I suggest you sit in the drawing room until it arrives?' She ushered her charming guest to a chair and table in the window seat.

Ambrosine, looking very much better after her rest, appeared too. 'Dame Miriam? If I may? I just had to tell you, I saw your Viola, just after the war . . .' She clasped her hands to her breast. 'I was transported!'

As Inigo was also with her, Meg withdrew to the kitchen. Dame Miriam had seemed enchanted by Ambrosine's memory of her Viola, so Meg was free to focus on suitable refreshments for a great actress.

'She's asked for tea,' Meg explained to Susan. 'And because she's so like a fairy, I seem to think she can only eat fairy-sized food.' Meg filled a plate with tiny meringues and eclairs.

Susan had made sandwiches and had cut them into fingers, no crusts, very easy to eat and a choice of fillings. 'That Inigo will eat anything left over, you mark my words. Lads that age have all got hollow legs.'

Meg put three cups and saucers on the tray with the teapot, milk and sugar, in case anyone else was invited, and took it through. Susan followed with a tall cake stand bearing a selection of food which could have been elevenses, lunch, afternoon tea, or all three.

When Meg went back a few minutes later with more hot water, Ambrosine and Dame Miriam were chatting away like best friends. It seemed they had an acquaintance in common and lots else besides.

'Delightful for Dame Miriam to have someone to talk to about her glory days in the theatre,' said Inigo, popping into the kitchen to reassure them nothing else was required. 'They're getting on like a house on fire!'

'I just hope Ambrosine doesn't get overtired,' said Meg to Susan when they were alone again.

'She's a tough one,' said Susan. 'Now, Meg, what's all this about her making over her share of Nightingale Woods to you?'

How on earth did Susan know about that? Meg thought. She had told absolutely no one – not even her best friends. Then she sighed. Family retainers, especially those like Susan, always seemed to know everything.

Chapter Thirty-Five

Meg and Louise were in the office the following morning. Meg was there to be near the telephone in case Justin rang. Although every moment of every day was filled, all Meg could think about was him, although when they heard a car drive up, she didn't go out. It was the throaty roar of a motorbike that Meg was longing to hear.

Then Meg heard a familiar voice and rushed into the hall.

'Lizzie!' she said, hugging her friend life-threateningly hard. Then she turned to the little girl who was hiding behind her mother, possibly startled by the whirlwind who had just appeared. 'Letty?' Meg said gently. 'You won't remember me but I'm a very good friend of your mother's.'

Letty nodded obligingly but held on firmly to her mother's leg. Meg turned back to her old friend. 'You remember my mother? Louise?'

Louise had followed her daughter at a more sedate pace. 'I certainly remember you, Lizzie. We met in London.'

When her mother and Lizzie had exchanged greetings, Meg had one burning question. 'How did you get here so soon? We only sent up the smoke signals yesterday!'

Lizzie laughed. 'I know, but this is an emergency! With everything that is going on at the family pile, I thought I ought to do something pronto! That and wanting to get away from all the fallout from the biggest wedding of the year being cancelled.' She paused. 'The family chauffeur brought me. Hugo arranged it. His parents don't know; it was easier that way. As long as the chauffeur is back in time to bring my mother in law . . .'

'Lady Fussy-Knickers,' Meg said as an aside to Susan and Cherry, who had appeared. 'You didn't feel obliged to come with her and save your driver a journey?'

Lizzie shook her head. 'Nothing would induce her to share a car with a small child, and I quote. Anyway, I know Nessa won't want to see her. Where is she?' Lizzie went on. 'Is she OK?'

'She's upstairs,' said Louise. 'She's trying to see if she can find something suitable to wear in my wardrobe. She brought almost nothing to wear with her.'

'Mum has far more dresses and skirts than I do,' Meg explained.

'It seems I've arrived in the nick of time,' said Lizzie, obviously delighted. 'I brought my sewing machine. I have an electric one now.'

Louise laughed. 'I'll take you up!' She held her hand out to the little girl, who had now released her grip on her mother. 'Are you coming, Letty?'

Letty nodded and took the hand.

'I'm coming too,' said Meg, knowing that Cherry would fetch her if Justin did happen to ring while she was upstairs.

After Lizzie and Vanessa had greeted each other with laughter and a few tears, Louise excused herself. 'Can I take Letty down to the kitchen for a drink and a snack?'

'Of course!' said Lizzie. 'If she'll go.'

Louise crouched down in front of Letty. 'Would you like a drink? I bet you're thirsty after your long car journey.'

Letty considered. Possibly she was a bit thirsty.

'Come with me down to the kitchen,' Louise went on, 'and we'll find you some milk or squash. Maybe something to eat as well?'

Lizzie, Meg and Vanessa watched in amazement as Letty went with Louise, holding her hand, apparently completely happy.

'Isn't that lovely?' said Lizzie. 'She can be a bit nervous with older women. Obviously, my mother-in-law is terrifying and my mother tries far too hard and wants to be hugged and kissed all the time. Letty is affectionate but she usually needs to get used to people. Your mother obviously hit exactly the right note!'

'I'm afraid we call your mother-in-law Lady Fussy-Knickers,' said Meg.

Lizzie laughed. 'Our names for her aren't nearly as friendly.'

'Although one way or another she's got us a lot of new business so we're grateful to her too,' Meg went on. 'Nessa, did you find anything of Mum's you fancied wearing?'

'You mother has offered me a couple of lovely dresses, but they're all a bit long.'

'That's where I come in!' said Lizzie. 'Now, let's have a look . . .'

As she watched Lizzie pin up Louise's dresses while Vanessa stood on a chair, Meg explained her and Letty's accommodation. 'All the rooms on the top floor were part of the nursery quarters of the house. There are bars on the windows and I hope they don't make you feel like you're in a prison.'

'Do you remember that fateful weekend when we all stayed in the nursery for Hugo's party?' asked Lizzie. 'Those nursery quarters were enormous!'

'These aren't as big but still quite spacious.' Meg looked at her watch. She was restless now. Supposing Cherry couldn't shout loud enough to tell her if Justin rang?

Lizzie obviously guessed what Meg was feeling. 'Now, don't run off yet, Meggy,' she said, her mouth full of pins. 'I know that you won't have bought yourself a new dress for ages.' She gestured to a rather large suitcase and a cotton garment bag that someone had kindly brought upstairs.

Meg looked anxiously at her friend's luggage. 'Mum has given me a couple of nice things . . .'

'And I've been sewing for you. I know your meas-urements and unless you've changed hugely . . .' Lizzie got up from pinning Vanessa's hem and opened the suitcase. 'Here!'

She held up a short, high-waisted dress with a scoop neck, fitted sleeves with a deep frill at the elbows. 'Try it on. It's supposed to be a Dolly Rocker.'

'Oh, it's lovely, Meg!' said Vanessa.

Meg decided to stop thinking about Justin and try on the dress.

It fitted perfectly. 'Gosh! I feel so – modern!' said Meg. 'And the last time I bought anything was from the market in France, when I was with Alexandra.' She sighed. 'It feels a lifetime ago, now.'

'I bet it does,' said Vanessa, who was definitely more cheerful this morning.

Lizzie hadn't finished with adding to Meg's ward-robe. 'I also made this.' Lizzie turned to the garment bag and unzipped it. She lifted out a dress. 'I had the material left over from a dress I made for Patsy. She insisted I did something with the bits.'

The dress was in pale gold brocade with a dark blue velvet bodice. It had an A-line skirt coming out from under the bust. It was for parties and wouldn't look out of place at a ball.

'It's beautiful, Lizzie,' said Meg. 'But when would I ever wear anything like this?' She felt mean saying so, but it was the truth.

'David told me there was going to be a party after the performance, definitely,' Lizzie said.

'But I'd be working – Nessa could wear it though?'

'Try it on. Let me have the satisfaction of seeing you in it.'

'I'll borrow something from your mother,' said Vanessa. 'Let me help you with it . . .'

Meg did feel quite unlike herself in the beautiful dress. It was very stylish and made her look taller, slender, elegant.

'I don't look like me at all,' she said, looking at herself in the mirror on the door of a wardrobe. She couldn't help wondering what Justin would think about her in it.

'You look so beautiful!' said Lizzie. 'I imagined you'd look like that. It's so satisfying that my design worked so well. Patsy will be thrilled. I must remember to take a photograph. I've borrowed Hugo's camera.'

'It is quite thrilling looking so different,' said Meg, who couldn't stop staring at the elegant stranger in front of her who looked a bit like she did.

'Can we show David? And your mother?' asked Lizzie.

Meg was doubtful. 'I'm not walking through the hotel looking like this. Suppose someone saw me?'

Lizzie shook her head, smiled and sighed. 'Honestly, Meg, why would you mind anyone seeing you looking so beautiful?'

'I'm staff, Lizzie!'

'You're practically family from what I hear. Anyway, even staff are allowed to look lovely sometimes.'

Was this the moment to tell Lizzie and Vanessa about Ambrosine's gift to her, which would make her part-owner of Nightingale Woods? No, thought Meg. Wait until it's all definite with everything signed.

Meg gave Lizzie a hug. 'Thank you so much for making it for me. I absolutely love it!'

'And you promise you'll wear it at the party after the performance?' Lizzie persisted.

'I promise!' said Meg. 'Mum and David will have to wait until then to see me in it anyway. We're full tonight for dinner.'

'And what about Justin?' asked Vanessa.

'He'll have to wait too!'

There was a brief silence.

'And what about Simon?' said Lizzie to Vanessa.

Vanessa just shook her head and left the room, tears beginning to fall again.

'She does love him, doesn't she?' said Lizzie.

'I really think she does,' Meg agreed. 'If you remember, she told us before, when you were getting married, that she'd been in love with him since she was a little girl.'

'Simon needs to know that,' said Lizzie. 'If only we could find a way to tell him.'

Chapter Thirty-Six

Meg, Lizzie, Letty and Louise were coming out of the kitchen into the hall just as Dame Miriam came in through the front door of Nightingale Woods, accompanied as usual by Inigo and her enormous handbag.

'And who is that little fairy?' she said, looking at Letty. 'Darling! You are so enchanting! Is this your mother?'

Lizzie blushed deeply while Louise introduced them.

'I insist this little one is in the play!' said Dame Miriam. 'She can be one of my courtiers!'

'I don't think she could learn lines,' said Lizzie, doubtfully.

'She'll only need to look pretty, which she can do just by being there!' said Dame Miriam. 'I wonder if we could get her a costume?'

'My friend Lizzie is an expert seamstress—' began Meg.

'And she's here as second wardrobe mistress,' said David, who had followed Dame Miriam in.

Dame Miriam crouched down to Letty's level. 'Will you be in the play, darling? You'd wear a beautiful dress and dance around on stage with the other fairies? Would you like that?'

Letty considered, and then agreed that yes, she would.

'That's settled!' said Dame Miriam. Then she said, 'Meg, you should go and look at the theatre. It's nearly set up for tomorrow and I think this is our most beautiful venue yet! Truly magical.' She paused, 'Inigo, darling . . .

Chased from the kitchen by Cherry and Susan, Meg did as Dame Miriam had suggested. Apart from anything else, her favourite bench looked out on to the natural amphitheatre. She wanted to think as well as see what 'the theatricals' had been up to. Where was Justin? Why hadn't he been in touch?

Once at her favourite spot, all thoughts of Justin went from her head. It was if her favourite spot had been transported to fairyland.

There was the bench well placed to admire the garden, in an alcove backed by roses, jasmine and a scented clematis. The fragrance was heavenly.

Where once had been an empty stretch of rough grass, with trees at the far edges, was now a forest floor, and the trees now surrounded it. As she looked, Meg realised that there was a stage and painted scenery that blended with the real trees. A huge artificial moon hung in the sky, and tiny lights, like fireflies, were dotted everywhere on invisible wires, filling the sky with stars. At ground level huge exotic shrubs were actually flats, painted to look real and possibly there so actors could appear from behind them. Other plants, toadstools and rocks made the set look both real and a little bit frightening.

There were rows of seats set out and now she looked more closely, Meg spotted a huge tarpaulin, like a circus tent, stretched over the stage. It had looked like a starry sky. That must be in case the rain came back.

In spite of sounds of banging, the odd shout and other indications that it was a stage set, it was magical.

'Good, isn't it?' said a young man, who appeared to be one of the building team. 'Our best yet, I reckon.'

'I can't believe what I'm seeing!' said Meg. 'I come here almost every day but this looks as if it's been here forever.'

'Thank you! Dame Miriam loves it, and that makes the whole difference. I reckon you could guarantee we'd come here every year, if you wanted.'

'I think that would be brilliant. Although it wouldn't be up to me, of course.'

'You're Meg, right? Head chef? Inigo says the food is also the best yet, too.'

'Why, thank you!' Meg said, delighted, and was still smiling as the young man loped off to make some adjustment he deemed was required.

'So, who was that young man I just caught you chatting to?' said a deep voice with a hint of a laugh in it.

'Justin!' said Meg and flung herself into his arms.

It was a long time before they decided they'd kissed enough. Eventually they let each other go.

'Oh, Meggy, I've missed you so much!' said Justin. 'I thought I'd find you here. I was so glad I was right.'

'It hasn't been that long,' said Meg, momentarily forgetting how painful she had found their short separation. 'But where have you been?' What have you been doing?'

'Missing you,' he said, looking as if he was about to kiss her all over again.

Meg giggled, so happy she could hardly breathe. 'And in your spare time?'

'Bits and pieces, this and that, but all done now.'

'Will you be able to buy Colin out of Nightingale Woods? But, more importantly, do you really want to?' she asked. 'Haven't you always wanted your own restaurant?'

'Yes, I will be able to, and yes, I have always wanted my own restaurant – but I'll have one, right here. You don't have to be in London to be a successful restaurateur these days. With you as my pastry chef, the sky is the limit for us.'

She gave a little cough and swallowed to cover up the fact that his words were making her feel gooey and weak and very much in love.

He pulled her on to his knee and she rested her head on his shoulder. He was wearing his motorbike leathers and she could smell petrol and road dust on him. For some reason she found this very sexy. Then reality struck her. 'Oh my God, dinner!'

'I'm sure it's all under control,' said Justin into her ear, not letting her go.

'But I have to check! You know that, Justin.'

He sighed. She slid off his lap and they walked back to the house hand in hand.

Chapter Thirty-Seven

It was early the following morning when Meg took a tray of tea and toast to the staff dining room, which, until a few days ago, had been a storeroom. Vanessa, Lizzie and Letty were there. It was Saturday, the day of the play.

'This is like when we lived together in Alexandra's house in London,' said Lizzie, handing her daughter a finger of toast and Marmite.

'A bit,' said Vanessa, having had a gulp of tea, 'only then I wasn't terrified of what would happen when my mother turned up.'

'She knows you're here,' said Lizzie soothingly. 'But you don't have to greet her on the doorstep the moment she arrives at the hotel.'

'You don't have to greet her at all, if you don't want to,' said Meg. 'There are lots of good hiding places at Nightingale Woods.'

'Why does Nessa want to hide?' asked Letty.

The three women exchanged glances.

'Is Gan-Gan cross with you, Nessa? I can help you hide if you like,' said Letty, helping herself to more toast.

'Thank you, sweetie,' said Vanessa. 'That's very kind.'

'Only I can't help if the play is on because I'm being a fairy,' Letty went on.

'You are,' said Lizzie, 'and I must get on with your costume.'

'Will I have wings?' asked Letty.

Meg saw Lizzie's slightly agonised expression at the prospect of having to make wings as well as a dress. 'I don't think Titania – she's the Queen of the Fairies – has wings, so you may not have them,' she said. 'It wouldn't do to have something that she hasn't got.'

Letty's face fell, but only a little bit. She cheered up when Louise appeared a few moments later.

'You're up early!' said Louise. 'Couldn't you sleep?'

'I'm early because it's the day of the play, of course,' said Meg. 'I probably woke Nessa, however.'

'I wasn't sleeping anyway,' said Vanessa.

'And I'm up early because Letty woke up,' said Lizzie.

'OK,' said Louise. 'I'm afraid I've got bad news for you all. Alexandra telephoned last night and she doesn't think they're going to be able to make the play. She has car problems. But she'll come as soon as she can. She hopes to get here in a couple of days.'

'Oh,' said Meg, suddenly feeling a little flat.

'That is a shame,' said Lizzie. 'It means I may not see her.'

'I'm sure she'd go and visit you at home,' said Meg.

'Yes, of course she would,' said Lizzie, putting on a smile.

'Right,' said Louise. 'I'm now going to make you all more tea, and then Letty and I are going to pick flowers for Ambrosine. Do you need to have your clothes on to do that, or will you be all right in your dressing gown and slippers?'

Lizzie opened her mouth, possibly to volunteer an opinion, but her daughter forestalled her. 'I'll be all right in my dressing gown and slippers.'

When the flower team had gone to find secateurs and buckets, Lizzie said, 'I love my daughter very much, but I do wish she didn't wake up so early, especially now.' She looked at her friends a little shyly. 'I'm pregnant again.'

'Oh, Lizzie!' said Meg. 'That's wonderful!'

'We're delighted, of course, but it does mean I'm dreadfully tired all the time.'

'Will you manage being a wardrobe mistress? Making Letty a costume? You haven't got long.'

'It'll take me minutes! The company have given me a lovely bit of crystal nylon. I don't even have to hem it! She'll look just like a real fairy.'

'And we all know what they look like,' said Meg.

'Of course we do!' said Lizzie. 'I think Louise has been distracted from the tea. Shall I make some more?'

'You sit down,' said Meg firmly. 'I'll make it. And then, scrambled eggs? I can just do it for us. Justin said he'd do breakfast with Susan.'

'He's very dashing, isn't he?' said Lizzie.

Meg blushed. 'I suppose so,' she mumbled.

'He's a dish!' said Vanessa. 'Almost as gorgeous as—' She paused and gulped.

'Simon,' said Lizzie quietly.

'I've burnt my boats, haven't I?' said Vanessa. 'He'll never speak to me again. He must hate me now.

Mummy said I've practically left him standing at the altar.'

'No such thing,' said Meg, brisk now. 'Don't even think about any of that today. Just focus on enjoying yourself and being David's assistant.'

'Did I hear my name?' said David, entering the room wearing a very colourful dressing gown.

'You did,' said Meg. 'Now you all stay here while I make you breakfast to eat. And get you more tea!'

Justin was in the kitchen when Meg got there and, having greeted Meg, a process which took a little while, agreed to make scrambled eggs and bring it through to the staff dining room.

Shortly afterwards, although it was only seven o'clock, the actors who were staying in the hotel were starting to appear. Inigo came to collect Dame Miriam's breakfast. As David said over eggs and toast, performance day had dawned!

Justin and Meg had done the lunchtime service together and she realised what a good team they made, although, thinking back, they had worked well together for that first big, important banquet, even though they were hardly speaking. They shared a brief, hard kiss before Meg left to go and check what was going on in the office.

Vanessa was in the hall and Meg was about to speak when they both heard noises which indicated one thing: Lady Lennox-Stanley was about to emerge through the front door.

They fled to the office and ducked down behind the desk, giggling hysterically. 'It's her,' Meg hissed to a confused Louise. 'Lady Fussy-Knickers. She's here!'

'I can't meet her. She'll kill me!' said Vanessa, no longer giggling, holding on to the waste-paper basket for moral support.

'I'd better go out then,' said Louise, and went to greet one of Nightingale Woods' most important guests.

When the coast was clear, and Lady Lennox-Stanley had been safely escorted to the Yellow Room (newly refurbished with its own bathroom and a delightful view of the gardens and the hills of Dorset beyond, as the brochure declared), Meg and Vanessa stood up and brushed down their clothes.

'I'll do office work for you,' said Vanessa. 'Then I won't feel so stupid hiding in here.'

'I thought you were going to be helping David?' said Meg.

'I asked him earlier, but he didn't have anything for me really. I just need to keep out of sight of my mother. I don't want a scene right now. Although I do know one is inevitable.'

Meg glanced at her friend, close to tears, and then looked at the desk, snatching up the handwritten menu she and Justin had discussed earlier. She handed it to Vanessa.

'Could you type this out three times, please? We can't use carbon copies and Dame Miriam needs her own copy.'

'Oh, of course I can do that. I did them before when I was here.'

Meg smiled and rubbed her friend's arm in a supportive way, glad that Vanessa didn't ask who the third menu was for. Meg had just felt typing only two copies wouldn't take up enough time.

Putting card into the typewriter and scrutinising Justin's slapdash handwriting to make sure she had everything right seemed to calm Vanessa down, and quite soon Meg felt she could leave her to go into the kitchen to see how the plans for dinner were going.

Justin was very firm. 'I'm going to let you make the desserts – they are your forte – but then you're coming out of the kitchen.'

'But, Justin, you know how full we are! Two sittings for dinner, the party—'

'Which is being catered by my old hotel.'

Meg had known this but had chosen to ignore it. 'There's still a lot to do for just you and Susan.'

Justin frowned and put his hands on her shoulders. 'You deserve the time off, Meggy. If it wasn't for you, none of this would be happening. You deserve to see the play like a proper paying member of the audience.'

Not entirely sure she was happy with the situation, Meg let herself be shooed from the kitchen. At least she'd been allowed to make a couple of really fabulous confections for the dessert trolley.

Lizzie seemed to be lying in wait for her. 'Come on! You're going to change into the dress I made you,' she said.

'To watch the play in?' said Meg. 'We'll be sitting in the garden. The dress is too grand for that, surely?'

'David told me that people really dress up for these plays,' said Lizzie. 'They treat it like Glyndebourne, especially with Dame Miriam in it.'

'Really?'

Lizzie nodded. 'And the party is straight afterwards.'

Vanessa appeared from the office. 'Are you going to help Meg get dressed? Can I come?'

'Actually, Nessa, you couldn't be very kind and go up to the attics? You can use the back stairs. Meg's mum has got Letty, but I know there are things she needs to do. You could take Letty to join the other actors in a little while?' She took a breath. 'Your mother has gone up to get changed. You'll be quite safe.'

Lizzie wasn't usually bossy, Meg realised, but now she seemed very determined. Vanessa obviously reached the same conclusion and made for the back stairs with no further argument.

'I am capable of getting dressed on my own, you know,' said Meg as Lizzie accompanied her to the flat.

'I know, but I need to tell you – I had a message from Hugo.'

'Oh, did he ring? Nessa has been in the office—'

Lizzie shook her head. 'He sent a message with Lady Fussy-Knickers' chauffeur. Hugo and Vanessa have known the chauffeur since they were children. He often used to get them out of scrapes.'

Meg nodded. 'That's very useful. But can't you tell me what he said? You don't need to come with me.'

They were at the foot of the fire escape that led to the door of the flat.

'I'm still coming. I might need to make last-minute alterations and I want to make sure you don't leave on your chef's trousers by mistake. Also,' Lizzie went on, 'I've been longing to take my scissors to your hair.'

Meg shrieked. 'Have you become a hairdresser since I last saw you?'

Lizzie laughed. 'I suppose I have!'

When Meg, showered and in her bra and pants, was sitting on her bed with a towel round her shoulders, with Lizzie snipping at her hair, the plan was explained.

'You remember that Simon is Hugo's best friend, don't you?' she asked.

'Of course. Simon was Hugo's best man,' said Meg, frowning slightly.

'Sorry,' said Lizzie. 'I think being pregnant has gone to my brain. Well, Hugo is going to bring Simon to the play tonight.'

'Really? Oh my goodness! That's wonderful! Nessa will be thrilled – if she doesn't die of shock.'

'Yes, but the thing is, Hugo doesn't know exactly when they'll get here. I've told David already, and he says he'll get good seats out of my mother-in-law's sightline. He'll make Nessa sit inside and you and he will sit at the end. Then, when Hugo and Simon turn up, you and David can nip out, and Simon will sit next to Nessa.'

'OK. It sounds a bit complicated.'

'It's not really,' said Lizzie. 'It's probably just the way I've explained it. Anyway, if they don't arrive during the play, and only turn up when the party is going strong, they'll find you. But you've got to stick to Nessa like a leech, in case she leaves early, which she'll want to do because she's avoiding her mother – aren't we all? And, well, she's unhappy.' Lizzie seemed excited. 'But Simon was so relieved to hear from Hugo. He had been devastated when Nessa called off the wedding. He thought it was something he'd done.'

Meg allowed herself to think of Justin, how she'd long to go to him the moment he appeared at the party, if he couldn't make the play. 'I'll do my best to keep Nessa under guard,' she said, not sounding enthusiastic.

Lizzie obviously realised what Meg was feeling. 'I'd love to help the lovers get together myself, but I'll have to field Letty the moment she's done her bit. She'll be tired and I don't want her to have a tantrum, especially with her grandmother here. Imagine the horror on Lady Lennox-Stanley's face, seeing her only grandchild face down in the mud, drumming her fists and screaming.'

Meg smiled. 'She might feel Letty's a kindred spirit! And it's fine. I'm really happy to keep my eye on Nessa.' She paused. 'Tell me one thing, does Letty really call her Gan-Gan?'

'I'm afraid so!'

A few moments later, Lizzie whisked Meg's face for hair with a tissue. 'What about that?' she said. She had snipped and combed and moved Meg about. She held up the mirror that Meg had avoided looking in.

'Who is that girl?' said Meg, staring at herself. Lizzie hadn't done much but suddenly Meg's eyes looked enormous and her cheekbones sharp. 'I look really – I don't know – as if I don't live in the country.'

Lizzie laughed. 'I'll take that as a compliment. But I'm glad I've got my dressmaking scissors, and not just the kitchen ones that Alexandra used to use.'

'I'm afraid she still does,' said Meg.

'Really? And her a countess and all.' Lizzie laughed. 'Such a shame she's been delayed.'

'I know! But they'll be here soon, if not today.' Meg was still staring at her reflection. 'I can't believe it's me.'

'The right fringe does a lot. You do look fab. Now, what about make-up?'

'I don't wear much—' Meg began.

'You don't need much,' said Lizzie. 'Just a little mascara . . .'

'I really am like Cinderella,' said Meg as they walked back across the courtyard. 'I worked in the kitchen and now I'm transformed!'

'Hmph,' said Lizzie. 'I had to do a teeny bit more than wave a wand over a couple of white mice and a pumpkin, but I am very satisfied with my efforts.'

'And while I may be transformed, I do need to just check things are OK. Someone may have schmushed my Black Forest gateau.'

It was an excuse to see Justin in the kitchen, but, to her disappointment, he wasn't there. When asked,

Susan couldn't say where he was and was so uninterested that Meg almost suspected her of knowing more than she admitted to.

But her gateau was still a cream- and chocolate-covered delight, and with this she had to be satisfied.

Meg was about to look for Vanessa in the attics when she appeared from the office with Louise. They were both wearing long dresses and had their hair styled.

'I've left Letty with Inigo,' said Vanessa. 'He came up just before we were about to get ready and, like an angel, took her away. I think Letty plans to marry him.'

'Fine by me,' said Lizzie. 'You both look lovely, by the way. But I must get the smallest fairy in the show into her costume.'

'Oh, darling!' said Louise as she caught sight of Meg. 'You look – beautiful!'

David came down the stairs at that moment, looking very handsome and actor-like in his dinner jacket. He stopped when he saw her. 'Meggy, you look absolutely stunning.'

Meg was blushing. 'It's all down to Lizzie. A lovely dress and a new haircut.'

'And Vanessa,' David said, turning his attention to her. 'You look equally lovely. I do like your dress. And the little locket on that black velvet ribbon makes your skin look like Dorset cream!'

'The dress is one of mine,' said Louise. 'But the locket is Nessa's. I just gave her the ribbon.'

369

'Golly, Ness!' said Meg. 'You look like a princess.'

'You both look like princesses,' said David. Then he held out his arms, crooked, ready to hook into the arms of his companions. 'Ladies? Shall we process to the entertainment?'

Chapter Thirty-Eight

Inigo had reserved three seats at the end of a row for them. Meg made sure she was at the end.

'It really is like being transported to fairyland,' Vanessa said to David. 'I've been hiding from my mother all day so haven't seen any of this.' She gestured to the surroundings. 'It's magical!'

'The fact that it's stopped raining and it's a beautiful evening really does help,' David said. 'The rain seems to have really brought the fragrance out of the roses and the fig tree. It smells like Harrods' cosmetic department.'

'Far better than that,' said Meg. 'I can't wait to see Letty. I know Lizzie made her a costume in about five minutes flat.'

'Easier when you're dealing with a very small fairy,' said David, and then laughed.

'I wonder where my mother is sitting,' said Vanessa. 'Can you look, Meg?'

Meg scanned the audience and then spotted Lady Lennox-Stanley. She was sitting next to Basil Knott-Dean and seemed very happy. Considering she was supposed to be devastated by her daughter calling off the wedding of the season at very short notice, she was bearing up surprisingly well.

'She's two rows ahead of us, and in the middle,' Meg reported. 'If she sees you, you'll have plenty of time to make a quick getaway.'

Vanessa laughed.

'Now, quiet, children. The play's about to start,' said David.

There was music and then the curtain, drawn by long ropes attached to the trees, was hauled up out of the way.

Because Meg's mind was so full, in the beginning she found it hard to lose herself in the play, but when Dame Miriam, as Titania, came on, she was entranced.

The elderly lady with a large handbag who was fussed over by everyone was no more and in her place was a beautiful and powerful fairy queen. She commanded her fairies (including a tiny Letty who looked as if she might take flight at any moment) and ultimately her husband Oberon with perfect control.

But all the actors were brilliant. Meg and the entire audience clapped and clapped until their hands were sore. There was only one disappointment: Simon and Hugo hadn't yet appeared, and Meg was upset for Vanessa's sake.

People were still shouting 'bravo' and 'encore' when the stage hands, dressed in black from head to toe, began to turn what had been a theatre into a party venue. What had been a stage and an area for the audience was now a covered dance floor with a raised platform for a band. There were suddenly little lights in the trees and draped around the supports for the canvas roof. Meg realised they must have put the lights there earlier and just turned them on now, but to her it looked as if Tinkerbell from *Peter Pan* had flown about with her wand, creating magic.

Everyone was already in very high spirits, dancing, drinking champagne, toasting each other and pairing up.

'It's nearly the end of the season,' David said. 'Everyone is getting a bit demob happy. No one has to worry about misbehaving or having a hangover. It's just a celebration.'

'Almost all the cast members can play instruments,' David explained. 'When a production is travelling round the country, they try to keep the company as small as they can. But Russell has got in a proper band for this party.'

'It's such a shame Alexandra will miss all this,' said Meg. 'I know I keep saying that!'

'Never say die, Meggy!' he replied. 'Now where's that Nessa got too?'

They spotted Vanessa dancing with Inigo and little Letty. She seemed to have forgotten about trying to keep out of sight of her mother.

'She's having fun,' said Meg, pleased.

'Uh-oh,' said David sharply. 'Who's that cutting in? Oh good Lord!'

Meg ran forward, ready to rescue Vanessa if necessary. She was in time to see a tall dark stranger wrap his arms around Vanessa and kiss her, long and hard.

'What on earth is going on?' demanded Lady Lennox-Stanley, suddenly right by the couple, obviously furious.

'I'm claiming my bride,' said Simon. 'And if she'll still have me, we're going to elope! My darling Vanessa, will you still marry me?'

'Oh, Simon!' said Vanessa. 'All I want is to be married to you! But I couldn't face that enormous wedding!'

Lady Lennox-Stanley stood there, gaping. Eventually she enquired of no one in particular, 'If you're getting married after all, does it mean we don't have to send all the wedding presents back?'

Utterly delighted to see her friend united with the love of her life, Meg turned to David, but instead found herself being hugged by Alexandra.

'Lexi!' Meg said. 'You made it! Did you see the play?'

'I'm afraid not but I caught the main drama! Isn't Simon gorgeous? And good for Nessa. Eloping is so much more romantic than having a big society wedding.'

Alexandra's husband, Antoine, stepped forward. 'Hello, Meg. You are looking particularly charming tonight, if I may say so.' He kissed her on both cheeks.

Meg sighed happily. 'Are your children here as well?'

Antoine nodded. 'They are somewhere about, but more to the point, where is Justin?'

Meg's high spirits descended. 'Doing something in the kitchen, I expect. Seriously,' she went on, hoping she didn't sound too bereft and eager to change the subject, 'do you really not know where the children are?'

'All is well. They were kidnapped by some very charming young people who apparently work as stage hands, musicians and actors,' said Antoine. 'They went very willingly.'

'Next year Henri could join the band,' said Alexandra, 'and of course Félicité could paint scenery. But perhaps Stéphie is a little young to have a holiday job. Although she'd be very fed up, having to stay at home with us.'

Antoine shrugged. 'Perhaps! Meg? Could I have the pleasure of this dance?'

Meg shook her head. 'I've got things to do. You really want to dance with your wife anyway.'

Seeing them waltzing around the floor, Meg knew that she was right. They were so in tune with each other's movements, so completely and utterly in love. She looked around for David, so she could share this observation with him, but he had gone.

Inigo stood in his place. 'David told me to tell you that he's been summoned by Dame Miriam and that you're welcome to join them.' He looked at Meg. 'You don't fancy a trot round the floor with me, do you? At the risk of me trampling on you?'

Meg laughed. 'Not really,' she said. 'There's a lovely girl over there and I'm sure you wouldn't trample on her.'

Then Meg spotted Ambrosine. She and her colonel were sitting down, watching the party, looking very content. Meg ran over. 'Ambrosine! How are you? You're not getting too tired, are you?'

Ambrosine made a swishing gesture. 'The colonel here will hardly let me take a step unaccompanied. I am thoroughly enjoying myself. We're saving ourselves for a spirited tango later.'

Meg gasped and then realised she was being teased. She stood with Ambrosine and her beau, watching the party, not quite sure what she should do. Maybe she should go and look for Justin?

She saw David and Dame Miriam in the semicircle of chairs where she was sitting, holding court in the most gracious way imaginable, still every inch a queen although she was no longer dressed as Titania, Queen of the Fairies.

Then the band struck up 'Some Enchanted Evening' and Dame Miriam turned to David.

'She's asking him to dance,' said Ambrosine. 'I bet he's a lovely dancer.'

They watched as tall David led the diminutive actress on to the floor. They danced beautifully together. Dame Miriam was looking so happy and Meg knew David would be enjoying himself enormously.

''E's a damned good-looking chap, *non*?' said a man with a French accent.

'Maxime!' said Meg. 'You came with Alexandra?'

'We came in separate cars. Antoine's car was extremely full.' He kissed Meg on both cheeks and then Meg made the introductions.

'*Enchanté, madame*,' he said to Ambrosine and kissed her hand.

Ambrosine spoke to him in French and introduced the colonel. To Meg's surprise, the colonel spoke fluent French too. She made her excuses and left them chatting happily.

She was delighted for David that Maxime had come and knew it wouldn't be long until they found each other.

She felt suddenly tired. Justin was nowhere to be seen and she felt sad and let down. What was the point of her new dress if Justin wasn't going to see her in it? He was obviously busy, and they would catch up with each other tomorrow, but it was now that she wanted him. Her feet ached, and the fact that Vanessa now wasn't going to be in her little flat so he could have spent night with her was just depressing. She felt tears gather in the back of her throat and she had to concentrate on not dissolving into a heap of self-pity.

She heard footsteps running up behind her and turned sharply. It was Justin, slightly out of breath. 'There you are!'

'Yes!' She tried to smile and hoped her tears, nearer now, wouldn't betray her feelings of abandonment.

'I've been scouring the party for you but there are so many people it took me a while.' He frowned. 'Are you OK?'

'Oh yes! I'm just a bit tired, that's all.'

'Not too tired, I hope. I have a little walk planned for us.'

Meg wanted to say, 'No need to walk anywhere, Vanessa and Simon have run away to get married and my flat is empty,' but she couldn't. It sounded so brazen somehow. She loved him and was sure that he loved her too, but at that moment, she didn't feel comfortable asking him to go to bed with her, more or less.

He held out his hand. 'If you're really exhausted, I could get out my motorbike and give you a backie, but it is rather noisy.'

Suddenly she laughed and her doubts and fears dissipated. 'A backie? Is it really called a backie, like when we were children and rode about on bicycles?'

'Well, most people call it riding pillion but I thought the idea might scare you.' He looked at her in a way that made Meg feel desired and protected at the same time.

He held out his hand again. 'Come!'

Chapter Thirty-Nine

❦

As Justin took her hand, all the magic and the beauty of the night returned. No longer was Meg a tired chef at the end of a long day. She was a girl walking on a beautiful summer's night with the man she loved.

'Is it far?' she asked after a little while. Ahead she could see that the path was too narrow for them to walk hand in hand and although the moon was full its light was obscured by trees.

'Not really.' He pulled her closely to his side. 'I have a torch but, frankly, the moon gives us better light.'

Suddenly they turned a corner and there in front of them was a house, its windows glowing with light.

'Oh my goodness! Why didn't I know this house was here?' asked Meg, intrigued and enchanted.

'It's the gamekeeper's cottage,' said Justin. 'It's too far away from the house for you to come across, normally.' He laughed. 'Just as well, or you'd have made it guest accommodation – in the middle of the woods, like in Hansel and Gretel. But it's safe. Come on in. The door's not locked.'

The wooden door opened on to a room filled with lamplight. There seemed to be a light on every surface and there was a fire flickering in the grate.'

'I had to get all this lit and then come and find you before the fire went out.'

'But it's summer!' said Meg, entering the house.

'I know, but these old cottages can be damp and smell a bit mouldy. Besides, I love a fire in summer. Otherwise people feel obliged to wear cardigans.'

Meg started to laugh. 'Cardigans! Honestly, Justin!'

'It would be a shame to wear a cardigan over that lovely dress, Meggy.'

'I'm not even sure I own a cardigan,' said Meg. 'I'd have had to borrow one from my mother.'

'I obviously knew that,' he said. 'Hence the fire. Come and sit by it. There should really be a wooden settle there, but they are very uncomfortable. This sofa, on the other hand, is fine. I'll pull it round.'

Meg found herself putting her hands out to warm in the firelight. 'It isn't cold outside at all, but having a fire is lovely. This cottage reminds me of where Lizzie lives.'

'Is that a good thing?' asked Justin, who seemed a little on edge.

'It's a very good thing,' said Meg, smiling up at him. 'Why don't you sit down next to me?'

'Music first!' He went to the table where a wind-up gramophone stood. 'There's no electricity in this house. I didn't have time to organise that. I bought this gramophone and a pile of seventy-eight records in a little junk shop.'

Soon the house was filled with rather scratchy jazz music.

'Our own private party!' said Meg, relaxing more as every moment passed.

'I've got food,' he said. 'You can't expect a chef to do anything romantic that doesn't involve food.'

Although she didn't say it, Meg felt the situation was indeed romantic. 'A four-course meal?' she suggested instead.

'I'm afraid not. Are you hungry? Have you had anything to eat this evening?'

Meg hadn't really noticed at the time but now she remembered that she hadn't. 'I'm starving.'

'It's only a picnic but Susan helped me make it so it's ample.'

He disappeared into the kitchen and came out with a hamper. He pulled up a little table and put the hamper on it, but still he wouldn't sit down. He went back to the kitchen and came back with a bottle of champagne and glasses. Only when he'd put on another record and opened the bottle and filled the glasses did he sit down.

'Are we celebrating something?' asked Meg, indicating the champagne.

'I do hope so!' said Justin. He seemed to be getting more and more flustered, completely lacking in his usual swagger and confidence.

'Well, what is it? What do you want to celebrate? The play? Nightingale Woods?'

'Oh, Meg! It's not like you to be dense. I'm going to ask you to marry me. The champagne is to celebrate our engagement!'

A smile spread across Meg's face and her heart swelled with happiness. 'So, if you do actually ask me to marry you, and I say no, I'm not allowed the champagne?' she said solemnly, her heart singing.

He nodded. And to her relief, he didn't get down on one knee, he just sat on the sofa next to her and took hold of her hands. 'Will you marry me, Meggy?'

She took a deep breath. 'Of course I will!'

'Thank goodness for that. I wasn't at all sure that you'd say yes. I can be such a grumpy, difficult so-and-so.'

She laughed but she didn't deny it.

Then he took her into his arms and they kissed long after the music had stopped.

'If we don't drink the champagne soon, it'll go flat,' said Meg eventually, breathless with happiness.

'It won't,' said Justin, but he did let her go and hand her a glass. 'To us!' he said.

'To us, and to Nightingale Woods.' Then Meg asked: 'Can I choose another record?'

'Of course. I'll get out the food.'

Meg looked through the pile of old 78s for a while and eventually put on 'A Nightingale Sang in Berkeley Square'. She came back to the sofa to see that there was now a table in front of it and a lavish picnic had been spread out. One of the plates bore little tartlets filled with glossy strawberries.

'I made those!' she said. 'They're for the dessert trolley.'

'Only the best for my lovely fiancée,' said Justin, and handed her a plate of chicken salad.'

'I think I recognise this, too,' she said, tucking in. 'Made specially for Dame Miriam.'

'As I said, only the best.'

They ate and drank for a while, then Justin said, 'Do you like this little house?'

'I love it, of course! It's delightful.' He was looking rather oddly at her. 'Why do you ask?'

'Because it's yours. I arranged to buy it from the estate and it's in your name – or will be when all the legal stuff is complete.'

Meg didn't know what to say. 'But Justin? I'll soon have a third of Nightingale Woods. I don't need this as well.'

He exhaled and appeared to prepare himself to say something difficult. 'I know that you'll have a share of the hotel, but I thought you might like to have a home that wasn't part of the business. It's somewhere we can be when we want to get away from work for a bit.'

'Oh, Justin,' said Meg, choking back a tear. 'I don't know what to say.'

'You don't have to say anything. One more record and then I'm going to take you upstairs to bed.'

A moment or two later the sweet notes of 'Some Enchanted Evening' filled the little house. Justin pulled Meg up from the sofa, took her into his arms and danced with her until the music stopped. 'I love you, little Meg. I think I always have, from the moment I found you in the kitchen, so brave, so fierce, so utterly adorable.'

'And I love you too!' Then she took his hand and led the way to the staircase.

Have you read them all?

Living Dangerously
For Polly, life is complicated enough without a relationship.
Surely, love is only a distraction . . .

The Rose Revived
May, Sally and Harriet decide to kick-start their own business.
Is it too much to hope for the same in their romantic lives?

Wild Designs
When Althea loses her job, she decides to transform her life
and pursue her passion for gardening.

Stately Pursuits
Hetty is drawn into a fight to save a crumbling stately home.

Life Skills
When Julia goes to work on a pair of hotel boats,
her past follows her . . .

Thyme Out
Perdita runs into her ex-husband unexpectedly. Can love
blossom between them for a second time?

Artistic Licence
Thea runs off to Ireland with a charming artist and finds herself
having to choose between two men.

Highland Fling
Jenny Porter dashes off to Scotland and gets caught in a
complicated love triangle . . .

Paradise Fields
Which man can Nel trust to help preserve the meadow
and farmers' market she loves?

Restoring Grace
Ellie and Grace embark on restoring a stately
home, but have to reckon with the help of the disconcertingly
attractive Flynn Cormack.

Flora's Lot
Flora joins the family antique business and finds herself fending off
dinner invitations from the devastatingly handsome Henry.

Practically Perfect
Anna decides to renovate a beautiful cottage that is perfect on the
outside and anything but on the inside.

Going Dutch
Jo and Dora live on a barge boat and have both sworn off men until
they meet Marcus and Tom . . .

Wedding Season
Complications ensue when wedding planner Sarah agrees to
plan two weddings on the same day.

Love Letters
When the bookshop where she works has to close, Laura agrees to
help organise a literary festival, with complicated results . . .

A Perfect Proposal
Fed up with living her life for others, Sophie jets off to
New York for the trip of a lifetime.

Summer of Love
Sian moves to the country with her young son to start a new life.

Recipe for Love
Zoe is invited to compete in a televised cookery competition.
There is only one problem: one of the judges is too tasty to resist . . .

A French Affair
When Gina inherits a stall in the French House and meets
the owner, the last thing she is thinking about is love . . .

The Perfect Match
Bella is dismayed when the man who broke her heart,
many years ago, turns up in her life again.

A Vintage Wedding
Beth, Lindy and Rachel set up a business organising beautiful vintage
weddings. Could their own happy endings be right around the corner?

A Summer at Sea
Emily decides to spend the summer cooking
on a 'puffer' boat in Scotland.

A Secret Garden
Lorna and Philly work at a beautiful manor house in the Cotswolds.
Could everything change when they discover a secret garden?

A Country Escape
Fran has a year to turn a very run-down dairy farm into profit.
What could possibly go wrong?

A Rose Petal Summer
Will this be the summer Caro and the young man she met in
Greece many years previously finally fall in love?

A Springtime Affair
Gilly falls for the charming Leo, while her daughter Helena
accepts a helping hand from Jago.
Can both these men be too good to be true?

A Wedding in the Country
It is London in the 60s, and Lizzie is so thrilled by her new,
exciting life that she forgets all about her mother's
marriage plans for her . . .

A Wedding in Provence
Alexandra spends her summer in Provence
looking after three hostile children and their impossibly
good-looking father . . .

Keep in touch with

STEP INTO THE WORLD OF KATIE FFORDE AT

www.katiefforde.com

Be the first to hear Katie's news by signing up to her email newsletter, find out all about her new book releases and see Katie's photos and videos.

You can also follow Katie on Twitter and Instagram or visit her dedicated Facebook page.

 @KatieFforde   /KatieFforde    @ffordekatie